# PRAISE FOR *PACIFIC EDGE*

"What distinguishes [*Pacific Edge*] from dozens of over-heated ecological-disaster scenarios is [Mr. Robinson's] sense of scale. He never equates the fate of a particular hill with the fate of civilization. Instead, through a blend of dirt-under-the-fingernails naturalism and lyrical magical realism, he invites you to share his characters' intensely personal, intensely local attachment to what they have."

— *The New York Times Book Review*

"Kim Stanley Robinson writes with a love and understanding and evocation of the natural world comparable to that of John Muir or William Henry Hudson. In *Pacific Edge* he is concerned with their preservation. One need not fully agree with the politics of any of his characters— as diverse as the people themselves—to enjoy their richly told story and have one's mind stirred by the many ideas presented."

— Poul Anderson

"Robinson gets into what he's best at, the evocation of people in love, people at odds, the delicate inside surfaces of social involution. The end of the book is supremely achieved, without the need to call on God, or a new order of being, or anything else at all but the courageous and perpetual inadequacy of the human heart."

— *Sunday Times* (London)

Tor books by Kim Stanley Robinson

*The Blind Geometer*
*Escape from Kathmandu*
*The Gold Coast*
*Icehenge*
*The Memory of Whiteness*
*Pacific Edge*
*The Planet on the Table*
*A Short, Sharp Shock*

*KS Robinson*

# PACIFIC EDGE

## KIM STANLEY ROBINSON

*for Helen,*

*w/best from*

*S.*

*San Francisco*

*1992*

TOR®

A TOM DOHERTY ASSOCIATES BOOK
NEW YORK

PACIFIC EDGE

Copyright © 1990 by Kim Stanley Robinson

A Tor Book
Published by Tom Doherty Associates, Inc.
49 West 24th Street
New York, N.Y. 10010

ISBN: 0-812-50056-3

First edition: November 1990
First mass market printing: June 1991

Printed in the United States of America

0  9  8  7  6  5  4  3  2  1

*for my parents*

# 1

Despair could never touch a morning like this.

The air was cool, and smelled of sage. It had the clarity that comes to southern California only after a Santa Ana wind has blown all haze and history out to sea—air like telescopic glass, so that the snowtopped San Gabriels seemed near enough to touch, though they were forty miles away. The flanks of the blue foothills revealed the etching of every ravine, and beneath the foothills, stretching to the sea, the broad coastal plain seemed nothing but treetops: groves of orange, avocado, lemon, olive; windbreaks of eucalyptus and palm; ornamentals of a thousand different varieties, both natural and genetically engineered. It was as if the whole plain were a garden run riot, with the dawn sun flushing the landscape every shade of green.

Overlooking all this was a man, walking down a hillside trail, stopping occasionally to take in the view. He had a loose gangly walk, and often skipped from one step to the next, as if playing a game. He was thirty-two but he looked like a boy, let loose in the hills with an eternal day before him.

He wore khaki work pants, a tank-top shirt, and filthy tennis shoes. His hands were large, scabbed and scarred; his arms were long. From time to time he interrupted his ramble to grasp an invisible baseball bat and swing it before him in a sharp half swing, crying, "Boom!" Doves still involved in their dawn courtship scattered before these homers, and the man laughed and skipped down the trail. His neck was red, his skin freckled, his eyes sleepy, his hair straw-colored and poking out everywhere. He had a long face with high pronounced cheekbones, and pale blue eyes. Trying to walk and look at Catalina at the same time, he tripped and had to make a quick downhill run to recover his balance. "Whoah!" he said. "Man! What a day!"

He dropped down the hillside into El Modena. His friends trickled out of the hills in ones and twos, on foot or bicycle, to converge at a torn-up intersection. They took up pick or shovel, jumped into the rough holes and went to work. Dirt flew into hoppers, picks hit stones with a *clink clink clink*, voices chattered with the week's gossip.

They were tearing out the street. It had been a large intersection: four-lane asphalt streets, white concrete curbs, big asphalt parking lots and gas stations on the corners, shopping centers behind. Now the buildings were gone and most of the asphalt too, hauled away to refineries in Long Beach; and they dug deeper.

His friends greeted him.

"Hey, Kevin, look what I found."

"Hi, Doris. Looks like a traffic light box."

"We already found one of those."

Kevin squatted by the box, checked it out. "Now we've got two. They probably left it down here when they installed a new one."

"What a waste."

From another crater Gabriela groaned. "No! No! Telephone lines, power cables, gas mains, PVC tubing, the traffic light network—and now another gas station tank!"

"Look, here's a buncha crushed beer cans," Hank said. "At least they did some things right."

* * *

As they dug they teased Kevin about that night's town council meeting, Kevin's first as a council member. "I still don't know how you let yourself get talked into it," Gabriela said. She worked construction with Kevin and Hank; young, tough and wild, she had a mouth, and often gave Kevin a hard time.

"They told me it would be fun."

Everyone laughed.

"They told him it would be fun! Here's a man who's been to hundreds of council meetings, but when Jean Aureliano tells him they're fun, Kevin Claiborne says, 'Oh, yeah, I guess they are!'"

"Well, maybe they will be."

They laughed again. Kevin just kept wielding his pick, grinning an embarrassed grin.

"They won't be," Doris said. She was the other Green on the council. Having served two terms she would be something like Kevin's advisor, a task she didn't appear to relish. They were housemates, and old friends, so she knew what she was getting into. She said to Gabriela, "Jean chose Kevin because she wanted somebody popular."

"That doesn't explain Kevin agreeing to it!"

Hank said, "The tree growing fastest is the one they cut first."

Gabriela laughed. "Try making sense, Hank, okay?"


The air warmed as the morning passed. They ran into a third traffic light box, and Doris scowled. "People were so wasteful."

Hank said, "Every culture is as wasteful as it can afford to be."

"Nah. It's just lousy values."

"What about the Scots?" Kevin asked. "People say they were really thrifty."

"But they were poor," Hank said. "They couldn't afford not to be thrifty. It proves my point."

Doris threw dirt into a hopper. "Thrift is a value independent of circumstances."

"You can see why they might leave stuff down here," Kevin said, tapping at the traffic boxes. "It's a bitch to tear up these streets, and with all the cars."

Doris shook her short black hair. "You're getting it backwards, Kev, just like Hank. It's the values you have that drive your actions, and not the reverse. If they had cared enough they would have cleared all this shit out of here and used it, just like us."

"I guess."

"It's like pedaling a bike. Values are the downstroke, actions are the upstroke. And it's the downstroke that moves things along."

"Well," Kevin said, wiping sweat from his brow and thinking about it. "If you've got toeclips on, you can get quite a bit of power on your upstroke. At least I do."

Gabriela glanced quickly at Hank. "Power on your upstroke, Kev? Really?"

"Yeah, you pull up on the toeclips. Don't you get some thrust that way?"

"Shit yeah, Kev, I get a lot of power on my upstroke."

"About how much would you say you get?" Hank asked.

Kevin said, "Well, when I'm clipped in tight I think I must get twenty percent or so."

Gabriela broke into wild cackles. "Ah, ha ha HA! This, ha! —this is the mind about to join the town council! I can't wait! I can't wait to see him get into some heavy debate with Alfredo! Fucking *toeclips*—he'll be talking TOECLIPS!"

"Well," Kevin said stubbornly, "don't you get power on your upstroke?"

"But twenty percent?" Hank asked, interested now. "Is that all the time, or just when you're resting your quads?"

Doris and Gabriela groaned. The two men fell into a technical discussion of the issue.

Gabriela said, "Kevin gets into it with Alfredo, he'll say toeclips! He'll say, 'Watch out, Fredo, or I'll poison your blood!' "

Doris chuckled, and from the depths of his discourse Kevin frowned.


Gabriela was referring to an incident from Kevin's grade school days, when he had been assigned with some others to debate the proposition, "The pen is mightier than the sword." Kevin had had to start the debate by arguing in favor of the proposition, and he had stood at the head of the class, blushing hot red, twisting his hands, rocking back and forth, biting his lips, blowing out every circuit—until finally he said, blinking doubtfully, "Well— if you had just the pen—and if you stuck someone—they might get blood poisoning from the ink!"

Heads to the desks, minutes of helpless howling, Mr. Freeman wiping the tears from his eyes—people falling out of their chairs! No one had ever forgotten it. In fact it sometimes seemed to Kevin that everyone he had ever known had been in that classroom that day, even people like Hank, who was ten years older than him, or Gabriela, who was ten years younger. Everybody! But it was just a story people told.


They dug deeper, ran into rounded sandstone boulders. Over the eons Santiago Creek had wandered over the alluvial slopes tailing out of the Santa Ana Mountains, and it seemed all of El Modena had been the streambed at one time or another, because they found these stones everywhere. The pace was casual; this was town work, and so was best regarded as a party, to avoid irritation at the inefficiency. In El Modena they were required to do ten hours a week of town work, and so there were opportunities for vast amounts of irritation. They had gotten good at taking it less than seriously.

Kevin said, "Hey, where's Ramona?"

Doris looked up. "Didn't you hear?"

"No, what?"

"She and Alfredo broke up."

This got the attention of everyone in earshot. Some stopped and came over to get the story. "He's moved out of the house, on to Redhill with his partners."

"You're kidding!"

"No. I guess they've been fighting a lot more lately. That's what everyone at their house says. Anyway, Ramona went for a walk this morning."

"But the game!" Kevin said.

Doris jabbed her shovel into dirt an inch from his toe. "Kevin, did it ever occur to you that there are more important things than softball?"

"Well sure," he said, looking dubious at the proposition.

"She said she'd be back in time for the game."

"Good," Kevin said, then saw her expression and added quickly, "Too bad, though. Really too bad. Quite a surprise, too."

He thought about Ramona Sanchez. Single for the first time since ninth grade, in fact.

Doris saw the look on his face and turned her back on him. Her stocky brown legs were dusty below green nylon shorts; her sleeveless tan shirt was sweaty and smudged. Straight black hair swung from side to side as she attacked the ground. "Help me with this rock," she said to Kevin sharply, back still to him. Uncertainly he helped her move yet another water-rounded blob of sandstone.

"Well, if it isn't the new council at work," said an amused baritone voice above them.

Kevin and Doris looked up to see Alfredo Blair himself, seated on his mountain bike. The bright titanium frame flashed in the sun. Without thinking Kevin said, "Speak of the devil."

"Well," Doris said, with a quick warning glance at Kevin, "if it isn't the new mayor at leisure."

Alfredo grinned rakishly. He was a big handsome man, black-haired, moustached, clear clean lines to his jaw, nose, forehead. It was hard to imagine that just the day before he had moved out of a fifteen-year relationship.

"Good luck in your game today," he said, in a tone that implied they would need it, even though they were only playing the lowly Oranges. Alfredo's team the Vanguards and their team the Lobos were perpetual rivals; before today this had always been a source of jokes, as Ramona was on the Lobos. Now Kevin wasn't sure what it was. Alfredo went on: "I'm looking forward to when we get to play you."

"We've got work to do, Alfredo," Doris said.

"Don't let me stop you. Town work benefits everyone." He laughed, biked off. "See you at the council meeting!" he yelled over his shoulder.

They went back to work.

"I hope when we play them we beat the shit out of them," Kevin said.

"You always hope that."

"True."

Kevin and Alfredo had grown up on the same street, and had shared many classes in school, including the class assigned to debate the proposition. So they were old friends, and Kevin had had many opportunities to watch Alfredo operate in the world, and he knew well that his old friend was a very admirable person—smart, friendly, popular, energetic, successful. Good at everything; everything came easily to him and everyone liked him.

But it was too nice a day to let the thought of Alfredo wreck it.

Besides, Alfredo and Ramona had broken up. Obscurely cheered by the thought, Kevin hauled a boulder up into a hopper.

When they stopped for lunch they were about eye-level with the old surface of the intersection, which was now a chaotic field of craters, pocked by trenches and treadmarks, with wheelbarrows and dumpsters all over. Kevin squinted at the sight and grinned. "This is gonna make one hell of a softball diamond."

After lunch the spring softball season began. Players biked into Santiago Park from all directions, bats over handlebars, and they fell collectively into time-honored patterns; for softball is a ritual activity, and the approach to ritual is also ritualized. Feet were shoved into stiff cleats, gloves were slipped on, and they walked out onto the green grass field and played catch in groups of two and three, the big balls floating back and forth, making a dreamy knitwork of white lines in the air.

The umpires were running their chalk wheelbarrows up the foul lines when Ramona Sanchez coasted to the third base side and dumped her bike. Long legs, wide shoulders, Hispanic coloring, black hair. . . . The rest of the Lobos greeted her happily, relieved to see her, and she smiled and said, "Hi, guys," in almost her usual way; but everyone could see she wasn't herself.

Ramona was one of those people who always have a bright smile and a cheery tone of voice. Doris for one found it exasperating. "She's a biological optimist," Doris would grouse, "it isn't even up to her. It's something in her blood chemistry."

"Wait a second," Hank would object, "you're the one always talking about values—shouldn't optimism be the result of will? I mean, *blood chemistry?*"

And Doris would reply that optimism might indeed be an act of will, but that good looks, intelligence and great athletic skill no doubt helped to make it a rather small one; and these qualities were all biological, even if they weren't blood chemistry.

Anyway, the sight of Ramona on this day was a disturbing thing: an unhappy optimist. Even Kevin, who started to play catch with her with the full intention of behaving normally, thus giving

her a break from unwanted sympathy, was unnerved by how subdued she seemed. He felt foolish trying to pretend all was well,
and since she ignored his pretense he just caught and threw, warming her up.

Judging by the hard flat trajectory of her throws, she was
considerably warm already. Ramona Sanchez had a good arm; in
fact, she was a gun. Once Kevin had seen one of her rare wild
throws knock a spoke cleanly out of the wheel of a parked bike,
without moving the rest of the bike an inch. She regularly broke
the leather ties in first basemen's gloves, and once or twice had
broken fingers as well. Kevin had to pay close attention to avoid
a similar fate, because the ball jumped across the space between
them almost instantaneously. A real gun. And not in a good mood.

So they threw in silence, except for the leather smack of the
glove. There was a certain companionableness about it, Kevin
felt—a sort of solidarity expressed. Or so he hoped, since he
couldn't think of anything to say. Then the umpires called for the
start of the game, and he walked over and stood beside her as she
sat and jammed on her cleats. She did it with such violence that
it seemed artificial not to notice, so Kevin said, hesitantly, "I
heard about you and Alfredo."

"Uh huh," she said, not impressed.

"I'm sorry."

Briefly she twisted her mouth down. That's how unhappy I
would be if I let myself go, the look said. Then the stoic look
returned and she shrugged, stood, bent over to stretch her legs.
The backs of her thighs banded, muscles clearly visible under
smooth brown skin.

They walked back to the bench, where their teammates were
swinging bats. The team captains gave line-up cards to the scorer.
All activity began to spiral down toward the ritual; more and more
that was not part of it fell away and disappeared, until when one
team took the field—first basemen rolling grounders to the infield-
ers, pitcher taking practice tosses, outfielders throwing fly balls
around—everything extraneous to the ritual was gone. Kevin, the

first batter of the new year, walked up to the plate, adrenaline spiking through him. Players called out something encouraging to him or the pitcher, and the umpire cried "Play ball!"

And the batter stepped into the box, and the first pitch of the season rose into the air, and the shouts ("Get a hit!" "Start it off right!" "Hey batter, hey batter!") grew distant, faded until no one heard them, not even those who spoke. Time dilated and the big fat shiny new white ball hung up there at the top of its arc, became the center of all their worlds, the focus—until it crossed the plate, the batter swung, and the game began.

It was a great game as far as Kevin was concerned: the Lobos kept the lead throughout, but not by much. And Kevin was four for four, which would always be enough to make him happy.

In the field he settled down at third base to sharp attention on every pitch. Third base like a razor's edge, third base like a mongoose among snakes: this was how the announcer in his head had always put it, ever since childhood. Occasionally there was a sudden chance to act, but mostly it was settling down, paying attention, the same phrases said over and over. Playing as a kind of praying.

So he was lulled a bit, deep in the rhythms of what was essentially a very ordinary game, when suddenly things picked up. The Oranges scored four runs in their final at-bat, and now with two outs Santos Perez was coming to bat. Santos was a strong pull hitter, and as Donna prepared to pitch, Kevin settled into his cleat-scored position off third base, extra alert.

A short pitch dropped and Santos smashed a hot grounder to Kevin's left. Kevin dove instantly but the ball bounced past his glove, missing it by an inch. He hit the dirt cursing, and as he slid forward on chest and elbows he looked back, just in time to see the sprinting Ramona lunge out and snag the ball.

It was a tremendous backhand catch, but she had almost over-balanced to make it, and now she was running directly away from first base, very deep in the hole. There was no time to stop and set, and so she leaped in the air, spun to give the sidearm throw some momentum, and let it fly with a vicious flick of the wrist. The ball looped across the diamond and Jody caught it neatly on one hop at first base, just ahead of the racing Santos. Third out. Game over.

"Yeah!" Kevin cried, pushing up to his knees. "Wow!"

Everyone was cheering. Kevin looked back at Ramona. She had tumbled to the ground after the throw, and now she was sitting on the outfield grass, long, graceful, splay-legged, grinning, black hair in her eyes. And Kevin fell in love.

Of course that isn't *exactly* how it happened. That isn't the whole story. Kevin was a straightforward kind of guy, and crazy about softball, but still, he was not the kind of person who would fall in love on the strength of a good play at shortstop. No, this was something else, something that had been developing for years and years.

He had known Ramona Sanchez since she first arrived in El Modena, when they were both in third grade. They had been in the same classes in grade school—including, yes, the class with the famous debate—and had shared a lot of classes in junior high. And Kevin had always liked her. One day in sixth grade she had told him she was Roman Catholic, and he had told her that there were Greek Catholics too. She had denied it disdainfully, and so they had gone to look it up in the encyclopedia. They had failed to find a listing for "Greek Catholic," which Kevin could not understand, as his grandfather Tom had certainly mentioned such a church. But having been proved right Ramona became sympathetic, and even scanned the index and found a listing for "Greek Orthodox Church," which seemed to explain things. After that they sat before the screen and read the entry, and scanned through other articles, talking about Greece, the travels they had made (Ramona had been to Mexico, Kevin had been to Death Valley), the possibilities of buying a Greek island and living on it, and so on.

After that Kevin had had a crush on Ramona, one that he never told anyone about—certainly not her. He was a shy boy, that's all there was to it. But the feeling persisted, and in junior high when it became the thing to have romantic friends, life was a dizzying polymorphous swirl of crushes and relationships, and everyone was absorbed in it. So over the course of junior high's three years, shy Kevin gradually and with difficulty worked himself up to the point of asking Ramona out to a school dance—to Homecoming, in fact, the big dance of the year. When he asked her, stammering with fright, she made him feel like she thought it was an excellent idea; but said she had already accepted an invitation, from Alfredo Blair.

The rest was history. Ramona and Alfredo had been a couple, aside from the brief breaks that stormy high school romances often have, from that Homecoming to the present day.

In later years, however, as El Modena High School's biology teacher, Ramona had developed the habit of taking her classes out to Kevin's construction sites, to learn some applied ecology—also carpentry, and a bit of architecture—all while helping him out a little. Kevin liked that, even though the students were only marginally more help than hassle. It was a friendly thing, something he and Ramona did to spend time together.

Still, she and Alfredo were partners. They never married, but always lived together. So Kevin had gotten used to thinking of Ramona as a friend only. A good friend, sort of like his sister Jill—only not like a sister, because there had always been an extra attraction. A shared attraction, it seemed. It wasn't all that important, but it gave their friendship a kind of thrill, a nice fullness—a kind of latent potential, perhaps, destined never to be fulfilled. Which made it romantic.

A lifelong thing, then. And before the softball game, while warming Ramona up, he had been conscious of seeing her in a

way that he hadn't for years—seeing the perfect proportions of
her back and legs, shoulders and bottom—the dramatic Hispanic
coloring, the fine features that made her one of the town
beauties—the grace of her strong overhand throw—her careless
unselfconsciousness. Deep inside him memories had stirred, memories of feelings he would have said were long forgotten, for he
never thought of his past much, and if asked would have assumed
it had all slipped away. And yet there it was, stirring inside him,
ready at a moment's notice to leap back out and take over his life.

So when he turned to look at her after her spectacular play, and
saw her sprawled on the grass, long brown legs akimbo so that he
was looking at the green crotch of her gym shorts, at a white strip
of their underlining on the inside of one thigh—her weight on one
straightened arm, white T-shirt molded against her almost flat
chest—brushing hair out of black eyes, smiling for the first time
that afternoon—it was as if all Kevin's life had been a wind-up,
and this the throw. As if he had stepped into a dream in which all
emotions were intensified. *Whoosh!* went the air out of his lungs.
His heart thudded, the skin of his face flushed and tingled with
the impact of it, with the *recognition* of it, and yes—it was love.
No doubt about it.

To feel was to act for Kevin, and so as soon as they were done
packing up equipment and changing shoes, he looked for Ramona.
She had become unusually silent again, after the rush of congratulations for her game ender, and now she was biking off by herself.
Kevin caught up with her on his little mountain bike, then matched
her speed. "Are you going to the council meeting tonight?"

"I don't think so."

Not going to see Alfredo sworn in as mayor. It was definitely
true, then. "Wow," he said.

"Well, you know—I just don't feel like being there and having lots of people assume we're still together, for photos maybe even. It would be awkward as hell."

"I can see that. So . . . What're you gonna do this afternoon?"

She hesitated. "I was thinking of going flying, actually. Work some of this out of my system."

"Ah."

She looked over at him. "Want to join me?"

Kevin's heart tocked at the back of his throat. His inclination was to say "Sure!" and he always followed his inclinations; thus it was a measure of his interest that he managed to say, "If you really feel like company? I know that sometimes I just like to get off by myself. . . ."

"Ah, well. I wouldn't mind the company. Might help."

"Usually does," Kevin said automatically, not paying attention to what he was saying, or how it failed to match with what he had just said before. He could feel his heart. He grinned. "Hey, that was a hell of a play you made there."


At a glider port on Fairhaven they untied the Sanchezs' two-person flyer, a Northrop Condor, and after hooking it to the take-off sling they strapped themselves in and clipped their feet into the pedals. Ramona freed the craft and with a jerk they were off, pedaling like mad. Ramona pulled back on the flaps, the sling uncoupled, they shot up like a pebble from a slingshot; then caught the breeze and rushed higher, like a kite pulled into the wind by an enthusiastic runner.

"Yow!" Kevin cried, and Ramona said, "Pedal harder!" and they both pumped away, leaning back and pushing the little plane up with every stroke. The huge prop whirred before them, but two-seaters were not quite as efficient as one-seaters; the extra muscle did not quite make up for the extra weight, and they had to grind at the tandem pedals as if racing to get the craft up to two hundred feet, where the afternoon sea breeze lifted them dizzily. Even a two-seater weighed less than thirty pounds, and gusts of the wind could toss them like a shuttlecock.

Ramona turned them into this breeze with a gull's swoop. The feel of it, the feel of flying! They relaxed the pace, settled into a long distance rhythm, swooped around the sky over Orange County. Hard work; it was one of the weird glories of their time, that the highest technologies were producing artifacts that demanded more intense physical labor than ever before—as in the case of human-powered flight, which required extreme effort from even the best endurance athletes. But once possible, who could resist it?

Not Ramona Sanchez; she pedaled along, smiling with contentment. She flew a lot. Often while working on roofs, absorbed in the labor, imagining the shape of the finished home and the lives it would contain, Kevin would hear a voice from above, and looking up he would see her in her little Hughes Dragonfly, making a cyclist's *whirr* and waving down like a sweaty air spirit. Now she said, "Let's go to Newport and take a look at the waves."

And so they soared and dipped in the onshore wind, like their condor namesake. From time to time Kevin glanced at Ramona's legs, working in tandem next to his. Her thighs were longer than his, her quads bigger and better defined: two hard muscles atop each leg, barely coming together in time to fit under the kneecap. They made her thighs look squared-off on top, an effect nicely balanced by long rounded curves beneath. And calf muscles out of an anatomical chart. The texture of her skin was very smooth, barely dusted by fine silky hair. . . .

Kevin shook his head, surprised by the dreamlike intensity of his vision, by how well he could *see* her. He glanced down at the Newport Freeway, crowded as usual. From above, the bike lanes were a motley collection of helmets, backs, and pumping legs, over spidery lines of metal and rubber. The cars' tracks gleamed like bands of silver embedded in the concrete, and cars hummed along them, blue roof red roof blue roof.

As they cut curves in the air Kevin saw buildings he had worked on at one time or another: a house reflecting sunlight from canopies of cloudgel and thermocrete; a garage renovated to a cottage; warehouses, offices, a bell tower, a pond house. . . . His work, tucked here and there in the trees. It was fun to see it, to point it out, to remember the challenge of the task met and dealt with, for better or worse.

Ramona laughed. "It must be nice to see your whole resumé like this."

"Yeah," he said, suddenly embarrassed. He had been rattling on.

She was looking at him.

Tall eucalyptus windbreaks cut the land into giant rectangles, as if the basin were a quilt of homes, orchards, green and yellow crops. Kevin's lungs filled with wind, he was buoyant at the sight of so much land, and all of it so familiar to him. The onshore breeze grew stronger over Costa Mesa, and they lofted toward the Irvine Hills. The big interchange of the San Diego and Newport freeways looked like a concrete pretzel. Beyond it there was a lot of water, reflecting the sunlight like scraps of mirror thrown on the land: streams, fish ponds, reservoirs, the marsh of Upper Newport Bay. It was low tide, and a lot of gray tidal flats were revealed, surrounded by reeds and clumps of trees. They could smell the salt stink of them on the wind, even up where they were. Thousands of ducks and geese bobbed on the water, making a beautiful speckled pattern.

"Migration again," Ramona said pensively. "Time for change."

"Headed north."

"The clouds are coming in faster than I thought they would." She pointed toward Newport Beach. The afternoon onshore wind was bringing in low ocean clouds, as often happened in spring. The Torrey pines loved it, but it was no fun to fly in.

"Well, what with the council meeting it won't do me any harm to get back a little early," Kevin said.

Ramona shifted the controls and they made a wide turn over Irvine. The mirrored glass boxes in the industrial parks glinted in the sun like children's blocks, green and blue and copper. Kevin glanced at Ramona and saw she was blinking rapidly. Crying? Ah—he'd mentioned the council meeting. Damn! And they'd been having such fun! He was an idiot. Impulsively he touched the back of her hand, where it rested on the control stick. "Sorry," he said. "I forgot."

"Oh," she said, voice unsteady. "I know."

"So . . ." Kevin wanted to ask what had happened.

She grimaced at him, intending it to be a comic expression. "It's been pretty upsetting."

"I can imagine. You were together a long time."

"Fifteen years!" she said. "Nearly half my life!" She struck the stick angrily, and the Condor dipped left. Kevin winced.

"Maybe it was too long," she said. "I mean too long with nothing happening. And neither of us had any other partners before we got together."

Kevin almost brought up their talk over the encyclopedia in sixth grade, but decided not to. Perhaps as an example of a previous relationship it was not particularly robust.

"High school sweethearts," Ramona exclaimed. "It is a bad idea, just like everyone says. You have a lot of history together, sure, but you don't really know if the other person is the best partner you could have. And then one of you gets interested in finding out!" She slammed the frame above the controls, making Kevin and the plane jump.

"Uh huh," he said. She was angry about it, that was clear. And it was great that she was letting it out like this, telling Kevin what she felt. If only she wouldn't emphasize her points with those hard blows to the frame, so close to the controls.

Also there was hardly any resistance in his pedals. They were turning the same chain together, and she was pumping away furiously, more than enough for both of them. And they were shuddering through little sideslips every time she pounded a point home.

Kevin swallowed, determined not to interrupt her thoughts with mundane worries.

"I mean you can't help but wonder!" she was saying, waving a hand. "I know Alfredo did. I'm not all that interesting, I suppose—"

"What?"

"Well, there's only a few things I really care about. And Alfredo is interested in *everything*." Bang. Right above the flaps. "There's so many things he's into that you can't even *believe it*." Bang! "And he was always so God-damned *busy!*" BANG BANG BANG!

"You have to be, to be a hundred," Kevin said, watching her hands and cringing. With the slips they were losing altitude, he noted. Even pumping as hard as she was.

"Yeah, sure you do. And he could be two hundreds! He could be a millionaire if they still had them, he really could! He's got just what it takes."

"Must take a lot of time, huh?"

"It takes your whole life!" WHAM.

Kevin pedaled hard, but he was just spinning around, as if his pedals weren't connected to a chain at all.

"At least that's what it felt like. And there we were not going anywhere, high school sweethearts at thirty-two. I don't care that much about marriage myself, but my parents and grandparents are Catholic, and so are Alfredo's, and you know how that is. Besides I was getting ready to have a family, you know every day I'm helping out with the kids in our house, and I thought why shouldn't one of these be ours?" Bang! "But Alfredo was not into it, oh no. I don't have time! he'd say. I'm not ready yet! And by the time he's ready, it'll be too late for me!" BANG! BANG! BANG!

"Uck," Kevin said, looking down at the treetops apprehensively. "It, uh, it wouldn't take that much time, would it? Not in your house."

"You'd be surprised. A lot of people are there to help, but still, you always end up with them. And Alfredo . . . well, we talked about it for years. But nothing ever changed, damn it! So I got pretty bitchy, I guess, and Alfredo spent more and more time away, you know. . . ." She began to blink rapidly, voice wobbling.

"Feedback loop," Kevin said, trying to stick to analysis. A relationship had feedback loops, like any other ecology—that's what Hank used to say. A movement in one direction or another could quickly spiral out of control. Kind of like a tailspin, now that Kevin thought about it. Harder than hell to re-stabilize after you fell into one of those. In fact people were killed all the time in crashes caused by them. Uncontrolled feedback loop. He tried to remember the few flying lessons he had taken. Mostly he was a grinder when he went flying. . . .

But it could work both ways, he thought as some resistance returned to his pedals. Upward spiral, a great flourishing of the spirit, everything feeding into it—

"A very bad feedback loop," Ramona said.

They pedaled on. Kevin pumped hard, kept his eye on the controls, on Ramona's vehement right fist. He found her story rather amazing in some respects. He didn't understand Alfredo. Imagine the chance to make love with this beautiful animal pumping away beside him, to watch her get fat with a child that was the combination of him and her. . . . He breathed erratically at the thought, suddenly aware of his own body, of his balls between his legs—

He banished the thought, looked down at Tustin. Close. "So," he said, thinking to go right at it. "You broke up."

"Yeah. I don't know, I was getting really angry, but I probably would have stuck it out. I never really thought about anything else. But Alfredo, he got mad at me too, and . . . and—"

She started to cry.

"Ah, Ramona," Kevin said. Wrong tack to take, there. The direct approach not always the best way. He pedaled hard, suddenly doing the work for both of them. Enormous resistance, she didn't seem to be pedaling at all now. Not a good moment to bother her, though. He gritted his teeth and began to pedal like a fiend. Their flyer dropped anyway, sideslipping a bit. Incredible resistance in the pedals. They were dropping toward the hills behind Tustin. Directly at them, in fact. Ramona's eyes were squeezed shut; she was too upset to notice anything. Kevin found his concern distracted. Fatal accidents in these things were not all that infrequent.

"I'm sorry," he panted, pumping violently. "But . . . uh . . ." He took a hand from the frame to pat her shoulder, briefly. "Maybe . . . um . . ."

"It's okay," she said, hands over her face, rubbing hard. "Sometimes I can't help it."

"Uh huh."

She looked up. "Shit, we're about to run into Redhill!"

"Um, yeah."

"Why didn't you say something!"

"Well . . ."

"Oh Kevin!"

She laughed, sniffed, reached over to peck his cheek. Then she started to pedal again, and turned them towards home.

Kevin's heart filled—with relief, certainly—but also with affection for her. It was a shame she had been hurt like that. Although he had no desire to see her and Alfredo achieve a reconciliation. None at all. He said, very cautiously, "Maybe it's better it happened now, if it was going to."

She nodded briefly.

They circled back in toward El Modena's little gliderport. A Dragonfly ahead of them dropped onto it, heavy as a bee in cold weather. Skillfully Ramona guided them in. The afternoon sun lit the treetops. Their shadow preceded them toward the grassy runway. They dropped to an elevation where the whole plain seemed nothing but treetops—all the streets and freeways obscured, most of the buildings screened. "I fly at this altitude a lot," Ramona said, "just to make it look like this."

"Good idea." Her small smile, the trees everywhere—Kevin felt like the breeze was cutting right through his chest. To think that Ramona Sanchez was a free woman! And sitting here beside him.

He couldn't look at her. She brought them down to the runway in a graceful swoop, and they pedaled hard as they landed, as gently as sitting on a couch. Quick roll to a stop. They unstrapped, stood unsteadily, flexed tired legs, walked the plane off the strip toward its berth.

"Whew," she said. "*Estoy cansada.*"

Kevin nodded. "Great flight, Ramona."

"Yeah?" And as they stored the plane in the gloomy hangar, she hugged him briefly and said, "You're a good friend, Kevin."

Which might have been a warning, but Kevin wasn't listening. He still felt the touch. "I want to be," he said, feeling his voice quiver. He didn't think it could be heard. "I want to be."


El Modena's town council had its chambers in the area's oldest building, the church on Chapman Avenue. Over the years this structure had reflected the town's fortunes like a totem. It had been built by Quakers in 1886, soon after they settled the area and cultivated it in raisin grapes. One Friend donated a big bell, which they put in a tower at the church's front end; but the bell's weight was too much for the framing, and in the first strong Santa Ana wind the whole building fell down, *boom!* In similar fashion grape blight destroyed the economy, so that the new town was virtually abandoned. So much for El Modena One. But they changed crops, and then rebuilt the church, in the first of a long sequence of resurrections; through the barrio and its hidden poverty (church closed), through suburbia and its erasure of history (church a restaurant)—through to the re-emergence of El Modena as a town with a destiny of its own, when the council bought the restaurant and converted it into a cramped and weird-looking city hall, suitable for renting on any party occasion. Thus it finally became the center of the community that its Quaker builders had hoped it would be nearly two centuries before.

Now the white courtyard walls were wrapped with colored streamers, and Japanese paper lanterns were hung in the courtyard's three big willows. The McElroy Mariachi Men strolled about playing their loose sweet music, and a long table was crowded with bottles of Al Shroeder's atrocious champagne.

Uneasily Kevin pedaled into the parking lot. As a contractor he had appeared before the council countless times, but walking into the yard as one of the council members was different. How in the hell had he got himself into it? Well, he was a Green, always had been. Renovate that sleazy old condo of a world! And this year they had needed to fill one of their two spots on the council, but most of the prominent party members were busy, or had served before, or were otherwise prevented from running. Suddenly—and Kevin didn't really know who had decided this, or how—they were all encouraging him to do it. He was well-known and well-liked, they told him, and he had done a lot of visible work in the community. Very visible, he said—I build houses. But in the end he was won over. Green council members voted all important issues as an expression of the group, so there wasn't that much to it. If there were things he didn't know, he could learn on the job. It wasn't that hard. Everyone should take their turn. It would be fun! He could consult when he needed to.

But (it occurred to him) he would most need to consult when he was actually up there behind the table—just when consulting was impossible! He brushed his hair with his fingers. Just like him, he thought morosely, to think of that only now. It was too late; the job was his. Time to learn.

Doris biked in with an older woman. "Kevin, this is Nadezhda Katayev, a friend of mine from Moscow. She was my boss when I did the exchange at their superconductor institute, and she's over here for a visit. She'll be staying with us."

Kevin shook hands with her, and they joined the crowd. Most of the people there were friends or acquaintances. People kidded him as usual; no one was taking the evening very seriously. He was handed a cup of champagne, and a group from the Lobos gathered to toast the day's game, and the political stardom of their teammates. Several cups of champagne later he felt better about everything.

Then Alfredo Blair entered the courtyard, in a swirl of friends and supporters and family. The McElroys tooted the opening bars of "Hail to the Chief," and Alfredo laughed, clearly having a fine time. Still, it was odd to see him at such an event without Ramona there, serving as the other pole of a powerful eye magnet. A sudden vision, of long legs pumping beside his, of her broad expressive face tearful with rage, pounding the ultralite's frame—

The party got louder, charged along. "There's a madman here," Doris observed, pointing to a stranger. They watched him: a huge man in a floppy black coat, who sidled from group to group with a strange rhinocerine grace, disrupting conversation after conversation. He spoke, people looked confused or shocked; he departed and barged in elsewhere, hair flying, champagne splashing out of his cup.

The mystery was solved when Alfredo introduced him. "Hey Oscar, come over here! Folks, this is our new town attorney, Oscar Baldarramma. You may have seen him in the interview process."

Kevin had not. Oscar Baldarramma approached. He was huge—taller than Kevin, and fat, and his bulk rode everywhere on him: his face was moonlike, his neck a tree trunk, and an immense barrel chest was more than matched by a round middle. His curly black hair was even more unruly than Kevin's, and he wore a dark suit some fifty years out of date. He himself looked to be around forty.

Now he nodded, creasing a multiple chin, and pursed thick, mobile lips. "Nice to meet the other rookie on the team," he said in a scratchy flat voice, as if making fun of the phrase.

Kevin nodded, at a loss for words. He had heard that the new town attorney was a hotshot from the Midwest, with several years of work for Chicago under his belt. And they needed a good lawyer, because El Modena like most towns was always getting sued. The old council had taken most of six months to replace the previous attorney. But then to choose this guy!

Oscar stepped toward Kevin, lowered his head, waggled his eyebrows portentiously. A bad mime couldn't have been more blatant: *Secrecy. Confidential Matter.* "I'm told you renovate old houses?"

"That's my job."

Oscar glanced around in spy movie style. "I've been permitted to lease an elderly house near the gliderport, and I wondered if you might be interested in rebuilding it for me."

Oh. "Well, I'd need to take a look at it first. But assuming we agree on everything, I could put you on our waiting list. It's short right now."

"I would be willing to wait."

It seemed a sign of good judgment to Kevin. "I'll drop by and look the place over, and give you an estimate."

"Of course," the big man whispered.

A tray was passed around and they all took paper cups of champagne. Oscar stared thoughtfully into his. "A local champagne, I take it."

"Yeah," Kevin said, "Al Shroeder makes it. He's got a big vineyard up on Cowan Heights."

"Cowan Heights."

Doris said sharply, "Just because it isn't from Napa or Sonoma doesn't mean it's terrible! I think it's pretty good!"

Oscar gazed at her. "And what is your profession, may I ask?"

"I'm a materials scientist."

"Then I defer to your judgment."

Kevin couldn't help laughing at the expression on Doris's face. "Al's champagne sucks," he said. "But he's got a good zinfandel—a lot better than this."

Oscar went slightly cross-eyed. "I will seek it out. A recommendation like that demands action!"

Kevin snorted, and Nadezhda grinned. But Doris looked more

annoyed than ever, and she was about to let Oscar know it, Kevin could tell, when Jean Aureliano called for silence.

Time for business. Alfredo, who had already spent six years on the council, was sworn in as the new mayor, and Kevin was sworn in as new council member. Kevin had forgotten about that part, and he stumbled on his way to the circle of officials. "What a start!" someone yelled. Hot-faced, he put his hand on a Bible, repeated something the judge said.

And yet in the midst of the blur, a sudden sensation—he was part of government now. Just like sixth grade civics class said he would be.

They moved into the council chambers, and Alfredo sat at the centerpoint of the council's curved table. As mayor he was no more than first among equals, a council member from the town's most numerous party. He ran their meetings, but had one vote like the others.

On one side of him sat Kevin, Doris, and Matt Chung. On the other side were Hiroko Washington, Susan Mayer, and Jerry Geiger. Oscar and the town planner, Mary Davenport, sat at a table of their own, off to the side. Kevin could clearly see the faces of all the other members, and as Alfredo urged the spectators to get seated, he looked them over.

Kevin and Doris were Greens, Alfredo and Matt were Feds. The New Federalists had just outpolled the Greens as the town's most numerous party, for the first time in some years; so they had a bit of a new edge. Hiroko, Susan and Jerry represented smaller local parties, and functioned as a kind of fluctuating middle, with Hiroko and Susan true moderates, and Jerry a kind of loose cannon, his voting record a model of inexplicable inconsistency. This made him quite popular with some Modeños, who had joined the Geiger Party to keep him on the council.

Alfredo smacked his palm against the table. "If we don't start soon we'll be up all night! Welcome to new member Kevin Claiborne. Let's get him right into it with the first item on the agenda—ah—the second. Welcoming him was the first. Okay, number two. Re-examining order to cut down the trees bordering Peters Canyon Reservoir. An injunction against complying with the order was issued, pending review by this council. And here we are. The request for the injunction was made by El Modena's Wilderness Party, represented tonight by Hu-nang Chu. Are you here, Hu-nang?''

An intense-looking woman stepped up to the witness's lectern. She told them forcefully that the trees around the reservoir were old and sacred, and that cutting them down was a wanton act of destruction. When she began to repeat herself Alfredo skillfully cut her off. "Mary, the order originated from your people—you want to comment first on this?''

The town planner cleared her throat. "The trees around the reservoir are cottonwoods and willows, both extremely hydrophilic species. Naturally their water comes out of the reservoir, and the plain fact is we can't afford it—we're losing approximately an acre foot a month. Council resolution two oh two two dash three instructs us to do everything possible to decrease dependency on OC Water District and the Municipal Water District. Expanding the reservoir helped, and we tried to clear the area of hydrophilic trees at the time of expansion, but the cottonwoods are especially quick to grow back. Willows, by the way, are not even native to the area. We propose to cut the trees down and replace them with scrub oaks and adapted desert grasses. We also plan to leave one big willow standing, near the dam.''

"Comments?" Alfredo said.

Everyone on the council who cared to comment approved Mary's plan. Jerry remarked it was nice to see El Modena cut down some trees for once. Alfredo asked for comments from the audience, and a few people came to the lectern to make a point, usually repeating an earlier statement, sometimes in an inebriated version. Alfredo cut those off and put it to a vote. The order to cut down the trees passed seven to zero.

"Unanimity!" Alfredo said cheerily. "A very nice omen for the future of this council. Sorry, Hu-nang, but the trees have a drinking problem. On to item number three: proposal to tighten the noise ordinance around the high school stadium, ha! Who's the courageous soul advocating this?"

And so the meeting rolled on, filling Wednesday night as so many meetings had before. A building permit battle that became a protest against town ownership of the land, a zoning boundary dispute, an ordinance banning skateboards on bike trails, a proposal to alter the investment patterns of the town funds . . . all the business of running a small town, churned out point by point in a public gathering. The work of running the world, repeated thousands of times all over the globe; you could say that this was where the real power lay.

But it didn't feel like that, this particular night in El Modena—not to Kevin. For him it was just work, and dull work at that. He felt like a judge with no precedent to guide him. Even when he did know of precedents, he discovered that they were seldom a close enough fit to the current situation to really provide much help. An important legal principle, he thought fuzzily, trying to shake off the effects of Al's champagne: precedent is useless. Often he decided to vote with Doris and figure out the whys and wherefores later. Happily there was no mechanism for asking them to justify their votes.

At about the fifth of these votes, he felt a strong sinking sensation—he was going to have to spend every Wednesday night for the next two years, doing just this! Listening very closely to a lot of matters that didn't interest him in the slightest! How in the *hell* had he gotten himself into it?

Out in the audience people were getting up and leaving. Doris's old boss Nadezhda stayed, watching curiously. Oscar and the council secretary took a lot of notes. The meeting droned on.

Kevin's concentration began to waver. The long day, the

champagne. . . . It was nice and warm, and the voices were all so calm, so soothing. . . .

Sleepy, yes.

Very, very sleepy.

How embarrassing!

And yet intensely drowsy. *Completely* drowsy. At his first council meeting. But it was so nice and warm. . . .

Don't fall asleep! Oh my God.

He pinched himself desperately. Could people see it when you clamped down on a yawn? He had never been sure.

What were they talking about? He wasn't even sure which item on the agenda they were discussing. With an immense effort he tried to focus.

"Item twenty-seven," Alfredo said, and for a second Kevin feared Alfredo was going to look over at him with his raffish grin. But he only read on. A bunch of water bureaucracy details, including nominations by the city planning office of two new members for the watermaster. Kevin had never heard of either of them. Still befuddled, he shook his head. Watermaster. When he was a child he had been fascinated by the name. It had been disappointing to learn that it was not a single person, with magical powers at his command, but merely a name for a board, another agency in an endless system of agencies. In some basins they merely recorded, in others they set groundwater policy. Kevin wasn't sure what they did in their district. But something, he felt, was strange. Perhaps that he had not recognized the names. And then, over at the side table, Oscar had tilted his head slightly. He was still watching them with a poker face, but there was something different in his demeanor. It was as if a statue of the sleeping Buddha had barely cracked open an eye, and glanced out curiously.

"Who are they?" Kevin croaked. "I mean, who are these nominees?"

Alfredo handled the interruption like Ramona fielding a bad hop, graceful and smooth as ever. He described the two candidates.

One was an associate of Matt's. The other was a member of the OC Water District's engineering board.

Kevin listened uncertainly. "What's their political affiliation?"

Alfredo shrugged. "I think they're Feds, but what's the big deal? It's not a political appointment."

"You must be kidding," Kevin said. Water, not political? Drowsiness gone, he glanced through the rest of the text of Item 27. Lots of detail. Ignoring Alfredo's request to explain himself, he read on. Approval of water production statements from the wells in the district, approval of annual report on groundwater conditions (good). Letter of thanks to OCWD for Crawford Canyon land donated to the town last year. Letter of inquiry sent by town planning board to get further information on the Metropolitan Water District's offer to supply client towns with more water—

Doris elbowed him in the ribs.

"What do you mean?" Alfredo repeated for the third time.

"Water is always political," Kevin said absently. "Tell me, do you always put so many things into one item on the agenda?"

"Sure," Alfredo said. "We group by topic."

But Oscar's head shifted a sixteenth of an inch to the left, a sixteenth of an inch to the right. Just like a Buddha statue coming alive.

If only he knew more about all this. . . . He chose at random. "What's this offer from MWD?"

Alfredo looked over the agenda. "Ah. That was something a few sessions ago. MWD has gotten their Colorado River allotment upped by court decision, and they'd like to sell that water before the Columbia River pipe is finished. The planning office has determined that if we do take more from MWD, we can avoid the penalties from OC Water District for overdrafting groundwater, and in the end it'll save us money. And MWD is desperate—when the Columbia pipe's done it'll be a real buyer's market. So in essence it's a buyer's market already."

"But we don't pump that much out of the groundwater here."

"No, but the pump taxes for overdrafting are severe. With the water from MWD we could replenish any overdraft ourselves, and avoid the tax."

Kevin shook his head, confused. "But extra MWD water would mean we would never overdraft."

"Exactly. That's the point. Anyway, it's just an inquiry letter for more information."

Kevin thought it over. In his work he had had to get water permits often, so he knew a little about it. Like many of the towns in southern California, they bought the bulk of their water from Los Angeles's Metropolitan Water District, which pumped it in from the Colorado River. But much more than that he didn't know, and this. . . .

"What information do we have now? Do they have a minimum sale figure?"

Alfredo asked Mary to read them the original letter from MWD, and she located it and read. Fifty acre feet a year minimum. Kevin said, "That's a lot more water than we need. What do you plan to do with it?"

"Well," Alfredo replied, "if there's any excess at first, we can sell it to the District watermaster."

If, Kevin thought. At first. Something strange here. . . .

Doris leaned forward in her seat. "So now we're going into the water business? What happened to the resolution to reduce dependency on MWD?"

"It's just a letter asking for more information," Alfredo said, almost irritably. "Water is a complex issue, and getting more expensive all the time. It's our job to try and get it as cheaply as we can." He glanced at Matt Chung, then down at his notes.

Kevin's fist clenched. They were up to something. He didn't know what it was, but suddenly he was sure of it. They had been trying to slip this by him, in his first council meeting, when he was disoriented, tired, a little drunk.

Alfredo was saying something about drought. "Don't you need an environmental impact statement for this kind of thing?" Kevin asked, cutting him off.

"For an inquiry letter?" Alfredo said, almost sarcastically.

"Okay, okay. But I've stood before this council trying to get permission to couple a greenhouse and a chicken coop, and I've had to make an EIS—so somewhere along the line we'd surely have to have one for a change like this!" Sudden spurt of anger, remembering the frustration of those many meetings.

Alfredo said, "It's just water."

"Fuck, you *must* be kidding!" Kevin said.

Doris jabbed him with an elbow, and he remembered where he was. Oops. He looked down at the table, blushing. There was some tittering out in the audience. Got to watch it here, not just a private citizen anymore.

Well. That had put a pause in the conversation. Kevin glanced at the other council members. Matt was frowning. The moderates looked concerned, confused. "Look," Kevin said. "I don't know who these nominees are, and I don't know any of the details about this offer from MWD. I can't approve item twenty-seven in such a state, and I'd like to move we postpone discussing it until next time."

"I second the motion," Doris said.

Alfredo looked like he was going to make some objection. But he only said, "In favor?"

Doris and Kevin raised their hands. Then Hiroko and Jerry did the same.

"Okay," Alfredo said, and shrugged. "That's it for tonight, then."

He closed the session without fuss, looked at Matt briefly as they stood.

They *had* hoped to slip something by, Kevin thought. But what? Anger flushed through him again: Alfredo was tricky. And all the more so because no one but Kevin seemed to recognize that in him.

Their new town attorney bulked before him. Buddha standing. "You'll come by to see my house?"

"Oh yeah," Kevin said, distracted.

Oscar gave him the address. "Perhaps you and Ms. Nakayama could come by for breakfast. You can see the house, and I might also be able to illuminate some aspects of tonight's agenda."

Kevin looked at him quickly. The man's big face was utterly blank; then his eyes fluttered up and down, wild as crows' wings. *Significance*. The moonlike face blanked out again.

"Okay," Kevin said. "We'll come by."

"I shall expect you promptly at your leisure."


Biking home in the night, the long meeting over. Kevin had had to take some tools over to Hank's, and Doris and Nadezhda had gone directly home, so now he was alone.

The cool rush of air, the bouncing headlamp, the occasional whirr of chain in derailleur. The smell everywhere of orange blossoms, cut with eucalyptus, underlaid by sage: the braided smell of El Modena. Funny that two of the three smells were immigrants, like all the rest of them. Together, the way they could fill him up. . . .

Freed of the night's responsibilities, and still a little drunk, Kevin felt the scent of the land fill him. Light as a balloon. Sudden joy in the cool spring night. God existed in every atom, as Hank was always saying, in every molecule, in every particulate jot of the material world, so that he was breathing God deep into himself with every fragrant breath. And sometimes it really felt that way, hammering nails into new framing, soaring in the sky, biking through night air, the black hills bulking around him. . . . He knew the configuration of every dark tree he passed, every turn in the path, and for a long moment rushing along he felt spread out in it all, interpenetrated, the smell of the plants part of him, his body a piece of the hills, and all of it cool with a holy tingling.

* * *

Kevin's thighs had stiffened up from the afternoon's flight, and feeling them, he saw Ramona's legs. Long muscles, smooth brown skin, the swirl of fine silky hair on inner thigh. Wham, wham, the frame of the ultralite shuddering under all that anger and pain. Still wrapped up with Alfredo, no doubt of that. Hmmm.

Long day. Four for four, boom, boom! His wrists remembered the hits, the solid vibrationless smack of a line drive. Thoughtlessly around the roundabout, up Chapman. Overlying the physical memories of the day, the meeting. Oh, man—stuck on that damned council for two whole years! Anger coursed through him again, at Alfredo's subterfuge, his smoothness. Buddha standing, the weird mime faces of their new town attorney. Something going on. It was funny; he had caught that from right as near sleep as he could have been. He knew he was slow, his friends made fun of him about it; but he wasn't stupid, he wasn't. Look at his houses and see. Would he have noticed that crammed item on the agenda if he had been fully awake? Hard to say. Didn't matter. Pattern recognition. A kind of subconscious resistance. Intelligence as a sort of stubbornness, a refusal to be fooled. No more classrooms falling off their chairs.

He took the left to home, pumped up the little road. He lived in a big old converted apartment block, built originally in a horseshoe around a pool. He had done the conversion himself, and still liked it about the best of any of his work; big tented thing bursting with light, home to a whole clan. His housemates, the neighbors inside, the real family.

Last painful push on the thighs, short coast to the bike rack at the open end of the horseshoe. Upstairs Tomas's window was lit as always, he would be up there before his computer screen, working away. Figures crossed before the big kitchen windows, Donna and Cindy no doubt, talking and pounding the cervecas, watching the kids wash dishes.

The building sat in an avocado grove at the foot of Rattlesnake Hill, one of the last knobs of the Santa Ana Mountains before the long flat stretch to the sea. Dark bulk of the hill above, furry with scrub oak and sage. His home under the hill. His hill, the center of his life, his own great mound of sandstone and sage.

He slipped the front tire of his mountain bike into the rack. Turning toward the house he saw something and stopped. A motion.

Something out there in the grove. He squinted against the two big squares of kitchen light. Clatter of pots and voices. There it was; black shape, between trees, about mid-grove. It too was still, and he had the sudden feeling it was looking back at him. Tall and man-shaped, sort of. Too dark to really see it.

It moved. Shift to the side, then gone, off into the trees. No sound at all.

Kevin let out a breath. Little tingle up his spine, around the hair on the back of his neck. What the . . . ?

Long day. Nothing out there but night. He shook his head, went inside.

# 2

*2 March 2012, 8 A.M. I decided that as a gesture to its spirit I would write my book outdoors. Unfortunately it's snowing today. The balcony above ours makes a sort of roof, however, so I am sticking to my resolve. Roll out computer stand, extension cords, chair. Sit bundled in down booties, bunting pants, down jacket, down hood. Plug in and pound away. The mind's finest hour. My hands are cold.*

*"Stark bewölkt, Schnee." We haven't seen the sun all year, even the Zürchers are moaning. Suddenly a dream comes back to me: Owens Valley in spring bloom.*

*Writing a utopia. Certainly it's a kind of compensation, a stab at succeeding where my real work has failed. Or at least an attempt to clarify my beliefs, my desires.*

*I remember in law school, thinking that the law determined the way the world was run, that if I learned it I could change things. Then the public defender's office, the case loads, the daily grind. The realization that nothing I did there would ever change things. And it wasn't much better at the CLE, or doing lawsuits for the Socialist Party, miserable remnant that it was. So many attacks from so many directions, we were lucky if we could hold on to the good that already existed. No chance to improve things. Nothing but a holding action. Really it was a relief when this post-doc of Pam's gave me the chance to quit.*

*Now I'll change the world in my mind.*

*Our balcony overlooks a small yard, surrounded by solid brick buildings. A massive linden dominates smaller trees and shrubs. Wet black branches thrust into a white sky. Below me are two evergreens, one something like a holly, the other something like a juniper; the birds are clustered in these, fluffed quivering feather-balls, infrequently cheeping. Between two buildings, a slice of Zürich: Grossmünster and Fraumünster and their copper-green spires, steely lake, big stone buildings of the university, the banks, the medieval town. Iron sound of a tram rolling downhill.*

*I'm writing a utopia in a country that runs as efficiently as Züri's blue trams, even though it has four languages, two religions, a nearly useless landscape. Conflicts that tear the rest of the world apart are solved here with the coolest kind of rationality, like engineers figuring out a problem in materials stress. How much torque can society take before it snaps, Dr. Science? Ask the Swiss.*

*Maybe they're too good at it. Refugees are pouring in,* Ausländer *nearly half the population they say, and so the National Action party has won some elections, become part of the ruling coalition. With a bullet. Return Switzerland to the Swiss! they cry. And in fact yesterday we got an* einladung *from the* Fremdenkontrolle der Stadt Zürich. *The Stranger Control. Time to renew our* Ausländerausweise. *It's down to every four months now. I wonder if they'll try to kick us out this time.*

*For now, all is calm. White flakes falling. I write in a kind of pocket utopia, a little island of calm in a maddened world. Perhaps it will help make my future seem more plausible to me—perhaps, remembering Switzerland, it will even seem possible.*

*But there's no such thing as a pocket utopia.*

The next morning Nadezhda joined Kevin and Doris for the visit to Oscar Baldarramma. They biked over in heavy traffic (voices, squeaky brakes, whirring derailleurs) and coasted down Oscar's street, gliding through the spaced shadows of liquid amber trees, so that it seemed the morning blinked.

Oscar's house was flanked by lemon and avocado trees. Unharvested lemons lay rotting in the weeds, giving the air a sweet-sour scent. The house itself was an old stucco and wood suburban thing, roofed with concrete tiles. A separate garden and bike shed stood under an avocado tree at the back of the lot, and a bit of the house's roof extended before the shed: "Carport," Kevin said, eyeing it with interest. "Pretty rare."

Oscar greeted them in a Hawaiian shirt slashed with yellow and blue stripes, and purple shorts. He ignored Doris's exaggerated squint, and led them inside for a tour. It was a typical tract house, built in the 1950s. Doris remarked that it was a big place for one person, and Oscar promptly hunched over and took a long sideways step, waggling his eyebrows fiercely and brandishing an invisible cigar: "Always available for boarding!"

Kevin and Doris stared at him, and he straightened up. "Groucho Marx," he explained.

Kevin and Doris looked at each other. "I've heard the name," Doris said. Kevin nodded.

Oscar glanced at Nadezhda, who was grinning. His mouth made a little O. "In that case . . ." he murmured, and turned to show them the next room.

When the tour was finished Kevin asked what Oscar wanted done.

"The usual thing." Oscar waved a hand. "Big clear walls that make it impossible to tell if you're indoors or out, an atrium three stories tall, perhaps an aviary, solar air conditioning and refrigeration and waste disposal, some banana trees and cinnamon bushes, a staircase with gold bannisters, a library big enough to hold twenty thousand books, and a completely work-free food supply."

"You don't want to garden?" Doris asked.

"I detest gardening."

Doris rolled her eyes. "That's silly, Oscar."

Oscar nodded solemnly. "I'm a silly guy."

"Where will you get your vegetables?"

"I will buy them. You recall the method."

"Huh," Doris said, not amused.

They viewed the back yard in a frosty silence. Kevin tried to get Oscar to speak seriously about his desires, but had little success. Oscar spoke of libraries, wood paneling, fireplaces, comfortable little nooks where one could huddle on long winter nights. . . . Kevin tried to explain that winter nights in the region weren't all that long, or cold. That he tended to work in a style that left a lot of open space, making homes that functioned as nearly self-sufficient little farms. Oscar seemed agreeable, although he still spoke in the same way about what he wanted. Kevin scratched his head, squinted at him. Buddha, babbling.

Finally Nadezhda asked Oscar about the previous night's council meeting.

"Ah yes. Well—I'm not sure how much you know about the water situation here?"

She stood to attention, as if reciting a lesson. "The American West begins where the annual rainfall drops below ten inches."

"Exactly."

And therefore, Oscar went on, much of the United States was a desert civilization; and like all previous desert civilizations, it was in danger of foundering when its water systems began to clog. Currently some sixty million people lived in the American West, where the natural supplies of water might support two or three. But even the largest reservoirs silt up, and most of the West, existing not just on surface water, had mined its groundwater like oil—thousands of years of accumulated rainfall, pumped out of the ground in less than a century. The great aquifers were drying up, and the reservoirs were holding less each day; while drought, in their warming climate, was more and more common. So the search for water was becoming desperate.

The solution was on a truly gigantic scale, which pleased the Army Corps of Engineers no end. Up in the Northwest, the Columbia River poured enormous amounts of water into the Pacific every year. Washington, Oregon and Idaho squawked mightily, remembering how Owens Valley had withered when Los Angeles gained the rights to its water; but the Columbia carried more than a hundred times the water those states were ever expected to need, and their fellow states to the south were truly in need. The Corps of Engineers loved the idea: dams, reservoirs, pipelines, canals— a multi-billion-dollar system, rescuing the sand-choked civilizations of the south. Grand! Lovely! What could be nicer? "It's what we've done in California for years; instead of moving to where the water is, we move the water to where the people are."

Nadezhda nodded. "We have this tradition in my country too. There was a plan to turn the Volga River right around, the whole thing, and send it south for irrigation purposes. Only when it seemed that world weather patterns might be shifted was the plan abandoned." She smiled. "Or maybe it was just lack of funds. Anyway, in your situation, where water will soon be plentiful again, what did that item on last night's agenda mean?"

"I'm not sure, but there were two parts I found interesting. One, the inquiry to Los Angeles's Metropolitan Water District, which supplies most of our town's water from their Colorado River pipeline. Second, the nominations for the watermaster. On the one hand, it looks like an attempt to bring more water to El Modena; on the other, an attempt to control its use when it arrives. You see?"

His guests nodded. "And what about this offer from Los Angeles?" Nadezhda said.

A ghost of a smile crossed Oscar's face. "When the federal courts made the original apportionment of the Colorado River's water to the states bordering it, they accidentally used a flood year's estimate of the river's annual flow. Every year after that they came up short, and the states fought like dogs over what water there was. To solve the problem the court cut all the states' shares proportionally. But California—the MWD, to be precise—recently won back the rights to their original allotment."

"Why is that?"

"Well, first, because they had been using their rights the longest, and most fully, and that solidifies their claim. And secondly, it's felt that the Columbia pipeline will solve the competing states' problems, so they won't need the Colorado's water. So, the MWD has more water than they have had for years, and since these rights are made more secure by usage, they're anxious to have their new water bought up and used as quickly as possible. All of their clients in southern California are being offered more water. Most are refusing it, and so MWD is getting anxious."

"Why are most refusing it?"

"They have what they need. It's a method of growth control. If they don't have the water, they can't expand without special action. The Santa Barbara strategy, it's called."

"But your mayor wants this water."

"Apparently so."

"But *why?*" Kevin said.

Oscar pursed his lips. "Well, you know what *I* heard."

Suddenly he jerked to left and right, peering about in a gross caricature of a check for spies. Low conspirator's voice: "I was dining at Le Boulangerie soon after my arrival in town, when I heard voices from the next booth—"

"Eavesdropping!" Doris exclaimed.

"Yes." Oscar grimaced horribly at her. "I can't help myself. Forgive me. Please."

Doris made a face.

Oscar went on: "Later I discovered the voices were those of your mayor, and someone named Ed. They were discussing a new complex, one which would combine labs with offices and shops. Novagene and Heartech were mentioned as potential tenants."

"Alfredo and Ed Macey run Heartech," Doris told him.

"Ah. Well."

"Did they say where they wanted to build?" Kevin asked.

"No, they didn't mention location—although Mr. Blair did say 'They want that view.' Perhaps that means in the hills somewhere. But if one were contemplating a new development of any size in El Modena, it would be necessary to have more water. And so last night when I saw item twenty-seven, I wondered if this might not be a small first step."

"The underhanded weasel!" Doris said.

"It all seemed fairly public to me," Oscar pointed out.

Doris glared at him. "I suppose you're going to claim a lawyerly neutrality in all this?"

Kevin winced. The truth was, Doris has a prejudice against lawyers. We're suffocating in lawyers, she would say, they're doing nothing but creating more excuses for themselves. We should make all of them train as ecologists before they're let into law school, give them some decent values.

They do take courses in ecology, Hank would tell her. It's part of their training.

Well they aren't learning it, Doris would say. Damned parasites!

Now, in Oscar's presence, she was icily discreet; she only used the adjective "lawyerly" with a little twist to it, and left it at that.

Though he certainly heard the inflection, Oscar eyed her impassively. "I am not a neutral man," he said, "in any sense of the word."

"Do you want to see this development stopped?"

"It is still only a matter of conjecture that one is proposed. I'd like to find out more about it."

"But if there is a large development, planned for the hills?"

"It depends—"

"It depends!"

"Yes. It depends on where it is. I wouldn't like to see any empty hilltops razed and built on. There are few of those left."

"Hardly any," Kevin said. "Really, to get a view over the plain in El Modena, there's only Rattlesnake Hill. . . ."

He and Doris stared at each other.

\* \* \*

Oscar served them a sumptuous breakfast of French toast and sausages, but Kevin had little appetite for it. His hill, his sandstone refuge . . .

When they were done Nadezhda said, "Assuming that Rattlesnake Hill is Alfredo's target, what can you do to stop him?"

Oscar rose from his chair. "The law lies in our hands like a blackjack!" He took a few vicious swings at the air. "If we choose to use it."

"Champion shadow boxer, I see," Doris muttered.

Kevin said, "You bet we choose to use it!"

"The water problem has potential," Oscar said. "I'm no expert in it, but I do know California water law is a swamp. We could be the creature from the black lagoon." He limped around the kitchen to illustrate this strategy. "And I have a friend in Bishop we should talk to, her name's Sally Tallhawk and she teaches at the law school. She was on the State Water Resources Control Board until recently, and she knows more than anyone about the current state of water law. I'm going there soon—we could talk to her about it."

Nadezhda said, "We need to know more of the mayor's plans."

"I don't know how we'll get them."

"I do," Kevin said. "I'm just going to go up to Alfredo's place and ask him!"

"Direct," Oscar noted.

Doris said, "Alternatively, we could crawl under his windows and eavesdrop until we learn what we want to know."

Oscar blinked. "Nothing like a little confrontation," he said to Kevin.

"Doesn't Thomas Barnard live in this area?" Nadezhda asked.

"That's my grandfather," Kevin said, surprised. "He lives up in the hills."

"Perhaps he can help."

"Well, maybe. I mean, true, but . . ."

Kevin's grandfather had had an active career in law and politics, and had been a prominent figure in the economic reforms of the twenties and thirties.

"He was a good lawyer," Nadezhda said. "Powerful. He knew how to get things done."

"You're right." Kevin nodded. "It's a good idea, really. It's just that he's a sort of hermit, now. I haven't seen him myself in a long time."

Nadezhda shrugged. "We all get strange. I would like to see him anyway."

"You know him?"

"We met once, long ago."

So Kevin agreed, a bit apprehensively, to take her up to see him.

Before they left Oscar showed them his library, contained in scores of cardboard boxes; one whole room was full of them. Kevin glanced in a box and saw a biography of Lou Gehrig. "Hey Oscar, you ought to join our softball team!"

"No thank you. I detest softball."

Doris snorted. "What?" Kevin said. "But why?"

Oscar shifted into a martial arts stance. Low growl: "The world plays hardball, Claiborne."


The world plays hardball. Sure, and he could handle it. But not his hill, not Rattlesnake Hill!

It was not just that it stood behind his house, which was true, and important; but that it was his place. It was an insignificant little round top at the end of the El Modena hills, broken dirty sandstone covered with scrub, and a small grove of trees which had been planted by his grandfather's grade school class, many years before. It stood there, the only empty hilltop in the area, because it had been owned for decades by the Orange County Water District, who left it alone.

And no one seemed to go up there but him. Oh, occasionally he'd find an empty beer dumpie or the like, thrown away on the summit. But the hill was always empty when he was there—quiet except for insect creaks, hot, dusty, and somehow filled with a sunny, calm presence, as if inhabited by an old Indian hill spirit, small but powerful.

He went up there when he wanted to work outdoors. He took his sketchpad, up to his favorite spot on the western edge of the copse of trees, and he'd sit and look out over the plain and sketch rooms, plans, interiors, exteriors. He'd done that for most of his life, had done a fair amount of homework there in his schooldays. He had scrambled up the dry ravines on the western side, he had thrown rocks off the top, he had followed the track of an old dirt road that had once spiraled up it. He went there when he was feeling lazy, when he only wanted to sit in the sun and feel the earth turning under him. He went there with women friends, at night, when he was feeling romantic.

Now he went up there and sat in the dirt, in his spot. Midday, the air hot, filled with dust and sage oils. He brushed his hands over the soil, over the sharp-edged nondescript sandstone pebbles. Picked them up, rubbed them together in his hands. He couldn't seem to achieve his usual feeling of peace, however, his feeling of connection with the ground beneath him; and the ballooning sense of lightness, the kind of epiphany he had felt while bicycling home the other night, eluded him completely. He was too worried. He could only sit and touch the earth, and worry.

At work he thought about it, worried about it. He and Hank and Gabriela were busy finishing up two jobs, one down in Costa Mesa, and he worked on the trim and clean-up in a state of distraction. Could they really want to develop Rattlesnake Hill? "It's that view they're after." If they were going to build, they would need more water. If they were going to have a view, in El Modena . . . there really wasn't any other choice! Rattlesnake Hill. A place where

—he realized this one morning, scraping caulking off of tile—where when you were there, you felt quite certain it would never change. And that was part of its appeal.

Usually when Kevin was working he was happy. He enjoyed most of the labor involved in construction, especially the carpentry. All of it, really. The direct continual results of his efforts, popping into existence before his eyes: framing, wiring, stucco, painting, tilework, trim, they all had their pleasures for him. And as he did the designs for their little team's work, he also had the architect's pleasure of seeing his ideas realized. With this Costa Mesa condo rehab, for instance, a lot of things had been uncertain: would you really be able to see the entire length of the structure, rooms opening on rooms? Would the atrium give enough light to that west wing? No way to be sure until it was done; and so the pleasure of work, bringing the vision into material being, finding out whether the calculations had been correct. Solving the mystery. Not much delayed gratification in construction. Immediate gratification, little problem after little problem, faced and solved, until the big problem was solved as well. And all through the process, the childlike joys of hammering, cutting, measuring. Bang bang bang, out in the sun and the wind, with clouds as his constant companions.

Usually. But this week he was too worried about the hill. Touch-up work, usually one of his favorite parts, seemed pale diversion, finicky and boring. He hardly even noticed it. And his town work was positively irritating. They would be digging out that street forever at their pace!

He had to get some answers. He had to go up and confront Alfredo, like he had said he would that morning at Oscar's. No way around it.


So one afternoon after town work he pedaled up into the hills, to the house on Redhill where a big group of Heartech people lived. Alfredo's new home.

The house was set on a terrace, cut high on the side of the hill above Tustin and Foothill. It was a huge white lump of Mission Revival, a style Kevin detested. To him the California Indians were noble savages, devastated by Junípero Serra's mission system. Thus Mission Revival, which every thirty years or so swept through southern California architecture in a great nostalgic wave, seemed to Kevin no more than a kind of homage to genocide. Any time he got the chance to renovate an example of the style he loved to obliterate it.

One small advantage to Mission Revival was it was always easy to find the front door—in this case a huge pair of oak monsters, standing in the center of a massive wall of whitewashed adobe, under a tile-roofed portico. Kevin stalked up the gravel drive and yanked on a thick rope bellpull.

Alfredo himself answered, dressed in shorts and a T-shirt. "Kevin, what a surprise. Come on in, man."

"I'd rather talk out here, if you don't mind. Do you have time?"

"Sure, sure." Alfredo stepped out, leaving the door open. "What is it?"

No really indirect approach to the issue had suggested itself to Kevin, and so he said, "Is it true that you and Ed and John are planning to build an industrial park on Rattlesnake Hill?"

Alfredo raised his eyebrows. Kevin had expected him to flinch, or in some other way look obviously guilty. The fact that he didn't made Kevin uneasy, nervous—a little bit guilty himself. Perhaps Oscar had misoverheard.

"Who told you that?"

"Never mind who—I just heard it. Is it true?"

Alfredo paused, shrugged. "There're always plans being talked around—"

Ah ha!

"—but I don't know of anything in particular. You would know if there was something up, being on the council."

Anger fired through Kevin, quick and hot. "So that's why you tried to slip that water stuff past us!"

Alfredo looked puzzled. "I didn't try to slip anything past anyone. Some business was taken care of—or we tried—in front of the whole council, in the ordinary course of a meeting. Right?"

"Well, yeah, that's right. But it was late, everyone was tired, I was new. No one was watching anymore. It was as close to slipping the thing under the door as you could get."

"A council meeting is a council meeting, Kevin. Things go on right till the last moment. You're going to have to get used to that." Alfredo looked amused at Kevin's naïveté. "If someone wanted to slip something by, it could have been shoved in among a bunch of other changes, it could have been done in the town planner's office and presented as boilerplate—"

"I guess you wish you had done it that way, now."

"Not at all. I'm just saying we didn't try to slip one by you." Alfredo spoke slowly, as if doing his best to explain a difficult matter to a child. He moved out onto the gravel drive.

"I think you did," Kevin said. "Obviously it isn't something you'd admit now. Anyway, what are you doing trying to turn some of our open land into a mall?"

"What mall? Look here, what are you talking about? We're making an inquiry about the extra water MWD is offering, because it makes sense, it saves us money. That's part of our job on the council. Now as to this other thing, if someone is exploring the possibilities of a multi-use center, what's the problem? Are you saying we shouldn't try to create jobs here in El Modena?"

"No!"

"Of course not. We need more jobs—El Modena is small, we don't generate much income. If some businesses moved here everyone would benefit. You might not need your share increased, but other people do."

"We already make enough from town shares."

"Is that the Green position?"

"Well . . ."

"I didn't think so. As I recall, you said increased efficiency would increase the shares."

"So it would!"

Alfredo walked further down the drive, to the low mounds of an extensive cactus garden. Standing there they had a view over all of Orange County's treetopped plain. "It gets to be a question of how we can become more efficient, doesn't it. I don't think we can do it without businesses to *be* efficient. But you—sometimes I think if you had your way you'd empty out the town and tear it down entirely." He gestured at the cacti. "Back to mustard fields and scrub hills, and maybe a couple of camps down on the creek."

"Come on," Kevin said scornfully. In fact, he had quite often daydreamed about just such a return to nature when tearing old structures down. But he knew it was just a fantasy, a wish to live the Indians' life, and he never mentioned it to others. It was disconcerting to hear Alfredo read his mind like that.

Alfredo saw his confusion. "You can only go so far with negative growth before it becomes harmful, Kevin. I realize there's a lot of momentum in your direction these days, and believe me, I think it's been a good thing. We needed it, and things are better now because of it. But any pendulum can swing too far, and you're one of those trying to hold it out there when it wants to swing back. Now that you're in a position of responsibility you've got to face it—the people who talked you into joining the council are extremists."

"We're talking about your company here," Kevin said feebly.

"We are? Well heck, say that we are. At Heartech we make cardiovascular equipment and blood substitutes and related material. It helps everyone, especially the regions still dealing with hepatitis and malaria. You were in Tanzania for your work abroad, you've got to know the kind of help it does!"

"I know, I know." Heartech was an important part of Orange

County's booming medtech industry, doing state-of-the-art work. It was right at the legal limits on company size; most of its long-time workers were hundreds, which meant that the company paid an enormous amount of money into Tustin's town shares, which were then redistributed out among the town's citizens, as part of their personal income. And Heartech helped a lot of liaison companies in Africa and Indonesia as well. No doubt about it, it was a good company, and Alfredo believed in it passionately. "Listen," he said, "let's follow this through. Don't you think biotechnology is valuable work?"

"Of course," Kevin said. "I use it every day."

"And the medical aspects of it save lives every day."

"That's true. Sure."

"Now wouldn't it be a good thing if El Modena contributed to that?"

"Yeah, it would. That would be great."

Alfredo spread his hands, palms up.

They looked at cacti.

Kevin, beginning to feel the way he did when he rode the Mad Hatter's Teacups in Disneyland, tried to gather his thoughts. "Actually, it seems to me it isn't so important where it happens . . ." Ah yes: where. "I mean where exactly do you have in mind, Alfredo?"

"Where what? Sorry, I've lost track of what you're talking about."

"Well, if you're thinking of building in the hills. Are you?"

"If there were people thinking about a development in the El Modena Hills, it would be a matter of attracting the best tenants possible. Things like that are important when you're competing with places like Irvine."

So he was thinking of the hills! "You should be mayor of Irvine," Kevin said bitterly. "Irvine is just your style."

"You mean they make money there? They attract business, they have big town shares?"

"Yes."

"But that's what our town council is for, right? I mean, there are people in this town who could use it, even if you can't."

"I'm not against the town shares growing!"

"Good. I'm glad to hear it."

Kevin exhaled noisily, frustrated. Feeling completely dizzy, he said, "Well—still—"

"So we should do what we can, right?"

"Yeah, sure—"

"I think we're more in agreement than you realize, Kevin. You build things, I build things. It's really the same thing."

"Yeah, but, but if you're tearing up wilderness!"

"Don't worry about that. There isn't any wilderness in El Modena in the first place, so don't get too romantic about it. Besides, we'll all be working out anything that happens here in the next couple of years, so we'll bang out a consensus just like always. Don't let your friends make you too paranoid about it."

"My friends don't make me paranoid. You make me paranoid."

"I don't appreciate that, Kevin. And it won't help in the long run. Look, I build things to make money, and so do you. We're in the same business, aren't we? I mean, aren't you in the construction business?"

"Yeah!"

Alfredo smiled. "Well, there you have it. We'll work it out. Hey, I've got to get going—I've got a date—down in Irvine, in fact." He winked, went into the house.

Ka . . . CHUNK.

Kevin faced the door, and after a moment's thought he slammed his fist into his palm. "It's completely different!" he shouted. "I do renovation!" Or else we tear down a structure and put another one in its place. And it always fits the land better. It's entirely different!

But there was no one there to argue with.

He let out a long breath. "Shit."

What had happened? Well, maybe Alfredo and his partners were planning a development. Maybe they weren't. Maybe it was up in the hills. Maybe it wasn't. He had learned that much.

He pulled his bike from the rack, observed his hands shaking. Alfredo was too much for him; try as he might, Alfredo could run rings around him. Chagrined at the realization, he turned the bike and headed downhill.

He needed help. Doris, Oscar, Oscar's friend in Bishop; Jean and the Green party organization; Nadezhda. Perhaps even Ramona, somehow. He shied away from the thought—the implication that his dislike for Alfredo had non-political components—it was a political matter, nothing more!

And Tom.

Once home he went looking for Nadezhda. "Do you still want to meet my grandfather?"


Kevin's grandfather lived in the back country, on a ridge in the broken hills north of Black Star Canyon. Kevin led Nadezhda and Doris up a poorly kept trail to his place, winding between sage and scrub oak and broken ribs of sandstone. Nadezhda was inquisitive about everything: plants, rocks, Tom's livelihood. She had a beautiful low voice, and had learned her English in India, so that the musical lilt of the subcontinent filled all her sentences.

"Well, Tom takes his ten thousand and lets it go at that. He's got a garden and some chickens, and he does some trapping and beekeeping and I don't know what all. He really does keep to himself these days. Didn't used to be that way."

"I wonder what happened."

"Well, he retired. And then my grandma died, about ten years ago."

"Ten years."

A switchback, and Kevin looked down at her. Next to Doris she seemed slight as a bird, graceful, cool, fit. No wonder Doris admired her. Ex-head of the Soviet State Planning Commission, currently lecturer in history on a school freighter, which was up in Seattle—

"He can get ten thousand dollars a year without working?"

"At his age he can. You know about the income magnitude thing?"

"A legal floor and ceiling on personal income, yes?"

"Yeah. Tom takes the floor."

She laughed. "We have a similar system. Your grandfather was a big advocate of those laws when they were introduced. He must have had a plan."

"No doubt. In fact he told me that once, when I was a kid."

Hiking with Grandpa, up the back canyons. Up Harding Canyon to the little waterfall, bushwhacking up crazy steep slopes to the ridge of Saddleback, up the dirt road to the double summit. Birds, lizards, dusty plants, endless streams of talk. Stories. Sandstone. The overwhelming smell of sage.

They topped a rise, and saw Tom's house. It was a small weather-beaten cabin, perched on the ridge that boxed the little canyon they had ascended. A big front window looked down at them, reflecting clouds like a monocle. Walls of cracked shingle were faded to the color of sand. Weeds grew waist high in an abandoned garden, and sticking out of the weeds were broken beehive flats, rain barrels, mountain bikes rusted or disassembled, a couple of grandfather clocks broken open to the sky.

Kevin thought of homes as windows to the soul, and so Tom's place left him baffled. The way it fit the ridge, disappeared into the sandstone and sage, was nice. A good sign. But the disarray, the lack of care, the piles of refuse. It looked like the area around an animal's hole in the ground.

Nadezhda merely looked at the place, black eyes bright. They walked through a weedy garden to the front door, and Kevin knocked. No answer. They stepped around back to the kitchen door, which was open. Looked in; no one there.

"Well, we might as well sit and wait a while," Kevin said. "I'll try calling him." He went to the other side of the ridge, put both hands to his mouth and let loose a piercing whistle.

There was a tall black walnut up the ridge, with a bench made of logs underneath it; Doris and Nadezhda sat there. Kevin wandered the yard, checking the little set of solar panels in back, the connections to the satellite dish. All in order. He pulled some weeds away from the overrun tomatoes and zucchini. Long black and orange bugs flew noisily away; other than that there was a complete, somehow audible silence. Ah: bees in the distance, defining the silence they buzzed in.

"Hey."

"Jesus, Grandpa!"

"What's happening, boy."

"You frightened me!"

"Apparently so."

He had come up the same trail they had. Bent over, humping some small iron traps and four dead rabbits. He'd been only feet from Kevin's back when he announced his presence, and not a sound of approach.

"Up here to weed?"

"Well, no. I brought Doris and a friend. We wanted to talk with you."

Tom just stared at him, bright-eyed. Stepped past and ducked into his cabin. Clatter of traps on the floor. When he re-emerged Doris and Nadezhda had come over from the bench and were standing beside Kevin. Tom stopped and stared at them. He was wearing pants worn to the color of the hillsides, and a blue T-shirt torn enough to reveal a bony white-haired chest. The hair edging his bald pate was a tangle, and his uncut beard was gray and white and brown and auburn, stained around his mouth. A dust-colored old man. He always looked like this, Kevin was used to it; it was, he had thought, a part of aging. But now Nadezhda stood before them neat as a bird after a bath, her silvery hair cut so that even when windblown it fell perfectly into place. One of her enamel earrings flashed turquoise and cream in the sun.

"Well?"

"Grandpa, this is a friend of Doris's—"

But Nadezhda stepped past him and extended a hand. "Nadezhda Katayev," she said. "We met a long time ago, at the Singapore Conference."

For an instant Tom's eyebrows shot up. Then he took her hand, dropped it. "You look much the same."

"And you too."

He smiled briefly, slipped past them with a neat, skittish movement. "Water," he said over his shoulder, and took off down a trail into a copse of live oak. His three guests looked at each other. Kevin shrugged, led the women down the trail. There in the shade Tom was attaching a pump handle to a skinny black pump, then pumping, slowly and steadily, his back to them. After quite a while water spurted from the pump into a tin trough, and through an open spigot into a five-gallon bucket. Kevin adjusted the bucket under the spigot, and then the three of them stood there and watched Tom pump. It was as if he were mute. Feeling uncomfortable, Kevin said, "We came up to talk to you about a problem we're having. You know I'm on the town council now?"

Tom nodded.

Kevin described what had happened so far, then said, "We don't really know for sure, but if Alfredo is interested in Rattlesnake Hill, it would be a disaster—there just aren't that many empty hills left."

Tom squinted, looked around briefly.

"I mean in El Modena, Tom! Overlooking the plain! You know what I mean. Shit, you planted the trees on top of Rattlesnake Hill, didn't you?"

"I helped."

"So don't you care what happens to it?"

"It's your backyard now."

"Yeah, but—"

"And you're on the council?"

"Yeah."

"Stop him, then. You know what to do, you don't need me."

"We do too! Man, when I talk to Alfredo I end up saying black is white!"

Tom shrugged, moved the full bucket from under the spigot and replaced it with an empty one. Stymied, Kevin moved the full bucket onto flat ground and sat beside it.

"You don't want to help?"

"I'm done with that stuff, Kevin. It's your job now." He said this with a friendly, birdlike glance.

Second bucket filled, Tom pulled out the pump handle and put it in a slot on the pump's side. He lifted the two buckets and started back toward the cabin.

"Here, let me take one of those."

"That's okay, thanks. I need the two for balance."


Following Tom up the trail to his cabin, Kevin looked at the old man's bowed back and shook his head, exasperated. This just was not the Grandpa he had grown up with. In those years there had been no more social animal than Tom Barnard; he was always talking, he organized camping trips for groups from town constantly, and he had taken his grandson up into the canyons and over the Santa Ana Mountains, and the San Jacintos, and back into Anza Borrego and Joshua Tree, and over to Catalina and down into Baja and up into the southern Sierras—and talking the whole way, for hours at a time every day, about everything you could possibly imagine! Much of Kevin's education—the parts he really remembered—had come from Tom on their hikes together, from asking questions and listening to Tom ramble. "I hated capitalism because it was a lie!" Tom would say, fording Harding Canyon stream with abandon. "It said that everyone exercising their self-interest would make a decent community! Such a lie!" Splash,

splash! "It was government as protection agency, a belief system for the rich. Why, even when it seemed to work, where did it leave them? Holed up in mansions and crazy as loons."

"But some people like to be alone."

"Yeah, yeah. And self-interest exists, no one can say it doesn't—the governments that tried got in deep trouble, because that's a lie of a different kind. But to say self-interest is all that exists, or that it should be given free rein! My Lord. Believe that and nothing matters but money."

"But you changed that," Kevin would say, watching his footwork.

"Yes, we did. We gave self-interest some room to work in, but we limited it. Channeled it toward the common good. That's the job of the law, as we saw it then." He laughed. "Legislation is a revolutionary power, boy, though it's seldom seen as such. We used it for all it was worth, and most liked the results, except for some of the rich, who fought like wolverines to hold on to what they had. In fact that's a fight that's still going on. I don't think it will ever end."

Exactly! Kevin thought, watching his strangely silent grandfather toil up the trail. The fight will go on forever, and yet you've stepped out of it, left it to us. Well, maybe that was fair, maybe it was their turn. But he needed the old man's help!

He sighed. They got to the cabin and Tom ducked inside. One bucket of water went into a holding tank. The other was brought out into the sun, along with the four dead rabbits. Big knife, slab of wood, tub for the blood and guts. Great. Tom began the grisly task of skinning and cleaning the little beasts. Hardly any meat on them; hardly any meat on Tom. Kevin went around the side and fed the chickens. When he returned Tom was still at it. Doris and Nadezhda were seated on the ground under the kitchen window. Kevin didn't know what to say.

* * *

"This conference in Singapore you met at—what was it about?"
Doris finally said, breaking a long silence.

"Conversion strategies," Nadezhda said.

"What's that?"

Nadezhda looked up at Tom. "Maybe you can explain it more
clearly," she said. "My English is not so good to be explaining
such a thing."

Tom glanced at her. "Uh huh." He went into the kitchen
with the skinned rabbits; they heard a freezer door open and shut.
He came back out and took the tub of entrails over the Emerson
septic tank, dumped them in, shut the lid and clamped it down.

Nadezhda shrugged at Doris, said, "We were finding ways
to convert the military parts of the economy. The big countries
had essentially war economies, and switching to a civilian economy
without causing a depression was no easy thing. In fact, no one
could afford to change. So strategies had to be conceived. We had
a big crowd in Singapore, though some there opposed the idea.
Do you remember General Larsen?" she said to Tom. "U.S. Air
Force, head of strategic defense?"

"I think so," Tom said as he walked by her. He went out
into his garden and started plucking tomatoes.

Nadezhda followed him. She picked up his basket, followed
him around as he shifted. "I am thinking people like him made
aerospace industries the hardest to change."

"Nah."

"You don't think so?"

"Nah."

"But why?"

Long silence.

Then Tom said, "Aerospace could be sicced on the energy
problem. But who needs tanks? Who needs artillery shells?"

He lapsed back into silence, rooted under weeds in search of another tomato. He glanced at Nadezhda resentfully, as if she had tricked him into speaking. Which, Kevin thought, she had.

"Yes," Nadezhda said, "conventional weapons were hard. Remember those Swiss plans, for cars built like troop movers?" She laughed, a low clear chuckle, and even elbowed Tom in the arm. He smiled, nodded. She said, "What about those prefab schoolrooms, made by the helmet and armor plants!"

Tom smiled politely, got up and went into the kitchen.

Nadezhda followed him, talking, taking down a second cutting board and cutting tomatoes with him, going through his shelves to find spices to add to oil and vinegar. Talking all the while. Occasionally in passing she put a hand to his arm, or while cutting she would elbow him gently, as old friends might: "Do you remember? Don't you remember?"

"I remember," he said, with that small smile. He glanced at her.

"When the engineers got the idea of it," she said to Doris and Kevin, "their eyes lit up. It was the best problems they were ever having, you could hear it in their voices! Because everything helped, you see? With all that military work redirected to survival problems, conflicts caused by the problems were eased, which reduced the demand for weapons. So it was a feedback spiral, and once in it, things changed very quickly." She laughed again, suffused with nervous energy, doing her best, Kevin saw, to arc that energy into Tom; to charm him, cajole him—seduce him. . . .

Tom merely smiled that brief glancing smile, and offered them a lunch of tomato salad. "All there is." But he was watching her, out of the corner of his eye; it seemed to Kevin that he couldn't help it.

They ate in silence. Tom wandered off to the pump with his buckets. Nadezhda went with him, talking about people they had known in Singapore.

Doris and Kevin sat in the sun. They could hear voices down at the pump. At one point Nadezhda exclaimed "But we acted!" so sharply they could make it out.

Muttered response, no response.

When they returned she was laughing again, helping with one bucket and telling a story. Tom was as silent as before. He still seemed friendly—but remote, watching them as if from a distance. Glancing frequently at Nadezhda. He took one bucket down to the Emerson tank, began working there.

Eventually Kevin shrugged, and indicated to the women that he thought it was time to leave. Tom wandered back as they stood. "You sure you won't help us?" Kevin asked, catching Tom's gaze and holding it.

Tom smiled. "You get 'em this time," he said. And to Nadezhda: "Nice to see you again."

Nadezhda looked him in the eye. "It was my pleasure," she said. She smiled at him, and something in it was so appealing, so intimate, that Kevin looked away. He noticed Tom did the same. Then Nadezhda led them down the trail.

# 3

*23 March. There is no such thing as a pocket utopia.*

*Consider the French aristocracy before the revolution—well fed, well clothed, well housed, well educated—brilliant lives. One could say they lived in a little utopia of their own. But we don't say that, because we know their lives rested on a base of human misery, peasants toiling in ignorance and suffering. And we think of the French aristocracy as parasites, brutal, stupid, tyrannical.*

*But now the world is a single economy. Global village, made in Thailand! And we stand on little islands of luxury, while the rest—great oceans of abject misery, bitter war, endless hunger. We say, But they are none of our affair! We have our island.*

*The Swiss have theirs. Mountain island with its banks and its bomb shelters—as fast as some Swiss take refugees in, other Swiss kick others out. Schizoid response, like all the rest of us.*

*Spent the morning at the* Fremdenkontrolle, *one office of the police station on Gemeinderstrasse. Clean, hushed. Marble floors and desktops. Polite official. But, he explains slowly in high German so I will understand, the new laws. As you don't have a job. Tourist visa only. And as you have been here over a year already, this no longer possible is. No Ausweis. Yes, wife can stay till end of employment. Daughter too, yes.*

*But who'll take care of her? I wanted to shout. Of course that's part of the plan. Kick out one and the rest of the family will follow, even if they have work. Efficient.*

*So we sit at the kitchen table. Pam's post-doc has seven months to go. She needs to finish—even with it it'll be hard to find work in the States, with all regulatory agencies under a hiring freeze. She's thinking about that, I can see. Eight years' work, and for what. I'll have to take Liddy, too—Pam can't work and care for her both. We have a month to get out. Meaning six months apart. The post-docs from China have to do worse than that all the time. But with Liddy so young.*

*We can protest, I say. Pam shakes her head, mouth bitter. Picks up In'tl Herald Tribune. Southern Club defaulting on all debt. Prediction of twenty-five percent reduction in world population called optimistic by. Civil war in India, in Mexico, in. Deforestation in. World temperature up another degree Centigrade since. Species going extinct—*

*I've already read it.*

*Pam throws the paper aside, looking beat. Never seen her so grim. Stands to wash dishes. I watch her back and can see she's crying. Six months.*

*We are the aristocracy of the world. But this time the revolution will bring down more than the aristocracy. Could be everything. Crumpled newspaper, compartmentalized disaster. Catastrophe by percentage points.*

*We can avoid it, I swear we can. Must concentrate on that to be able to continue.*

When the heart dies, you can't even grieve.

Tom rolled out of bed feeling old. Antediluvian. Contemporary of the background radiation. Eighty-one years old, actually. Well-propped by geriatric drugs which he abused assiduously, but still. He groaned, limped to the bathroom. Came awake and the great solitude settled on him again.

Standing in the doorway, looking out at the sage sunlight and not seeing a thing. Depression is like that. Sleep disrupted, affect blocked, nothing left but wood under the skin and an urge to cry. The best pills could do was to take the last feeling away and make it all wood. Which was a relief, although depressing in its own way if you considered it.

It was this: when his wife died he had gone crazy. And while he was crazy, he had decided never to become sane again. What was the point? Nothing mattered any more.

Say two strong trees grow together, in a spiraling of trunks. Say one of the trees dies and is cut away. Say the other is left twisted like a corkscrew, an oddity, always turning in an upward reach, stretch, search. Leafy branches bobbing, searching the air for something lost forever.

So the great solitude settled on him. No one to talk to, nothing interesting to do. Even the things he had enjoyed doing alone were not the same, because the solitude in them was not the same as the great solitude. The great solitude had seeped into everything, into the sage sunlight and the rustle of leaves, and it had become the condition of his madness, the definition of it, its heart.

He stood in the doorway, feeling it.


Only now he had been disturbed. A face from the past. Had he really lived that life? Sometimes it was flatly impossible to believe. Surely every morning he woke up an entirely new creature, oppressed by false visions of false pasts. The great solitude provided a continuity of sorts, but perhaps it was just that he had been condemned to wake up every morning in the body of yet another creature under its spell. The Tom Barnard who ran buffeted in the storms of his twenties. Later the canny lawyer chopping away at the law of the land, changing it, replacing it with laws more just, more beautiful. We can escape our memes just as we escaped our genes! they had all cried then. Perhaps they were wrong on both accounts, but the belief of the moment, of that particular incarnation . . .

A face from a previous incarnation. My name is Bridey Murphy, I can speak Gaelic, I knew a Russian beauty once with raven hair and a wit like the slicer for electron microscopes. Sure you did—Anastasia, right? And he's your grandson, too, the builder. Sure. A likely story. We can escape our genes, perhaps it was true. If he himself woke a new creature every morning, why expect his daughter's son to bear any resemblance to any incarnation along the way? We live with strangers. We live with disjunctures; he had never done any of it; just as likely to have been raising bees in some bombed-out forest, or lying flat on his back in an old folks' home, choking for breath. Incarnations too, no doubt, following other lines. That he had carved this line to this spot, that the world had spun along to this sage sunlight and the great solitude; impossible to believe. He would never become sane again.

But that face. That tough sharp voice, its undercurrent of scorn. He had liked her, in Singapore, he had thought her . . . attractive. Exotic. And once he and his young wife had climbed up through the cactus on the back side of Rattlesnake Hill, to watch a sunset and make love in a grove of trees they had helped to plant some incarnations before, in a dream of children. Sylphlike naked woman, standing between trees in the dusk. And jumping across time, a ghost of joy. Like an arrow into wood, *thunk*. Pale smooth skin, dark rough bark, and in that vision a sudden spark, the ghost of an epiphany.

They shouldn't be allowed to take that hill.

Bridey Murphy, the canny lawyer, stirring inside. "God damn it," he cried, "why didn't you leave me alone!"

He limped back inside and threw on his clothes. He looked at the cascading sheets on the bed and sat on it and cried. Then he laughed, sitting there on his bed. "Shit," he said, and put on his shoes.


So he came down out of the hills. Through trees, sunbeams breaking in leaves, scuffing the trail, watching for birds. At Black Star Canyon road he got on his little mountain bike and coasted down to Chapman. Coming through the cleft in the hills he looked to the right, up Crawford Canyon to Rattlesnake Hill. Scrub and cactus, a little grove of live oak, black walnut and sycamore on its round peak. The rest of the hills in view were all built up, exotic trees towering over homes, sure. Height equals money equals power. A miracle any hill was left bare. But OC Water District had owned Rattlesnake Hill before El Modena incorporated, and they were tough. Toughest watermasters in California, and that was saying a lot. So they had kept it clear. But a year or two before, they had deeded it over to the town; they hadn't needed it to fulfill their task, and the task was all that mattered to them. So now El Modena owned it, and they would have to decide what it was for.

Farther down Chapman he passed Pedro Sanchez, Emilia Deutsch, Sylvia Waters and John Smith. "Hey, Tom Barnard! Tom!" They all yelled at him. Old friends all. "Doesn't anything ever change down here?" he said to them, braking to a halt. Big smiles, awkward chat. No, nothing ever changed. Or so it seemed. Nothing but him. "I'm off to find Kevin." "They're playing a game," Pedro told him. "Down on Esplanade." Invitations to come over for dinner, cheery good-byes. He biked off, feeling strange. This had been his town, his community. Years and years.

Down on the Esplanade diamonds a softball game was in progress. The sight of it stopped him, and again the wood in him was pierced by ghost arrows. He had to stop.

There on a rise behind the Lobos dugout lolled Nadezhda Katayev and a tall fat man, laughing at something. He gulped, felt his pulse in him. Out of the habit of talking; a great wash of something like grief passed through him, lifted the wood, buoyed it up. Grief, or . . .

He pedaled down and joined them. The man was the new town attorney, named Oscar. They were deciding which movie star each ballplayer most resembled. Nadezhda said Ramona looked like Ingrid Bergman, Oscar said she looked like Belinda Brav.

"Nah she's prettier than that," Tom murmured, and felt a little creak of surprise when they laughed.

"What about me?" Oscar said to Nadezhda.

"Um . . . maybe Zero Mostel."

"You must have had quite an interesting career as a diplomat."

"What about Kevin?" Tom said.

"Norman Rockwell," Nadezhda decided. "Hay in his mouth."

"That's not a movie star."

"Same thing."

"A cross between Lyle Sims and Jim Nabors," Oscar said.

"No crosses allowed," Nadezhda ruled. "One of the Little Rascals, anyway."

Kevin came to bat, swung at the first pitch and hit a sharp line drive to the outfield. By the time they got the ball back in he was standing on third, with a grin splitting his face. You could see every tooth he had.

Nadezhda said, "He's like a little kid."

"Nine years old forever," Tom said, and cupped his hands to yell "Nice hit!" Automatic. Instinctual behavior. Couldn't stop it. So much for changing your memes.

Kevin saw him and laughed, waved. "Little Rascals for sure," Nadezhda said.


They watched the game. Oscar lay back on the grass, rubbing one pudgy hand over the cut blades, looking up at clouds. The seabreeze kept them cool. Fran Kratovil biked by, and seeing Tom she stopped, came over with a look of pleased surprise, greeted him, chatted a while before taking off. Old friends. . . .

Kevin came to bat again, lined another sharp hit. "He's hitting well," Tom said.

"Hitting a thousand," Oscar said.

"Wow."

"Hitting a thousand?"

They explained the system.

"He has a beautiful swing," she noted.

"Yes," Tom said. "That's a buggy whip swing."

"Buggy whip?"

"Quick wrists," Oscar said. "Flat swing, high bat speed. It looks like the bat has to bend to catch up with the rest of the swing."

"But why a buggy whip?"

Silence. Hesitantly, Tom said, "A buggy whip was a flexible pole, with a switch at the end. So it makes sense—a quick bat would look more like that than like a bull whip, which was like a piece of rope. Funny—I don't suppose anyone has actually seen a buggy whip for years, but they still have that name for the swing."

The other team came to bat, and got a rally going. "Ducks on the pond!" someone yelled.

"*Ducks* on the *pond?*"

"Runners in scoring position," Oscar explained. "From hunting."

"Do hunters shoot ducks when they're still on the water?"

"Hmm," Tom said.

Oscar said, "Maybe it means that knocking the runners in is easier than shooting ducks in the air."

"I don't know," Tom said. "It's more a question of potential. RBI time, you know."

"RBI time!" someone in the dugout yelled.


Then Doris came blasting over a grassy rise and coasted down to them, skidding to a halt.

"Hey, hi, Tom." She was excited. "I went to the town offices and checked through the planner's files to see if there were any re-zoning proposals in the works, and there are! There's one for Rattlesnake Hill!"

"Do you remember what the change was?" Oscar asked.

Doris gave him a look. "Five point four to three point two."

The two men thought about it.

Nadezhda said, "Is that an important change?"

"Five point four is open space," Oscar replied. He had rolled onto his side, and was lying on the grass with his massive head propped on one hand. "Three point two is commercial. How much are they proposing to change?"

Doris glared at him, incensed at his evident lack of concern. "Three hundred and twenty acres! It's the whole Water District lot—land I thought we were going to add to Santiago Creek Park. And damned if they aren't trying to slip it by in a comprehensive zoning package."

"It's stupid for Alfredo to try to slip all this stuff by," Tom said, thinking about it. "There's no way it'll work for long."

Oscar agreed. For the zoning change alone there would certainly have to be an environmental impact statement, and a rubber stamp town vote at the least—perhaps a contested town vote; and much the same would be true of any increase in the amount of water bought from MWD.

"The smart way to do it," Tom said, "would be to explain what you had in mind for the hill, and once that was generally approved of, get the necessary legislation through for it."

"It's almost as if . . ." Oscar said.

"As if he needs to do it this way." Tom nodded. "That's something to look for. If you can find out why he's trying to do the groundwork first, you might have found something useful." He gazed mildly at Doris and Oscar. Oscar rolled back onto his back. Doris gave Oscar a disgusted look, and fired away on her mountain bike.

After the game Oscar returned to work, and Nadezhda asked Tom to show her the hill in question. They went by Kevin and Doris's house, where Nadezhda was staying, then through the back garden to the bottom slope of the hill. An avocado grove extended up it fifty yards or so. "This is it. Crawford Canyon down there to the left, Rattlesnake Hill above."

"I thought so. It really is right behind their house."

Working in the grove was Rafael Jones, another old friend. "Hey, Tom! Everything okay?"

"Everything's fine, Rafe."

"Man, I haven't seen you in years! What brings you down here?"

Tom pointed a thumb at Nadezhda, and the other two laughed. "Yeah," Rafael said, "she's shaking up our house too." He was part of Kevin and Doris's household, the senior member and the house farmer; he ran their groves, and the garden. Tom asked him about the avocados and they chatted briefly. Feeling exhausted at the effort, Tom pointed uphill. "We're off to the top."

"Okay. Good to see you again, Tom, real good. Come on down and have dinner with us sometime."

Tom nodded and led Nadezhda up a trail. The irrigated greens gave way abruptly to deer-colored browns. It was May, which in southern California was the equivalent of late summer. Time for golden hills. Hesitantly Tom explained; southern California springtime, when things bloomed, occurred from November through February, corresponding to the rainy season. Summer's equivalent would be March through May; and the dry brown autumn was June through October. Leaving no good equivalent for winter proper, which was about right.

He really had forgotten how to talk.

Up the trail, wending between scrub oak, black sage, purple sage, matilija poppy, horehound, patches of prickly pear. The sharp smells of the hot shrubs filled the air, dominated by sage. The ground was a loose light-brown dirt, liberally mixed with sandstone pebbles. Tom stopped to search for fossils in the outcrops of sandstone, but didn't find any. They were there, he told Nadezhda. Shark teeth from giant extinct species, scores of mollusk-like things, and the teeth of a mammal called a desmostylian, which had no close relatives either living or extinct—kind of a cross between a hippo and a walrus. All kinds of fossils up here.

Occasionally they disturbed a pheasant, or a crowd of crows. From time to time they heard the rustling of some small animal getting out of their way. The sun beat on their necks.

First a flat ridge, then up to the hill's broad top. The wind struck them coolly. They walked to the little grove of black walnut and sycamore and live oak at the hill's highest point, and sat in the shade of a sycamore, among big brown leaves.

Nadezhda stretched out contentedly. Tom surveyed the scene. The coastal plain was hazy in the late afternoon light. There was Anaheim Stadium, the big hospital in Santa Ana, the Matterhorn at Disneyland. Other than that, treetops. Below them the houses and gardens of El Modena caught the light and basked in it, looking like the town's namesake in Tuscany.

He asked her about her home, ignoring the ghosts in the grove. (A young couple, in there laughing. Beyond them children, planting foot-high trees.)

She was from Sebastopol in the Crimea, but spoke of India as her home. After many years there, she had moved back to Moscow. "That was hard."

"India changed you?"

"India changes everyone who visits it, if they stay long enough, and if they stay open to it. So many people—I understood then how it would be possible to overrun the Earth, and soon. I was twenty-four when I first arrived. It gave me a sense of urgency."

"But then you went back to Moscow."

"Yes. Moscow is nothing compared to India, ah! And then my government was strange regarding India. Work there and when you came back you found no one was listening to you any more. You were tainted, you see. Made untouchable." She laughed.

"You did a lot of good work anyway."

"I could have done more."

They sat and felt the sun. Nadezhda poked a twig through

dead leaves. Tom watched her hands. Narrow, long-fingered. He felt thick, old, melancholy. Be here now, he thought, be here now. So hard. Nadezhda glanced at him. She mentioned Singapore, and it came back to him again, stronger than ever. She had been one of the leaders of the conference. They had had drinks together, walked the crowded, hot, color-filled streets of Singapore, arguing conversion strategies just as fast as they could talk. He described the memory as best he could, and she laughed. It was the same laugh. She had a kind of Asian face, hawk-nosed and imperious. Cossack blood. The steppes, Turkestan, the giant spaces of central Asia. Slender, fashionable, she had dressed in Singapore with liberal flourishes of Indian jewelry and clothing. Still did. Of course now she sailed with Indians again.

He asked about her life since then.

"It has not been so very interesting to tell. For many years I lived and worked in Moscow." Her first husband had been assigned to Kazakhstan and she had done regional economic studies, until he was killed in the riots of a brief local insurgency. Back to Moscow, then to India again, where she met her second husband, a Georgian working there. To Kiev, back to Moscow. Second husband died of a heart attack, while they were on vacation. Scuba diving in the Black Sea.

Children?

A son in Moscow, two daughters in Kiev. "And you?"

"My daughter and her husband, Kevin's folks, are in space, working on solar collectors. Have been for years. My son died when he was young, in a car accident."

"Ah."

"Kevin's sister is in Bangladesh. Jill."

"I have five grandchildren now, and a sixth is coming in a month." She laughed. "I don't see them enough."

Tom grunted. He hadn't seen Jill in a year, his daughter in five. People moved around too much, and thought that TV phones made up for it. He looked up at the sun, blinking through leaves.

So she had had two husbands die on her. And here she was laughing in the sunlight, making patterns with dead leaves and twigs, like a girl. Life was strange.

Back down the hill, in the sunset's apricot light. Tuscany in California. Kevin and Doris's house glowed in its garden, the clear panels and domes gleaming like a lamp lighting the surrounding trees. They went inside and joined the chaos of dinnertime. The kids dashed around shrieking. Sixteen people lived in the building, and at dinner time it seemed most of them were kids. Actually only five. Rafael and Andrea were clearly delighted to see him; they had worked together on El Modena's town charter, and yet it had been years. . . . They embarrassed Tom by getting out the good china and trying to get the whole house down to the table. Tomas, however, wouldn't leave his work screen. Tom knew Yoshi and Bob, they had been teachers when Kevin was in school. And he was acquainted with Sylvia and Sam, Donna and Cindy. But what a crowd! Even before the great solitude had descended, he couldn't have lived in such a constant gathering. Of course it was a big place, and they seldom got together like this. But still . . .

After dinner Tom poured cups of coffee for him and Nadezhda, and they went out to the atrium, where chairs were set around the fishpond. Overhead the skylight's cloudgel fluttered a bit in the breeze, and from the kitchen voices chattered, dishes clattered. The atrium was dark and cool, the cloudgel clear enough to reveal the stars. The open end of the old horseshoe shape of the apartment complex gave them a view west, and they were just enough up the side of the hill that the lights from the town bobbed below, like the lamps of night fishermen on a sea. They sipped coffee.

Doris rushed in, slammed the door, stomped off to the kitchen. "Where's my dinner?" she shouted.

About fifteen minutes later Kevin came in, looking pleased. He had been flying with Ramona, he said, and they had gone out to dinner afterward.

Doris brought him right back to earth with her news of the zoning proposal. "It's definitely Rattlesnake Hill they're after."

"You're kidding," Kevin said feebly. He collapsed onto one of the atrium chairs. "That bastard."

"We're going to have a fight on our hands," Doris predicted grimly.

"We knew that already."

"It's worse now."

"Okay, okay, it's worse now. Great."

"I'm just trying to be realistic."

"I know, I know." They went into the kitchen still discussing it. "Who the fuck ate everything?" Doris roared.

Nadezhda laughed, said quietly to Tom, "Sometimes I am thinking perhaps my Doris would not be unhappy if those two got back together."

"*Back* together?"

"Oh yes. They have had their moments, you know."

"I didn't know."

"Nothing very much. And a long time ago. When they first moved into this house, apparently. They almost moved into a room together, but then they didn't. And then Doris came over to work for me for a time. She told me about it then, when she was really feeling it. Then when she returned things were not working out so much, I guess. But I think she is still a bit in love with him."

Tom considered it. "I guess I hadn't noticed." How could he, up in the hills? "She does watch him a lot."

"But then there is this Ramona."

"Yeah, that's what Kevin just said. But I thought she lived with Alfredo."

Nadezhda filled him in on the latest. Telling him about the affairs of his own townspeople, and with a buoyant, lively curiosity. With pleasure. And she made it all so . . . suddenly he wanted to feel like she did, he wanted that *engagement* with things.

"Ah," he said, confused at himself. Hawk-nosed Asian beauty, gossiping to him in the dark atrium. . . .

They sat and watched stars bouncing on the other side of the cloudgel. Time passed.

"Will you be staying here tonight?" she asked.

The house had several spare rooms, but Tom shook his head. "It's an easy ride home, and I prefer sleeping there."

"Of course. But if you'll excuse me, I think I will be going to bed."

"Sure, sure. Don't mind me. I'll be setting off in a while."

"Thanks for taking me up on the hill. It's a good place, it should be left alone."

"We'll see. I was glad to go up there again myself."

She walked up the stairs to the second floor, then around the inner balcony to the southeast curve of the horseshoe, where the best guestroom was. Tom watched her disappear, thinking nothing. Feelings fluttered into him like moths banging into a light. Creak of wood. So long since he had done any of this! It was strange, strange. Long ago it had been like this, as if he slept years every night, and woke up in a new world every morning. That voice, laughing on the streets of Singapore—was it really them? Had it happened to him? Impossible, really. It must be. And yet . . . a disjuncture, again—between what he felt to be true, and what he knew to be fact. All those incarnations made his life.

He stood slowly. Tired. It would be a long ride home, but suddenly he wanted to be there. Needed to be there.


The next couple of weeks were warm and humid, and there was a dull feeling of tension in the air, as if more and more static electricity were building, as if any day a Santa Ana wind would come pouring over the hills and blow them all into the sea.

Tom didn't come back down into town, and eventually

Nadezhda got in the habit of going to see him. Sometimes he was there, sometimes he wasn't. When she found him at home they talked, in fits and starts; when he wasn't there she worked in his garden. Once she saw him slipping away as she hiked up the last stretch of trail, and realized he was having trouble adjusting to so much company. She stopped going, and spent her days with Doris or Kevin or Oscar, or Rafael and Andrea, or her other housemates. And then one evening Tom showed up at the house, to have a cup of coffee after dinner. Ready to talk for an hour or two, then slip away.

Kevin and Ramona fell into a pattern of a different sort; they got together in the late afternoon after work, every few days, to go flying, and then perhaps have dinner. While in the air they talked over the day's work, or something equally inconsequential. Out of nowhere, it seemed, Kevin had found an instinct for avoiding certain topics—for letting Ramona choose what to talk about, and then following along. It was a sort of tact he had never had; he hadn't cared enough, he hadn't been paying enough attention to the people he was with. But on these flights he was *really* paying attention, with the same dreamlike intensity he had felt on their first flight. Every excursion aloft was a whole and distinct adventure, the most important part of his day by far. Just to soar around the sky like that, to feel the wind lift them like a gull . . . to see the land, lying below like a gift on a plate!

And there was something wonderful about working so hard in tandem, harnessed to the same chain, legs pumping in the same rhythm. The physicality of it, the things they learned about each other's characters while at the edge of physical endurance—the constant reminder of their bodies, of their animal reality . . . add that to their softball games, and the swim workouts they sometimes joined in the mornings, and there wasn't much they didn't know about each other, as animals.

And so Kevin paid attention. And they pumped madly in the seats of the Ultralite, and soared through the air. And pointed out the sights below, and talked about nothing but the present moment.

"Look at that flock of crows," Kevin would say, pointing at a cloud of black-dot birds below.

"Gangsters," Ramona would reply.

"No, no! I really like crows!" She would laugh. "I do, don't you? They're such powerful flyers, they don't look pretty but they do it with such efficiency."

"Fullbacks of the air."

"Exactly!" There were thousands of crows in Orange County, living in great flocks off the fruit of the groves. "I like their croaky voices and the sheen on their wings, and that smart look in their eye when they watch you"—he was discovering all this in himself only at the moment he spoke it, so that it felt marvelous to speak, to discover—"and the way they hop sideways all shaggy and awkward. I really love them!"

And Ramona would laugh harder at each declaration. And Kevin would never speak of other things, knowing it was what she wanted. And she would fly them around the sky, more graceful than the crows, as graceful as the gulls, and the sweat would dry white on their skins as they worked like dervishes in the sky. And Kevin's heart . . . well, it was full. Brimming. But he had an instinct, now, telling him what to do. Telling him to bide his time.

Thus the most important part of his life, these days, was taking place two or three hundred feet in the air. Of course he was concerned about the workings of the town council, and it took up a fair amount of time, but from week to week he didn't worry about it much. They were waiting for Alfredo to make his next move, and doing what they could to find out more about his intentions. Doris had a friend in the financial offices of her company, who had a friend in a similar job with Heartech, and she was digging carefully there to find out what the rumors were in Alfredo's base of operations. There were rumors of a move, in fact. Perhaps they could get more details out of this friend of a friend; Doris was excited by the possibility, and put a lot of work into it, talking, acting innocent and ignorant, asking questions over lunches.

Then the re-zoning proposal appeared on the agenda, and it included the re-zoning of the old OCWD tract. Doris and Kevin walked into the council meeting like hunters settling into a blind.

It was a much more modest affair than the inaugural meeting; the people who had to be there were there, and that was it. The long room was mostly empty and dark, with all the light and people crowded into the business end of things. Alfredo ran the meeting through its paces with his usual efficiency, only lightly peppering things with jokes and asides. Then he came to item twelve. "Okay, let's get to the big stuff—re-zoning proposals."

Petitioners in the audience laughed as if that were another of his jokes. Kevin hunched forward in his seat, put his elbows on the table.

Doris, seeing the way Kevin's hands were clenched, decided she had better do the talking. "What about this change for the Crawford Canyon lots, Alfredo?"

"They're the lots that OCWD used to own. And the land up above it, across from Orange Hill."

"That's called Rattlesnake Hill," she said sharply.

"Not on the maps."

"Why a zoning change? That land was supposed to be added to Santiago Park."

"No, nothing's been decided about that land, actually."

"If you go back to the minutes of the meeting where those Crawford Canyon condos were condemned, I think you'll find that was the plan."

"I don't recall what was discussed then, but nothing was ever done about it."

"Going from five point four to three point two is a big change," Jerry Geiger noted.

"It sure is!" Kevin said loudly. "It means you could do major commercial building. What's the story, Alfredo?"

"The planning commission wanted to be able to consider that land as a possibility for various projects, isn't that right, Mary?"

Mary looked down at her notes. "Three point two is a general purpose classification."

"Meaning you could do almost anything up there!" Kevin exclaimed.

He was losing his temper already. Doris scowled at him, tried to take back their side of the argument. "It's actually commercial zoning, isn't it, Mary?"

"It allows commercial development, yes, but doesn't mandate it—"

Face red with emotion, Kevin said, "That is the *last empty hill in El Modena!*"

"Well," Alfredo said calmly. "No need to get upset. I know it's more or less in your backyard, but still, for the good of the town—"

"Where I live has nothing to do with it!" Kevin exclaimed, sliding his chair back as if he might stand. "What the fuck does that have to do with anything?"

A shocked silence, a titter. Doris elbowed Kevin in the side and then stepped hard on his foot. He glanced at her, startled.

"Don't you need an EIS for a change like that?" she said quickly.

"Zoning changes in themselves don't require impact statements," Alfredo said.

"Oscar, is that right?" Doris asked.

Oscar nodded slowly, doing his sleeping Buddha routine. "They are not required, but they can be requested."

"Well I request one!" Kevin said. "Anything could be done up there!"

"I second the request," Doris said. "Meanwhile, I want to have some things on record. Who made this re-zoning proposal, and why?"

An odd, expectant silence. Finally Alfredo said, gently, "As Kevin pointed out, this land includes one of the last empty hilltops in the area. As such, the land is extremely valuable. *Extremely* valuable. When we condemned those condos under the hill, I thought it was so we would be able to put the land to use that would better serve the whole town. That's what I said at the time. Now, if the land is made part of Santiago Park, that's nice for the park, and for the people living in the immediate area—"

Kevin's chair scraped the floor.

"We all live in the immediate area," Doris said, smacking her knee into Kevin's and wishing she had a cattle prod.

"Okay, okay," Alfredo said. "Some people are closer than others, but we're all in the neighborhood. And that's the point. That land is valuable to all of us, and Matt and I think all of us are concerned to see that it is used in the best way possible for the good of the town."

"Do you have a specific plan for it?" Jerry Geiger asked suddenly.

"Well, no. We only want the possibility to be there."

"Does this explain the request to buy more water from MWD?" Jerry asked, looking interested.

"Well, if we had the water . . ." Alfredo said, and Matt picked up the thought:

"If we had the water and the land was zoned for commercial use, then we could begin to look seriously at how to make use of the situation."

"You haven't looked seriously up till this point," Jerry said, sounding sardonic—though with Jerry it was hard to be sure.

"No, no. We've talked ideas, sure. But . . ."

Alfredo said, "Of course nothing can done unless the infrastructural possibility is there. But that's what our job is, to make sure the possibilities are there."

"Possibilities for what?" Kevin said, his voice rising. Doris attempted to step on his foot again, but he moved it. "First you're thinking about upping the water from MWD, supposedly because it saves us money. Then we're given a zoning change with no explanation, and when we ask for an explanation we get vague statements about possibilities. I want to know what exactly you have in mind, Alfredo, and why you're going about all this in such an underhanded manner.''

For a split second Alfredo glared at him. Then he turned away and said in a relaxed, humorous voice, "To repeat this proposal, made before the full council in the course of a normal council meeting, we are interested in re-zoning these lots so that we can then discuss using them in some way. Currently they are zoned five point four, which is open land and only open land—''

"That's what they should be zoned!" Kevin said, nearly shouting.

"That's your opinion, Kevin, but I don't believe it's generally shared, and I have the right to express my belief by proposing a change of this sort. Don't you agree?"

Kevin waved a hand in disgust. "You can propose all you want, but until you explain what you mean to do you haven't made a full proposal. You've only just tried to slip one by. The question is, what do you have in mind to do on that land? And you haven't answered it.''

Doris tightened the corners of her mouth so she wouldn't smile. There was something to be said for the mad dog approach, after all. Kevin's bluntness had taken Alfredo aback, if only for a moment. He was searching for an answer, and everyone could see it.

Finally Alfredo said, "I haven't answered that question because there is no answer to it. We have no specific plans for that land. We only want to make it possible to think about it with some expectation that the thought could bear fruit. It's useless to think about it unless we zone the land in a way that would make development legal. That's what we're proposing to do.''

"We want an EIS," Doris said. "It's obvious we'll need one, since as you say the re-zoning would mean a great deal for that land. Can we vote on that?"

They voted on it, and found they were unanimously in favor

of an environmental impact statement on the proposed zoning change. "Of course," Alfredo said easily. "These are facts we need to know."

But the look he gave them as they got up at the end of the meeting, Doris thought, was not a friendly one. Not friendly at all. She couldn't help smiling back. They had gotten to him.

Not long after that the Lobos had their first game of the season with the Vanguards, and from the moment Kevin stepped into the batter's box and looked out at Alfredo standing on the pitcher's mound, he could see that Alfredo was going to pitch him tough. The council meetings, Kevin and Ramona's flights over the town—if Alfredo had not seen them himself, he had surely heard of them, and what did he think of that? Kevin had his suspicions. . . . Even the fact that Kevin was still batting a thousand, a perfect seventeen for seventeen—oh, yes. Alfredo had his reasons, all right.

And he was a good pitcher. Now softball is a hitter's game, and a pitcher isn't going to strike a batter out; but that doesn't mean there's nothing he can do but serve it up. If the pitcher hits the back of the square of carpet that marks the strike zone with a high-arced pitch, it becomes damned difficult to hit the ball hard. Alfredo was good at this kind of pitch. And he had honed the psychological factor, he had the look of a power pitcher, that Don Drysdale sneer of confident disdain, saying *you can't hit me*. This was a ludicrous look for a softball pitcher to have, given the nature of the game, but somehow on Alfredo it had its effect.

So he stared in at Kevin with that contemptuous grin, seeming both not to recognize him and to personally mark him out at the same time. Then he threw up a pitch so high that Kevin immediately decided not to swing at it.

Unfortunately it landed right in the middle of the carpet. Strike one. And in their league batters got only two strikes, so Kevin was only a pitch away from striking out.

Alfredo's sneer grew wider than ever, and his next pitch was ridiculously high. Kevin judged it would fall short, and held up. He was right by no more than an inch, whew! One and one.

Unfazed, Alfredo threw up another pitch just like the previous one, only a touch deeper, and with a sudden jolt of panic Kevin judged it would be a strike. He swung hard, and was more surprised than anyone when he saw the ball flying deep into right-center field, rocketed by the desperation of Kevin's swing. Whew! He ran to second and smiled at his teammates, who were cheering loudly from the dugout. Alfredo, of course, did not turn around to look at him. Kevin laughed at his back.

In subsequent innings Alfredo walked Kevin twice. He was ridden hard for this failure by Kevin's teammates, and he got noticeably sharper as he urged on his own teammates. Meanwhile the rest of the Lobos were hitting him unusually well also. So it was not a good game for Alfredo, and the Lobos were ahead 9-4 when the Vanguards came up for the last time. Alfredo himself led off, and hit a single up the middle. He stood on first shouting to his teammates, clapping with an excess of energy.

The next batter, Julie Hanson, hit a hard line drive over Kevin's head. Kevin went to cover third, and then he was in that weird moment when things were happening all around him and he was very much a part of it, but not doing a thing: watching Mike race over and cut the ball off, seeing Alfredo barrel around second on his way to third, seeing Mike throw the ball hard toward him. He straddled the base to take the throw on one bounce. The ball tailed off to the right and he jumped out to stop it, and at the same moment he caught it *boom!* Alfredo slammed into him, knocking him head over heels into foul territory.

Dazed, Kevin shook his head. He was on hands and knees. The ball was still in his glove. He looked over at Fred Spaulding, who had his thumb up in the out sign. People were converging on them from all directions, shouting loudly. Alfredo was standing on third base, yelling angrily himself—something about Fred's umpiring. A crowd was gathering, and someone helped Kevin to his feet.

He took the ball from his glove and walked over to Alfredo, who eyed him warily. Without planning to he flipped the ball against Alfredo's chest, where it thunked and fell to the ground. "You're out," he said harshly, hearing his voice in a way he usually didn't.

He turned to walk away, was suddenly jerked around by the arm. He saw it was Alfredo and instantly lashed out with a fist, hitting Alfredo under the ear at about the same time that Alfredo's right struck him in the mouth. He fell, and then he and Alfredo and several others were in a chaotic clump of wrestling bodies, Alfredo screaming abuse, Kevin cursing and trying to get an arm free to swing again, Fred shouting at them to stop it and Mike and Doris and Ramona doing the same, and there were hands all over him pulling him away, restraining him. He found himself held by a bunch of hands; he could have broken free of them, but they were friends' hands for the most part, recognizable as such by feel alone. Across a stretch of grass Alfredo was similarly held. Alfredo glared furiously across the gap, shouting something at Fred. Nothing anyone said was comprehensible, it was as if he stood under an invisible bell jar that cut off all meaning, but in the cacophony he suddenly heard Ramona shriek "*What do you think you're doing!*" He took his eyes from Alfredo for an instant, afraid she meant him. But Ramona was transfixing Alfredo with a fierce look, it was him she was yelling at. Kevin wondered where he'd hit him. His right knuckles were throbbing.

"Fuck that!" Alfredo was shouting at Fred, "Fuck that! He was in the baseline, what'm I supposed to do? It's perfectly legal, it happens all the time!"

This was true.

"He's the one that started something," Alfredo shouted. "What the fuck is this?"

"Oh shut up, Alfredo," Ramona interjected. "You know perfectly well you started it."

Alfredo spared only a second to glare at her, but it was a cold, cold glare. He turned back to Fred: "Well? Are you going to do your job?"

A bunch of people from both teams began shouting accusations again. Fred pulled a whistle from under his shirt and whistled them down. "Shut up! Shut up! Shut up! I'm going to stop the game and give you both defeats if you don't get back to your dugouts! Come on, this is stupid. Move it!" He walked over to the clump of Lobos holding Kevin, and said, "Kevin, you're out of the game. This whole thing is your fault."

Loud contradictions from Kevin's teammates.

"—when you're in the baseline!" Fred carried over them. "The runner has the right to the baseline, and fielders have no complaint if they get run into while standing in it. So there was no call to throw the ball at him. Go sit it out. There's only a couple outs to go anyway, and I want to get this game finished so the next one can begin! Move it!"

Kevin found himself being pulled back toward the dugout. He was sitting on the bench. His throat was sore—had he been shouting too? Must have been.

Ramona was sitting next to him, hand on his arm. Suddenly he was aware of that touch, of a strong hand, trembling slightly, supporting him. She was on his side. Publicly. He looked at her and raised his eyebrows.

She took her hand away, and now it was his body that was quivering. Perhaps it had been his all along.

"That bastard," she said, with feeling. She stared across at Alfredo, who stood in his dugout still shouting at Fred.

Kevin could only swallow and nod.

After the game—which the Lobos held on to win—Kevin walked away a bit dazed, and considerably embarrassed. To be kicked out of a softball game, my Lord. It happened occasionally, especially between certain rival teams who tended to drink beer during the game. But it was rare.

He heard Alfredo's voice all the way across the field, and turned to look for him, surprised by the intensity of his dislike. That little figure over on the hillside, surrounded by its friends . . . a bundling, a node of everything he despised. If only he could have gotten in one more punch, he would have flattened him—

"Hi, Kev."

He jumped, afraid his thoughts could be read on his face. "Hi, Ramona."

"Pretty exciting game."

"Yeah."

"Here, come with me. I have to teach the afternoon class, but it ends early and then we can go flying."

"Sure." Kevin had been planning to return to work too, but they were finishing the Campbell house, and Hank and Gabriela could take care of clean-up for the afternoon.

They biked over to the high school, and Kevin showered in the gym. The old room brought back a lot of memories. His mouth hurt, the upper lip was swelling on one side. He combed his hair, futile task, and went up to Ramona's class. She was already into a lecture, and Kevin said hi to the kids and sat in the back.

The lecture had to do with population biology, the basic equations that determined population flux in a contained environment. The equations were nonlinear, and gave a rough model for what could be seen in the outside world, populations of a given species rising and falling in a stable but unpredictable, non-repeating cycle. This concept was counter-intuitive and Ramona took a long time explaining it, using examples and moving into a conversational style, with lots of questions from the students.

Their lab took up the whole top floor of one building, and the afternoon light poured in all the western windows and shattered blue in Ramona's black hair. She brought Kevin into the discussion and he talked about the variety of biologic systems used in modern architecture, settling on the example of Chinese carp in an atrium pool. These fish were among the steadiest in terms of numbers, but the equations still held when describing fluctuations in their population, and they were put to immediate use in deciding the size of the pool, the number of fish to be harvested, and so on.

Still, the nonlinearity of the equations, the tendency for populations to suddenly jump up or down, confused some of the students. Kevin could understand this, as it always struck him as a mystery as well.

Ramona dragged out a Lorenz waterwheel to give them a concrete example. This was a simple waterwheel with twelve buckets around its rim, and it could turn in either direction. When the water was turned on from a hose hung above the wheel, the slowest stream of water wouldn't move the wheel at all; slowly the top bucket filled and then water dribbled over its side to the tub below. At a moderate flow the top bucket filled and tilted off to one side, and after that the wheel turned in a stately circle, buckets emptying on the bottom and partially filling under the hose. This was what they all expected, this was what common sense and experience from the outside world would suggest was normal. Thus it was even more of a surprise when Ramona turned up the water from the hose, and the wheel began to turn rapidly in one direction, slow down, speed up, *reverse direction*—

The class gasped at the first reversal, laughed, chattered. The wheel moved erratically, buckets sometimes filling to the brim, sometimes flashing under the hose. Chaotic movement, created by the simplest of inputs. Ramona moved from wheel to blackboard, working through the equations that described this oddity, which was actually quite common in nature. Then she set the students to exercises to demonstrate the issue for themselves, and they crowded around computer screens to see the results of their work in spectacularly colored displays.

Kevin sat at the back and watched her work. Despite her ease and laughter there was something objective, even formal in her manner. The kids were relaxed but respectful around her, and if they horsed around excessively a laser glance from her dark eyes would be enough to put them back to the task. Remembering their own days in high school—in the very same room—Kevin had to laugh: she had been a hell-raiser then. Maybe that was an advantage, now that it was her job to keep control. Station to station, running each student through the work, making sure they understood, moving on with instructions for further experiments onscreen. . . . It was clear she was a good teacher, and that was a pleasure to see. It was important for a teacher to have a certain distance, she should be liked and admired but also at a distance, a strong personality presenting a strong and coherent portrait of the world. This is the way the world is! the strong teacher says in every phrase and glance; not to downplay the complexity of the world, but to present a clear and distinct single view of it, which students could then work against in building their own views. It wasn't so important that the teacher present all sides of a case, or pretend to neutrality in controversial issues. Over the years the multiplicity of teachers that every student got would take care of that. What was more important was that a teacher advocate a vivid, powerful set of ideas, to be a force, to make an impact. Population biology was still a seething mass of theoretical controversy, for instance, but Ramona argued the case for her beliefs as firmly as if speaking to a dissertation committee judging her—outlining other opinions, but then countering them with the ones she believed in. And the students listened. Kevin too.

Then class was done, and they were out in the late afternoon's honey light. The color of high school swim team workouts. "Come on, we just have enough time to tour El Toro before dinner. I've got to make the meal tonight, you can help."

"Sure." They were going to have to gain altitude fast to catch up to Kevin.

\* \* \*

Dear Claire:

I am here.

I arrived three weeks ago, and was offered my choice of housing: I could lease a small empty tract house, or I could take up residence in a large communal home which had some empty rooms. I went to visit the communal home, and found it occupied by a number of extraordinarily friendly, healthy, energetic and beautiful people. Naturally I chose the small empty tract house. Note address below.

The town is indeed as arcadian as I thought when visiting for the interviews—idyllic or bucolic, depending on mood. Part of it lies just under foothills; then these same foothills form the middle of the town, geographically, though they are sparsely populated; and behind the foothills there is a section of high canyon within the town limits. Most of the town seems to consist of gardens, truck farms, nurseries—in any case, land in cultivation—except for that given over to bike paths, swimming pools or sport fields. Orchards are popular. Although we are in Orange County, the trees seem mostly to be lemon, avocado, olive—I promise at first opportunity I will open the tree guide you gave me, and figure out which. I know you will want to know.

There is just as much sun as legends say, perhaps more. Three weeks of it and I feel a bit stunned. Imagine the effect of lifetimes of it, and you will more fully understand the local culture.

They bike to excess. In fact there is no public transport except for car rentals on the freeways, which are expensive. Motorbikes are even more expensive. Obviously the feeling is that your own legs should move you. People here have strong legs.

On the other hand they don't know who Groucho Marx is. And as far as I can determine, not only is there no live theater in El Modena—the whole county is bare of it! Yes, I'm in the Gobi. I'm in Nova Zemlya. I'm in—yes—*I'm in Orange County*. I'm in the land where culture consists of a vigorous swim workout, followed by a discussion of the usefulness of hand paddles.

I witnessed this very discussion the other day, when my nev

friend Kevin urged me to come by the pool. I dropped by and saw about thirty people, swimming back and forth. Back and forth, and back and forth. And so on. Very, very energetically. The exercise certainly creates some beautiful bodies—something I'd rather watch than have, as you know.

At one point Kevin leaped out salmonlike and invited me to join them. I explained that an allergy, alas, prevented me from doing so.

Oh too bad, he said. Allergic to chlorine?

To exertion.

Oh, wow—what a shame!

I suggested to him that they were wasting a fine energy source. Look, I said, if you were only to tie lines to your ankles, and have the lines wound on spools that offered a little resistance, then it might be possible to store some small fraction of the calories used to swim across the pool. One or more solar panels could be retired from service, the constellations made less cluttered. Kevin nodded thoughtfully. Good idea! he said. But he bogged down in design difficulties, and promised he would get back to me.

Kevin, by the way, is the builder I've hired to renovate my new domicile; he's a bioarchitect. Yes, the latest thing, it's my style now. In fact I saw several examples of Kevin's work before hiring him, and he is very good—a sort of poet of homes, with a talent for spacious, sculpted interior space. My hopes are high.

Having seen his work, it was at first disconcerting to meet Kevin himself, because in person he strikes one as a very ordinary carpenter: tall, lanky, loose in a way that makes you immediately confident that he can field grounders with the best of them. He grins a lot. In fact he wandered through my whole house grinning, on his first visit; but with a squint that could have indicated Deep Thought. I hope so. In any case, a new friend. He laughs at my extravagances, I at his, and in our mutual amazement we are both well entertained.

And actually Kevin is the emperor of intellect, compared to

his partner Hank. Hank is short and balding, with forearms as thick as his neck. He's in his mid-forties, though he looks older than that. Apparently he was once a student in the seminary of that Native American church down in New Mexico, and it shows. He is prone to sudden spells of gaping. He'll be working at a maniac's pace (the only one he has) when *bang* he'll stop whatever he is doing and stare open-mouthed at it, entranced. Say he is sawing a two-by-four when he's transfixed, perhaps by a knot in the wood. Seconds pass; a minute or two may pass. Then: We are whorls of pattern, he'll say in an awed tone, tossed out by the surging universe.

What's the matter, Hank? Gabriela will call from across the house. Find a bug?

Once when they were talking I heard him say, Hard to believe they've broken up, I remember when those two was so close they would've held water.

Another time he was describing a fight Kevin and the town's mayor had on the softball diamond (a famous fight, this; these people gossip so much they make Chicago seem like a city of mutes—you won't believe that, but it's true), and he said, Alfredo was so worked up it's lucky he has two nostrils.

People are always dropping by to talk to him, I'm not sure why. As far as I can tell they seem in want of advice, although about what I couldn't guess. Hank is always happy to see them, and they chat as he works, or go out and sit in the driveway, sometimes for a good part of the day. Between that and the gaping I would say he is not the driving element in the team.

And the way their third partner Gabriela stares at him! He never ceases to amaze her. She's younger than the men are, hired straight out of school a year or two ago, to keep up their energy, Hank explained. She has a piercing eye, and a sharp tongue as well, and a wild laugh, usually inspired by her two partners. They can lay her flat on the floor.

It may be a while before work on my house is completed.

Other entertainment: I am joined here by a fellow exile, a Soviet woman named Nadezhda Katayev. She is here visiting an acquaintance of hers, one Doris Nakayama. Doris works in superconductors, and has perhaps been affected by too close contact with her materials. She is cool, tough, humorless; boggled by my bulk and confused by my speech. But she does have this friend Nadezhda, who, if she were not in her seventies and the spitting image of my grandmother, would soon be the object of my advances. Maybe she will be anyway. We loaf around town together like two aging diplomats, assigned to a backwater post in the twilight of our careers.

Our latest expedition was to a garden party. Ah yes, I thought: country culture. A pastoral Proustian affair, drinks in the topiary, flower-beds and hedges, perhaps even a maze. Nadezhda and I biked over together, me dressed in colonial whites, trundling along with other cyclists gazelling by me on both sides, and Nadezhda in a flower print dress which constantly threatened to get caught in the spokes of her bike.

We were greeted at the door of the Sanchez's big communal house by our hostess Ramona Sanchez, who was dressed in her usual outfit of gym shorts and a T-shirt, plus giant canvas gardening gloves. Yes, this was a garden party; meaning we all were supposed to go out and work in the garden.

So I spent the better part of an afternoon sitting in my whites on newly turned earth, making repartee with dissected worms and keeping close track of the progress of my blisters. The only consolations were the beer, Nadezhda's mordant commentary, muttered to me in delicious counterpoint to her polite public pronouncements, and the sight of Ramona Sanchez's long and leggy legs. Ramona is the town beauty; she looks like either Ingrid Bergman or Belinda Brav, depending on whether you take my word or Nadezhda's. Currently she is the focus of a great deal of gossip, as she recently broke up with her long-time mate Alfredo the mayor. My friend Kevin is interested in taking Alfredo's place, but then so am I—the difference being that Ramona appears to reciprocate some of Kevin's regard, while for me she has only a disinterested friendliness.

Though she did join me to weed for a half hour or so. I argued the civil rights of the poor decimated or bimated worms, writhing around us. Ramona assured me in her best biology teacher style that they were beneath pain, and that I would approve the sacrifice when I ate the food that resulted from it. A specialty of the area? I asked, squinting with trepidation. Luckily she only meant the salad.

Well, you get the idea. It really exists! Arcadia! Bucolica! Marx's "idiocy of rural life"! I don't think I truly believed it until now.

Not that the town is free of trouble! My daily workload reminds me constantly that in fact it exists entangled in intricate webs of law. Their system is a mix, combining a communalism of the Santa Rosa model—land and public utilities owned in common, residents required to do ten hours a week of town work, a couple of town-owned businesses in operation to use all the labor available, that sort of thing—with aspects of the new federal model: residents are taxed more and more heavily as they approach the personal income cap, and they can direct 60 percent of their taxes to whatever services they support the most. Businesses based in town are subject to the same sort of graduated system. I am familiar with much of this from my years in Bishop, which has a similar system. As usual in these set-ups, the town is fairly wealthy, even if it is avoided by businesses looking for the best break possible. From all the income generated, a town share is distributed back out to the citizens, which comes to about twice the national income floor. But people still complain that it isn't higher. Everyone wants to be a hundred. And here they believe that a properly run town could make everyone hit the cap as a matter of course. Thus there is the kind of intense involvement with town politics typical of these set-ups, government mixed with business mixed with life-styles, etc.

And so there is also the usual array of Machiavellian battles. Prominent among these at the moment is an attempt by the mayor to appropriate an empty hilltop for his own company's offices. He's got at least an even chance of succeeding, I'd say; he appears popular, and people want the town shares larger. Moving Heartech into town would certainly do that, as it's a very successful medtech company, right at the legal limit for company size.

The opposition to the mayor comes mainly from Kevin and his friends, and they are getting a quick education, with little or no help from the Green party brass, a fact I find faintly suspicious. Most recently they got the council to order an EIS for the zoning change that would make development possible, and they thought this was a big victory. You see what I mean about naïveté! Naturally the town planner, a functionary of the mayor's, went out and hired Higgins, Ramirez and Bretner to do the EIS, so we'll get another LA Special in a few weeks from the infamous HRB, urging the creation of an environment by development as soon as possible. And my friends will learn that an EIS is just one more cannon on the battlefield, to be turned in different directions depending on who holds it. I'm going to take them up to Sally and let her educate them.

But enough for this time, or too much.

Do write again. I know it is a lost and dead form of communication, but surely we can say things in correspondence that calls would never allow. As for instance, I miss you. In fact I miss almost all of my life in Chicago, which has disappeared like a long vivid dream. "I feel as if great blocks of my life have broken off and fallen into the sea," isn't that how Durrell puts it in the *Quartet?* I suppose I should consider El Modena my Cycladean isle, removed from the Alexandrian complexities of Chi and my life there; here I can do my work in peace, far from the miseries of the entanglement with E, etc. And there's something to it. Waking every morning to yet another sunny day, I do feel a Grecian sense of light, of ease. It is no accident that the old real estate hucksters called this coast Mediterranean.

So, I will sit under my lemon trees, recover, write my reflections on a hillside Venus. Anxiously await your next. Thanks for sending the latest poems as well. You are as clear as Stevens; forge on with that encouragement in mind. Meanwhile I remain,

Your Oscar

# 4

*"Light cracks on the black gloss of the canal, and a gondola oar squeaks under us. Standing on the moonlit bridge, laughing together, listening to the campanile strike midnight, I decide to change Kid Death's hair from black to red—"*

Something like that. Ah yes—the vibrant author's journal in The Einstein Intersection, *young mind speaking to young mind, brilliant flashes of light in the head.* No doubt my image of Europe owes much to it. But what I've found . . . could half a century have changed that much? History, change—rate constants, sure. It feels so much as if things are accelerating. A wind blows through the fabric of time, things change faster than we can imagine. Punctuated equilibrium, without the equilibrium. Hey, Mr. Delany, here I am in Europe writing a book too! But yesterday I spent the morning at the Fremdenkontrolle, *arguing in my atrocious German which always makes me feel brain-damaged,* getting nowhere. They really are going to kick me out. And in the afternoon I did laundry, running around the building in the rain to the laundry room, Liddy howling upstairs at a banged knee. Last load dry and piled in the red basket, jogging round the front I caught my toe on a board covering the sidewalk next to some street work, fell and spilled clothes all over the mud of the torn-up street. I sat on the curb and almost cried. What happened, Mr. Delany? How come instead of wandering the night canals I'm dumping my laundry in the street? How come when I consider revisions it's not *"change Kid Death's hair from black to red"* but *"throw out the first draft and start the whole thing over"?*

*And only two weeks before Liddy and I leave.*

*What a cheat utopias are, no wonder people hate them. Engineer some fresh start, an island, a new continent, dispossess them, give them a new planet sure! So they don't have to deal with our history. Ever since More they've been doing it: rupture, clean cut, fresh start.*

*So the utopias in books are pocket utopias too. Ahistorical, static, why should we read them? They don't speak to us trapped in this world as we are, we look at them in the same way we look at the pretty inside of a paperweight, snow drifting down, so what? It may be nice but we're stuck here and no one's going to give us a fresh start, we have to deal with history as it stands, no freer than a wedge in a crack.*

> *Stuck in history like a wedge in a crack*
> *With no way out and no way back—*
> *Split the world!*

*Must redefine utopia. It isn't the perfect end-product of our wishes, define it so and it deserves the scorn of those who sneer when they hear the word. No. Utopia is the process of making a better world, the name for one path history can take, a dynamic, tumultuous, agonizing process, with no end. Struggle forever.*

*Compare it to the present course of history. If you can.*

One Saturday morning before dawn, Kevin, Doris, and Oscar biked down to the Newport Freeway, shivering in chill wet air. They checked out a car from a sleepy state worker and took off.

The freeway was dead at that hour, in all lanes. Quickly they hummed up to the car's maximum speed, in this case about sixty miles an hour. "Another piece of shit," Doris said. Kevin yawned; traveling in cars always made him sleepy. Doris complained about the smell, opening the windows and cursing the previous users.

"Spoken like a solid citizen," Oscar said.

She gave him an ugly look and stared out the window.

Hum of the motor, whirr of the tires, whoosh of the cool air. Finally Doris rolled the windows up. Kevin fell asleep.

They took the Riverside Freeway up the Santa Ana Canyon, passing under huge live oak trees on the big canyon floor. In Riverside they switched to highway 395 and headed north, up California's back side.

The sun rose as they traveled over the high desert north of Riverside. Long shadows striped the bare harsh land. Here and there in the distance they spotted knots of date palms and cottonwoods. These oases marked the sites of new villages, scattered in rings around the towns of Hisperia, Lancaster, Victorville. None of these villages were big, but taken together they accounted for a percentage of the diaspora out of the LA basin. You could say that "Greater Los Angeles" now extended out across the Mojave, making possible a much reduced density—even some open land —in the heart of the old monster itself.

Kevin woke up. "How do you know this Sally Tallhawk?" he asked Oscar.

"She was one of my teachers in law school."

"So you haven't seen her for a while?"

"Actually we get together pretty frequently. We have a good time."

"Uh huh. And she's on the state water board?"

"She was. She just left it. But she knows everyone on it, and she knows everything we might need to know about California water law. And it's the state laws that determine what the towns can or cannot do, when it comes to water usage."

"You aren't kidding—I hear that all the time when I try to get building permits."

"Well, you can see why it has to be that way—water is a regional concern. When towns had control over water there were some horrible local fights."

"Still are, as far as I can tell."

The country they were crossing got higher, wilder. To their left the Sierra Nevada's eastern escarpment jumped ten thousand feet into the sky. To their right lower ranges, the Slate and the Panamint, and then the White Mountains, rose burnt and bare. They passed Owens Lake, a sky-colored expanse with a crusty white border, and were in Owens Valley.

High and narrow, tucked between two of the tallest ranges on the continent, Owens Valley was a riot of spring color. Orchards made a patchwork of the valley floor (apples, almonds, cherries, pears), and many of the trees were in bloom, each branch thick with blossoms, every tree a hallucinatory burst of white or pink. Behind them stood wild slopes of granite and evergreen.

They passed Lone Pine, the largest town in the valley at almost a hundred thousand people. Beyond Lone Pine they tracked through the strange tortured shapes of the Alabama Hills, some of the oldest rock in North America. After Independence, another big town, they came to Bishop, the cultural center of the valley.

The main street of Bishop, which was simply highway 395 itself, formed the town's "historic district." Kevin laughed to see it: an old Western drive-thru town, composed of motels, Greyhound bus stations, drive-in food stops, steak restaurants, auto parts shops, hardware stores, pharmacies, the rest of the usual selection. Bishop clearly treasured it.

Away from Main Street the town had been transformed: sixty thousand people lived in some of the most elegant examples of the new architecture Kevin had ever seen, as well as some of the most bizarre. In the northwest quarter of town sprawled the University of California campus. After they dropped off their car at the depot, the three travelers walked over to it.

The land at the university had been donated partly by the city of Los Angeles, partly by the Bishop reservation of the Paiute and Shoshone Indians. The buildings imitated the local landscape: two rows of tall concrete buildings stood like mountain ranges, over low wooden structures tucked among a great number of pines. They found a map of the campus along one walkway, located

Kroeber College and walked to it, passing groups of students sitting on the grass, eating lunch.

Before some low wooden offices Oscar stopped them and pointed to a woman sitting in the sun, eyes closed. "That's Sally Tallhawk."

She was in fact tall, but not particularly hawkish—she had the broad face of the Paiutes, with thick black eyebrows. She wore a long-sleeved shirt (sleeves rolled up onto big biceps), jeans, and running shoes. A small pair of gold-rimmed bifocals made her seem quite professorial.

She heard their approach, rose to greet them. "Hey, Rhino," she said to Oscar easily, and they shook hands left-handed. Oscar introduced Kevin and Doris, and she welcomed them to Bishop. Her voice was low and rapid. "Look here," she said, "I'm off to the mountains, I was just about to leave."

"But we came all this way to talk to you!" Oscar exclaimed. "And we have the festival games tomorrow night."

"It's just an overnighter I have in mind," she said. "I want to check snow levels in Dusy Basin. I can get you folks all the equipment you need from the department, and you can come along." Imperiously she quelled Oscar's protest: "I'm going up into the mountains, I say! If you want to talk to me you'll have to come along!"

So they did. An hour later they were at the trailhead at South Lake, putting packs on their backs. And then they were hiking, up onto the wild sides of California's great backbone. Kevin and Doris glanced at Oscar, then at each other. How would Oscar handle the hard work of hiking?

As it turned out he toiled upward without complaint, sweating, heaving for breath, rolling his eyes behind Tallhawk's back; but listening intently to her when she spoke. Occasionally he looked at Kevin and Doris, to make sure they could hear, to make sure they were enjoying themselves. They had never seen him so solicitous. The work itself didn't seem to bother him much at all. And yet Sally Tallhawk was leading them at a rapid pace.

After two or three hours they rose out of the pine forest, into a mixed zone where patches of dark green lodgepole pine stood here and there, among humps of bare dark red granite. They came to the shores of a long island-filled lake, and hiked around it. Snow patches dotted the north faces of the peaks that towered around them, and white reflections shimmered in the dark blue water.

"You see how much water pours down into Owens Valley," Tallhawk said, waving a wide hand, wiping sweat from one eye. "And yet under the old laws, all of it could be piped away to Los Angeles."

As they hiked she told the old story, of how the LA Department of Water and Power had obtained the water rights for all the streams falling out of the east side of the Sierra into Owens Valley—in effect draining the yearly snowfall of the watershed off to LA.

"Criminals," Doris said, disgusted. "Where were their values?"

"In growth," Oscar murmured.

There had been a man working for the Federal Bureau of Reclamation, Sally said, making a survey of the valley's water resources. At the same time he was being paid as a consultant by LA, and he passed along everything he learned to LA, so that they knew which streams to gain the rights to. And so Owens Valley was sucked dry, its farms and orchards destroyed. The farmers went out of business and LA bought up their land. Owens Lake dried up completely, and Mono Lake came close, and the groundwater level fell and fell, until even the desert plants began to die.

"I can't believe they could get away with it!" Doris said.

Tallhawk only laughed. "They ended up with the peculiar situation of a city in one county being the major landowner in another county. This was so disturbing that laws were passed in Sacramento to make any repetition of that kind of ownership impossible. But it was too late for Owens Valley."

Telling this story took a while. By the time Tallhawk was done they were above Long Lake, into wild, rocky territory, where the ponds were small, and bluer than seemed possible. Shadows were cast far to the left, toward a jagged skyline Sally identified as the Inconsolable Range. Oscar huffed and puffed, showing a surprising endurance. They were all in a rhythm, walking in a little line—a little line of tiny figures, hiking across a landscape of blasted stone, dwarfed by the huge bare mountains that now surrounded them on three sides.

The trail wound over a knob called Saddlerock, then turned left, up a monstrous trench in the Inconsolable Range. They were in shadow now, and the scattered junipers with their gnarled cinnamon branches and dusky green needles seemed like sentient things, huddled together to watch them pass.

They started up an endless series of switchbacks that ascended the right wall of the enormous trench, stomping through snow more and more often as they got higher. Tallhawk pounded up the trail at a steady pace, and they rose so quickly they could pop their ears. Eventually the trail was completely filled with snow, tromped down by previous hikers. At times they looked back down at the route they had taken, at a long string of lakes in late afternoon shadow; then the trail would switch back, and they stared directly across at the sharktooth edge of the Inconsolable Range, rising to the massive pyramid of Mount Agassiz. They were far above treeline now, it was nothing but rock and snow.

Finally they topped the right wall of the great trench, and the trail ran over the saddle of Bishop Pass. At the high point of the broad pass they walked by the King's Canyon park boundary sign, and into the Dusy Basin.

To their left the broad ridge curved up to the multiple peak of Agassiz, a wild broken wall of variegated granite. Here Mesozoic volcanic sediments had metamorphosed under the pressure of rising granitic masses called plutons, and all of that had folded together, light and dark rock mixing like the batter in a marble cake. They trod over shattered fields of dark Lamarck granodiorite, and then over bands of the lighter alaskite, which zigzagged up and striped the great wall of Agassiz, and provided the thunderbolts in Thunderbolt Peak. And as they hiked Tallhawk's voice babbled like the sound of a distant low brook, enumerating every stone, every alpine flower tucked in the granite cracks.

Not too long after they started down the other side of the pass, they came to the highest lake in Dusy Basin, which was unnamed. Its shores were fiercely rocky, but there was one tiny grassy spot suitable for a campsite, and they threw down their packs there. Sally and Doris began to put up the tents; Oscar flopped flat on his back, looking like a beached whale; Kevin got out the gas stove and cooking utensils, quick with hunger. They chattered as they worked, looking around them all the while. Oscar complained about Sally's idea of a pretty campsite and they all laughed, even him; the place was spectacular.

In the evening light the wild peaks glowed. Mount Agassiz, Thunderbolt Peak, Isosceles Peak, Columbine Peak, The Black Giant—each a complete masterpiece of form alone, each a perfect complement to the others. Huge boulders stood scattered on the undulating rock floor of Dusy Basin, and down at its bottom there was a narrow string of ponds and trees, still half-buried in snow. The sun lay just over the peaks to the west. The sky behind the mountains was twilight blue, and all the snow on the peaks was tinted a deep pink. Chaos generating order, order generating chaos; who could say which was which in such alpenglow?

As they made camp the conversation kept returning to water. Sally Tallhawk, it was clear, was obsessed with water. Specifically, with the water situation in California, a Gordian knot of law and practice that no one could ever cut apart. To learn the system, manipulate it, explain it—this was her passion.

In California water flows uphill toward money, she told them. This had been the primary truth of the system for decades. Most states used riparian water law, where landowners have the right to water on their land. That went back to English common law, and a landscape with lots of streams in it. But California and the other Hispanic states used parts of appropriative water law, which came from dry Mexico and Spain, and which recognized the rights of those who first made a beneficial, consumptive use of water—it didn't matter where their land was in relation to it. In this system, later owners of land couldn't build anything to impede the free passage of water to the original user. And so money—particularly old money—had its advantage.

"So that's how LA could take water from Owens Valley," Doris said.

The tents were up, sleeping bags out. They gathered around Kevin and the stove with the materials for dinner.

"Well, it's more complex than that. But essentially that's right."

But in the end, Tallhawk told them, the water loss did Owens Valley a kind of good. LA tried to compensate for its appropriation by making the valley into something like a nature preserve. And so the valley missed all the glories of twentieth century southern California civilization. Then, when water loss threatened the native desert plants of the valley, Inyo County sued LA, and the courts decided in Inyo's favor. This led to new laws being passed in Sacramento, laws that gave control of Inyo's water back to it. But by this time feelings about growth and development had changed, and the valley towns went about rebuilding according to their own sense of value. "The dry years saved us from a lot of crap."

Oscar said to Kevin and Doris, "You'll have to remember that if we lose this case."

Doris shook her head irritably. "It's not the same. We won't be able to go back from a situation like ours."

Tallhawk said, "You can never be sure of that. We're working now on the final arrangements for the removal of the Hetch Hetchy dam, for instance. That was the biggest defeat ever for the environmental movement in California, right back at its start—a valley described as a second Yosemite, drowned so San Francisco could have a convenient water supply. John Muir himself couldn't stop that one. But now we're making them store the water in a couple of catchments downstream, and when that's done they'll drain Hetch Hetchy and bring that valley back out into the light of day, after a century and a half. The ecologists say the valley floor will recover in fifty to a hundred years, faster if they truck some of the mud out into the San Joaquin as fertilizer. So you see—some disasters can be reversed.''

"It would be better to avoid disaster in the first place," Kevin said.

"Undoubtedly," Tallhawk said. "I was just reminding you that there's not too many things that are irrevocable, when you're talking about the waterscape. Water flows forever, so there is a resilience there we can rely on.''

"Glen Canyon next, eh?" Oscar said.

"My God, yes!" Tallhawk cried, and laughed.

The sun disappeared. It got cold fast. The sky turned a dark velvet blue that seemed to crackle where it met the glowing white snow ridges. Steam rose from the pot on the stove, and they could smell the stew.

"But in El Modena . . ." Kevin said.

"In El Modena, I don't know.''

Then the stew bubbled over, and it was declared ready. They spooned it into cups and ate. Tallhawk had brought a bottle of red wine along, and they drank it gratefully.

"Can't we use water to stop Alfredo's plan?" Kevin asked as he finished eating.

"Maybe.''

It was strange but true, she told them: Orange County had a lot of water. It was one of the best water districts in the state, in terms of groundwater conservation.

"What does that mean, exactly?" Kevin asked.

"Well, do you understand what groundwater is?''

"Water under the ground?''

"Yes, yes. But not in pools.''

She stood, waved her arms at the scene, talking as she pulled her down jacket from her pack. Walked in circles around them, looking at the peaks.

Soil is permeable, she said, and the rock below soil is also permeable, right down to solid bedrock, which forms the bottom of groundwater basins. Water fills all the available space in permeable rock, percolating everywhere it can go. And it flows downhill as it does on the surface, not as quickly, but just as definitely. "Imagine Owens Valley is a big trench between the ranges, which it is. Filled almost halfway up with rock and soil eroded out of the mountains. The San Joaquin Valley is the same way, only much bigger. These are immense reservoirs of water, then, only the water level lies below the soil level, at least in most places. Geologists and hydrologists have charted these groundwater basins everywhere, and there are some *huge* ones in California.

"Now some are self-contained, they don't flow downstream. There's enormous amounts of water in these, but they're only replenished by rainfall, which is scarce out here. If you pump water you empty basins like those. The Ogdalilla basin under Oklahoma was one of those, and it was pumped dry like an oil field, which is why they're so desperate for the Columbia's water now.

"Anyway, you have to imagine this underground saturation, this underground movement." She stretched her arms forward and reached with her fingers, in a sort of unconscious groundwater dance. "The shapes of the basin bottoms sometimes bring the water closer to the surface—if there's an underground ridge of impermeable bedrock, and the groundwater is flowing downhill over this ridge, water gets pushed to the surface, in the very top of a giant slow-motion waterfall. That's how you get artesian wells."

Silence as she walked around the camp. Now it seemed they could hear the subterranean flow, murmuring beneath them, a deep bass to the wind's tremolo.

"And El Modena?" Kevin said.

"Well, when a groundwater basin drains into the sea, there's a strange situation; the water doesn't really drain very much, because there's water pressure on both sides. Fresh water forces itself out if there's flow coming in from upstream, but if not . . . well, the only thing that keeps sea water from reversing the flow and pushing into the ground under the land is the pressure of the fresh water, pouring down.

"Now Orange County's basin doesn't have a whole lot of water coming into it any more. Riverside takes a lot before it reaches Orange County, as do all the other cities upstream. And agriculture in Orange County itself took a lot of water from the very start of settlement. They pumped more than was replenished, which was easy to do. But the pressure balance at the coastline was altered, and sea water began to leach inland. Wells near the coast turned salty. There's no way to stop that kind of intrusion except to keep the basin full, so that the pressure outward is maintained. So the Orange County Water District was formed, and their job was to keep the groundwater basin healthy, so all their wells wouldn't turn to salt. This was back in the 1920s. They were given the taxing and allocation powers necessary to do the job, and the right to sue cities upstream. And they went at it with a kind of religious fervor. They did it as well as any water district in California, despite all the stupidity going on above ground in that area. And so you have a healthy basin under you."

They had finished eating. They cleaned up the cups and the pot; their hands got wet, and quickly they got cold. They scrambled to get into the down jackets and bunting pants that Tallhawk's department had provided. Then they sat on their groundpads, sleeping bags bunched around them, making a circle around the stove, which served as their campfire. The great arc of peaks still glowed with some last remnant of light, under a dark sky. Sally pulled out a small bottle of brandy and passed it around, continued:

"It means that you live on an enormous pool of water, renewed all the time by OCWD. They buy water from us and from LA, and pour most of it right into the ground. Store it there. They keep the pressure regulated so very little of it is lost to the sea; there's a balance of pressures at the coastline. So the artesian wells that gave Fountain Valley its name will never come back, and no one there would want them to! But you have the water you need. It's strange, because it's a desert coastline with hardly any rainfall. But the OCWD planned for a population increase that other forces balked—the population increase never occurred, and so there's water to spare now. Strange but true."

"So water won't help us stop them?" Kevin said, disappointed.

"Not a pure scarcity. But Oscar says you have a resolution banning the further purchase of water from LA. You could try to stand on that."

"Like Santa Barbara?"

"Santa Barbara slowed development by turning off the tap, yes. But they're in a different situation—they stayed out of the California Water Project, and they don't buy water from LA, and they don't have much of a groundwater basin. So they're really limited, and they've made a conscious decision not to change that. It works well if you have those initial conditions. But Orange County doesn't. There's a lot of water that was brought into the area before these issues were raised, and that water is still available."

Kevin and Doris looked at each other glumly.


They listened to the wind, and watched the stars pop into existence in a rich blue sky. On such a fine night it was a shame to get into the tents, so they only shifted into their sleeping bags, and lay on the groundpads watching the sky. The snow patches scattered among the rocks shone as if lit from within. It seemed possible to feel them melt, then rush into the ground beneath them, to fall down the slope into Le Conte Canyon and seep a slow path to the sea, in invisible underground Columbias. Kevin felt a stirring in him, the full-lunged breathlessness that marked his love for El

Modena's hills, extending outward to these great peaks. Interpenetration with the rock. He was melting like the snow, seeping into it. In every particulate jot of matter, spirit, dancing . . .

"So what do you suggest, Sally?" Doris finally said.

"We'd like our town to end up as nice as Bishop," Kevin added. "But with people like Alfredo running things . . ."

"But he's not really running things, right?"

"No, but he is powerful."

"You've got to expect a lot of resistance to what you're trying to do. Saving the land for its own sake goes against the grain of white American thought, and so it's a fight that'll never end. Why not grow if we can, why not change things completely? A lot of people will never understand the answer to that question, because to them a good life only means more things. They have no feeling for the land. We have an aesthetic of wilderness now, but it takes a certain kind of sensibility to feel it."

"So in our case . . ." Kevin prompted, feeling anxious.

"Well." Tallhawk stood up, reached for the nearly empty brandy bottle. "You could try endangered species. If there is any kind of endangered species inhabiting your hill, that would be enough. The Endangered Species Act is tough."

"I don't think Rattlesnake Hill is like to have any," Doris said. "It's pretty ordinary."

"Well, look into it. They stopped a freeway down near your area because of a very ordinary-looking lizard that happens to be rare.

"Then the California Environmental Quality Act is a good chance. Under the terms of the act, environmental impact reports come early in the process, and once you have one, you can use it."

"But if it's not particularly favorable to us?" Oscar asked, sounding sleepy.

"You could consider going to the National Trust for Land, or the Nature Conservancy—they lend assistance to movements like yours, and they have the money to fight large developers. You could maybe convince them to bid against the development if it comes to that.''

"The town itself owns all the land," Doris said.

"Sure. But these groups can help you with lobbying and campaigning when the issue comes to a vote, and they could even pay to lease it.''

"That would be good.''

"But there's nothing we could use to stop them before a referendum?" Kevin asked. "I'm just scared Alfredo would win. He's good at that.''

"Well, the environmental stuff I mentioned. Or you could see if the hill has some unique water properties, like a spring.''

"It doesn't," Kevin said.

"You could try drilling a spring on the sly.''

She laughed at the long silence.

"Well it's a thought, right? Here, have some brandy. One swallow left each. You'll think of something. If not, let me know and we'll come down and threaten this guy. Maybe we can offer you a discount on Owens Valley water if you leave the hilltop alone. Inyo County influencing southern Californian politics, I like that!" She laughed. "Or find a sacred ancient Indian burial mound or the like. Except I don't think the Gabrielinos were into that kind of thing. Or if they were, we don't know about it.''

Kevin shook his head. "The hillside is basically empty. I've been all over it. I've hung out on that hill ever since I was a kid, I've *crawled* all over it.''

"Might be fossils," Oscar said.

"You'd have to make a world-class find," Tallhawk said. "El Modena tar pits. I'd try to rely on something a bit more solid if I were you.''

They thought about it, listening to wind over rock, over snow. Listening to water seep into the ground.

"Ready for tomorrow's match?" Tallhawk asked Oscar.

Oscar was a Falstaffian mound, he looked like one of the

boulders surrounding them. "I've never been readier," he muttered.

"Match?" Kevin said. "What's this? Going to be in a chess match, Oscar?"

Tallhawk laughed.

"It is like chess," Oscar murmured, "only more intricate."

"Didn't you know the redneck festival starts tomorrow?" Tallhawk asked Kevin and Doris.

"No."

"Tomorrow is opening day for hunting season; in fact, we'll have to haul ass out of here to avoid getting shot by some fool. Bishop celebrates opening day with age-old customs. Jacked-up pick-up trucks painted in metallic colors, with gun racks in their back windows—fifty cases of whiskey, shipped in from Kentucky—tomorrow night'll be wild. That's one reason I wanted to come up here tonight. Get a last taste of quiet."

They lay stretched out in their bags.

Kevin listened to the wind, and looked around at the dark peaks poking into the night sky. Suddenly it was clear to him that Sally had had a reason to bring them up here to have this talk; that this place itself was part of the discourse, part of what she wanted to say. The university of the wilderness. The spine of California, the hidden source of the south's wealth. This hard wild place . . .

Around them the wind, spirit of the mountains, breathed. Water, the soul of the mountains, seeped downward. Rock, the body of the mountains, stood fast.

Held in a bowl like God's linked hands, they slept.

The next day they hiked back over the pass and down the trail, and drove a little gas car down to Tallhawk's house in Bishop to clean up.

As dusk fell they walked downtown, and found that Bishop

had filled with people. It seemed like the entire population of
eastern California must have been there, dressed in blue jeans,
pendletons, cowboy boots, cowboy hats, camouflaged flak jackets,
bright orange hunter's vests, square dancing dresses, rodeo chaps,
bordello robes, cavalry uniforms, animal furs, southern belle ball
gowns, Indian outfits—if it had ever been seen in the American
West before, it was there now. Main Street was packed with pick-
up trucks, all track-free, running on grain alcohol and making a
terrific noise and stink. Their drivers revved engines constantly to
protest the long periods of gridlock. "A traffic-jam parade," Oscar
said.

They ate at a coffee shop called Huk Finns, then walked in
a stream of people toward the Paiute reservation. Over the screech
of pick-ups burning rubber they heard occasional gunshots, and
the dark streets were illuminated by the glare of skyrockets bursting
overhead. Oscar sang loudly: "Oh the rocket's red glare, the bombs
bursting in air—"

"Where are we going?" Doris shouted at him.

"Bishop High School gymnasium," he replied.

Which was filling rapidly, with a rowdy, even crazed audience. Oscar led Kevin and Doris to a row of benches in the front
of the upper deck. The basketball court below was filled with a
large boxing ring. "Not boxing!" Doris said.

"Of course not," Oscar said, and walked off. Kevin and
Doris stared at each other, nonplussed. They sat for nearly fifteen
minutes, and nothing happened. Then into the ring stepped a
woman wearing a tuxedo jacket over a black body suit and dark
fishnet nylons, with high heels and a top hat. Tumultuous applause.
Inexpert spotlights bounced to left and right, finally settling on
her. She lifted an absurdly large microphone and said, "ARE YOU
READY?"

The crowd was ready. Doris stuck her fingers in her ears.
People standing were shouted down, and the aisles filled. There
were perhaps ten thousand people jammed into the place. "OKAY

THEN! FIRST MATCH: BRIDE OF GERONIMO VERSUS THE RHINOCEROS!''

"I'll be damned," Kevin said, his words completely drowned by the uproar. The spots swung around drunkenly as their operators searched for the entering contestants. By the time they found them, they were almost to the dark green mat of the ring: two large figures in long capes, one scarlet, the other incandescent blue. The crowd roared, the two contestants shook their fists over their heads: Oscar and Sally Tallhawk, no doubt about it.

Quickly the two contestants were in the ring and mugging it up, bouncing against each other chest to chest. The Mistress of Ceremonies—also the referee—tried to separate them, at the same time holding her mike where it would catch their dire threats. Tallhawk snarled as she detailed the ravages Oscar would suffer: "I'm using your scalp as a floormop! Your skin will make good window squeegees! And I need some new dingleberries to hang from my rear-view mirror!"

The crowd roared.

Oscar puffed out his cheeks, mumbled "Prediction is always dangerous, but the Rhino is reasonably confident the match will ultimately be decided in his favor."

The crowd gave him an ovation.

The MC let them at it.

They circled each other, knocking hands aside and snarling. The Bride grabbed the Rhino's wrist and pulled, and the Rhino flew through space and hit the ring ropes, which were very elastic. The Rhino fell deep into them, rebounded back and was kicked in the chest—he staggered, the Bride took a flying leap across the ring and landed on his shoulders, bearing him to the mat. She got a knee across his throat and pounded her elbow into his face. When she stood and threw her arms overhead the crowd screamed "GERONIMA!" and the MC announced, "THE BIG G SEEMS TO HAVE LEVELED THE RHINO WITH HER FAMOUS BLUBBERHAWK FROM SPACE MOVE."

But the Rhino, twitching in agony on the mat, reached out a hand and jerked both of Geronima's feet from under her, felling her like a tree, allowing him to stagger up and away.

It happened several times: Bride of Geronimo used Rhino for a punching bag, but when Rhino was prostrate and the Bride reaping the crowd's approval, the Rhino would resuscitate, barely, and deliver a stinging riposte. Once he pulled the rope on one side and let it go, which caused the rope on the other side to snap Geronima in the back and bring her down. In revenge she grabbed a lightbulb from the top of one of the rope poles, broke it and ground it into the Rhino's face, until the MC knocked her away with the mike. The Rhino kept both hands to his face, grunting in agony as Geronima chased him about the ring. Clearly he was blind. It was a prime opportunity; Mrs. G. raced around the ring, revving up for truly impressive leaps off the corner poles, attempting her Blubberhawk from Space kill—but each time as she dropped from the air the Rhino would trip, or stagger, or hear something above, and neatly sidestep away, looking absurdly light-footed for all his bulk—and Geronima would land flat on her face. Time after time this happened, until Geronima was raving with frustration, and the crowd was in a frenzy. Then Rhino reached into his back pocket and smeared something over his face. "AH HA!" said the MC. "LOOKS LIKE HE'S USING SOME OF THAT NEW PLASTIC SKIN TO REPAIR HIS FACE—YES— SEE HOW FAST IT'S HEALED—WHY—LOOK AT THAT! —HE'S OKAY!"

Rhino dodged another leap and muttered into the mike. "MY ALMANAC INDICATES THAT THE TIDE MAY HAVE TURNED, MISSUS GEE." And then he was all over the ring, sidestepping, looking right and left in grossly exaggerated glances, then leaping forward to box the Bride's ears or twist her to the mat. Finally he got behind her and began bouncing her off his knee. "UH OH!" the MC cried. "IT'S RHINO'S ATOMIC DROP! NO ONE CAN TAKE THAT FOR LONG!"

And indeed Geronima collapsed to the mat, flat out. Rhino nodded shyly to the roaring crowd. The MC gave him a kiss, which gave him an idea—he tiptoed after her and took a tug at her tux, which came apart at the seams. Now the crowd really loved him.

But the MC was incensed, and turned to stalk him. He stumbled backwards across the ring, tried to wake Geronima, but to no avail. The Bride was out. The Rhino began to fly about the ring, thrown by a voluptuous woman in a fishnet body stocking, who paused only to continue in her role of commentator: "NOW I'M FINISHING THIS NOSEY RHINO OFF WITH A TRIPLE-SPIN KIDNEY HAMMER." Rhino tried desperately to escape the ring, grasping at spectators through the ropes with eyes bugged out; but he was pulled back in and pounded. The Bride even roused herself to join the final carnage, before collapsing again after a single chop from the MC, who wanted no help. In the end the MC stood alone over the two prone wrestlers, and when she had caught her breath and straightened her hair, and tried on the torn tux and tossed it away as a bad job, she calmly announced the next bout. "UGLY GEORGE VERSUS MISTER CHICKENSHIT, COMING UP AS SOON AS WE GET THE LARD OFF THE CANVAS."


There were several more bouts scheduled, but Kevin and Doris left their seats and struggled through the crowd to an exit, then made their way down to the locker room doors on the ground floor. Oscar was just emerging, freshly showered and back in street clothes, blinking in a kind of Clark Kentish way. After signing autographs for a gang of youngsters he joined Kevin and Doris.

"That was great!" Kevin said, grinning at Oscar's owlish innocence.

Doris said, "Where's Sally?"

"Thank you," Oscar said to Kevin. "Sally has another match

later in the evening. Would you care to join me for something to drink? I find I am thirsty—I could even use another dinner, to tell the truth. I have to eat lightly before a match.''

''I believe it.''

So they went back to Main Street and Huk Finns. Oscar ordered corned beef and hash, and poured whiskey over the hash, to Doris's horror. But she joined in as they drank most of a bottle.

Kevin couldn't stop grinning. ''So Oscar, how'd you get into professional wrestling?''

''Just fell into it.''

''No, really!''

''I liked the money. Sally was already doing it, and she thought I had the necessary . . . talent.''

''Do you ever get hurt?'' Doris asked.

''Certainly. We make mistakes all the time. Once I missed on the Atomic Drop and caught Sally on the tailbone, and a couple minutes later she popped me right on the nose. Bled all over. We both got miffed, and it turned into a serious fight for a while. But those look dull compared to the tandem stuff.''

''You really ought to join our softball team,'' Kevin said. ''Your footwork is great, you'd do fine!''

Oscar shook his head, mouth full.

They left a bit unsteady on their feet, but in high spirits. Main Street was not quite as crowded as before, but there were still hundreds of people wandering about. They were passing a loud group when a tall man stopped them. ''Hey, ain't you the Rhino? Hey!'' he bellowed to his companions. ''This here's the Rhino, the guy who wrestles the Bride of Geronimo!''

''Fame,'' Doris said.

''Hey Rhino, let's try a takedown right here, whaddya say? I used to wrestle in high school, here, try some real wrestling moves.''

He grabbed for Oscar's wrist, but Oscar's wrist had moved.

''What's a matter, Rhino? Chicken?''

"Drunk," Oscar said.

For answer the man drove his shoulder at Oscar's chest, and missed; turned with a roar and charged again. Oscar shuffled to one side, avoiding him in the dark. The man cannoned into Kevin.

"Hey, fuck you," Kevin said, and punched the man in the nose.

Immediately they were in a free-for-all, swinging away amid shrieks and curses. Chaos in the dark. People came running to watch or to join the melee, and it only stopped when a whole gang of police drove up and strode among them, blowing their whistles and poking with nightsticks anyone who continued to fight. Soon the fighters were lined up and wristbanded.

"Anyone with a wristband stopped again will go to jail," the officer in charge told them. "The bands will come off in a couple days. Now go home and sober up."

Oscar and Kevin and Doris started toward Tallhawk's house. "That was stupid," Doris told Kevin.

"I know."

She glanced around. "Those guys are following us."

"Let's lose them now," Oscar suggested, and took off running.

Their belligerents followed in noisy but fairly efficient pursuit. It took them several blocks of twisting, turning, and flat-out running to shake them.

When they were free of pursuit they stood on a street corner, gasping. "This sure is fun," Doris said acidly.

Oscar nodded. "I know. But now I'm lost." He shrugged. "Oh well."

It took them another hour to find Tallhawk's house, and by that time Oscar was dragging. "This is far more exercise than I like," he said as he opened the door of the darkened house. He entered a study with a long couch, collapsed on it. "It always happens like this when I visit Sally. She's a maniac, essentially. The guest room is down the hall."

Kevin went to the bathroom. When he returned to the guest room, he found that it had only one bed, and a rather narrow one at that.

Doris was undressing beside it. "It's okay," she said unsteadily. "We can both fit."

Kevin swayed for a moment. "Um," he said. "I don't know—there's another couch out there, I think—"

Then she pressed against him, hugging him. "Come on," she said in a muffled voice. "We've done this before."

Which was true. He had looked down onto that head of black hair, in embraces just like this. Although. . . . And besides, he. . . . Drunkenly he kissed the part, and the familiar scent of her hair filled him. He hugged back, too drunk to think past the moment. He gave in to it. They fell onto the bed.

The trip back was long, and hung over. Kevin was tired, bored with the endless Mojave Desert, awkward and tongue-tied with his old friend Doris. Oscar slumped in his seat, a portrait of the sleeping Buddha. Doris sat looking out her window, thinking unreadable thoughts.

Images of Sally Tallhawk jumped Kevin as if out of ambush: striding around their campsite with the evening sun flush on her broad face, arms spread out as she talked in a low chant of water sluicing into the underworld, pooling, drawn inward, making its secret way to the sea. The ragged ridge of Thunderbolt Peak against a sky the color of the ocean, stripes of white rock like marble crisscrossing the dark basalt, hypnagogic visions of her dancing by the lakeshore with its black wavelets, throwing Oscar out onto it where he skated as if on ice—

Jerking back awake. Trying to nod off again. The car's monotonous hum. Off to their right, the weird illuminated black surface of one of the microwave catchments, receivers like immense stereo speakers flat on their backs, soaking rays, the photon space music, the lased power sent down from the solar panels soaring in their orbits. They were almost done setting out that array of orbiting panels, his parents' work would be finished. What would they do then? Space junkies, would they ever come down? Visit El Modena? He missed them, needed to talk to them. Couldn't they give him advice, tell him what to do, make it all as simple as it once had been?

No. But he should give them a call anyway. And his sister Jill as well.

Then, home at the house—having said a very awkward "good night" to Doris, pretending that there was no reason he should not go to his own room just as he always did—the TV was blinking.

It was a message from Jill.

"All right!" he said as he saw her face. That sort of coincidence was always cropping up between them. He would think of her, she would call.

She looked like him, but only in a way; all his hayseed homeliness had been transformed into broad, wild good looks, in that peculiar way that happens in family resemblances, where minute shifts in feature can make all the difference between plainness and beauty: big mobile mouth, upturned nose, freckles, wide blue eyes with light eyelashes and eyebrows, and auburn hair turning burnt gold under the Asian sun.

Now her little image said in the familiar hoarse voice, "Well, I've been trying to get you for the last couple of days because I'm moving out of Dakka to learn some tropical disease technique at a hospital in Atgaon, up in the northeast near the Indian border—in fact I've already moved out there, I'm just back to pick up the last of my things and slog through the bureaucracy. You wouldn't believe what a mess that is, it makes California seem like a really regulation-free place. I hate doing these recordings, I wish I could get hold of you. Anyway, Atgaon's about as far away from Dakka as you can get and still be in Bangladesh, it takes all day to get there, on a new train built on a big causeway to keep it above the floodplain. It must go over a hundred bridges, it's a really wet country.

"Atgaon is a market town on the Tista River, which comes down from Sikkim. The hospital is the most important thing in town, it's associated with the Institute for the Study of Tropical Diseases, and getting to be one of the leaders in the area—like, this is the place they developed the once-a-year malaria pill. The whole thing was started by the Rajhasan Landless Cooperative Society, one of the land reform groups, which is pretty neat. They do tons of clinical work, and they have a bunch of good research projects. I'm going to work on one concerning hepatitis-B-two. Meanwhile I'm helping out in the emergency room and in clinic visits, so it's mostly busy, but I like it—the people are nice and I'm learning a lot.

"I'm living in a little bungalow of my own on the hospital grounds. It's pretty nice, but there are some surprises. Like my first day there I turned on the light and tossed my bag on the bed, and a gigantic centipede came clattering out at me! I took a broom and smacked the thing with the handle and cut it in half, and *both sides started to crawl away in different directions*. Can you believe it? I was freaked and put a bed post on one half of the thing in place, while I pulverized the other half with the broom handle. Then I did the same to the half under the post. What a *mess*. Later they told me to check out bedsheets and clothes before using them—I told them hey, I know!"

She grinned her sister grin, and Kevin laughed. "Oh, Jill—" he said. He wanted to talk, he needed to talk!

He stopped the tape, tried to put a call through to Bangladesh. It wouldn't go; she wasn't there in Dakka to answer.

Feeling odd, he started the tape again.

". . . Happy to know that there's a woman's softball league out here, can you believe it? Apparently there was an exchange program, nurses here went to Guam, and some from Guam came here, and the ones here started softball games, and when the nurses visiting Guam came back they were hooked on it too, so they kept it going. Now it's grown, they've got some fields and a five-village league and everything. I haven't seen Atgaon's field yet, but they say it's a good one. They're proud of having a woman's league, women in the rural areas are just getting out from under Islamic law, and now they're doing all kinds of work, and involved in the land reform, and infiltrating the bureaucracy too, which means in a few years they'll have taken over! And playing sports like this together, it's new for them and they love it. Team spirit and all that. The big sport around here is cricket, of course, and women are doing that too, but there's also this little softball league.

"Anyway, they figured since I was American I must play softball, and they got me out to play catch with them, and now I'm not only on a team but have been appointed head umpire for the season, because they were having trouble with their umpires taking sides. It's the last thing I would have expected when I came. But I guess I shouldn't be surprised, I mean you can go to the El Toro mela every summer, so why not softball over here? Everything everywhere, that's what it's coming to.

"Well, I'm going to get off, this is costing me fun times in Dakka. There aren't any phones like this in Atgaon—the hospital has a recorder but no transmitter, so I'll try to make some letters there, and send them when I can. Meanwhile you can send letters like this to me in Dakka, and I'll get to play them eventually. I hope you will, it's not as good as really talking but it's better than nothing. Say hi to everyone there, I love you."

The image flickered out.

Kevin sat in his dark room, staring at static on the screen. He could hear Tomas in the next room, tapping away at his computer's keyboard. He could go and talk to Tomas, who would take a break for something like that. Or he could go down to the kitchen, Donna and Cindy would be down there soaking it up and talking to people on TV. Or Sylvia and Sam. Friends were the real family, after all. Family were not actually family until they were friends too. And yet, and yet . . . his sister. Jill Claiborne. He wanted to talk to his sister.

# 5

*May. Hard buds on the branches, vibrant green in the rain. Barely a day's sun all April. I can't remember.*

Pam came home last night tired and footsore after running two experiments at once. She thinks she can finish the lab work early and do the writing up in the States. Shorten separation. So she's in Pamela Overdrive. I made dinner and she threw the paper down in disgust, told me about her day. "The probe compound and internal standards diffused out of the water sample into the headspace until an equilibrium between the liquid and gas phases was reached."

"Uh huh."

"And that depends on the water solubility and the volatility of the two compounds."

As she went on I stared at her. *What Chemists Say To Spouses/ What Spouses Understand.* Blah blah blah, Tom, blah blah blah.

She saw the doggie look on my face, smiled. "So how'd the book go?"

"The same." It's not fair, really. I can't understand a word she says when she talks of her work, while for me, on this project at least, she is a crucial sounding board. "I'm thinking of alternating chapters of fiction with essay chapters which discuss the political and economic problems we need to solve."

"My God." Wrinkled nose, as if something gone bad in fridge.

*"Hey, H.G. Wells did it."*

*"Which book?"*

*"Well—one of the major utopian novels."*

*"Still in print?"*

*"No."*

*"Libraries have it?"*

*"University libraries."*

*"So Wells's science fiction adventures are still in every library and bookstore, while this major utopia with the essays is long gone, and you can't even remember the title?"*

*I changed the subject.*

*Think I might pass on the essays.*

*Six months, four months. Three months? Go quickly, mysterious experiments. Go well. Please.*

Kevin woke from a dream in which a huge bird was standing on the limpid water of a rapid stream, wings outstretched as it spun on the clear surface, keeping a precarious balance. Foggily he shook his head, grinned at himself. "Sally Tallhawk," he said, rolling out the syllables. The strategies she had listed while wandering around her sublime campsite filled his thoughts, and feeling charged with energy he decided to visit Jean Aureliano before work and confer.

Jean's office was on the saddle between Orange Hill and Chapman Hill. Kevin blasted up the trail in fifth gear and skidded into her little terrace. Her office was a low set of rooms built around a tiny central stone garden, with open walls and pagoda corners on the low roof. Kevin had done some work on it. When he walked into her office she looked up from the phone and smiled at him, gestured at him to take a seat. Instead he wandered around looking at the prints on the walls, Chinese landscape paintings in the Ming dynasty style, gold on green and blue. Jean spoke sharply, arguing with someone. She had iron gray hair, cut short in a cap over a solid, handsome head. Big-boned and heavyset, she moved like a dancer and had a black belt in karate. For many years now she had been the most powerful person in El Modena, and one of the most powerful in Orange County, and she still looked it. The smoldering glare of the Hispanic matriarch was currently fixed on whoever was on the other end of the line, and Kevin, glancing at her quickly, was glad it wasn't him.

"Damn it," she said, interrupting a tinny whine coming over the phone, "the whole Green alliance is breaking up on the shoals of extremists like you, we're in the modern world now—no, no, don't give me that, there's no going back, all this talk of watershed sovereignty is so much nostalgia, it's no wonder there's shrieks of protest from all sides! You're tearing the party apart and losing us the mandate we've had! Politics is the art of the possible, Damaso, and if you set impossible goals then what kind of politician are you? It's stupid. What? . . . No. Wrong. Marx can be split into two parts, the historian and the prophet. As a historian he was great and we use his paradigm every day, I don't contest that, but as a prophet he was wrong from the start! By now anyone who calls themselves a Marxist in that sense has *elote* for brains. . . . Damaso, I can't believe you sometimes. *Los pobres,* come on, you think you help them with this balkanization?—*Chinga* yourself!" And then a long string of sulphurous Spanish.

Angrily she hit the phone, cutting off the connection. "What do you want?" she said to Kevin without looking up.

Nervously Kevin told her.

"Yes," she said. "Alfredo's great plan. From the crown of creation to the crown of the town. I've been keeping track of it and I think you and Doris are doing a good job."

"Thanks," Kevin said, "but we've been trying to do more. We talked to a water lawyer from UC Bishop—"

"Tallhawk?"

"Uh huh."

"Yeah, she's a good one. What did she say?"

"Well, she said we were unlikely to stop this development on the water issue alone."

Jean nodded. "But we've got resolution two-oh-two-two to hang onto, there."

"Yeah. But she gave us some suggestions for other avenues to take, and one of them was to use the various requirements of the California Environmental Quality Act. Oscar said you would know about that and how it was going—you could ask to see their EIS when it comes in."

"Yeah that's right, we'll do that. The problem is that they'll probably be able to minimize the environmental impact on that little hill, it barely touches Santiago Park, and with all the other hills already built up—" She made a quick gesture at her office.

"Wouldn't that be a point in our favor?"

"More likely a precedent. But we'll do what we can about it."

"Oscar said that if you mobilized the party machinery to fight the proposal . . ."

"Exactly. We should be able to crush it, and I'll certainly be trying, believe me." She stood up, strode around the office, flung open one sliding wall door, stepped half out onto the porch. "Of course if it comes to a referendum you can never be sure. It's just impossible to tell what the people in this town will vote for and what they won't. A lot of people would be happy if the town were making more money, and this would do that, so it's a dangerous thing to bring to a vote. What I'm saying is that it would be a lot safer if we could stop it in the council itself, right there at the zoning. So you and Doris have to keep at the moderates. We all do."

They discussed Hiroko Washington, Susan Mayer, and Jerry Geiger in turn; Jean knew them intimately from her years as mayor, and her assessment was that their chances of convincing the three were fairly good. None could be counted on for sure, but all were possibilities. "We only need to get two. Keep after it every way you can, and I'll be doing the same up here." There was a look on her face—determined, stubborn, ready to fight. As if she were going in for her black belt trial again.

* * *

Reassured, Kevin left her office and coasted down to work. He and Hank and Gabriela were beginning the renovation of Oscar's house, and the other two were already hard at it, tearing out interior walls. Oscar emerged from his library from time to time to watch them. "You look like you're having fun," he observed.

"This is the best part of carpentry!" Gabriela exclaimed as she hammered plaster away from studs, sending white dust flying. "Yar! Ah! Hack!"

"You're an anarchist, Gabriela."

"No, I'm a *nihilist*."

"I like it too," Hank said, eyeing a joint in exposed framing. He took an exploratory slam at it.

"Why is that?" Oscar asked.

Hank squinted, stilled. "Well . . . carpentry is so precise, you always have to be very careful and measured and controlled, and you're always having to juke with edges that don't quite meet and make everything look perfect—it's such a perfectionist thing, even if you're just covering up so it looks right even though it ain't—anyway . . ." He looked around as if tracking a bird that had flown into the room. "Anyway, so you get to the part of the job that is just destructive—"

"Yar!" Bang. "Ha!" Bang. "Hack hack hack!" BANG. BANG. BANG.

"I see," Oscar said.

"It's like how Russ and his vet friends are always going duck-hunting on the weekends. Same principle."

"Fucking schizophrenics," Gabriela said. "I went over there one time and they had some duck they had found while they were hunting, it had busted a wing or something so they brought it home so they could nurse it back to health, had it in a box right next to the bag of all the other ones they'd blasted to smithereens that same day."

"I understand," Oscar said. "No one breaks the law as happily as a lawyer."

"We want to wreck things," Gabriela said. "Soldiers know all about it. Generals, how do you think generals got to be generals? They just have more of it than the rest of us."

"Should call you General Gabby, eh?" Hank said.

"Generalissimo Gabrielosima," she growled, and took a vicious swing at a stud. BANG!


Around noon Oscar made them all sandwiches, and after lunch he followed Kevin around, poring over the plans Kevin had drawn up for the renovation, and asking him questions. Each answer spawned more questions, and in the days that followed Oscar asked more, until it became a regular cross-examination.

"What don't you like about these old places you work on?"

"Well, they're pretty poorly built. And, well, they're dead."

"Dead?"

"Yeah, they're just boxes. Inert. They don't do anything, except protect you from wind and rain. Hell, you can do that with a box."

"And you like the new houses because they're alive?"

"Yeah. And the whole system is so neat, so . . . ingenious. Like this cloudgel." He pulled at a long roll of clear fabric, stretched it between his fists, let it contract. "You put panels of this stuff in the roof or walls, and if the temperature inside the room is low, then the cloudgel is clear, and sunlight is let in. At around seventy degrees it begins to cloud up, and at eighty it's white, and reflecting sun away. So it thermostats, just like clouds over the land. It's so *neat*."

"Spaceship technology, right?"

"Yeah. Apply it here, along with the other stuff, and you can make a really efficient little farm of a house. Stick in a nervous system of sensors for the house computer, run a tube down into the earth for cool air, use the sunlight for heat and to grow plants and fish, sling a couple of photovotaic cells on the roof for power, put in an Emerson tank—you know, depending on how far you want to go with it, you can get it to provide most of your daily needs. In any case you're saving lots of money.''

"But what about styling? How do you keep it from looking like a lab?"

"Easy! Lot of panels and open space, porches, atriums, French windows—you know, a lot of areas where it's hard to say if you're inside or out. That's what I like, anyway.'' He tapped one of the sketches scattered on the kitchen table. "There's this architect in Costa Mesa putting homes on water, they float on a little pond that stabilizes the temp and allows them to rotate the house in relation to the sun, and do a lot of aquaculture—''

"You row across to it?"

"Nah, there's a bridge.''

"Maybe I want one of those.''

"Please.''

"But what about food? Why a farmhouse?"

"Why not? Don't you like food?''

"It's obvious I like food. But why grow it in my house? To me it seems no more than fashion.''

"Of course it's a fashion. House styles always are. But it makes so much sense, given the materials at hand. Extra heat is going to be generated in the south-facing rooms, especially in this part of the country. And the house computer has the capacity for millions of times more work than you've given it so far. Why not put that heat and attention to work? See here, three small rooms on the south front, so you can vary temperatures and crops, and control infestations better.''

"I want no bugs in my house.''

"Nobody does, but that's greenhouses for you. Besides the computer is actually pretty good at controlling them. Then look, a pool in a central skylighted atrium. Panels adjustable so the skylight can be opened to make it a real atrium.''

"I have no central atrium."

"Not yet, but look, we're just gonna knock a little hole in your ceiling here—"

"We're going to knock a giant fucking hole in your ceiling!" Gabriela said as she walked by. "Don't let him fool you. You ain't gonna have a roof any bigger'n a cat's forehead by the time we're done."

"Ignore her. See, cloudgel skylight over a pool."

"I don't know if I like the idea of water in my house."

"Well, it's a good idea, because it's so stable thermally. And you can grow fish and provide a good bit of your protein."

"I detest fishing."

"The computer does it. First thing you know they're fillets in your fridge. Chinese carp is the usual staple."

"I don't like the idea of eating my house guests."

From the next room: "He don't like the idea of a computer than can kill occupants!"

"Good point."

"You get used to it. Then here, we'll enclose the area under the old carport, make it a breakfast room and part of the greenhouse, keep that peach tree in one wall, it'll be great. I love that kind of room."

"Is that why you like this work? To create rooms like that?"

"I like making the whole house. Changing bad to good. Man, I go into some of those old condo complexes, and my God—six hundred square feet, little tiny white-walled rooms with cottage cheese ceilings, cheap carpet over plywood floors, no light—they were like rats in a cage! Little white prison cells, I can't believe people lived like that! I mean they were more prosperous than that, weren't they? Couldn't they have done better?"

Oscar shrugged. "I suppose they could have."

"But they didn't! Now I go into one of those places and blast some space and light into them, do the whole program and in the end you can house just about as many people, but the feel of living there is completely different."

Oscar said, "You have to believe that you can live in a more communal situation without going crazy. You have to be willing to share space."

"I always make sure everyone has a room of their own, that's important to me."

"But the rest of it—kitchens, living rooms, all that. Social organization has to change for you to be able to redo those big places."

"So it's like Doris says—it's a matter of values."

"Yes, I think that's right."

"Well, I like our values. Seeing homes as organisms—there's an elegance to that, and if you can still make it beautiful . . ."

"It's a work of art."

"Yes, but a work of art that you live in. If you live in a work of art, it does something to you. It . . ." Kevin shook his head, unable to express it. "It gives you a good feeling."

From the next room Gabriela hooted. "It *gives* you a good *feeling?*"

Oscar called to her, "The aestheticization of *la vie quotidienne!*"

"Oh, now I get it! Just what I was going to say!"

Hank appeared in the doorway, saw and two-by-four in his hands. "It's Chinese, really. Their little gardens, and the sliding panels and the indoor-outdoor, and the communal thing and the domestic life as art—they've been doing it for thousands of years."

"That's true," Kevin said. "I love Chinese landscaping."

But now Hank was entranced by the two-by-four in his hand. "Uh oh, I appear to have sawed this one a little sigogglin." He made a face, hitched up his pants, walked back out under the carport.

One time after the day's work they bought some dumpies of beer and went up onto Rattlesnake Hill to look for endangered species. This was Kevin's idea, and they gave him a hard time about it, but he held fast. "Look, it's one of the best ways to stop the whole thing dead in its tracks, all right? There were some horned lizards down in the Newport Hills stopped a whole freeway a few years back. So we should try it."

And so they did, hiking up from Kevin and Doris's, and stopping often to inspect plants along the way. Jody was their botanist, and she brought along Ramona for a back-up. It was a hot afternoon, and they stopped often to consult with the beer.

"What's this tree, I don't remember seeing a tree quite like that."

It was a short twisted thing, with smooth gray bark runnelled by vertical lines. Big shiny leaves hid clumps of berries. "That's a mulefat tree," Jody said.

"How the hell did a tree get a name like that?"

"Maybe it burns well."

"Did they burn mule fat?"

"I don't think so. Pass that dumpie over."

Kevin wandered around as the rest sat to observe the mulefat tree. "What about this?" he said, pointing to a shrub with thread-like needles bushing everywhere on it.

"Sage!" they all yelled at him. "Purple sage," Jody amended. "We'll also see black sage and regular gray sage."

"About as endangered as dirt," Hank said.

"Okay, okay. Come on, you guys, we've got the whole hill to go over."

So they got up and continued the search. Kevin led them, and Jody identified a lot of plants. Gabby and Hank and Oscar and Ramona drank a lot of beer. A shrubby tree with oval flat leaves was a laurel sumac. A shrub with long stiff needles poking in every direction was Spanish broom. "Make it bigger and it's a foxtail pine," Hank said. Ramona identified about half the plants they ran across: mantilija poppy with its tiny leaves; horehound, a plain shrub; periwinkle with its broad leaves and purple flowers, a fine ground cover on the hill's north side; a tree that looked like a Torrey pine but was actually a Coulter pine; and on the crown of the hill, in the grove Tom had helped plant so long ago, a pair of fine black walnuts, with the bark looking broken, and the small green leaves in neat rows.

On the west side of the hill there were some steep ravines leading down into Crawford Canyon, and they clambered up and down, scrabbling for footholds in the loose sandstone and the sandy dirt. "What about this cactus?" Kevin said, pointing.

"Jesus, Kevin, that's prickly pear," Jody said. "You can get that stuff pickled down at the Mexican deli."

"That's it!" Gabriela cried. "Pickled cactus gets so popular that they're cutting it down everywhere to supply the market, and so suddenly it's endangered up here, yeah!"

"Ah shut up," Kevin said.

"Hey, here's some wildlife," Hank said from some distance away. He was on his hands and knees, his face inches from the dirt.

"Ants," Gabriela said as they walked over. "Chocolate covered ants get popular, and so suddenly—"

"No, it's a newt."

So it was; a small brown newt, crawling across an opening between sage bushes.

"It looks like rubber. Look how slow it moves."

"That's obviously a rare fake newt, put here to get Kevin's hopes up."

"It does look fake."

"They should be endangered, look how slow they are." The newt was moving each leg in turn, very slowly. Even blinking its little yellow eyes took time.

"The battery's running down."

"All right, all right," Kevin said, walking away angrily.

They followed him down the hill.


"That's all right, Kevin," Ramona said. "We've got a softball game tonight, remember?"

"True," Kevin said, perking up.

"Hey, are you still hitting a thousand?"

"Come on, Gabby, I don't want to talk about it."

"You are, you are! What is it, thirty for thirty?"

"Thirty-six for thirty-six," Ramona said. "But it is bad luck to talk about it."

"That's all right," Kevin said. "I'm not gonna mind when it ends anyway, it's making me nervous."

And this was true. Batting a thousand was not natural. Hit as well as possible, some line drives should still be caught. To keep firing them into empty places on the field was just plain weird, and Kevin was not comfortable with it. People were razzing him, too, both opponents and his own teammates. Mr. Thousand. Mr. Perfect. Heaven Kevin. It was embarrassing.

"Strike out on purpose, then," Hank suggested. "Get it over with. That's what I'd do."

"Damned if I will!"

They laughed at him.

Besides, each time he walked to the plate, that night or any other, and stood there half-swinging his bat, and the pitcher lofted up the ball, big and white and round against the black and the skittering moths, like a full moon falling out of the sky—then all thought would fly from his mind, he became an utter blank; and would come to standing on first or second or third, grinning and feeling the hit still in his hands and wrists. He couldn't stop it even if he wanted to.


Another day as they were finishing work Ramona cruised by and said to Kevin, "Want to go to the beach?"

His heartbeat tocked at the back of his throat. "Sure."

Biking down the Newport Freeway the wind cut through him, and with clear road ahead he shifted into high gear and started pumping hard. Ramona drafted him and after a while took the lead, and they zipped down the gentle slope of the coastal basin pumping so hard that they passed the cars in the next lane, and all for the fun of going fast. On the narrow streets of Costa Mesa and Newport Beach they had to slow and negotiate the traffic, following it out to the end of Balboa Peninsula. Here apartment blocks jumbled high on both sides of the street. Nothing could be done to reduce the population along such a fine beach, and besides the ocean-mad residents seemed to enjoy the crowd. Many of the old crackerbox apartments had been joined and reworked, and now big tentlike complexes quivered like flags in the wind, sheltering co-ops, tribes, big families, vacation groups, complete strangers —every social unit ever imagined was housed there, behind fabric walls bright with the traditional Newport Beach pastels.

They coasted to the end of the peninsula, under rows of palm trees. Scraps of green tossed overhead in the strong onshore breeze. They came to the Wedge and stopped. This was the world's most famous body surfing beach. Here waves from the west came in at an angle to the long jetty at the Newport Harbor channel, and as the waves approached the beach, masses of water built up against the rocks. Eventually these masses surged back out to sea in a huge backwash, a counterwave which crossed subsequent incoming swells at an angle, creating peaks, fast powerful cusps that moved across the waves very rapidly, often just at the point they were breaking. It was like something out of a physics class wave tank, and it was tremendously popular with body surfers, because the secondary wave could propel a body across the face of the primary wave with heartstopping speed. Add an element of danger—the water was often only three feet deep at the break, and tales of paralysis and death were common—and the result was a perfect adrenalin rush for the OC ocean maniac.

Today, however, the Pacific was pacific, almost lakelike, and the Wedge Effect was not working. This was fine with Ramona and Kevin, they were happy just to swim. Cool salt tang, the luxurious sensuality of immersion, flotation, the return to the sea. Kevin sharked over the rippled tawny sand on the bottom, looked up through silver bubbles at the surface, saw its rise and fall, its curious partial reflectivity, sky and sand both visible at once. Long graceful body in a dark red suit, swimming overhead with powerful strokes. Women are dolphins, he thought, and laughed a burst of silver at the sky. He ran out of air and shot to the surface, broke into blinding white air, eyes scored by salt and sun, delicious stinging. "Outside," Ramona called, but she was fooling; no waves of any size out there, only flat glary blue, all the way to the horizon. Nothing but shore break. They grunioned around in that for a long time, mindless, lifted up and down by the moon. After that their suits were full of sand, they had to swim out again to flush them clean.

Back on the beach. Sitting on sand, half dry. Salt crust on smooth brown skin. The smell of salt and seaweed, the cool wind.

"Want to walk out the jetty?"

Onto the mound of giant boulders, stepping carefully. Rough uneven surfaces of basalt and feldspar gleamed in the light, gray and black and white and red and brown. Between the rocks the swells rose and fell, sucking and slapping the barnacles.

"We used to come out here all the time when we were kids."

"Us too," Ramona said. "The whole house. Boulder ballet, we called it. Only on the other jetty, because my mom always took us to Corona del Mar." Newport Harbor's channel was flanked on both sides by jetties, the other one was some two hundred yards across the water.

"It was always the Wedge for us. There was something magical about walking out this jetty when I was a kid. A big adventure, like going to the end of the world."

They stepped and balanced, hopped and teetered. Occasionally they bumped together, arm to arm. Their skin was warm in the sun. They talked about this and that, and Kevin felt certain boundaries disappearing. Ramona was willing to talk about anything, now, about things beyond the present moment. Childhoods in El Modena and at the beach. The boats offshore. Their work. The people they knew. The huge rocks jumbled under them: "Where *did* they come from, anyway?" They didn't know. It didn't matter. What do you talk about when you're falling in love? It doesn't matter. All the questions are, Who are you? How do you think? Are you like me? Will you love me? And all the answers are, I am like this, like this, like this. I am like you. I like you.

"We used to race out to the end sometimes, running over these rocks! Crazy!"

"Yeah, we're a lot more sensible now," Ramona said, and grinned.

They came to the end, where the causeway of stone plunged into the sea. The horizon stood before them at eye level, a hazy white bar. Sunlight broke on the sea in a billion points, flickering like gold signal mirrors, sending a Morse of infinite complexity.

They sat on a flat boulder, side by side. Ramona leaned back on both hands, jacking her elbows forward. Muscley brown forearms bulged side to side, muscley brown biceps bulged front to back. Triceps stood out like the swells between the jetties.

"How's things at your house?"

"Okay," Kevin said. "Andrea's back is bothering her. Yoshi is sick of teaching English, Sylvia's worried that the kids have chicken pox. Donna and Cindy are still drinking too much, and Tomas still spends all his time at the screen. The usual lunacy. I bet Nadezhda thinks we're bedlam."

"She's nice."

"Yeah. But sometimes the house is just howling, and the look on her face . . ."

"It can't be any worse than India."

"Maybe. Maybe it bothers me more than her. I tell you, some nights when the kids are wild I wonder if living in small families isn't a good idea."

"Oh no," Ramona said. "Do you think so? I mean, they're so isolated."

"Quieter."

"Sure, but so what? I mean, you've always got your room. But if it were only you and a partner and kids! Try to imagine Rosa and Josh doing that! Rosa doesn't do a thing to take care of

Doug and Ginger, she's always working or down here surfing. So those kids are there and they're really into being entertained constantly, and sometime I know Josh would just go crazy if he were in a little house all by himself. He almost does already.''

"A lot of them did, I guess. Mothers.''

"Yeah. But at our place Josh can get me or my mom to take the kids while he goes out to swim or something, and we can talk with him, and he tells us about it and feels better, and by the time Rosa's back he's having a good time and he doesn't care. Unless he's really pissed at her. But they manage. I don't think their marriage would survive if they lived by themselves.''

Kevin nodded. "But what about other couples who're different? What you're saying is that marriages are less intense now because people tend to live in groups. But what about the really good marriages? Then reducing the intensity is just diffusing something good.''

"Diffusing it, yeah, spreading it around. Maybe we need to have that kind of good diffused out. The couple won't suffer.''

"No? Well. Maybe not.'' What about us, then? Kevin wanted to say. He had never even found someone he felt like trying with. And she and Alfredo, fifteen years? What went wrong? "But . . . something is gone, I think. Something I think I'd like.''

Ramona frowned, considering it. They watched swells run up and down the seaweedy, mussel-crusted band of rock at sea level. Talked about other things. Felt light crash into their skin.

Ramona pointed north. "Couple of big ships coming.''

"Oh, I love to watch those.'' He sat up, shaded his eyes with a hand. Two tall ships had risen over the horizon, converging on the harbor from slightly different angles, one from San Pedro, and the other rounding Catalina from the north. Both were combinations of square rigged and fore-and-aft rigged, the current favorite of ship designers. They resembled the giant barkentines built in the last years of sailing's classic age, only the fore-and-aft sails were rigid, and bulged around the masts in an airfoil shape. Each ship had five masts, and the one rounding Catalina had an isosceles mast for its foremast, two spars rising from the hull to meet over-head.

Suddenly all the yards on both ships bloomed white with sail, and the little bones of white water chewed by their sharp bows got larger. "Hey they're racing!" Kevin said. "They're racing!"

Ramona stood to watch. The onshore breeze was strength-ening, and the two ships were on a reach across it, so their sails bulged toward shore. Stunsails bloomed to each side of the highest yards, and from a distance it seemed the ships flew over the water, gliding like pelicans. Working freighters only, so big they could never be really fast, but those stacks of white sail, full-bellied with the wind! Complex as jets, simple as kites, the two craft cut through the swells and converged on the harbor, on each other. It seemed possible the windward ship might try to steal the other's wind, and sure enough the leeward ship began to luff off a bit, toward the beach. Perhaps the pilot would have to try swinging behind the windward ship, to trade places and reverse the tactic; a dan-gerous maneuver, however, as they might never catch up. "Isos-celes is trying to push them into the beach," Ramona observed.

"Yeah, they're caught inside. I say Isosceles has them."

"No, I say Leeward's closer, they'll slip right around the jetty here, we'll probably be able to step aboard."

"Bet."

"Okay."

On the end of the other jetty a group of kids were standing and shouting at the sight. The wind pushed at them, Kevin raised his arms to feel it. That something so free and wild should be harnessed to the will: the ancient elegance of it made him laugh.

"Go, Isosceles!" "Go, Leeward!" And they shouted and bumped shoulders like the kids on the other jetty. As the ships got closer they could see better how big they were. The channel couldn't take any larger, it looked as if the mainyards would stretch from one jetty to the other, great silver condor wings of alloy. The crews of the two ships were standing on the windward rails as ballast, and someone on each ship hurled amplified insults across the ever-narrowing gap of water between them. It really did look as though they would reach the channel mouth in a dead heat, in which case Isosceles would be forced to luff off, according to race protocol. Ramona was gleefully pointing this out to Kevin when a long silver spar telescoped out from the windward side of Isosceles' bow, and an immense rainbow-striped balloon spinnaker whooshed into existence like a parachute, dragging the whole great ship behind it. Swells exploded under the bow. "Coming through!" they heard the tinny loudspeaker from Isosceles cry, and with a faint Bronx cheer the Leeward sloughed off. Its stunsails rolled up into their spars, and the spars telescoped back in under the yards. Sail was taken in everywhere, without a single sailor aloft, and the ship settled down into the water like a motorboat with the throttle cut. When Isosceles turned into the channel entrance, to the cheers of spectators on both jetties, its sails too disappeared, rolling up with the faint hum of automated rigging and tackle blocks. Three of the five topsails and the isosceles top section served to propel it down the channel at a stately five miles an hour, and the bare spars stood high against the hills of Corona del Mar. Leeward followed it in, looking much the same. The crews waved back at them.

"They're so *beautiful*," Kevin said.

"I wonder if one of them is Nadezhda's ship," Ramona said. "It's due soon."

They sat down again, leaned back against the warm rock side by side, arms touching. A thick rain of light poured down on them, knitting tightly with the onshore wind. Photon by photon, striking and flaking off, filling the air so that everything—the sea, the tall ships, the stone of the jetties, the green light tower at the other jetty's end, the buoys clanging on the groundswell, the long sand reach of the beach, the lifeguard stands and their streaming flags, the pastel wrack of apartments, the palm fronds swaying over it all—everything floated in a white light, an aura of salt mist, ethereal in the photon rain. In every particulate jot of being . . . Kevin settled back like a sleepy cat. "What a day."

And Ramona leaned over, black hair blinding as a crow's wing, and kissed him.

Over the next weeks matters progressed on the Rattlesnake Hill issue, but slowly and amorphously, so that it was hard to keep a sense of what was happening. A letter came back from LA's Metropolitan Water District, outlining their offer of more water. What it came down to was a reduced rate if they purchased more. Mary and the town planner's office immediately made inquiries with the OCWD concerning sell-through rates. Clearly they were hoping that El Modena could buy the extra water from LA, and then give what they didn't use to OCWD by pouring it into the groundwater basin. This would get them credits from OCWD that they could use against pump taxes, and the net result might be a considerable savings, with a lot of water in reserve.

Oscar shook his head when he heard about it. "I believe I'd like to look into this one a little more," he murmured. First of all, he told Kevin, town resolution 2022 would have to be overthrown or some sort of special dispensation made, which would take council action or a town vote. And then the whole maneuver would tend to put the town in the water business, buying it here and selling it there, and the State Water Resources Control Board was likely to have some thoughts about that, no matter what the district watermaster said. If it came to a town vote that superficially looked like it was only about saving money, Oscar wanted to talk to Sally Tallhawk about her suggestion concerning Inyo County's water. Inyo now owned the water that used to belong to Los Angeles, and it was possible they could work out some kind of deal, and buy even cheaper water from Inyo than the MWD was offering, with some use stipulations included that would keep the water from fueling a big development. Certainly Inyo would appreciate the irony of altering the shape of development in southern California, after the years of manipulation they had suffered at the hands of LA.

So Oscar was busy. Kevin for his part dropped by to talk with Hiroko, Susan, and Jerry, to see what they were thinking about the matter. Jerry had let his law practice lapse so that he could help run a small computer firm located down on Santiago Creek where it crossed Tustin Avenue, and Kevin found him there one day, eating lunch by the creek. He was a burly man in his early sixties, who looked as calm and sensible as you could ever want, until you noticed a glint in his eye, the only indication of a secret sense of humor, a sort of anarchist's playfulness that the town had come to know all too well.

He shrugged when Kevin asked him about the hill matter. "Depends what it is. I need to see Alfredo's plans, what it would do for the town."

"Jerry, that's the last empty hill in the whole area! Why should he take that hill? I notice you're content to have your business down here on the flats."

Jerry swallowed a bit of sandwich. "Maybe I'm not content. Maybe I'd like to take some offices up there in Alfredo's complex."

"Ah, come on. Here you are down by the creek for lunch, I know you appreciate the way this town has been working, what it stands for. Why else would you be here?"

"I was born here."

"Yah, well . . ." Kevin sighed. Talking to Jerry was hard. "All the more reason you should want to protect it. It's a miracle the water district held onto that hill for so long, and now that we've got it, it would be a shame to make it look like all the rest of them. Think about it."

"I'll think about it." He swallowed. "Know what I heard?"

"What?"

"I heard Alfredo's being pressed into trying for this move. Needs to do it."

Kevin thought about that as he rode over to see Susan Mayer. Susan was chief scientist at the El Modena Chicken Farm, which supplied much of northern Orange County with chickens. Kevin found her out in the farm's lab, cursing a gc/mass spec: an athletic woman in her forties, one of the best swimmers in town. "I don't really have time to talk about it now, Kevin, but I assure you I know just what you're worried about. Alfredo is a nice man, and good for the town, but sometimes it seems like he should be in Irvine or Anaheim where the stakes are higher." She wouldn't say more than that. "Sorry, I've got to get to work on this, it looks like we might have an outbreak in one of the coops. We'll have to wait and see about the hill stuff until we know more anyway, right?"

Sigh. On to Hiroko, botanist and orchard farmer. Also a landscape gardener, and she was out on a job. Kevin found her and gave her a hand digging up a front yard, and they had a good long talk as they worked. Hiroko had been on the council on and off for about twenty years, and so nothing much in that area excited her any more. But she seemed sympathetic, and skeptical about Alfredo and his big plans, as she put it. Kevin left her feeling good. If they could count on Hiroko, then it would only take one more to have a majority on the council. Susan and Jerry were both possibles, and so . . .

He told Doris what Jerry had said about Alfredo needing to make the move. "Hmm," Doris said. "Okay, I'll see if pretending I know that for sure will pull anything more out of John." She was working the hardest of them all, pumping her connections for more news from inside Heartech. Her friend John heard a lot in the financial office of her own firm, Avending, and his friend over in Heartech's offices knew even more. The next time she talked to him, she said something about Alfredo having to make a move. "Yeah, it's an outside thing," John said, "Ann's sure of it. They've always had a source of outside money, she says. That's why it's ballooned so fast."

Apparently Heartech's growth had been even more rapid than it appeared to the public. And some of that growth was being absorbed by a hidden backer, so that Heartech would remain within legal company size, and avoid any special audits from the IRS.

Or so the rumors had it. "They're iceberging in the black, Ann says," John told Doris in low voice.

"Unbelievable," Doris said. If it were true, then they would have the best weapon possible to stop any office-building by Heartech. Proving it, however . . . "But if they build this development they're going to come under the microscope! No way they can fund it themselves—they'll either have to apply for government help or have a partner."

"True," John said a week later. "And Doris—I'm sorry to tell you, but . . ."


Dear Claire:

    . . . Yes, I went to Opening Day in Bishop, and provided the usual entertainment for the masses with Sally. Our match was witnessed by Kevin and Doris; the sturdy Doris was either appalled or disgusted, she couldn't decide which. She had little spare time to scorn the Grand Sport, however, as she and Kevin spent at least part of the weekend recomplicating an old relationship. They were lovers long ago, Nadezhda told me, and currently Doris seems both attracted to and exasperated by Kevin, while he, it seems to me, relies on her rather more than he realizes. They spent a night in Sally's guest room, and afterwards the currents swirling around under the surface of things would have spun a submarine. This, at the same time that Kevin is enthusiastically exploring the consequences of Ramona the Beauty's freedom. It's getting pretty complicated in Elmo. . . .

    . . . Yes, Nadezhda is still here, though she won't be for long; her ship is in Newport Harbor, and in two or three weeks it will depart, taking her with it. That will be a sad day. We have done a lot together, and it has been a delight. Often she calls to ask if I want to cruise the town, and if I agree I am dragged all over Orange County in a kind of parody of an educational tour. She's like Ben Franklin on drugs. What are you doing here? Why are you doing it this way and not that? Is it really true that mustard grass was part of the original ground cover on this plain? Couldn't you use bigger cells? Aren't you thinking the mayor is pushing things too fast? Is it true what they say about Kevin and Ramona? She peppers them with questions till they reel, then bikes away muttering about slowness, ignorance, sleepwalking. What zombies, she'll mutter if they're unresponsive. What sheep! On the other hand, when she runs into people who know what they are doing and enjoy talking about it, she gets them going for hours, and bikes away glowing. Ah, what energy, what ingenuity, what boldness! she will cry, face flushed, eyes bright. And so the people here love her, while at the same time being slightly afraid of her. With her combination of fire and wisdom, of energy and experience, she seems like some higher life form, some next step in evolution. Old but young. Those geriatric drugs must really be something. Maybe I'd better start taking them now.

Certainly her presence has put the jumper cables to Tom Barnard, who was living a hermit's life in the hills before her arrival. Now he comes into town pretty regularly. Many people here know him, especially among the older generations, and Nadezhda has worked hard at getting him re-involved in their lives, in her usual energetic fashion. They're doing a lot of socializing together. Also, we've started to get him seriously involved in the struggle over the plans for Rattlesnake Hill.

Developments (so to speak) in the hill battle abound, as Kevin and Doris try to put Sally's suggestions into action. They may even drill a spring. This was Sally's suggestion, and I am sure she was joking, but she played it like a wooden Indian, and they took her seriously. Far be it from me to disabuse them, and explain that a drilled spring (or *well*, as we call it) will not stop development.

One night in the midst of this activity Doris came home from work slamming doors and snarling. I had just dropped by their house to talk to Kevin, and found no one home but the kids. I was the only adult there, an unusual situation that neither Doris nor I would have wanted, I am sure.

However, I asked what was wrong. She shouted her reply; a friend in the financial department of her company, Avending, had told her that Avending was negotiating with Heartech, the mayor's company, over plans to propose a new complex in El Modena. Here we had been wondering who Alfredo and his partners would get to join them in building this complex, and it was Doris's own company!

I tried to make a joke. At least she would be within walking distance of her job, I said. She gave me her Medusa imitation, a very convincing one.

I'm quitting, she said. I can't work there anymore.

Something in the way she said it made me feel mischievous. I wanted to push at this virtue of hers, see how far it extended. I said, first you ought to find out what you can about their plans.

She stared at me. Do you think so?

I nodded.

I'd need some help.

I'll help you, I said, surprising both of us.

So she called her friend in the financial office, and spoke urgently with him for nearly half an hour. And then I found myself accompanying Fierce Doris to her place of employment, Avending of Santa Ana.

It was a small complex of labs and offices near the freeway. Doris led us in past a security guard, explaining I was a friend.

Once in her lab I stared around me, amazed! It was the biggest surprise of a pretty surprising night; the office part of the lab was filled with sculpture! Small pieces, large pieces, abstracts, human and animal figures . . . made of metals, ceramics, materials I couldn't identify. What is this? I said.

You know, we develop materials here, she said. Superconductors and like that. These are throwaways from various experiments.

You mean they just come out like this? I said stupidly.

She laughed shortly.

You sculpt them, I said.

Yes, that's right. I'm going to have to get all these home. . . .

You could have knocked me over with a feather, or at least a pillow. Who knows what depths these southern tidepools conceal? Any step might plunge you overhead in the brine. . . .

Doris went to work on the computer, and soon the printer was ejecting page after page of records. We need to do the rest in John's office, she said. That's tricky—I'm in my lab all the time at night, but there's no reason to be in his office. You'll have to keep a lookout for security, and the cleaning robots.

We tiptoed down the corridor into her friend's office. Again the computer, the print out. I kept watch in the hall while Doris xeroxed pages from a file cabinet. She began to fill boxes.

A cleaning robot hummed down the hall toward us. Feverishly I disarranged an office between us and it, hoping to slow it down. I didn't get out in time, and it bumped into me coming in the doorway. "Excuse me," it said. "Cleaning."

"Quite all right. Could you please clean this office?"

"Excuse me. Cleaning." It entered the office and uttered a little click, no doubt dismayed at the mess I had just made. I dashed past it, back to Doris.

She was done xeroxing, and about two hours later she was done printing out. We carried box after box into the parking lot, finishing just ahead of the cleaning robot's entrance.

Outside we had a bicycle built for two, with a big trailer attached behind. We piled that trailer so high with boxes that when we got on the bike, it was as if it were set in cement. There we were, absconding with Avending's entire history, and we couldn't move an inch. Both of us jumped up and down on the pedals; no movement. What would security say when they saw us? Thieves, escaping at zero miles an hour.

I had to get off and apply the Atomic Drop to the trailer to get us started, and then run around and leap into my saddle, to hop furiously on a pedal that moved like an hour hand. Unfortunately the right turn we took onto the street killed our momentum. It was necessary to apply three Atomic Drops in succession to get us moving again. After that it was a matter of acceleration. Once we got up to about five miles an hour, we found we could maintain it pretty well.

The next day Doris quit her job. Now she is getting Tom to help her go through the records she stole. It is unclear whether they will be of use, but Tom thinks it is possible the two companies have illegal sources of capital, or will obtain them to help finance the complex. Worth looking for, he says. And something in the records made him suggest that Hong Kong might be implicated. So our raid is justified. Fierce Doris strikes again!

She gave me one of her sculptures, in thanks for my help. Big slabs of a blue-green ceramic alloy: a female figure, tossing aloft a bird, a raptor in its first downstroke. A wonderful sense of movement. We stared at it, both embarrassed to speechlessness.

Have you been sculpting long? I asked.

A few years.

What inspired you to begin?

Well—I was running experiments on certain materials under pressure, and when they came out of the kiln, they looked funny. I kept seeing things in them, you know, like you see shapes in clouds. So I started to help bring the shapes out.

I'll put this in my atrium when they're done working, I said.

. . . Work on my house continues apace. Right now it looks like the Parthenon: roofless and blown apart. They assure me it will begin to coalesce soon, and I hope so, because some strange things have happened when I am home alone, and perhaps when the house is finished they will stop happening.

. . . Of course I still feel disoriented—unprotected, in the midst of growing a new shell, of building a new life. But the old life in Chicago seems more and more like a dream to me—a very long and vivid dream, admittedly—but a dream still, and like a dream it is growing less intense and less easy to remember as I drift further away. Strange, this life, isn't it? We think, nothing could ever get more real than this! Then *this* becomes nothing more than a darting fragmentary complex of pure mentation, while a new reality, more real than ever! steps in to obscure all previous candidates. I never get used to it. Well—write soon, please—I miss you—xx oo—

Your Oscar

# 6

*Been on plane four hours now. Liddy finally asleep. Tapping on lap keyboard. Might as well distract myself.*

*Strategies for changing history. Invent the history leading out of this world (please) into the world of the book. Causes of utopian process gaining upper hand.*

*Words scroll up and disappear forever, like days.*

*Lincoln not assassinated, no, no, we know it didn't happen that way, we know we can't take that road. Not useful. Someone appears to lead us, no! No Great Man theory here. No individual can save us. Together or not at all.*

*Together or nothing. Ah, Pamela—*

*Some group. In power or out. Act together. Say lawyers, the law? Still can't escape the feeling that there's where a difference could be made, despite my own experience. Remake the law of the land. Say a whole class of Harvard Law School, class of '12 goes out to fill posts of all kinds, government, World Bank, IMF, Pentagon. Save the twenty-first century. Plausible? No. A story. But at least it's possible, I mean we could do it! Nothing stopping us but inertia, ideology. Lack of imagination! Teachers, religious leaders . . . but there are few politically active people in any group. And to agree on a whole program of action, all of them. How implausible can something be before it's useless? It's conspiracy theory, really. We don't need that either.*

*History changed by a popular book, a utopia, everyone reads it and it has ideas, or vague pokes in the direction of ideas, it changes their thinking, everyone starts working for a better world—*

*Getting desperate. Marcuse: one of the worst signs of our danger is we can't imagine the route from here to utopia. No way to get there.*

*Take the first step and you're there. Process, dynamism, the way is the life. We must imagine the way. Our imagination is stronger than theirs! Take the first step and you're on the road.*

*And so? In my book?*

*Stare at empty screen. My daughter sighs in her sleep. Her sleeping face. It's a matter of touch, and if you can't touch the one you love—can't see her—*

*We're thirty-five thousand feet above the earth. People are watching a movie. The blue curve of the world, such a big place, so much bigger than we ever think, until something takes us. . . .*

*Words scroll up and disappear forever, like*

The night of Hank's Mars party they rode into the hills in a big group, bike lamps bobbing like a string of fireflies. The Lobos formed the core of the party, then Oscar was along, and Tom and Nadezhda, weaving dangerously on a bicycle built for two. They came to the end of the paved road near Black Star Canyon and left the bikes behind. Hank's backpack clinked as he led them up the dark trail. Oscar stumbled in the forest twilight: "Humanity lands on the fabled red planet, and we celebrate this feat by wandering in the dark like savages. It's *2001* run backwards. Ow!"

The air was warm. The sage and low gnarled oaks covering the canyon walls clattered and shooshed in irregular gusts of wind. A Santa Ana wind was arriving, sweeping down from the north, compressing over the San Jacintos, warming and losing moisture until it burst out of the canyons hot and dry. "Santa Ana!" Tom said, sniffing. He explained to Nadezhda, touched the back of her hand and she jumped. "Static electricity. It's a good sign."

An electric shock with every touch.

After a half hour's climb they came to Black Star Hot Springs, a series of small pools in a narrow meadow. Sycamore, live oak, and black walnut stood crowded on the flat canyon floor, surrounding the pools. Near the largest pool was a small cabin and pavilion. Hank had rented it from the town for the night, and he unlocked the door and turned on a lamp inside. Yellow window squares illuminated the steam bubbling off the pool's surface. Stiff live oak leaves clacked together. Branch rubbed on branch, adding ghostly creaks to the susurrous of leaf sound.

"Yow—it's hot tonight."

The large pool was two down from the source of the spring. Concrete steps and an underwater concrete bench had been built into it, and the rest of the bottom was a hard gritty sandstone not much different from the concrete in texture. The pool was about twenty feet across, and varied between three and five feet in depth. In short, a perfect hot springs pool.

Hank, Jody, Mike and Oscar put food and drink into the cabin's refrigerator. The rest shed their clothes and stepped into the pool. Abrupt splashes, squeals of pain, hoots of delight. The water was the temperature of a hot bath, deliciously warm once past the initial shock of it.

Oscar appeared at the pool's edge, a big white blob in the dim light. "Watch out," Kevin said. Oscar threw his massive head back; in the darkness he seemed three times the size of a man, broad-shouldered, barrel-chested, big-bellied, thick-legged. His friends stared despite themselves. Suddenly he crouched, threw his arms wide, mimed jumping out over them. Just the way he shifted on his feet and whipped his head around implied the whole action of running forward and leaping up, landing in a giant cannonball dive. "No, no! The pool! You'll crack the bottom!" He pawed the ground with a bare foot, shook his black curls ferociously, took a little run back, then forward to the pool's edge, then back again, arms outstretched like a surfer's, tilting with the absurd rhinocerine grace Kevin and Doris had seen in Bishop.

Hank and Jody and Mike came out of the cabin to see what the ruckus was about, and with a last great wind-up Oscar took off, into the air like a great white whale, suspended in a ball several feet above them. Then KERPLOP, and an enormous splash.

Wild shrieks. "My God," said Gabriela, "the water's two feet lower."

"And just think if Oscar weren't in the pool."

Doris, laughing hard, said "Oscar, you have to stay in so we aren't beached."

"Glug," Oscar said, spurting water from his mouth like an Italian fountain, an immense Cupid.

"What's the flow rate of this spring?" Mike said. "Ten gallons a minute? We should be back to normal by morning."

"We'll have to pour some tequila in," Hank said solemnly, carrying out a big tray filled with bottles and glasses. "A sacrifice. Here, start working on these."

Jody passed around glasses, leaning out over the water.

"You look like a cocktail waitress, stop working so hard, we can get this stuff."

"Hank's bringing out the masks, then we're done."

Hank brought out a stack of papier-maché masks he had made, animals faces of all kinds. "Great, Hank." "Yeah, I spent a couple months on these, every night." He gave them out, very particular about who got which one. Kevin was a horse, Ramona an eagle, Gabriela a rooster, Mike a fish; Tom was a turtle, Nadezhda a cat; Oscar was a frog, Doris a crow, Jody a tiger, and Hank himself was a coyote. All the masks had eyeholes, and mouths convenient for drinking. They walked around the pool inspecting each other and giggling. Masked heads, naked bodies: it was weird, bizarre, dangerous looking.

"Ribbit!"

They all joined in with the appropriate cry.

Jody stepped into the pool and whistled at its heat, her long body feline under the tiger mask. Hank hopped around handing people glasses, or bottles for those who needed them to be able to drink through their masks.

"This is Hank's own tequila," Tom told Nadezhda. "He grows the cactus in his garden and does all the extraction and fermentation and distillation himself." He took a gulp from his glass. *"Horrible* stuff. Here, Hank, give me some more of that."

"It tastes fine to me," Nadezhda said, then coughed hard.

Tom laughed. "Yeah, tequila is heavenly."

Hank stood at one end of the pool, looking perfectly natural, as if he always went naked and sported a coyote head. "Listen to the wind." He prowled around the pool's edge. Over the trickle of water they could hear the wind soughing, and suddenly the shape of the canyon was perfectly clear to them: the narrowing upstream, the headwall, the side canyons up above—all that, just in sound. Hank began humming, and some of them picked it up, the great "aum" shifting as different people joined in or stopped to breathe. Over this ground bass Hank muttered what sounded like random sentences, some intelligible, some not. "We come from the earth. We're part of the earth." Then a low breath chant, "Hi-ya *huh,* hi-ya *huh,* au-oom," and then more complex and various, a singsong poem in a language none of them knew, punctuated by exclamations. "We come from the earth like this water, pouring into the world. We are bubbles of earth. Bubbles of earth." Then another language, Sanskrit, Shoshone, only the shaman knew. He prowled around them like Coyote checking out a henhouse, growling. They could feel his physical authority; they stood in the pool milling around to face him, chanting too, getting louder until Coyote howled, and suddenly they were all baying at the moon, as loud as voices could ever be.

Hank hopped in the pool, hooted. "Man when you're wet that wind is cold!"

"Quick," Tom said, "more awful tequila."

"Good idea."

Jody went to get more from the cabin, and while she was

there she pulled the cabin's TV onto the deck and turned it on, with the sound off. It seemed a kind of lamp, the faces and command centers mere colored forms. Jody dialed up music, Chinese harps and low flute tones, whistling over the sound of the wind. Overhead the stars blinked and shivered, brilliant in the so-black sky; the moon wouldn't rise for a hour or two. Just over the treetops one of the big orbiting solar collectors shone like a jewel, like a chip of the moon or a planet ten times bigger than Jupiter.

Ramona stood in the shallow end, a broad-shouldered eagle, collarbones prominent under sleek wet skin. "The water gets too hot, but with the wind it feels really cold when you get out. You can't get it right."

"Reminds me of Muir's night on Shasta," the turtle said. "He was tough, his father was a Calvinist minister and a cruel man, he beat Muir and worked him at the bottom of wells. So nothing in the Sierras ever bothered him. But one time he and a friend climbed Shasta and got caught in a storm up there at the top, a real bad blizzard. It should have killed them, but luckily Shasta was more active in those days, and there was still a hot spring pool in the summit caldera. Muir and his friend found this pool and jumped in, but the water in it was like a hundred and fifty degrees, and full of sulphur gas. So they couldn't stay in it, but when they got out they started to freeze instantly. It was scald or freeze, no middle ground. All they could do to survive was keep dipping in and out of the pool, lying in the shallows and rolling over all night long, one side in the water and the other in the wind, on and on until their senses were so blasted that they couldn't tell the hot from the cold. Afterwards Muir said it was the most uncomfortable night he had ever spent, which is saying a lot, because he was a wild man."

"Sounds like our Hank," the tiger said. "One time we were up in the Sierras and a lightning storm struck, and I turned around and there was Hank climbing a tall tree—I said what the hell are you doing? and he said he wanted to get a better look."

Said the rooster, "One time we went to Yosemite and climbed to the top of Yosemite Falls, and Hank, he walked right out knee deep to where he could look over the edge! Three thousand feet down!"

"Hey," Hank said, "how else you gonna see it?"

They laughed at him.

"It was October, I tell you, the water was low!"

"How about that time we were on top of that water tower on the Colorado and these crazies hauled up in a motor boat and ran up the tower and dove off into the river—must have been fifty or sixty feet! And soon as they were finished Hank just leaned out over, and kept on leaning till he dove in too! Sixty feet!"

"I woulda done it before," Coyote said, "but it didn't occur to me till I saw those guys do it."

The rooster crowed with laughter. "Once we were riding a ski lift at Big Bear and Hank says to me Don't this look like a great take-off point, Gabby? It'd be just like dropping in on a big wave, wouldn't it? And before I could say no it wouldn't be anything like dropping in on a big wave he had *hopped out of the fucking ski lift,* dropped and turned thirty feet through the air and hit the slope flying!"

"Actually, I cut my forehead on the front of my skis on that one," Hank said. "Don't know how."

"What about the time you took Damaso climbing in Joshua Tree—"

"Oh, that was a mistake," Coyote said. "He got freaked and came off when we were crossing Hairball Ledge, and fell so fast I had to grab him by his *hair* as he slid by. A hundred feet up and we're hanging there by two fingertips and Damaso's *hair*."

"I feel comfortable again," the eagle announced, head bobbing on the water's surface. "Or at least safer."

She floated over to the horse. Instantly Kevin felt a dizzying stallion's rush of blood coursing through his side as hers touched him. Knees, whole thighs; she stayed there, pressed against him. The blood poured through him, spurting out of his heart in great booms, flushing out every capillary in his skin, so that he had to take in a big shivery breath to contain all the tingling. The power of the touch. Their shoulders brushed, and her newly emergent wet flesh felt as warm as the water. Steam caught the rose light from the TV screen. They were showing a close-up of Mars. The horse considered the idea of an orgasm through his side.

Oscar and Doris, frog and crow, were discussing the most dangerous things they had ever done, in a facetious style so that they spoke only of accidents. Getting caught under a bronze mold, flying with Ramona, wrestling the Vancouver Virgins, trying to rescue a college paper from a burning apartment. . . . Their claims for their own stupidity were matched only by their claims for the other's. Hearing this from across the pool, the cat nudged the turtle and made a tiny gesture in their direction. The turtle shook his head, nodded with his round head toward the horse and the eagle. The cat shrugged.

"I think it's time," Coyote declared. "Isn't Mars getting closer?"

"Should I turn up the sound?"

"NO."

Flute and Chinese harp, and the wind in the trees, served them as soundtrack for humanity's first touch of another planet. So often delayed, so often screwed up, the journey was finally coming to its end—which was also a beginning, of something none of them could see, exactly, though they all knew it was important. A whole world, a whole history, implied in a single image. . . .

From orbit the expedition had dropped several robot landers, in Hellas Basin where they planned to touch down, and all of these robots were equipped with heat-seeking cameras, which were now trained on the manned lander as it descended. The directors of the TV program had any number of fine images to choose from, and often they split the screen to provide more than one. The view from the lander as Hellas, the biggest of all craters, got closer and more distinct, its floor a rock-strewn plain of reddish sand. Or the view from the ground, looking up into a dark pink sky, where there was an odd thing, a black dot in the middle of a white circle, growing larger. It resolved to the lander and its parachute, then bloomed with white light as retro-rockets fired. The view shifted to a shot from orbit, in super telephoto, the lander a white spot of thistledown, drifting onto a desert floor. Ah yes—images that would become part of history forever and ever, created in this very moment, in the knife-edge present that is all we ever inhabit. The TV seemed huge.

Coyote shaman started chanting again, and some of the other animals provided the purring background hum. Everything—the stars shivering overhead, the black leaves clicking in the black sky, the deep whoosh of the wind, the wet chuckle of water, the weird Chinese music, their voices, the taste of cactus, the extraordinary square of rich red color, over against the dark mass of the pavilion—all fused to a single whole, a unit of experience in which nothing could be removed. The turtle, pulling out of it for a moment, had to admire the shaman's strange sense of ritual, of place. How better to be part of this moment, one of humanity's greatest? Then the lander fell closer to the ground and their voices rose, they saw the sand on the desert floor kick up, as if in a wind like the one swirling their wet skin, and the turtle felt a surge of something he had almost forgotten. Grinning inside his mask, he howled and howled. They all were howling. The lander dropped lower, throwing out clouds and clouds of dust and red sand. They screamed at the stars as it touched down, jumping and cheering wildly. "Yaay! Yaay!"

There were people on Mars.

After that the action on screen returned to the business of astronauts and commentators. Hank ran to the cabin and came back with a couple of light beachballs that he threw in the pool. They batted the balls around in volleyball style, talked, drank, watched the continuing drama of the astronauts suiting up. "What will they say, you know, their first words?"

"If they say something stupid like on the moon, I'll throw up."

"How about, 'Well, here we are.' "

"Home at last."

"The Martians have landed."

"Take me to your leader."

"If we don't turn the sound up we'll never know."

"That would be an odd thing to say."

"We'll find out tomorrow, leave it down. We're doing better than they will anyway, you know astronauts."

A ball in the middle of the pool rolled over slowly on the water, pushed seemingly by the steam that curled off the surface in lazy arabesques. Foggy yellow light. Images of raised arms, flexing shoulders, breasts and pecs, animal faces. They glowed in the dark, their bodies looked like translucent pink skins containing some sort of flame.

They sat in a circle, silent, resting, feeling the water flow over them, the wind course through them. Muscles relaxed to mush in the warmth, and minds followed. The eagle crossed the pool to sit by the horse again, moving slowly, in a sort of dream dance that threw up a wake of steam streamers. A sudden flurry of sycamore leaves spiraled down onto the pond, alighting it seemed just a fraction of an inch over the water on each side of the eagle as she turned and sat. Powerful torso twisting, revealing wide rangy shoulders, lats bulging out from ribs, flat chest. Glowing pinkly in the dark. One leaf perched on the eagle head.

The conversation broke into pieces. Fish and rooster wandered off on their own, towels in hand. Tom and Nadezhda talked about the Mars landing, about people they had known who had been involved in the effort, many years before—part of conversation strategy, after all. Coyote and tiger got out of the pool, sat facing each other, hands twined, chanting in time to the music: Hank small and compact, a bundle of thick wire muscles—Jody tall and curvey, big muscles, lush breasts and bottom. Kevin and Ramona watched them, knees touching.

The frog and the crow sat across from each other at the narrow end of the pool, occasionally batting the ball back and forth across the water, to keep it from floating down the exit stream and away. They didn't have much to say. The crow, in fact, was covertly watching horse and eagle. And from across the pool, in the midst of her relaxed talk with Tom, Nadezhda watched them all.

"Look at my fingertips," the horse said. "They're really pruning up."

"Mine too," the eagle replied. "My whole skin is doing it, I think." She sat on the concrete rim of the pool. She took off her mask, shook her head. Water sprayed out from her in a yellow corona. Hank had accomplished his reversal; it seemed to Kevin that this exposure of the face was infinitely more revealing and intimate than bare bodies could ever be.

She looked at him and he couldn't breathe. "I'm overheating," she said.

He nodded.

"Want to go for a walk?"

"Sure," he replied, and the stallion inside reared for the sky. "Moon should be up soon. We could take the middle canyon up to the ridge, get a view."

"Whatever."

They got out of the pool, went to the cabin, dried and dressed. Returned to the pool. "We're going for a walk," Ramona said.

They took off up the poolside trail. Soon after they left, Doris sat up on the pool rim herself. Her rounded body looked small and plump after Ramona's ranginess. "It is getting hot," she said to no one in particular, in a strained voice. She stood with a neat motion. The frog watched her silently. She walked quickly to the cabin, started dressing.

The cat slid over to the frog. "Don't you think you should join her?" she said quietly.

"Oh, no," the frog said, looking down at the water. "I think if she wanted that she would have asked."

"Not necessarily. If she asked you in front of us, and you said no . . ."

"But I don't think so. She wants . . . well. I don't know." He turned to the rim, picked up a bottle, drained it empty. "Whew." He surged out of the pool, causing a sudden little tsunami. He padded over to the picnic table, drank from another bottle. Turning, he saw that Doris was gone.

He took off his frog mask, dressed. The pool seemed to pulse with a light from its bottom that filtered up through a tapestry of reddish steam. The ripples on the surface were . . . something. But Doris was gone. Oscar felt his diaphragm contract a bit, and the corners of his mouth tighten. Perhaps she had wanted him to ask to join her. Never know, now. Unless—

The wind coursing over his wet head felt cool and dry. Despite the evaporative cooling he could tell it was a hot wind. It felt good to be out in it. All his body felt cool, warm, relaxed, melted. And perhaps. Well, if he could find her. Sooner the better, as far as that went. Brusquely he pulled on his shoes, walked to the pool, crouched beside Nadezhda. "I think I'll go take a look for her," he said softly.

The cat nodded. "She went up that same trail, by the pools. I think she'll appreciate it."

Oscar nodded, straightened. The sycamore overhead had a fractal pattern of such complexity that it made him dizzy. So many branches, all of them waving against the stars, not in concert but each in a rhythm of its own, depending on how far from the trunk it was . . . another drink of tequila, sure. Looking down he saw the trail as clear as the yellow brick road. He lumbered off along it, into the forest.


Tom and Nadezhda sat beside each other, masks off. The wind felt good on Tom's face. Hank and Jody were still chanting, voices ordering the night's sound, and feeling it fill him Tom joined in, *Aum*. Under his feet the sandstone was both slick and gritty at once. Between the leaves the sky to the east had a faint white aureole—desert dust in the wind, and the moon about to rise. Hank and Jody stood, short man, tall woman, and walked across the pavilion hand in hand, stopping only to pick up a towel.

"Well," Tom said. "Here we are." He laughed. On the screen the lander stood on the red rocky plain of Hellas. "Such an alien little car."

"Is that what they'll say when they step out?"

He shook his head. "That's what I say here. And now."

Nadezhda nodded gravely. "But they should say that. Why don't you get us another bottle of the tequila. I'm developing a taste for it."

"Uh oh." He went and got a full bottle from the table. "I'm kind of drunk, myself."

"Me too. If that's what it is. You're right, it feels a little different. But I like it."

"You do now."

"That's what counts. You know, I'm getting colder rather than warmer. It's like a bath you've been in too long."

"We could move upstream to the next pool. It's hotter."

"Let's do that."

She stood and stepped into the stream bed, walked upstream with small, hesitant steps. Even in the dark her silvery white hair shone like a cap. Slender as she was, in the dark she almost looked like a young girl. Tom blinked, grasped the neck of the bottle more firmly, followed her.

Odd to have a stream's water be the warmest part of the surroundings. Nadezhda was just a shape now between trees, her hair the most visible part of her. Something in the sight gave Tom a quiver: naked woman walking up a streambed in the dark, between trees. Wisps of steam were just visible. Ferns on the bank curled in black nautilus patterns, like fossils held up on stems for their viewing.

When he came to the next pool Nadezhda was standing on its concrete bench, knee deep in water, waist deep in steam. The moon was coming up over the east wall of the canyon, and to his dark-adjusted eyes it was as bright as any streetlight. He almost wished it weren't there. But then his pupils shrank and again it seemed dim, dark even. Nadezhda watched him. "You're right," she said. "It is warmer."

"Good." They sat side by side on the edge of the pool, feet on the concrete bench below. They passed the slim bottle back and forth. The wind had almost dried their bodies, but after a bit it felt cool, and they lowered themselves into the water.

"I hope Oscar finds Doris."

"I guess."

"Well, he has to try." She laughed. "Pretty bodies."

"Yeah. Especially Ramona and Jody."

She elbowed him. "And Kevin and Hank!"

"Yeah, okay."

"And Gabby and Mike and Doris and Oscar!"

He laughed. "It's true."

She took a slug from the bottle, shifted closer to him. "Except, I don't know, I am thinking they are a little unformed. Like porcelain, or infants. To be really beautiful a body has to have a bit more to it. Their skin is too smooth. Beautiful skin has to have some pattern to it." She pinched together the skin of his upper arm. "Like that."

He laughed. "Yeah, they need some wrinkles, show some character!" He laughed again. Here I am, he thought; here I am.

"I have a lot of character," Nadezhda said, and giggled.

"Me too."

"And, and their hair is always just one color. No mix."

"Pied beauty. Give thanks to God for dappled things. . . ."

"Pied beauty, yes. On a chest with some heft to it." Her fingers traced lines over him.

Tom's hand found wet warm silt, beside the concrete rim of the pond; he picked some up, drew his initials on Nadezhda's chest. "Hmm, TB, looks good but subject to confusion." He changed the two letters to boxes.

Nadezhda got a handful, put stripes on his cheeks and forehead, around his eyes. "You look scary," she said. "Like one of the holy wanderers in India."

"Aaar." He worked on her face too, pulling it closer to his. Just two stripes on each cheek. "Spooky."

"I bet they don't know how to kiss, either," she said, and leaned into him.

When they stopped Tom laughed. "No," he said, "I bet they don't know that."

As they fell further into it, they kept drawing patterns on each other. "Bet they don't know this." "Or this." "Or—oh—this."

The moon was half full. Tom could see Nadezhda well indeed, her body all painted and pulsing, glowing pinkly, warm as the water under him. A muddy kiss of her breast. Taste of the earth. He was too bemused to hold a thought in his head, there was too much to take in. The wind in the trees, the flow of hot water over his legs, the half moon all marred, the perfect stars, the body sliding up and down between his hands. He held skin and felt it slide over ribs like slats in a fence.

They heard the distant yowl of coyotes, yipping in astounding glissandos that no dog could even approximate—crazily melodic, exultant, moonstruck. From the direction of the cabin they heard a single cry of release, and looking at each other they laughed, laughed at the way everything was falling together in a pattern beyond any calculation or hope of repetition: we do these things once, then they're gone! The distant coyotes kept howling and the wind picked up, swirled the branches overhead, and Nadezhda hugged him as they moved together.

When they returned to the world she laughed with her breath, shortly. "Our blessing on all of them."

* * *

Kevin and Ramona, horse and eagle, walked up the canyon past the spring and into the darkness of dense night forest. If there was a trail here they couldn't see it. Kevin smiled, enjoying the twisting between trees, the stepping over fronds and fallen logs. It felt good to be out of the water and into the wind—his body was overheated at the core, and his face kept sweating so that the hot wind seemed cool, refreshing, comfortable.

He stopped as the canyon bottom divided into two forks, and Ramona came up beside him. Pressed against him. He knew these canyons from boyhood, but in the uncertain light, distracted as he was, he found it hard to concentrate on what he knew, hard to remember any of that—it was just forest, night. Moon would be up soon, then he would remember. Meanwhile he chose the left fork and they continued on. Should eventually get them onto a ridge, and then he would know their location.

It was rougher up this side canyon, which rose like a broken staircase; there was a rock with a long oak bannister. They used their hands to pull themselves up. A final scramble brought them up the headwall of the canyon, and they stood on a broad ridge, sloping slowly up to the long crest of the range that led to Saddleback. Here the ground was dry and crumbled—a layer of dirt over the sandstone below. Dwarfish scrub oaks and gnarly sage bushes dotted the ridge irregularly, and in most places it was easy to walk between them.

To the east the horizon glowed, then broke to white. Moonrise. Immediately the stars dimmed, the sky became less purely black—it was a pastel black now. Shadows jumped into existence like solid ghosts, and everything on the ridge suddenly looked different. The half spheres of the sage bushes crouching on the earth like hiding animals, the wind-tossed scrub oaks crabbed and threatening.

When the moon—big and fat, its dark half just as visible as the bright half—when this ball, half light, half dark, was almost

breaking free of the horizon, they saw movement in its face.
"What?" Then Kevin saw that the movement was on a ridge to
the east. Silhouetted against the moon, animals pointed their long
thin muzzles at the sky. A few dream seconds of silence later they
heard the cries.

Coyotes. "Hank gets around fast," Kevin whispered. The
weirdness of the sound, the impossible slides up and down, the
way the yips and barks and sliding yowls crossed over each other,
making momentary harmonies and disharmonies that never once
held still—all sent great shivers up Kevin's spine. The skin on his
arms and back goose-pimpled. Thoughtlessly he drew Ramona to
him (a little static shock). They embraced. This was something
friends often did in their town, but Kevin and Ramona never
had—given what was and what was not between them, it would
have been too much. So this was the first time. They drew back
to look at each other in the fey light, and even without color Kevin
could see the perfect coloring of Ramona's face, the rich skin,
raven hair—the whites of eyes and teeth . . . teeth that bit lower
lip and then they were kissing. The coyotes' ecstasy yipped from
inside them now, a complete interpenetration of inner and outer.
Their first true kiss. Kevin's blood transmuted to something lighter,
faster, hotter, freer—to wind. His blood turned to wind.


For Doris it was not like that. She left the hot springs angry and
then morose, and paid little attention to where she was going.
Upcanyon, yes, in the direction that Kevin and Ramona had gone.
But she would never follow them. It would be stupid. And anyway
impossible. But if only she could come upon Kevin and say to
him—shout at him—*why?* Why her and not me? We've made
love before, how many times? We've been good friends, we've
lived in that house together for how many years? A long, long,
long long time. And you never once looked at me like you do at
her. We had fun, we laughed, we made love, we seemed to be
enjoying ourselves, but still you were never all there, you never

committed anything. You were never *passionate*. Wanting. It was just floating along for you, a friendship, "Damn you," she said aloud. In the noise of the wind, canyon soughing like a great broken flute, no one would ever hear her. They were in conspiracy together, she and the wind and the canyon, covering for each other, protecting each other. No one could hear. Unless she screamed. And she would never do that. "Not me, I'm not the kind to scream. Shout, maybe, or perhaps a sharp, staccato, cutting remark. A stiletto of a remark. But no histrionics from Doris Nakayama, no, of course not," voice rising with every word, till she let out a little shriek, *"Aah!"* Clapped her hand over her mouth, bit her fingers, laughed angrily. She sniffed and spit the snot out on the ground. Dashed tears from her cheeks. It felt good to stumble through the trees ranting and raving, crashing through brush when there was no obvious way. "Stupid fool, I mean just because she's tall and beautiful and smart and a good fucking shortstop. And she's sweet, sure, but when will she make you laugh? When will she make you think or teach you anything? Ah, fuck, you're two peas in a pod. A very boring pod. The two of you together have no more wit than a rock. So I suppose you'll never miss it, you bastard."

The canyon forked and Doris bludgeoned her way to the left, up a steep side canyon that gave her a lot of opportunity to work off steam. She attacked the boulders like personal enemies. Overheated from the damned hot springs. Muttering to herself she walked straight into the middle of a sage brush, and a whole flock of sleeping doves shot away, cooing and clucking and landing in a bush nearby together. Their liquid calls pursued her as she continued up the defile. She smelled of sage now, the very smell of these hills, of this wind, of Orange County itself. Before the people and the oranges and the eucalyptus and the labs it had smelled like this. She crushed a twig of it between her fingers, smelled it. Hank and his loony ceremony, she hummed the *Aum,* smelled the sage running all through her. They were more her hills than anyone else's.

She topped the headwall of the canyon just as the coyotes began their mad song, and so she had just turned up the ridge when she saw the figures above her. Frightened, she dropped behind a bush. They would think she had followed them. All thought of getting Kevin alone and lambasting him disappeared as she crouched to the ground. Finally she dared to move, to peer around the side of the hemispherical sage. And so she saw them embrace and kiss: silhouetted figures in the moonlight, like a silver on black nineteenth-century etching entitled "Love". Careless of noise she turned and ran back down the ridge, tore down into another canyon.


Ramona broke away from their kiss. "What was that?"

"Huh?"

"Didn't you hear it? And I saw something move, out of the corner of my eye. Back the way we came."

"Maybe another coyote."

"It was bigger than that."

"Hmm."

The shape Kevin had seen in the night, after his first council meeting. He had forgotten it, but now he remembered. And there were mountain lions in the Santa Ana Mountains again, it was said—Kevin had never seen one. It was unlikely one would have come so close to people, though—the areas they liked were higher, up on the back side of Saddleback. Well, he wouldn't mention the possibility, for fear it would spoil the mood.

"Do you think it could have been a mountain lion?" Ramona said matter-of-factly.

"Nah." He cleared his throat. "Or at least, it isn't very likely."

The coyotes' yipping seemed to assure them that it was, on the contrary, entirely possible.

"Let's go down the next canyon over," Ramona suggested.

Kevin nodded, and they walked the top of the ridge, winding

between sage brushes. The rounded edge of the ridge curved in a big bow, until they had the moon at their backs. Their shadows stretched long before them, black and solid. The wind threw their hair across their faces. They stopped often to kiss, and each kiss was longer and more passionate, more a complete world in itself.

To their right, and so back in the general direction of the hot springs, they saw a rather shallow, wide canyon. "Look!" Ramona said, pointing down into it. At the first dip in the canyon floor there was a copse of big old sycamore trees. The biggest stood by itself, overlooking the canyon below, and there seemed to be a vine dropping from one high, thick branch. "It's the swing," she said. "It's Swing Canyon!"

"Sure enough!" Kevin said. "Hey, I know where we are now."

"Come on," she said, leading him down, looking over her shoulder with a girlish smile. "Let's go swing."


Down at the big tree they found the swing was the same as ever. It was not an ordinary swing, but a single thick rope, tied to a crook in a side branch, so that it hung well clear of the battered old trunk. The ground fell away in a smooth slope downcanyon, so it was possible to grasp the rope over a round knot and run down the slope, and when lifted off the ground one could put one's feet on a bar of wood holed and stuck above a knot at the bottom of the rope. And so one swung out into space in a long slow arc, above the brush-covered drop to the lower canyon.

They took turns doing this. Kevin rode into space feeling the mounting exhilaration of the kisses between rides, the rough contact of their bodies as they stopped each other, the windy joy of the rides themselves, out in the wind and the spinning moonlit shadows. At the end of each flight he felt lighter and lighter, as if casting off dross with each spin. He was escaping by degrees the pull of the earth. The wind was rushing downcanyon, so that each flight was pushed further out among the stars, and on the way back in he found he could face into the wind, spreadeagle his spirit and land light as a feather, to be caught in Ramona's strong arms. He felt they had joined the people on Mars, and flew in gravity two-fifths that of the world they had known.

"Here," Ramona said breathlessly at the end of one run. "We can do it together. Hold on from opposite sides, and run down and put our feet on each side of the bar." They kissed hard and their hands explored each other hungrily. "Do you think it'll work?" "Sure! I mean who knows? Let's try it."

"Okay." Kevin seized the rope. Ramona's hands closed just above his. They took off running. When the rope pulled them free of the earth their feet scrabbled for a hold on the bar, which teetered under them. Finally they balanced on it, and could take their weight off their arms. Standing together, face to face, flying through the night with the hot dry wind, they kissed long and hard, and their tongues spoke directly to each other in a language of touch so much more direct and powerful than the language of words that Kevin thought he might forget speech entirely. Ramona pulled away, laughed. They were spinning slowly. She pressed against him. "Do you remember when we were in third grade and we went behind the school and kissed?" she said in his ear. "No!" Kevin said, astonished. Had that really happened? She kissed his ear, thrust her tongue in it. That whole side of his body buzzed as if touched by some electricity of sex, he almost fell off. He held the big muscles of her bottom, larger than the full spread of his hand. She breathed in his ear, rubbed the hard band of her public bone over his thigh. They were spinning. The wind rushed by as they unzipped each other's pants. "I want to kiss you all over," Ramona said under her breath. She reached into his pants and squeezed him hard—Kevin gasped, the shock of it shot straight up his belly and spine, he very well might fall off, Ramona pulled her pants down and kicked them off into the night, pressed against him and they kissed, spinning. They had no weight at all, they were lofted like tufts of dandelion in the dry wind, spinning—

"Oh hey," Kevin said. "Here comes the ground." With a

rush they were stumbling up the slope, hanging onto the rope to keep from falling over, sliding over the soft dirt, slewing to one side. They fell together, collapsed onto the ground, let the rope fall away. Seemed Ramona's pants were actually still on, his too, how had that happened? Mind getting ahead of the game. Exquisite delay to get them off, over her butt, down her long legs, shove them to one side. Undressing twice? he noted hazily. Very nice idea. One of the best parts, after all, unbutton each other's buttons, pull each other free of all that raiment, reveal the naked self inside. When we are naked we are still clothed inside, but the beautiful, physical, sexual thereness of the flesh, pulsing warmly under the fingers, bodies pressed together, seeking maximum contact, skin to skin, everything touching everything and all those cloth barriers gone—it's easy to be overwhelmed by that. And to be inside her, to be the male half of a new creature the two of them made, to have such a female half there all around him. . . .

He looked up and saw that the rope was swinging idly in the wind, that it had knocked down some of the periwinkle blooms that spiraled up the sycamore trunk. Petals and whole flowers floated down diagonally in the wind and were landing all around them, on his back, in Ramona's face (eyes closed, mouth open in a girlish O of surprise), petals like leaves falling around them, little fingers on his back, piling up, drifting against their sides until they moved in a mound of periwinkle blossoms, a blanket of them. He saw a pure black mountain lion pad by, purring its approval. It levitated with a casual leap into the lowest fork of their tree, where it sprawled over both sides of a big branch, legs all akimbo, perfectly relaxed, staring at them with big moon eyes, purring a purr as deep and rasping as waves breaking on shingle, purring a purr that enveloped them like the sound of the wind in the branches. Kevin felt it deep inside, vibrating both him and Ramona completely as they plunged toward oblivion, the universal now. They were spinning.

\* \* \*

Oscar had lost the canyon trail immediately, almost falling in the little gurgling pool at the source of the spring; he had to sink to one knee abruptly to keep from pitching in. Spiraling blade fronds slapped him gently in the face. He stared transfixed at the roiled surface of the pool, which turned over itself as if a hose were spurting out water somewhere below the surface. So odd—here they were on a desert coastline, the mountains mostly bare and brown, and before his eyes water poured out of a hill. And steaming hot to boot. Where did it come from? Oh, he knew that. Law classes, surprising how much you had to understand for the law to make sense. And the way Sally taught that class, up in Dusy Basin and down on the campus; he felt he understood groundwater basins. He stood on the bony cracked hills, eons old, porous to water right down to the bedrock. So the ground beneath him was saturated, up to some level below him, a few feet, several hundred feet, depending on where he stood. Water down there slowly flowing, down its secret watersheds. A rib of bedrock, an underground upwelling. This was the top of one, pouring out a crack. A reservoir filled with stone. Underground waterfall. And hot because some cracks in deep bedrock were letting the earth's internal heat seep up. My God. Could it actually be that hot down there? Well, the crust was only a few miles thick, and after that it was a few *thousand* miles to the core. Essentially he was standing on a ball of molten lava, with something as thin as aluminum foil insulating him from it.

The spring water scalded his fingers, and hastily he pulled away. Uneasy at the heat, which seemed now to have a faint red glow to it, he stepped over the stream and upcanyon, aware suddenly of a Pellucidar below like the insides of a foundry, bright yellow spills of molten metal leaving intense afterimages in his sight. Except in reality the superheated rock below was under such gravitational pressure that it could be called neither a liquid or a solid, not if you wanted to be accurate. A slight variation, a bolide gravitational or magnetic, and the dark night might suddenly explode on him. Have to live with that.

The woods were dark. Black on black. Oscar blundered into branches that were like wooden arms trying to tackle him. He couldn't see well enough to move around out here, how did the others do it? The canyon floor was irregular and much of what he stepped on was soft. It made him squeamish and light-footed. Needed a flashlight. Definitely dark. Once a friend in Virginia had taken him out to see one of the caverns in the Shenandoah Mountains, and the guide there had shut down the light in one deep cavern, so they could see the purity of a complete lack of light. You couldn't see your hand right in front of your nose, nor distinguish any motions it made. It was simply a field of the richest, blackest black he had ever seen.

This wasn't like that. Overhead stars sparked between wind-tossed branches, and a single solar panel station blinked in the west like a streetlight seen from miles away. Presumably these were casting some light on the scene. How many candlepower was a star? Let's see, a lit candle some eight miles away is supposed to be visible. They did an experiment about that, in the early days, wandering out on a clear desert basin. One man tramped back and forth to find out at just what point he lost sight of the distant candle. Eight miles? Maybe it wasn't that far. What was stopping the light from being visible, anyway? What got in the way? Imagine that man out there wandering back and forth, a distant prick of light winking in and out of existence.

He could in fact see his hand in front of his face. Experiment proved this. Black octopuslike thing. But what stood before him, or at his feet: inky shapes on a field of sable velvet. It was possible to walk right into a tree. He proved that by experiment too. Subsequently he made his way with his hands stretched out before him, like a sleepwalker.

Nothing to see, but lots to hear. Airy voice of the wind scraping stone, hooting from time to time around sharp corners. The myriad shivery clicks of leaves overhead and around, a sound sometimes like water falling, but with the individual sounds sharper, more individualized—but so many of them. . . . The creaks of branches rubbing together, eucalyptus trees did that a lot, they were talkative trees. A scurrying underfoot that made him tread even more slowly, more lightly. Tiny creatures were rushing away as he approached, much as little people ran from city-stomping Godzillas in Japanese movies. And maybe some little guys with a superweapon like snake poison would try to bring him down. Necessary to move very slowly. Give them time to escape.

After a while he increased his pace again. Rattlers were likely to be asleep after all, and they were the only superpowers around. Maybe. Anyway he had to venture on. But it was probably best to give as much warning of his arrival as possible, so instead of trying to reduce the noise of his passage he increased it, swinging a stick around and hitting things with it. It also served as a blind man's cane, warning him of trees and the like. Best, clearly, to move by sense of sound and touch. He recalled an acquaintance's story, of walking by a lake at night in east Texas in early summer, stepping *squick, squick* at every step, as each step came down on one of millions of young frogs hopping about. Ick.

He came to the dim bulk of a canyon wall. So it was possible to see something. A bit confusing; apparently the canyon must fork here. He went right, and soon found himself struggling up through thickets of sage and other shrubs. One type was kind of a Spanish bayonet thing, a bunch of long, stiff, and very sharply pointed blades. Best to avoid. Really, this was stupid. What did he think he was doing? What did he expect to find? Surely no one else would have taken a route as crowded with vegetation as this. Bulldozer approach.

Still he struggled on through the tangled mass of branches. One advantage to hiking alone; you can do things so stupid that no two people together would ever carry on with it. Manzanita, or was it mesquite, anyway there was no way he could go through a nest of that stuff, no matter it was only thigh-high. Those branches were like steel. Go around. Keep going. Pure stubbornness, but after all he could turn around any time and get back to the hot springs easily, so why not? He could do this just for the fun of stupid stubbornness, mindless and pure. Holding to a course just because he was on one. Inertia. A gyroscope in the spirit, spinning madly. One time his friends had rated everyone in their group for strangeness, charm and spin. One to ten. Oscar was the only one given tens in all categories. Nice friends. But his placid moon-faced bulk, spinning? They must have been seeing in to this gyroscope.

The bushwhacking got more fun. This was life, after all— bashing around in the dark, fighting through tangles of very tough clutching branches, sometimes knee-high, sometimes well over-head. Allegory, Everyman, bungle in the jungle.

The moon rose, and everything changed. Something like a thick translucent white syrup poured into the canyon, making the trees into distinct beings, the mesquite patches into densely textured surfaces, as in an arty black-and-white photo of the sea's surface, or snow on a forest, or something equally dappled. The droopy long leaves of eucalyptus trees swung in the wind, clattering lightly together. A spiky-barked, spiky-leaved, dusty little tree stood in his path like a growth seen through a microscope. Bacillus scrub-oakus. Oak, he has a heart of oak, Hank said when recommending Oscar be hired as town attorney. Should have known that any town that consulted someone like Hank when hiring an attorney was going to be seriously weird. Shadows moved and jumped, quivered and bobbed. He could see just enough to see that everything was moving. The wind didn't seem as strong, or as loud. Moonlight thick as gel. Sage smell.

The moon itself was an intense white, its violent history marked all over it. A rabbit stirring a bowl of rice, the Chinese saw. Nothing so simple as a face. Moonfaced, like Oscar. Sister moon. Just tilt your head to the right a bit and there it was, the rabbit's two long laid-back ears as clear as could be. Bowl of rice, well it certainly could have been a bowl of pudding, that was guesswork. But the rabbit was there, looking down at him.

There was a rustle underfoot, and in the distance the wind made a sound like crying souls. Not like the wind at all. Must have been coursing through a hole in the sandstone to create such an eerie sound. Just like a cry. Shadows moved suddenly to the left and in the sudden depth of the third dimension that the moon added to the world he thought he saw a bulk shift between trees. Yes, there it was, something fast and big—

It crashed downcanyon, charging sightlessly at him—

Oscar threw out his hands reflexively. "Hey!"

"Aaa!" it cried, leaping back.

"Doris!" Oscar exclaimed, reeling his mind back in. "Excuse me—"

"*What?*—"

"It's me!"

"Who?" The panic in her voice was shifting to anger.

"Oscar!" he said, and then, "You remember, I was down at the pools—"

"Don't joke with me!" There was a wild note in her voice. She wiped her face with a hand. Something more than embarrassment at being frightened by their sudden encounter. Words burst out of her: "What are you doing following me?"

"I'm not! I mean—I—" A number of alternative explanations jammed on his tongue, as he struggled for the right tack to take with her in this fierce mood. "I was just out for a walk. I figured if I ran into you I'd have some company—"

"I don't want company!" she cried. "I don't like you following me, leave me alone!"

And she rushed downcanyon, crashing through sagebrush almost as much as he had.

He stood there in the moony dark, stunned by the dislike in her voice. His heart tocked in his ears, seemed to pound in the earth beneath him. Intense hurt, mood plummeting like a bird hit by shot. Thump thump, thump thump, thump thump. Not fair. Really. A lifetime's defenses went into action. No schoolmate's taunt could touch him. "Well," he said absently, in a John Wayne voice. "Guess I'll hafta carry on up this here mountain all by m'self." Muttering with all the voices, the whole cast of an imaginary movie, moving up the scrub-filled canyon. "Terrible vines here, ain't they Cap'n." "Yes, son, but they help hide us from the Injuns. Those Paiutes find us and it would be blubberhawk from space time."

It got steeper, and he found himself on hands and knees, to get under the thickest part of the brush. Sometimes he crawled right on his belly, heedless of the dirt shoving under his shirt and belt. Clean dry dirt. Some dry leaves, not many. The smell of sage was so strong that he gasped. Must've dropped the spice rack, Cap'n.

At the end of his struggle he found himself beached on a broad ridge. The moon bathed it in light, and the monochrome landscape was revealed to the eye: bony gray hills rose in long broad waves to the mountains around the bulk of Saddleback. Black canyons dropped into the depths between them. The moon was surrounded with a talcum of white light which blotted out the stars. The wind was strong, a hot breath rushing over him. Occasional treetops stuck up in the air, like black gallows or the ruins of old houses. There, in the corner of his eye, a movement.

He spun to face it, saw nothing. But that hadn't been just a branch waving in the wind. Had Doris returned to stalk him? Pound on him some more? Or—an absurd little ray of hope—apologize to him for her rudeness? Sure. "Doris?" The hope died. Not likely at best. Besides, it had been—

And there it was again, a smooth shape flowing between two bushes. Shadow in the moon's twilight. An animal.

And in the distance, floating on the wind, a weird yipping bark, yodeling away. Like the cry he had heard before, only . . . wolves?

"Not possible, Jones," he whispered. "The timber wolf was driven into the Tetons in my granddad's time."

Still, he hurried up the ridge, as it seemed the easiest route.

Possible to see farther, too. His ankle hurt. Up the ridge was a knob of hard sandstone boulders, thrusting up among the stars. Like a refuge. A lookout in every direction.

Getting there was a problem. He zigzagged between bushes and short trees, nearly fell off the ridge. A rose bush caught at his clothes, stabbed him, the roses were a bright light gray, most of the blooms just opening, branches extending all over like ropes. As he struggled out of them the blooms fanned open, dropped blown, their yellow quite clear and distinct even in this black-and-white world. Frightened, he hurried away and up the ridge. He tripped and fell to his knees. Two branches twined together, squeaked out the word "Beware! Bewaaare!" He broke them off—they were deadwood. They struggled for a minute in his hands before becoming a wooden broadsword, thick and solid. Behind him the black shadow slipped from bush to bush like quicksilver across glass. Its eyes were bright.

He stumbled into a cleared area of grass, saw that waist-high boulders had been placed in a circle on it. Maybe twenty of them, casting shadows blacker than themselves across the grass. One stone wobbled, rolled off. Wings dashed the air, dive-bombing him and flitting away. No sound to the wings at all. Owls were supposed to fly like that.

Suddenly the peak seemed a trap, a final aerie he couldn't escape from. A horror of sacrifice filled him, he turned off the ridge and down the head of a canyon. He ran under trees into sudden dark and fell. Cut, bruised, palm of hand burning. A tree stood over him triumphantly, its knobby arms waving in the attempt to free themselves from their paralysis and seize him. So many bony hands. Whaddyou get? bon-y fingers, he sang in his mind. He rolled in dried leaves and crunchy twigs. Dark. Ring of dimly glowing mushrooms, making a circle like the stone ring above. A rose bush wilted before him and the dread washed in again. He crashed away.

Now the canyon floor was fairly level. Eucalyptus trees filled the glade, and below it was as bare as a room. The trees dripped an herbicide that kept the area all to themselves. Easy walking. Suddenly low white shapes dashed about his knees, and he cried out in surprise. The shapes honked. They glowed like the mushrooms had. Ducks? Bigger, no, they were geese. Geese! He laughed, they scattered and scolded him with angry short honks. Nipped at his calves.

He allowed the little flock to guide him downcanyon. About ten of them, it seemed, scuttling about underfoot and honking impatiently. They guided him left, nipping. Up a gentle slope, side wall of the canyon nearly flat here, opening to the sky. Higher yet up the canyon's side, and the dark waving canyon bottom was filled with treetops. Ocean of round-topped waves. They came to a broad shelf, floored with silver sand. His breath was harsh in his throat. There was a yip and the geese all honked and gathered behind him, huddling there as if he would protect them. Low doggy shapes whipped around the shelf and stood—long tails, foxlike. Fox and geese? The geese turned as one and hissed at one of the creatures. Coyote, sure. Bigger than a fox. Geese and coyote. The coyote moved like a sheepdog with a recalcitrant flock of sheep. Geese and sheep, similar creatures. No doubt geese were smarter.

Several more coyotes appeared out of the darkness, herded Oscar and the geese to the back wall of the shelf. Here the sand was thick and bright, mica chips flashing moonlight, the geese standing out like cottonballs, dashing about complaining. They nipped back at the coyotes if pushed too far, noisy as they clacked and honked and hissed, in a language very expressive, very emotive. Clear as could be what they meant. The coyotes' tongue, on the other hand, was utterly alien. Sliding yips, how did they do it? Vocal chords like a pedal steel guitar.

The geese settled down, began to peck in the sand. They groomed their feathers with their bills, their long necks stretching in impossible curves, loops. Grooming each other or the coyotes who sprawled among them, calm and watchful. Oscar sat down heavily, crossed his legs. A coyote still ambling around their beach-like extrusion plopped down behind him, lay on its side, its back pressing Oscar's. He found he was weeping, he couldn't see anything but dim white blobs in the darkness. The moon set and the geese themselves provided the light, glowing like little moons. The coyote braced against him sighed heavily, squeaked softly with contentment, like a dog. Comfortable. A few more coyotes heard the sound, padded over to join them. The wind filled Oscar's chest until he thought it might burst him, or waft him away like a balloon. His eyes felt dry and sandy, his nose was clogged. He breathed in and out through his mouth, trying to keep from over-filling. Furry warmth, the tickle of a tail flicking against his ankle. Contentment spilled through him, he was an artesian well of contentment. The down under the feathers of the geese; nothing softer. They buzzed through their bills when they were happy. He lay on his side, feeling a warm exhaustion wash down through him, groundwater, muscles melting. One night when he was five years old, the shadow of the tree outside his window had waved on the floor, and he had felt something like this—felt how big the world was, and how charged everything was with meaning. It made you breathe so deep, made your chest fill so full! In and out, in and out, in the rhythm of the sand underneath him. Geese slept with their heads under one wing.

When he woke it was not from sleep, but from a dream so vivid and real that it seemed opening his eyes was like disappearing, turning into a ghost. Stepping from some bright world into a dimmer one. He was lying on sand, his side was damp and stiff. The night's wandering stood clear in his memory, including the flock of white geese and their guardian coyotes. But now the sandy shelf was bare. Paw prints everywhere. He was alone.

He sat up, groaning. The sky was the gray of his pearl gray suit, and seemed low and cloudy, though a few stars pricked it to show that it was actually the clear dome of the sky, cloud-gray in this moment of the dawn. Everything was still monochrome, grays everywhere, a million shades of it. There were thorny weeds edging the patch of sand. Bird song started in the canyon below, and small birds here and there joined in.

Moaning and groaning he stood, hiked down from the shelf. How . . . He lost the thought. All the intense emotions of the night before had drained away. The wind still gusted, but not inside him. He was calm, emptied, drained. Trees stood around him like great silent saints. He walked downcanyon. Eventually he would come on something. At times he felt sure he was still dreaming, despite a stubbed toe. Warm dry air, even at dawn.

Far down the canyon, where it opened up and joined a bigger one, he came upon a big bare sycamore tree, filled with sleeping crows. A tree very old, very big, mostly dead, no leaves except on one live strip that twisted greenly off to the side; and entirely filled with still black birds.

"Now wait a minute." He pinched himself. Bit the skin between thumb and forefinger. Yes, he was awake. He certainly seemed awake. Mountain canyon at dawn, Santa Ana Mountains. Yes, he was awake! Anyway this happened a lot, even down in town. There were a lot of crows around, flocks of really big ones, like ravens it seemed to him. Loud birds, pests, little Mongols of the air, dominating wherever they wanted to. He had seen a flock descend on a tree before; in fact they had their favorites, which they stopped in ritually at the end of the day, when heading back up to their night haunts—up to here, in fact, for this particular horde. A whole flock perched up there silently, sleeping, filling every branch like black fruit, on twisting gray branches against the gray sky. The green of the live strip beginning to show.

He took a deep breath and shook his head, feeling strange. He knew he was awake, nearly sober, relatively sane; but the sight was so luminous, so heavy with some meaning he couldn't express. . . .

An idea struck him, and he walked under the tree. Standing foursquare he looked up; then threw his arms wide and shouted, *"Hey!"*

The tree exploded with birds! Flapping black wings, cawing wildly, crows burst away to every point of the compass, loose-winged, straggle-feathered, leaving black images of their powerful downstrokes against the delicate tracery of bare gray branches. Cawing, they regrouped in a swirl above the tree, then flew off to the west, a dancing irregular cloud of winged black dots. Oscar stood dazed, face to the sky, mouth hanging open.

# 7

*Last week a nightmare. Landed at Dulles and arrested in Immigration. On a list, accused of violating the Hayes-Green Act. Swiss gov't must have told them I was coming, flight number and everything. What do you mean? I shouted at officious official. I'm an American citizen! I haven't broken any laws! Such a release to be able to speak my mind in my native tongue—everything pent up from the past weeks spilled out in a rush, I was really furious and shouting at him, and it felt so good but it was a mistake as he took a dislike to me.*

*Against the law to advocate overthrowing US gov't.*

*What do you mean! I've never done anything of the kind!*

*Membership in California Lawyers for the Environment, right? Worked for American Socialist Legal Action Group, right?*

*So what? We never advocated anything but change!*

*Smirk of scorn, hatred. He knew he had me.*

*Got a lawyer but before he arrived they put me through physical and took blood sample. Told to stay in county. Next day told I tested positive for HIV virus. I'm sure this is a lie, Swiss test Ausländer every four months and no problem there, but told to remain county till follow-up tests analyzed. Possessions being held. Quarantine possible if results stay positive.*

*My lawyer says law is currently being challenged. Meanwhile I'm in a motel near his place. Called Pam and she suggested sending Liddy on to folks in OC so can deal better with things here. Put Liddy on plane this morning, poor girl crying for Pam, me too. Now two days to wait for test results.*

*Got to work. Got to. At local library, on an old manual typewriter. The book mocks: how can you, little worm crushed in gears, possibly aspire to me? Got to continue nevertheless. In a way it's all I have left.*

*The problem of an adequate history bothers me still. I mean not my personal troubles, but the depression, the wars, the AIDS plague. (Fear.) Every day everything a little worse. Twelve years past the millenium, maybe the apocalyptics were just a bit early in their predictions, too tied to numbers. Maybe it just takes a while for the world to end.*

*Sometimes I read what I've written sick with anger, for them it's all so easy. Oh to really be that narrator, to sit back and write with cool ironic detachment about individual characters and their little lives because those lives really mattered! Utopia is when our lives matter. I see him writing on a hilltop in an Orange County covered with trees, at a table under an olive tree, looking over a garden plain and the distant Pacific shining with sunlight, or on Mars, why not, chronicling how his new world was born out of the healthy fertility of the old earth mother, while I'm stuck here in 2012 with my wife an ocean to the east and my daughter a continent to the west, "enjoined not to leave the county" (the sheriff) and none of our lives matter a damn.*

Days passed and Kevin never came down, never returned to feeling normal. Late that week, watching a news report on the Mars landing, it dawned on him that he was never going to feel *normal* again. This startled him, made him faintly uneasy.

Not that he wasn't happy. When he recalled the night in the hills with Ramona he got lighter, physically lighter, especially when working or swimming. Exhilaration resisted gravity as if it were a direct counterforce. "Walking on air"—this extravagant figure of speech was actually an accurate description of a lived reality. Amazing.

But it had been such a strange night. It felt like a dream, parts of it seemed to slip away each time he thought of other things, so that he didn't want to think of anything else, for fear the whole night might slip away. When he saw Ramona again, down at their streetwork, his heart skipped a beat, and shyly he looked down. Would she acknowledge it? Had it really happened?

Then when he looked up he saw that Ramona smile, a beacon of pleasure, black eyes looking right at him. She remembered too. If it was a dream, they had dreamed it together. Relief gave his exhilaration another lift, he slammed a pick into the broken asphalt and felt like he might be tossed aloft.

Now he was truly in love. And for the first time. Late bloomer indeed! Most of us first fall in love in our teens, it's part of the intensity of those years, falling for some schoolmate, not so much because of the qualities of the loved one but because of a powerful unspoken desire to be in love. It is part of the growth of the soul. And though the actual nature of the loved one is not crucially important, it would not be true to say that first love is thereby lessened, or less intensely felt. On the contrary—because of its newness, perhaps, it is often felt with particular strength. Most adults forget this in the flood of events that the rest of life pours over them, or perhaps they're disinclined to remember those years at all, filled as they were with foolishness, awkwardness, shame. Often enough first love was part of the awkwardness, inappropriately directed, poorly expressed, seldom reciprocated . . . we prefer not to remember. But remember with courage and you will feel again its biting power; few things since will have made you as joyfully, painfully alive.

Kevin Claiborne, however, had not fallen in love in adolescence—or, really, at any time thereafter. The desire never struck him, and no one he met inspired him to it. He had gone through life enjoying his sexual relationships, but something was missing, even if Kevin was only vaguely aware of it. Doris's angry attempts to tell him that, years before, had alerted him to the fact that there was something others felt which he did not. It was confusing, because he felt that he loved—loved Doris, his friends, his family, his housemates, his teammates. . . . Apparently it wasn't what she was talking about.

So the affair with Doris had ended almost as it began. And when Kevin felt romantic love for the first time, at the age of thirty-two, after years of work at home and abroad, after a thousand acquaintances and long years of experience with them, it was not because of the obscure adolescent desire to love *somebody*. Nor was it just forces in his own soul, though no doubt there was movement there too, as there always is, even if it is glacially slow. Instead it was a particular response, to Ramona Sanchez, his friend. She embodied what Kevin Claiborne loved most in women, he had known that for some time, somewhere in him. And when suddenly she became free and turned her attention to him—her affection to him—well, if Kevin's soul had been glacially slow, then it was now like a certain glacier in Alaska, which had crawled for centuries until one year it crashed down hundreds of yards, cutting off a whole bay.

It was a remarkable thing, this being in love. It changed everything. When he worked it was with an extra charge of satisfaction, feeling the sensual rush of the labor. At home he felt like a good housemate, a good friend. People relaxed around him, they felt they were having a good time, they could talk to him— they always could, but now he seemed to have more to give back. At the pool he swam like a champion, the water was like air and he flew through it, loving the exertion. And he was playing ball better than ever. The hitting streak extended without any worry, it was just something that happened. It wasn't very hard to hit a softball, after all. A smooth stroke, good timing, a line drive was almost inevitable. Was inevitable, apparently. He was 43 for 43 now, and everyone was calling him Mr. Thousand, making a terrible racket when he came to bat. He laughed, he didn't care, the streak didn't matter. And that made it easier.

And the time spent with Ramona. That morning in their torn-up street he understood what it would be like—she was there, he could look over at her whenever he wanted, and there she would be, graceful, strong, unselfconsciously beautiful—and when she looked at him, he knew just what it said. *I remember. I'm yours.*

My God. It was love.


For Doris, the days after their party were like a truly enormous hangover. She felt queasy, disoriented, dizzy, and very irritable. One night when Hank was over for dinner she said angrily to him, "God damn it, Hank, somehow you always get me to drink about ten times more of your damned tequila than I really want to! Why do you *do* that!"

"Well, you know," Hank said, looking sheepish. "I try to live by the old Greek rule, you know. Moderation in all things."

"Moderation in all things!" Doris shouted, disgusted.

The rest of the table hooted. "Moderation in all things," Rafael said, laughing. "Right, Hank, that's you to a T."

Nadezhda said, "I visited Rhodes once, where that saying was born. Cleobolus said it, around 650 B.C. The guide book I bought was a translation, and they had it 'Measure is in all the best.' "

Andrea smiled. "Doesn't have the same ring to it, does it."

"What the hell do you mean, Hank?" Doris demanded. "Just how does moderation in all things explain pounding twenty-five bottles of atrocious tequila?"

"Well, you know—if you say moderation in all things, then among all things you gotta include moderation itself, see what I mean? So you gotta go crazy once in a while, if you ask me."


Then Tom showed up, and after dinner he and Doris began poring over the records Doris had taken from Avending. At one point Tom shook his head. "First of all, a lot of this looks to be coded. It may just be a cipher, but if it's in cipher and coded too then we're shit out of luck."

Doris scowled.

"Besides," Tom went on, "even if we break the code—hell, even with the straight stuff—it won't make that much sense to me. I'm no financial records analyst, never have been."

"I thought you might be able to see at least some trends," Doris said.

"Well, maybe. But look, your friend John is not likely to have had access to Avending's most intimate secrets anyway, especially if they've been involved in some funny stuff. His clearance just wouldn't go that high."

"Well, shit," Doris said, "why did I bother to take this stuff in the first place!"

"Don't ask me."

Nadezhda said to Tom, "Don't you have any friends left in Washington who could be helping you with this kind of problem?"

Tom considered it. "Maybe. I'll have to make some calls. Here, while I'm doing that, sort this stuff into what's in English and what's coded. Where you can tell the difference."

"Actually John's clearance is pretty damn high," Doris said.

Tom just shook his head and got on the TV. For a while he talked to a small gray-haired black woman, leaning back in a rotating chair; then to a tall man with a shiny bald head; then to the blank screen, for three or four conversations. There was a lot of incidental chat as he renewed old acquaintances, caught up on news: "Nylphonia, it's me. Tom Barnard."

"I thought you were dead."

That sort of thing. Finally he got into a long conversation with a female voice and a blank screen, one punctuated several times by laughter. "That'll take hours," Tom said at one point. "We've got thousands of pages here."

"That's your problem," the voice said. "If you want us to help, you'll have to send it all along. Just stick them in front of the screen one at a time and I'll set my end to photo. I'm off to breakfast anyway, and I'll get back to you later when we've gone through them."

"You think it'll be worth it?"

"How do I know? But from what you've said, I think we'll be able to come up with something. That much data should reveal the shape of the company's financial relations, and if they're hiding things, that'll show in the shape of what they're not hiding. We'll show you."

"What about the coding?"

Laughter.

"Well, thanks, Em." Tom turned to Doris and Nadezhda. "Okay, we've got to put every one of these sheets of paper on the TV screen, and the better order they're in, the easier it'll be for my friends to analyze them."

So they set to work getting the data transferred. Kevin came in and took his turn. Each sheet sat on the screen for only a second before there was a beep from the phone. Even so it took them until well into the night to get everything photographed. "And to think most of this stuff is irrelevant," Doris said at one point.

"Worse for my friends than for us," Tom replied.

"Are we going to have to pay them for this?"

"You bet. But it's a whole network of friends we're plugging into, and some of them owe me. We'll figure something out after they've looked at this stuff."

"What exactly will they be looking for?" Kevin asked.

"Infractions of the laws governing company size, capital dispersion and that sort of thing. Corporate law is a gigantic body of stuff, see, very complex. The main thrust of the twenty-forty international agreements was to cut down on the size of corporations, cut them down so far that only companies remain. It's actually anti-corporate law, I mean that's what we were doing for twenty-five years. We chopped up the corporations and left behind a teeming mass of small companies, and a bunch of associations and information networks—all well and good, but there are projects in this world that need a lot of capital to be carried off, and so mechanisms for that had to be instituted, new banking practices and company teamwork programs, and that's where you get the morass of law dealing with that. Alfredo's lawyers are undoubtedly playing all those angles and it may be that Avending has been brought in in a legal way, or it could be that there's an illegal corporate ownership aspect to things. There's no reason why they shouldn't have used legal methods, it's not that hard and a lot safer for their project. But they might be cutting corners—hell, it might have been forced on them, by someone with some leverage. The way Alfredo has introduced the zoning and water stuff . . ."

"It's sure that Alfredo and his Heartech partners got to be hundreds damned fast," Doris said.

"And live like more than hundreds," Kevin added.

"Do they? Well, it's worth looking into."


A few days later the environmental impact statement was filed by Higgins, Ramirez and Bretner, and there it was in the town computer for anyone to call up and inspect. Kevin read it while eating lunch over at Oscar's house. By the time he was done reading, he had lost his appetite. Theatrically he cast a half-eaten sandwich onto the table. These days even getting angry felt sort of good. "What do they mean erosion on the western side? There's no erosion at all there!"

"Them ravines," Hank said. "Must be erosion, don't you think?"

"Yeah, but it's perfectly natural, I mean it isn't accelerated or anything. I know every inch of that hill and there's no unusual erosion at all there!"

Oscar came into the kitchen to make his own lunch. "Ah. HRB strikes again. Natural state equals erosion, litter, underuse. Sure." He read the TV screen while putting together a Reuben sandwich. "See the way alternative four is slanted. Construction of a commercial center, paths to the peak—this is probably the best description of what Alfredo has in mind that we've seen so far. Parking lot down at the head of Crawford Canyon. This will help stop erosion on the western slope, clean up the refuse on the peak, add sightly landscaping, and increase town awareness and enjoyment of the prospect.''

"Shit," Kevin said.

"That's an LA Special all right. Hmm. Other alternatives are generally downplayed, I see. Hill turned into park, how can they downplay that? Ah. Would be a small addition to Santiago Park, which is already underutilized, and some seventeen percent of town property. Indeed.''

"Shit!" Kevin said.

Oscar went back to his sandwich. Environmental impact statements had come a long way since the early days, he told Hank and Kevin. LA's Metropolitan Water Department had once submitted four unacceptable statements in a row, for instance, when attempting to finesse the fact that excessive mining of the groundwater in Owens Valley was going to destroy even the desert flora that had survived the earlier diversions of surface water. The obvious bias in those statements had been one factor in Inyo County's eventual victory over LA, in the Sacramento courts and legislature; and every agency forced to submit an EIS had learned a lesson from that. Alternative uses had to be described in detail. Obvious harmful effects could not be ignored. The appearance, at least, of a complete and balanced study had to be maintained. "The days of 'There is no environment here' are over. Consulting firms like HRB are extremely sophisticated—they make their reputations by writing statements that will stand up to challenges. Complete, but still getting the job done, you know—making whatever impression the agency that hired them wants.''

"Well, shit!" Kevin said.

Gabriela, walking through the kitchen on her way to the roof, said "Time to poison his blood, hey Kev?"

That night Kevin made a chicken stroganoff dinner, while the others checked out the California Environmental Quality Act and the town charter, looking for ways to challenge the EIS.

"Look, the land belongs to us!" Kevin said from the kitchen.

Tom grinned. "El Modena has a population of about ten thousand, so we're three ten-thousandth owners."

"Not enough," Doris said.

"No. But it is true that essentially this is a battle for the opinion of the rest of the owners. The rest of the state and the nation and the world have a say as well, and we might be able to manipulate those forces to our purpose, but the main thing is convincing the people in town to agree with us. The rest of the world doesn't care that much about Rattlesnake Hill."

Oscar had dinner with them fairly often, as his kitchen was in an inconvenient state of renovation. One night he came in with the tiniest hint of a smile on his face, and seeing him, Kevin said "Hey, what's up?"

Oscar lifted an eyebrow. "Well, you know I have been making inquiries with the State Water Resources Control Board."

"Yeah, yeah?"

Oscar accepted a glass of water from Doris, sat heavily by the pool. Things were a mess in Sacramento, he told them, as usual. On the one hand, Inyo County's victory over the city of Los Angeles had had the statewide effect of making each county the master of its groundwater. But groundwater basins paid no heed to county lines, and so use of the groundwater in many cases had to be adjudicated by the courts. In many cases state control was stronger than ever. The waterscape was simply bigger than local governments could effectively manage. And so there was a mixed effect; some counties now had control over water that had previously been mined out from under them, while other counties were suddenly feeling pinched. Into that mix came the new source of water from the north, controlled by the state, and funneled through the canals of the old Central Water Project. Confusion, disarray—in other words, the typical California waterscape, in its general feel. But many of the particulars were new.

"So," Oscar said, "it has taken me a while to find out what the board would make of this proposal of Alfredo's, to buy water from the MWD and then sell whatever excess there might be to the OCWD. Because no one on the board is inclined to talk about hypothetical cases. They have enough real cases to keep them occupied, and hypothetical cases are usually too vague to make a judgment on. But one of the board members is a good friend of Sally's, they were on the board together. I finally got her cornered long enough to listen to me, and she prevaricated for a long time, but it comes down to this—they wouldn't allow it."

"Great!"

"How does she mean that?" Tom asked.

"Buying water and selling it, or using it for other water credits, is not something the board allows municipalities to do any more—it's the state's prerogative."

"What about the MWD?"

"They've been turned into a kind of non-profit clearing house."

"You mean after all those years of manipulation and control and raking it in at the expense of Owens Valley and the rest of the south, LA is now collecting and distributing all that water as a non-profit operation?"

"That's right."

Tom laughed for a long time.

Oscar surged up out of his chair, went to the kitchen to refill his glass. "There's no swamp like water law," he muttered under the sound of Tom's laughter.


So Kevin was feeling good about things, and late one afternoon after a hard day's work at Oscar's place, he gave Ramona a call. "Want to go to the beach for sunset?"

"Sure."

It was that easy. "Hey, isn't your birthday sometime soon?"

She laughed. "Tomorrow, in fact."

"I thought so! We can celebrate, I'll take you to dinner at the Crab Cooker."

"It's a deal."

It seemed like his bike had a little hidden motor in it.

It was a fine evening at Newport Beach. They went to the long strand west of the 15th Street pier, walked behind the stone groins. The evening onshore wind was weak, a yellow haze lay in the air. The sun sank in an orange smear over Palos Verdes. The bluffs behind the coastal highway were dark and furry, and it seemed this beach was cut off from the world, a place of its own. Stars blurred in the salt air. They scuffed through the warm sand barefoot, arms around each other. Down the beach a fire licked over the edge of a concrete firepit, silhouetting children who held hot dogs out on coathangers bent straight. The twined scent of charred meat and lighter fluid wafted past, cutting through the cold wet smell of seaweed. Waves swept in at an angle, rushed whitely toward them, retreated hissing, left bubbling wet sand. We do this once, it never happens again.

At the Santa Ana River's mouth they stopped. A lifeguard stand stared blankly at the waves, which gleamed in the dark. They climbed the seven wooden steps which lifeguards could descend in a single leap. They sat on the damp painted plywood, watched waves, kissed until they were dizzy. Lay on the wood, on their sides, embracing and kissing until that was all that existed. How perfect the noise of surf was for making out; why should that be? A waft from the barbecue blew by. "Hungry?" "Yeah."

Biking lazily to the Crab Cooker, Kevin felt better than he could ever remember feeling. That happiness could be such a physical sensation! Ravenously he ate salad, bread, and crab legs. The white wine coursed through him like Hank's tequila. He was very aware of Ramona's hands, of the lips that had so recently been kissing his. She really was stunning.

They sat over coffee after dinner, talking about nothing much.

They concentrated on what had been theirs together, laying out
for their mutual inspection their long friendship, defining it, cele-
brating it.

Outside the night was cool. They biked in the slow lane of
the Newport Freeway, taking almost an hour to get home. Without
a word Ramona led the way down Fairhaven, past the gliderport
to her house, a squarish old renovated apartment block. They rolled
the bikes into the racks, and she led him by the hand into the
building. Through the atrium and by the pool, up the stairs to the
inner balcony, and around and up again, to her room. He had never
been in it before. It was a big square room—big enough for two,
of course—set above the rest of that wing of the house, so that
there were windows on all four sides. "Ooh, nice," he said,
checking out the design. "Great idea." Big bed in one corner,
desk in the other corner, shelves extending from the desk along
walls on both sides, under the windows. Occasional gaps on the
shelves were the only signs of the recently departed occupant.
Kevin ignored them. One corner of the room was taken up with
bathroom and closet nook. There were clothes on the floor, knick-
knacks here and there, a general clutter. Music system on a lower
shelf, but she didn't turn it on.

They sat on the floor, kissed. Soon they were stretched out
beside each other, getting clothes off slowly. Making love.

Kevin drifted in and out. Sometimes his skin was his mind,
and did all his thinking. Then something would happen, they would
stop moving for a moment, perhaps, and he would see his fingers
tangled in her black hair. Under her head the carpet was a light
brown, the nap worn and frayed. She whispered something wordless, moved under him. This is Ramona, he thought, Ramona
Sanchez. The surge of feeling for her was stronger than the physical
pleasure pouring through his nerves, and the combination of the
two was . . . he'd never felt anything like it. This was why sex
was so . . . he lost the thought. If they kissed at the same time
they moved together, he would burst. They were creeping across
the carpet, soon their heads would bump the wall. Ramona made

little squeaks at his every plunge into her, which made him want to move faster. Moving under him, tigerish . . . He held her in his arms, bumped the top of his head firmly against the wall, thump, thump, they were off into the last slide, breath quick and ragged and wordless, his mind saying Ramona, Ramona, Ramona.

Afterward he lay in her arms, warm except for where sweat dried on his back and legs. His face was buried in the fragrant hair behind her ear. I love you, I love you. The intensity of it shocked him. All his life, he thought, his happiness had been no more than animal contentment, like a cow in the sun. A carpenter roofing on a sunny day with a breeze, hitting good nails with a good hammer. Swinging the bat and barely feeling the ball when he struck it. Animal sensation, wonderful as far as it went. But now something in him had changed, and without being able to articulate it, he knew he would never be the same again. And he didn't want to be, either. Because he was lying on an old brown carpet next to his love, head against a wall, in an entirely new world.

"Let's go to bed," Ramona said. He sat back, watched her stand and walk to the bathroom. Such a strong body.

She returned, pulled him to his feet, led him to her bed. Pulled the covers down. They got in and drew a sheet over them. The ordinary reality of it, the sheer domesticity of it, filled Kevin up—the world sheered away and after a while they were making love again, using the springiness of the bed to rock into each other. Euphoria set every nerve singing, this was the best time yet. Their night in the hills had been so strange, after all. Kevin had not known how to think of it. It could have been a stroke of magic, falling through his life just once—a result of Mars, Hank's tequila, the sage hills themselves, intoxicating the whole party. But tonight was an ordinary night, in Ramona's every-night bed, with white cotton sheets that made her body dark as molasses, that made everything more real. He was there and so was she, lying beside him, one long leg spreadeagled over his, the other disappearing under sheets. Really there.

Her breathing slowed. She was getting drowsy. "Remember Swing Tree?" she asked, voice sleepy.

"Yes?"

"That one swing—the long one?"

"I think we must have been out there an hour."

She laughed softly. "All night. It felt like we did everything in that one ride. I thought we had our clothes off and everything."

"Me too!"

"So wonderful. The long swing."

"Happy birthday," Kevin whispered after a while.

"Wonderful presents."

She fell asleep.

Kevin watched her. His eyes adjusted to the dark. Far away in the house a door closed, voices sounded. Someone up late.

Then it was quiet. Time passed. Kevin kept looking at her, soaking her in. He was lying on his left side, head propped on his left hand. Ramona lay on her back, head turned to the side, mouth open, looking girlish. Kevin closed his eyes, found he didn't want to. He wanted to look at her.

She had really powerful shoulders, you could see where her bullet throws came from. Funny how flat-chested she was. Dark nipples made little breast shapes of their own. He remembered her once, laughing resentfully and saying, Alfredo's always looking at women with tits. Still she looked so female. Small breasts drew attention to the greyhound proportions of torso, flanks, hips, bottom, legs. She was perfectly proportioned as she was.

Time passed, but Kevin didn't grow tired. In a way he wanted to wake her and make love again. Then again, just to lie against her side while she slept . . . a long quiver shook him, he thought it might wake her. No chance—she was out.

His hand fell asleep, and he lowered his head. Her hair spilled over the pillow, black shot silk against the white cotton. Perhaps he dozed for a while. He shifted and felt her, looked at her again. Occasionally he had seen love stories on TV. I adore you, I worship you. He had watched them thinking, how stories exaggerate. But they didn't—in fact they couldn't express it at all—poor stories, trying to match the intensity of the real! They never got it, they never could. *Adore*—it was all wrong, it didn't explain it at all, it was just a word, an attempt to get beyond *love*. He loved his sister, his parents, his friends. He needed another word for this, no doubt about it.

The room was lightening. Dawn on its way. No! he thought. Too fast! The slow increase of illumination brought the room's dimensions into focus, made everything a bit translucent, as if it were a world made entirely of gray glass. In this light Ramona glowed with a dark, sensuous presence. She stirred, spoke briefly. Talking in her sleep. Kevin stared at her, drank her in, the fine skin, the occasional freckle or mole shifting over ribs, the sleek curve of her flank and hip. Outside birds chirped.

And day came, too quickly. Because when the sun cracked over the hills and the little studio room was fully lit, Ramona shifted, rolled, sighed, woke up. The night was over.


They took turns in the bathroom, and when Kevin came out she had on gym shorts and a T-shirt. "Shower?" he said.

She shook her head. "Not yet. You go ahead, I'll start up some coffee."

So he showered, wishing she was under the crash of warm water with him. Why not?

Then later as he sat on the floor beside the coffee-maker, she quickly showered herself. What the hell, he thought. Hadn't it been an invitation? . . . Well, whatever. Maybe she liked to shower alone.

Then she was out, hair slicked back with a comb, towel around her neck, dressed again. They sat on the floor in the sun, drinking coffee from her little machine. She asked him what his plans were for the day. He told her a little about Oscar's house, the progress of the work there.

There was a knock at the door. She looked surprised. It was

still a little before eight. She went to answer, coffee mug in hand. She opened the door.

"Happy birthday!" said a voice from the landing at the top of the stairs.

Alfredo.

"Thanks," Ramona said, and stepped outside. Closed the door behind her.

Kevin's diaphragm was in a hard knot under his ribs. He relaxed it, deliberately took a sip of coffee. He stared at the door. Well, Alfredo would have had to find out eventually. Hard way to do it, though. He could just hear their voices out there. Suddenly the door opened and he jumped. Ramona stuck her head in. "Just a sec, Kev. It's Alfredo."

"I know," Kevin said, but the door was closing. He could hear Alfredo's voice, sounding strained, upset. He was keeping it low, and so was she.

What were they saying? Curious, Kevin stood and approached the door. He still couldn't distinguish their words. Just tones: Alfredo upset, perhaps pleading. Certainly asking questions. Ramona flat, not saying much.

He wandered away from the door, feeling more and more uncomfortable. Fright and confidence both filled him, canceling each other out and leaving him nearly blank, except for a light oscillation, a confused feeling. A discomfort. This was strange, he thought. Very strange.

All the objects in the room had taken on a kind of lit *thereness*, as things will on a morning when you have had little or no sleep. There on her desk, a few books: dictionaries, *Webster's* and a yellow Spanish/English one. Several books in Spanish. A volume of the sonnets of Petrarch. He picked it up but couldn't concentrate enough to read even a line. Something by Ambrose Bierce. A sewing repair kit. Six or seven small seashells, with a few grains of sand scattered under them. A desk lamp with a long extendable metal arm. From this window one looked into the branches of the Torrey pine in their atrium. What could they be saying?

After perhaps fifteen minutes Ramona opened the door and came in alone. She approached him directly, took his hand. Her expression was worried, guarded. "Listen, Kevin. Alfredo and I, we have a lot of things to talk about—things that never got said, that need to be said now. He's upset, and I need to explain to him about us." She squeezed his hand. "I don't want you to just be sitting around in here trapped by us going over a bunch of old stuff."

Kevin nodded. "I understand." No time to think.

"Why don't you go ahead and go to work, and I'll come over later."

"Okay," he said blankly.

She walked him to the door. Alfredo would see his damp hair and assume they had showered together. In any case he knew Kevin had spent the night. Good. Kevin stopped her before she opened the door, gave her a kiss. She was distracted. But she smiled at him, and the previous night returned in a rush. Then she opened the door, and Kevin stepped out.

Alfredo was standing at one side of the landing, leaning against the railing, looking down. Kevin paused at the head of the stairs and looked at him. Alfredo looked up, and Kevin nodded a hello. Alfredo nodded back very briefly, his face pinched and unhappy. His glance shifted away, to the open door and Ramona. Kevin walked down the stairs. When he looked up Alfredo was inside, the door was closed.


Kevin went to work on Oscar's place. He and Hank and Gabriela worked on the roof, pulling out the old cracked concrete tiles to clear the way for the clerestory windows that would stand on top of the south-facing rooms. All day he expected Ramona to come biking down the street from Prospect, any minute now, for minute after minute after minute. Long time. Memories of the previous night struck him so strongly that sometimes he forgot what he was doing and had to stop right in the middle of things, looking around

to catch his balance. Sometimes this happened while he was working with Hank. "Shit, Kev, you're acting kinda like me today,
what's the problem?"

"Nothing."

"You okay?"

"Yeah, yeah."

"Flashbacking, eh?"

"I guess so."

The only person who biked up to the house was Oscar himself,
trundling home for lunch. He stared up at them for a while, then
went inside and made lunch for everyone. After they ate he ques-
tioned them about the day's work, ascended a creaking ladder to
take a look at it. Then he biked away, and they went back to work.

And still no Ramona. Well, perhaps she didn't know he was
at Oscar's. No, she knew. It was odd. Then again didn't she have
to teach today? Of course. So she couldn't come by till after three
or four. And what time was it now?

And so the afternoon ticked along, inching through a dull
haze of anxiety. What had Ramona and Alfredo said to each other?
If . . . It must have been a shock to Alfredo, to find Kevin there.
He couldn't have had any warning. Unless someone who had been
up at the hot springs had mentioned something and news had
spread, the way it tended to in El Modena. Still, there wouldn't
have been any warning about last night, or this morning. But why
had he come by to say happy birthday so damned early?

"You sure you're okay?" Hank asked as they put their tools
in Oscar's garden shed.

"Yeah, yeah."

He biked home, ate a dinner he didn't notice. Afterwards he
stood in the atrium for ten minutes fidgeting, then walked over to
Ramona's house. He couldn't help it.

Hesitantly he knocked at the kitchen door, looked in. Pedro,
Ramona's father, was in there washing dishes. "Come on in,"
Pedro said.

"Thanks. Is Ramona home?"

"I don't think so. She didn't eat here."

"Do you know where she is?"

"Nope. Actually I thought she was at your place. I haven't seen her today."

"Oh." Kevin shifted uncomfortably. Part of him wondered how much Pedro knew, but mostly he was thinking *where is she?* He found he couldn't talk very well. Pedro was shorter than Ramona but he had the same coloring, his black hair now sprinkled with white. A handsome man. The way he spoke reminded Kevin of Ramona, obviously the daughter had imitated him in years past. Now there was just the same crease between his eyebrows, a mild frown of concern as he chatted.

"I guess I'll try back tomorrow," Kevin said. "Will you tell her I dropped by?"

"Sure. Do you want me to have her call you when she gets in?"

"Yeah," he said gratefully, "do that."

But that was a mistake, because he spent the evening waiting for the phone to ring. Well into the night, in fact. And it never rang.

The next day he worked in the morning, and then spent the afternoon up at Tom's, working on the pump, which had broken. While he was there Tom got a call, and spent half an hour inside.

When Tom came back down to the pump he said, "My friends think there may be an outside connection in the Heartech-Avending deal."

"What does that mean?"

"Means Avending or Heartech might have an illegal source of capital. It might be here or it might be in Hong Kong, they're getting signs of both."

"Hong Kong?"

"The Chinese are using Hong Kong to generate money— they overlook all kinds of black conglomerates there, even though they've agreed to the international protocols that should make the conglomerates illegal. Then the Chinese zap them for a good bit of whatever profit they make.''

''So we might have something. That would be nice.''

''Nice? If my friends can pin it down, that would do your job for you! What's bugging you, boy?''

''Nothing. I'm just wondering how it will all turn out, that's all. Say, where's Nadezhda?''

''She's down at her ship. They'll be leaving before too long—I guess they've got a delay. Waiting for some stuff from Minnesota.''

Kevin listened to Tom talk about it for a while, but there was grit in his thinking, and he kept losing track of the conversation. Finally Tom said, ''Go home, boy, you must be tired. Get some rest.''


Then when he got home he found Ramona sitting in the kitchen, helping Denise and Jay with their homework. She looked up at him and smiled, and he felt a rush of relief so powerful that he had to sit. Until that moment he hadn't known how anxious he was.

Ramona set the kids to work on their own, led Kevin into the atrium. He caught her up in the dark and gave her a hug. She hugged back, but there was a stiffness in her spine, and she avoided his kiss. He pulled back frowning, the knot back in his stomach.

She laughed at his expression. ''Don't worry!'' she said, and leaned up to kiss him briefly.

''What happened? Where have you been? What did he want? Why didn't you call?''

Ramona laughed again, led him by the hand to poolside. They sat on the low chairs.

''Well, I've been talking to Alfredo,'' she said. ''I guess that answers all your questions at once. He came over yesterday morning to talk about things, apparently. Then when he found you there and realized we had spent the night together, he—well, he fell apart. He needed to talk anyway, and the more that sank in, the more he needed to.''

"About what?''

"About him and me. You know. What happened, what went wrong.''

"Does he want you two to get back together?'' Kevin asked, hearing the strain in his voice.

"Well.'' She looked away. "Maybe so. I'm not sure why, though, even after all the talking we did. I don't know.''

"And you?'' Kevin asked, pressing right to the point, too nervous to avoid it.

Ramona reach over, took his hand. "I . . . I don't know what I want, Kev.''

He felt his diaphragm seizing up, getting tighter with every breath, every absence of breath. Oh my God, he thought. Oh my God.

"I mean,'' she said, "Alfredo and I were together for a long time. We went through a lot together. But a lot of it was bad. Really bad. And you and I—well, you know how I feel about you, Kev. I love you. And I love the way we are together. I haven't felt the way I have the last week in a long time.''

I've never felt like I have in the last week! Kevin wanted to say, and he only just bit back the words, suddenly frightened of speech.

"Anyway,'' Ramona said, still squeezing his hand, "I don't know what to think. I don't know what I feel about things with Alfredo. He says he wants to get back together, but I don't know. . . .''

"Seeing us together,'' Kevin suggested.

"Yeah, I know. Believe me.'' And suddenly she was blinking rapidly, about to cry. What was this? Kevin's fright grew. "I don't know what to do,'' she exclaimed painfully. "I can't be sure about Alfredo, and I hate having anything happen between you and me, to get in the way when we were just beginning!''

Exactly, Kevin thought, squeezing her hand in turn. Don't let it! Should he say that, or would it just be more pressure? He shifted his chair closer to hers, tried to put an arm around her.

"But," she said, pulling herself together, putting a hand to his arm and forestalling him. "The fact is, it's happened. I can't just ignore it. I mean that's fifteen years of my life, there. I can't just tell him to leave me alone, not after all that—especially—well, especially"—losing it again, voice getting desperate—"especially when I don't know what I feel!" She turned to him beseechingly, said, "Don't you *see?*"

"I see." He couldn't swallow well. His diaphragm was as hard as if a block of wood had been inserted under his ribs. "But Ramona," he said, not able to stop himself, "I love you."

"Ah," she said, as if he'd stuck her with a pin; and suddenly he was terrified.

She threw herself up out of her chair as if to run away, collapsed against him as he stood, embraced him, head against his chest, breathing in convulsive gasps, almost sobs. Kevin held her against him, feeling her warmth, frightened in a way he had never been before. Another new feeling! It was as if he had been exiled from a whole enormous world of emotion, and now he was in it—but he wasn't sure he wanted to be, because this love that caused him to clutch Ramona to him so tightly—this love made him so *vulnerable*. . . . If she left. He couldn't think of it. Was this what it meant to be in love, to feel this horrible fear?

"Come upstairs," he said into her hair.

"No," she said, muffled into his shirt. "No." She composed herself, sniffed hard, pulled away from him, stood fully. Eye to eye she faced him, her wet eyes unblinking, her gaze firm. "I'm not going to sleep with anybody for a while. It's too . . . it's too much. I need to know what I think, what I want. I've got to have some time to myself. Do you understand?"

"I understand," he said, barely able to form the words. Such fear . . .

"I do love you," she said, as if she had to convince him of it, as if he were doubting her. Horrible!

"I know," he said weakly. He didn't know what to say. He was stunned. A new world.

She was watching his face, nodding. "You should know," she said firmly. Then, after a pause, "I'm going home now. I'll see you at the games and the street work and all. Please. Don't worry."

He laughed briefly, weakly. "Don't worry."

"Please?"

He took a deep breath. "Oh, Ramona . . ." His voice was unsteady, his throat suddenly clamped. "I won't be able to help it," he got out.

She sniffed, sighed. "I'm sorry. But I've got to have some time!" she cried softly, and darted forward to peck him with a kiss, and was off, across the dark atrium and out the door.

The following days were long. Kevin had never known this kind of tension, and it disagreed with him. At times he found himself wishing that Ramona and Alfredo had never broken up, that he had never thought of her as free, or gone up in the ultralite with her, or walked into the night hills with her, or spent the night in her room. Any of it. Better to leave him the way he had been before, happy in himself, in his own life! To have his happiness, even his ability to function, dependent on someone else . . . he hated it.

Two or three days passed, and he found out that Ramona had gone to San Diego to stay with friends. She left a short note on his house screen. Jody was substituting for her at school, and she expected to be away a week. Damn, he thought when he read the note. Why didn't you tell me? Why are you doing this? Make up your mind! Don't leave my whole life hanging like this!

Still, it was somewhat easier knowing that she wasn't in town.

He couldn't see her, and didn't have to decide not to try. Alfredo couldn't see her either. He could try to pretend that everything was normal, go on with daily life.

That Wednesday's town council meeting, for instance. It was an ordinary agenda on the face of it, fire-fighting equipment expenditures, the fate of the old oak on Prospect and Fairhaven, the raccoon problem along Santiago Creek, permission for a convenience store, *et cetera*. Alfredo led them through these matters with his usual skill, but without aplomb. To Kevin he seemed distracted and remote, his face still pinched. He never looked Kevin in the eye, but addressed him while tapping a pencil on his notes, looking down at them. Kevin for his part tried to appear as relaxed as he could, joking a bit with witnesses and the like. But it was an effort, an act. In reality he felt as nervous as Alfredo looked.

He wondered how many people at the meeting knew what was going on. Certainly many in town knew he and Ramona had been getting close. Oscar, over at his table with his moonlike impassive face; he wouldn't be telling people about it. Nor Hank, nor Tom and Nadezhda. Jody? Gabriela or Mike? It would only take one leak for the story to spread everywhere, that was town life for you. Were some of the audience here tonight to see Alfredo and him pick at each other? Ach . . . no wonder Alfredo looked so guarded. Oh well. Not worth worrying about, not with the agenda in that department already full.

He remembered something Tom had said. "Every issue is related to this zoning change issue now, because you're on a council of seven, and your ability to act is determined by your working relationship with the other six members. Some will be your opponents no matter what, but others are in the middle, undecided. Those are the ones you have to cultivate. You have to back them on the things they care about most. That's the obvious angle. But then there's the unobtrusive stuff, following up their remarks with something that reinforces what they said—asking them questions to defer to their areas of expertise—that sort of thing. It has to be subtle—very, very, very subtle. And continuous. You have to *think*, Kev. Diplomacy is hard work.''

So Kevin sucked on his coffee and worked. Hiroko Washington was impatient indeed with the witnesses who wanted the Santiago Creek raccoons left entirely alone. ''Just where do you live? Do you have kids there?'' she demanded of them. Jerry Geiger seemed down on the raccoon fans as well. It was doubtful Jerry could be influenced by anything, his memory was only one agenda item long, but still, both him and Hiroko . . .

''Have we got a population count on them?'' Kevin asked the Fish and Game rep.

''No, not a recent one.''

''Can you guess reliably from the data you have?''

''Well . . .''

''Aren't there maximum populations beyond which it's bad for them?''

''Sure.''

''So we may be near that number, and killing some would be good for the remaining raccoons?''

''Sure.''

''How long would it take to make a count?''

And so on. And once or twice he saw Hiroko nod vigorously, and it was she who moved that a new population count be made. And Jerry who seconded it.

Good. Diplomacy in action. One hand washes the other. Kevin pursed his lips, feeling cynical. But it was a cynical business, diplomacy. He was beginning to understand that.

And then they were on to the convenience store, and he lost his close focus on it, and it all seemed trivial. My God, is this what it meant to be a citizen in a democracy? Is this what he was actually spending the evenings of his only life doing? His whole existence stood in the balance, and they were arguing over whether or not to give permission to build a convenience store?

And so the tension came and went, obsession then distraction.

\* \* \*

How slowly time passed. Hours dragged like whole afternoons. He had trouble sleeping, nights seemed unbearably long. So much of life was wasted lying down, comatose. Sometimes, unable to sleep, he hated the very idea of sleep, hated the way his body forced him to live.

At work he kept forgetting what the next task was supposed to be. The June overcast extended into July, clouds rolling in from the sea every day. And he found himself standing on Oscar's roof shivering, staring up at clouds, feeling stunned.

Hank and Gabby, who knew now what was going on, left him alone. Sometimes Hank brought along some dumpies of beer, and at the end of the day they sat down on stacks of two-by-eights and drank them, not saying much of anything. Then it was home for another long night.

Kevin took to spending a lot of time at the TV, talking with the house's sister families around the world, catching up on what they were all doing. Awful the way people tended to ignore these humans who appeared on their screens once a month, in a regular rotation. Oh sure, there were occasional conversations over meals, but often the people on both sides of the screens avoided the commitments these screen relationships represented. Still, it only took paying attention, an inquiry, a hello; the translating machines went to work and there he was in another place, involved in distant lives. He needed that now, so he turned up the sound, faced the screen, said Hi, asked how people were doing. The Indonesian couple had just had their third child and were facing killer taxes. The South African family was complaining about their government's bungling trade policies. The big Russian household near Moscow was building a new wing onto their complex, and they talked to Kevin for almost two hours about it. He promised to be there next month to check in on how they were doing.

And then every night the screen would go blank, and he'd be left with his own household, whatever members of it were at home. They were a distraction, though he would have preferred to talk to Tom. But Tom was usually out with Nadezhda. So he wished his sister would call. He would try calling her, but she was never in Dakka. He didn't want to talk about it with his parents. Jill, however . . . he wanted to talk to her, needed to. But she was never home. He could only leave messages.

Life on pause. His hitting streak, going beyond all laws of chance and good fortune, began to seem like a macabre joke. He hated it. And yet it seemed vitally important that he keep it going, as if when the streak broke, he would too. Then he went to bat afraid, aware of the overwhelming likelihood of making an out. In one game, in his first at-bat he nubbed one but managed to beat it out. The next time he took a pitch on a full count, and Fred Spaulding called it a ball despite the funny bounce to one side that it took. The third time up he nubbed another one, directly in front of the plate. He took off running to first base thinking it's over now, it's over. But, as they told him afterward, the Tigers' catcher, Joe Sampson, slipped on the strike carpet and fell face first into the grass, fingers just inches from the ball. And since the fielder had never touched the ball, it couldn't be scored an error. It was a hit, even though the ball had traveled less than four feet.

"Holy moly," Hank said afterwards. "That was the lamest two-for-two I ever expect to see in the life of the universe!"

Kevin could only hang his head and agree. The streak was a curse in disguise. It was mocking him, it was out to drive him crazy. Better if it were ended. And nothing would be easier, actually. He could just go up to the plate and whiff at a couple and it would all be over, the pressure gone.

In the next game he decided to do it. He would commit streak suicide. So in his first at bat he squeezed his eyes shut, waited, swung, missed. Everyone laughed. He gritted his teeth, feeling horrible. Next pitch he squeezed his eyes shut harder than before, groaned, swung the bat hard. *Thump*. He opened his eyes, astonished. The right fielder was going to field the ball on a hop. His teammates were yelling at him to run. He jogged to first, feeling dazed, as if he had jumped off a building and a safety net had appeared from nowhere.

Of course he could keep his eyes open and miss for sure. But now he was scared to try.

When the inning was over he went to the dugout to get his glove, and Jody said, "Pressure getting to you, eh?"

"No!" Kevin cried.

Everyone laughed.

"Well, it's not!" Kevin insisted, feeling his face flush.

They laughed harder.

"That's all right," Jody said. "I'd be crazy by now. Why don't you just go up there next time and take two whiffs and get it over with?"

"No way!" Kevin cried, jumping away from her. Had she seen his eyes squeezed shut? Had all of them seen?

But they all were laughing cheerily. "That's the spirit," Stacey said, and slapped his shoulder in passing. They ran out onto the field chattering, Kevin's stress-out forgotten. But Kevin couldn't forget, couldn't loosen up. Here he was in a softball game, and his diaphragm was a block of wood inside him. He was falling apart.


The following week felt like either a month or a day, Kevin couldn't say which, but there he was in the council meeting again, so a week it was. Numbly he went through his paces, bored by the meeting, inattentive. It went smoothly, and near the end Matt Chung said, "We've got the information we need to proceed on the question of the proposal from the Metropolitan Water District, shall we use this time and go ahead on that? It'll be item two next week anyway."

No one objected, and so suddenly they were in the discussion. Should they buy the extra water from MWD or not?

Kevin tried to gather his thoughts.

While he was still at it Doris said, "Alfredo, what will we do with the extra water there will undoubtedly be?"

Alfredo explained again that it would be a smart move financially to pour it into the groundwater basin and get credits against their drafting from the OCWD.

Doris nodded. "Excuse me, Mr. Baldarramma, have you checked on the legality of such a move?"

Oscar nodded. "I have."

"And?"

"Wait a second," Alfredo interrupted, staring at Oscar. "Why did you do that?"

Oscar met his stare, said blandly, "As I understand it, my job as town attorney is to check the legal status of council actions."

"There's been no action on this yet."

"A proposal is an action."

"It is not! We've only just discussed this."

"Do you object to knowing the legal status of your suggestions?"

"Well no, of course not. I just think you're getting ahead of yourself here."

Oscar shrugged. "We can discuss my job description after the meeting, if you like. Meanwhile, would you like to hear the legal status of your suggestion concerning the use of this water?"

"Sure, of course."

Oscar moved a sheaf of paper in front of him, glanced at the members of the council. "Several years ago the State Water Resource Control Board responded to new laws passed by the California State Assembly by writing a new set of regulations governing water sales. The Revised California Water Code states that no California municipality can buy water and later sell it or use it as credit, unless said municipality has made the water available for consumption for the first time, and in that case, only for as long as is necessary to pay for the method of procurement. The right to buy and then sell water without using it is reserved to the state."

"So we couldn't sell any excess we had if we bought this water from MWD," Doris said quickly.

"That's right."

"So we'd have to use it all."

"Or give it to OCWD, yes."

A silence in the council chambers.

Doris pressed on. "So we don't need this water, and it won't save us money to buy it, because we can't resell it. And buying it would be breaking the council resolution of twenty twenty-two that ordered El Modena to do everything it could to reduce our water dependency on MWD. Look here, I move that we vote on this item, and turn it down. We simply don't need this water."

"Wait a second," Alfredo said. "The discussion isn't finished."

But the discussion was out of his hands, for the moment. Doris kept pressing, asked for a vote in every pause, inquired acidly whether there really was anything left to be said. Before too long Alfredo was forced to call for a vote. He and Matt voted to buy the water. The rest of the council voted against it.


Afterwards, walking over to the house to celebrate, the others were in fine spirits. "All right," Kevin said. At least something was going well. "That look on Alfredo's face when Oscar zapped him—ha." Fine. Fuck him.

In a deep voice Doris said, "'Do you object to knowing the legal status of your suggestions?'" She laughed out loud.

Tom was there at the house, sitting with Nadezhda and Rafael and Cindy and Donna by the pool. Kevin and Doris told him all about it. Kevin downed most of a dumpie of beer in one swallow. "So much for messing with our hill!" he said.

"Come on," Tom said. He laughed. "It only means they'll have to change their strategy."

"What do you mean?" Kevin said.

"They were trying to lay the groundwork for this development before they proposed it, to make things easier. Now that that's failed, they'll probably propose the development anyway, and try to convince the town it's a good thing. If they can do that then they can say, Hey, we need more water, we need different zoning. If the general concept has been approved then it'll happen."

"So," Kevin said, staring at the dumpie of beer.

"Hey, it's still a good thing." Tom slapped him on the arm. "Momentum, you know. But it's a battle won, not the war."


Four days later Kevin heard that Ramona was back in town. He heard it from Stacey down at the chickenhouse, accidentally, as Stacey was talking to Susan. That he had heard about it like that frightened him, and he jogged home with his package of breasts and thighs, desperately trying not to think about it. That she was back in El Modena and hadn't told him, hadn't come by his place first thing. . . .

He got home and called her up. Pedro answered, went to get her. She came on. "I hear you're back," Kevin said.

"Yeah, I just got in this morning." She smiled, as if there was nothing unusual happening. But it was just before sunset. Her eyes watched him guardedly. "Why don't you come over and we can talk."

He blanked the screen, rode over to her house.

She came out and met him in the yard, and they turned and walked down the path toward Santiago Creek. She was wearing jeans worn almost white, frayed at the cuffs. A white blouse with a scoop neck.

Suddenly she stopped him, faced him, took up his hands in hers, so that they hung between the two of them. Curious how held hands could make a barrier.

"Kevin—Alfredo and I are going to get back together. Stay together. He wants to, and I want to too."

Kevin disengaged his hands from hers. "But . . ." He didn't know what to say. Couldn't think. "But you broke up," he heard himself saying. "You gave it a try for years and years and it didn't work. Nothing's changed except you and I got started. We just started."

"I know," Ramona said. She bit her lip, looked down. "But . . ." She shook her head. "I don't want it to be like this." She looked off to one side. "But Alfredo came down to San Diego, and we talked about it for a long—"

*"What?"* Kevin said. "Alfredo came to San Diego?"

She looked up at him, eyes bright in the twilight. "Yes."

"But"—a twist in him, ribs pulled in—"Well shit! You said you were going to get away from us both and think about it and that's what I thought you were doing! And here you were off with him!"

"I meant to get away. But he followed me down there. He found out where I was staying and he went down there, and I told him to leave but he wouldn't, he refused to. He just stood out there on the lawn. He said he had to talk, and he wouldn't leave, all night long, and so we started to talk, and—"

Kevin took off walking, fast.

"Kevin!"

He ran. Around a corner he felt the muscles in his legs and he ran even harder. He sprinted as fast as he could for over a minute, right up Chapman and into the hills. On a sudden impulse, the instinct of an animal running for cover, he turned left and crashed up through the brush, onto Rattlesnake Hill.

He sat under the sycamores and black walnuts at the top.

Time passed.

He stared at the branches against the sky. He broke up leaves, stuck their stems in the earth. Occasionally he thought of crushing lines to say, in long imaginary arguments with Ramona. Mostly he was a blank.

\* \* \*

Much later he tromped down through cool wet midnight air to his house, weary and heartsick. He was completely startled to find Ramona sitting on the ground outside the back door of the house, head on her knees.

She looked up at him. She had been crying.

"I don't want it to be this way," she said. "I love you, Kevin, don't you know that?"

"How can I know that? If you loved me you'd stay with me."

She pressed her hands to the sides of her head. "I . . . I hate not to, Kevin. But Alfredo and I have been together for so long. And now he's really unhappy, he really wants us to be together. And I've put so much work into making that relationship go, I've tried so hard. I can't just give all those years up, don't you see?"

"It doesn't make sense. You tried hard all those years, right, and it didn't work, you were both unhappy. Why should it work now? Nothing's different."

She shivered. "Things are different—"

"All that's different is you and I fell in love! And now Alfredo is jealous! He didn't want you, but now that I do. . . ."

She shook her head, hard. "It's more than that, Kevin. He was coming over on my birthday to say all the same things he said afterwards, and he didn't even know about us."

"So he says now."

"I believe him."

"So what was I, then? What about you, what do *you* want?"

She took a deep breath. "I want to try again with Alfredo. I do. I love him, Kevin, I've always loved him. It's part of my whole life. I want to make it work, so that all those years—that part of me—my whole life . . ." Her mouth twisted. "He's part of what I am."

"So I was just a, a, a kind of crowbar to get Alfredo's thinking straight!"

Tears welled up in her eyes, spilled down her cheeks. "Not fair! I didn't want this!"

Kevin felt a grim satisfaction, he wanted her unhappy, he wanted her as miserable as he was—

She stood. "I'm sorry. I can't take this." She started to walk away and he grasped her arm. She pulled free. "Please! I said I'm sorry, please don't torture me!"

"*Me* torture *you!*"

But she was the one running away now, her white shirt a blur in the darkness.

His satisfaction dissipated. For a while he felt bad. Surely she hadn't wanted things to come to this. She hadn't planned it.

Still, he got angrier and angrier at her. And Alfredo, going down to San Diego to find her! Fucking hypocrite, he hadn't cared for her when he had her, only when he didn't, only when it looked like he might lose her. Jealousy, nothing more; jealousy. So she was a *fool* to go back to him, and he got even angrier at her. She should have sent Alfredo away when he showed up in San Diego, if she wanted to be fair! Instead a talk with him, many talks, a reconciliation. A happy return to some San Diego bed.

He couldn't sleep that night. A dull ache filled him. Other than that he couldn't feel anything.

Two days later the Lobos had a game. Kevin showed up late. He coasted down to the field and dropped his bike. Ramona biked in right behind him, and everyone else was already paired off and warming up, so without a word they put on their cleats and walked out to the outfield, to throw a ball back and forth. All without a word.

And so it comes to this: out on the far edge of a busy softball diamond, two people play catch, in silence. A man and a woman.

The evening sun casts long shadows away from them. The man throws the ball harder and harder with every throw, so that it looks like they're playing a game of Bullet. But the woman never says a word, or flinches, or steps back. She puts up her glove and catches each throw right in the pocket, on the thin leather over her palm. The ball smacks with a loud *pop* each time she catches it. Right on the palm. The man only throws the ball harder. The woman bites her lower lip. She throws the ball back almost as hard as it comes, with a smooth violent snap of the wrist. And the man only throws harder.

And so back and forth the white ball flies, straight and hard, like a little cannonball. *Smack. Smack. Smack. Smack. Smack.*

# 8

*In a camp in Virginia. Interned. Big mistake to antagonize that immigration officer. That a single official's enmity can result in this! But it's more than that, of course. A tidal wave of fear. Lawyer says private tests all negative, so this is just a ploy to hold me while they put together a case under the H-G Act. False positives. Meanwhile here in a kind of camp. Wooden dormitory barracks in rows, dead grass, dirt baseball diamonds, benches, fences. Barbed wire, yes. City of the dying. False positives, those bastards. Actually a lot of people here make the same claim. Some of them obviously wrong.*

*Summer in Virginia, hot, humid. Thunderstorms black with hail and lightning. The daily blitzkrieg of the news. War spilling into the Balkans like a bad summer re-run. TV apocalypse. Four planes blown up in transatlantic flights, and international flights soon to be severely curtailed. Pam will have to return by ship, if she can get home at all. World getting bigger as it falls apart. I can't write any more.*

As Tom had predicted, Alfredo was now forced to go public with his plans for Rattlesnake Hill. He and Matt took time on the town talk TV channel in the dinner hour before the Wednesday night council meeting, and they announced their proposal, walking around a large architect's model of the hill after it had been built up according to their plans. The model was covered with little dark green trees, especially on top—the copse already there would be allowed to remain, at least in part. And the structures were low, built around the hilltop in a sort of crown, stepped in terracelike levels and in some places, apparently, built into the hillside. The buildings were of pale blond brick, and what was not building was lawn. It was a beautiful model, attractive as all miniatures are, ingenious, detailed, small.

Matt went through the town finances, comparing El Modena's shares to those of the surrounding towns and discussing the downturn they had taken in the last ten years. He went over charts showing how the new complex would contribute to the town income, and then moved on to show briefly where Heartech and Avending would get the financing to build the complex. Timetables were presented, the whole program.

Finally Alfredo came back on. "In the end it's your town, and it's your land, so you all have to make the decision. All we can do is make the proposal and see what you think, and that's what we're doing. We think it would be a real contribution to El Modena, the restaurants and shops and promenades up there would really make the hill used, and of course the restaurants and shops down below would benefit as well. We've made proposals on the council concerning zoning and water resources that would make the project feasible on the infrastructural level. The environmental impact report has been made, and it says pretty much what we're saying here, that the hill will be changed, sure, but not in a degrading way. Nearly a quarter of the town's land is parkland just like the hill, immediately behind it—we could easily afford that hill, and use its prominence in Orange County's geography to make a stronger profile for the town as a civic and financial unit."

"Fuck," Kevin said, watching his screen. "What babble!"

Tom laughed. "You're catching on, boy."

Alfredo and Matt ended by asking those watching to spread the word, because few townspeople would be watching, and to speak to their council members in favor of the proposal, if they were so inclined. More detailed messages and plans and updates and mailings were promised.

"Okay, it's in the open," Tom said. "Time to start asking the hard questions in the council. You can still stop the whole thing right in council if the zoning proposal doesn't pass. If people want it then they'd have to elect a new council, and at least you'd have bought some time."

"Yeah, but if people want it, the council will probably go for it."

"Maybe. Depends on the council members—they don't have to pay any attention to polls if they don't want to, it's representative government after all, at least in this part of things."

"Yeah, yeah."

Kevin could barely talk about it. The truth was, since his talk with Ramona he just didn't care very much, about the hill or anything. He was numb. No more new worlds of feeling; just withdrawn, in a shell, stunned. Numb.


One night Tom got a call from his old friend Emma. "Listen, Tom, we've caught a good lead in this Heartech case you've put us on. We haven't followed it all the way yet, but it's clear there's a really strong relationship between your company and the American Association for Medical Technology."

"What's that?"

"Well, basically they're an umbrella organization for all the old profit hospitals in the country, with a lot of connections in Hong Kong."

"Ah ha!" Tom sat up. "Sounds promising."

"Very. This AAMT has been implicated in a number of building programs back on the East Coast, and in essence what they're up to is trying to take over as much of the medical industry as they can."

"I see. Well—anything I can do?"

"No. I've passed it to Chris, and she's going to be going

after it as part of her federal investigations, so it's coming along. But listen, I wanted to tell you—we broke cover to get the opening on this.''

"They know they're being investigated?''

"Exactly. And if Hong Kong is part of it, that could be bad news. Some of those Hong Kong banks are rough.''

"Okay, I'll keep my eyes open.''

"You do that. I'll get back to you when I have more, and Chris may be contacting you directly.''

"Good. Thanks, Em.''

"My pleasure. Good to have you back on the map, Tom.''


Doris was angry. Mostly she was angry at herself. No, that wasn't quite true. Mostly she was angry at Kevin. She watched his evident suffering in the affair with Ramona, and her heart filled with pity, anger, contempt. Stupid fool, to fall so hard for someone clearly in love with someone else! Kind of like Doris herself, in fact. Yes, she was angry at herself, for her own stupidity. Why care for an idiot?

Also she was angry at herself for being so rude to Oscar Baldarramma, that night in the hills. It had been a transference, and she knew it. He hadn't deserved it.

That was the important part. If people deserved it, Doris felt no compunction about being rude to them. That was the way she was. Her mother Ann had brought her up otherwise, teaching politeness as a cardinal virtue—just as Ann's mother had taught her, and her mother her, and so on and so forth back to the Nisei and Japan itself. But it hadn't taken with Doris, it went against the grain of her nature. Doris was not patient, she was not kind; she was sharp-tongued, and hard on people slower than she was. She had been hard on Kevin, perhaps—she had needled him, and he never appeared to mind, but who knew? No doubt she had hurt him. Yes, her mother's lessons still held, somewhere inside her—transformed to something like, People should not be subjected to anger they don't deserve. She had blown that one many a time. And never so spectacularly as with Oscar, up in the hills.

Which was galling. That night . . . two sights stuck in her mind, afterimages from looking into the sun of her own emotions. One, Kevin and Ramona, embracing on a moonlit ridge, kissing —okay, enough of that, nothing she could do about it. The other, though: Oscar's big round face, as she lashed out at him and ran. Shocked, baffled, hurt. She'd never seen him with an expression remotely like it. His face was usually a mask—over-solemn impassivity, grotesque mugging, all masks. What she had seen that night had been under the mask.

So, vastly irritated with herself and the apparently genetic imperative to be polite, she got on her bike after work one evening and rode over to Oscar's house. The front door was missing, as the whole southern exposure of the house was all torn up by Kevin's renovation. She went around to the side door, which led through a laundry room to the kitchen, and knocked.

Oscar opened the door. When he saw her his eyebrows drew together. Otherwise his face remained blank. The mask.

She saw the other face, moonstruck, distraught.

"Listen, Oscar, I'm really sorry about that night in the hills," she snapped. "I wasn't myself—"

Oscar raised a hand, stopping her. "Come in," he said. "I'm on the TV with my Armenian family."

She followed him in. On his TV screen was a courtyard, lit by some bare light bulbs hanging in a tree. A white table was crowded with bottles and glasses, and around it sat a gang of moustachioed men and black-haired women, all staring at the screen. Suddenly self-conscious, Doris said, "It must be the middle of the night there."

She heard her remarks spoken in the computer's Armenian. The crowd at the table laughed, and one said something. Oscar's TV then said, "In the summer we sleep in the day and live at night, to avoid the heat."

Doris nodded.

Oscar said, "It's been a pleasure as always, friends, but I should leave now. See you again next month."

And all the grinning faces on the screen said, "Good-bye, Oscar!" and waved. Oscar turned down the sound.

"I like that crowd," he said, moving off to the kitchen. "They're always inviting me to visit in person. If I did I'd have to stay a year to be sure I stayed in everyone's house."

Doris nodded. "I've got some families like that myself. The good ones make it worth the ones who never even look at the screen."

She decided to start again. "Listen, I'm really sorry about the other night—"

"I heard you the first time," he said brusquely. "Apology accepted. Really there's no need. I had a wonderful night, as it turned out."

"Really? Can't say I did. What happened to you?"

Oscar merely eyed her with his impassive stare. Ah ha, she thought. Maybe he is angry at me. Behind the mask.

She said, "Listen, can I take you out to dinner?"

"No." He blinked. "Not tonight anyway. I was just about to leave for the races."

"The races?"

"Yes. If you'd like to come along, perhaps afterwards we could get something. And there are hot dogs there."

"Hot dogs."

"Little beef sausages—"

"I know what hot dogs are," she snapped.

"Then you know enough to decide."

She didn't, actually, but she didn't want to give him the satisfaction of appearing curious. "Fine," she said. "Let's go."


He insisted they take a car, so they wouldn't be late. They tracked down to southern Irvine and parked at the edge of an almost full parking lot, next to a long stadium. Inside was a low rumbling.

"Sounds like a factory," Doris said. "What kind of racing is that?"

"Drag racing."

*"Cars?"*

"Exactly."

"But are they using gas?"

Roars from inside smothered Oscar's answer. Shit, Doris thought, he is mad at me. He's brought me here because he knows I won't like it."Alcohol!" Oscar said in a sudden silence.

"Fueling cars or people?"

"Both."

"But they aren't even *going* anywhere!" Road races at least had destinations.

Oscar stared at her. "But they go nowhere so fast."

All right, Doris said to herself. Calm down. Don't let him get to you. If you walk away then he'll just think you're a stuffy moralistic bitch like he already does, and he'll have won. To hell with that. He wasn't going to win, not tonight.

Oscar bought tickets and they walked into the stadium. People were crammed into bleachers, shouting conversations and drinking beer from dumpies and paper cups. Peanuts were flying around. Lots of dirty blue jeans, and blue-jean vests or jackets. Black leather was popular. And a lot of people were fat. Or very solid. Maybe that's why Oscar liked it.

They sat in the top bleachers, on numbered spots. Oscar got beers from a vendor. Suddenly he stood and bellowed, in a great rising baritone:

> Race-way!"
> national,
> In-ter-
> County,
> "Orange,

By the time he got to "In-ter-national," the whole crowd was bellowing along. Some kind of anthem. People turned to yell at Oscar, and one said bluntly "Who's that you got with you!" Oscar pointed down at Doris. "Dor-is Nak-ayama!" he roared, as if announcing a professional wrestler. "First timer!"

About thirty people yelled "Hi, Dor-is!"

She waved weakly.

Then cars rolled onto the long strip of blackened concrete below them. They were so loud that conversation was impossible. "Rail cars!" Oscar shouted in her ear. Immense thick back tires; long bodies, dominated by giant black and silver engines. Spindly rails extended forward to wheels that wouldn't have been out of place on a bicycle. Drivers were tucked down into a little slot behind the engine. They were big cars, something Doris realized when she saw the drivers' heads, little dot helmets. Even idling, the engines were loud, but when the drivers revved them they let out an explosive stutter of blasts, and almost clear flames burst from the big exhaust pipes on the sides. Bad vibrations in her stomach.

"Quarter miles," Oscar shouted. "Get up to two hundred miles an hour! Tremendous acceleration!"

His bleacher friends leaned in to shout more bits of information at her. Doris nodded rapidly, trying to look studious.

The two cars practiced starts, sending back wheels into smoking, screeching rotation, swerving alarmingly from side to side as the wheels caught at the concrete. The stink of burnt rubber joined the smell of incompletely burned grain alcohol.

"Burning rubber!" Oscar's friends shouted at her. "Heats the tires, and—" *blattt blattt screech!* "—traction!"

"Oscar's bike tires do that when he brakes," Doris shouted.

Laughter.

The two cars rumbled to the starting line, spitting fire. A pole with a vertical strip of lights separated them, and when the cars were set and roaring furiously, the lights lit in a quick sequence from top to bottom, and the cars leaped forward screeching, the crowd on its feet screaming, the cars flying over the blackened concrete toward the finish line in front of the grandstand. They flashed by and roared down the track, trailing little parachutes.

"They help them slow down," Oscar said, pointing.

"No, really?" Doris shouted loudly.

Two more cars trundled toward the starting line.

So the evening passed: an earsplitting race, an interval in which Oscar and his friends explained things to Doris, who made her commentary. The raw power of the cars was impressive, but still. "This is really silly!" Doris said at one point. Oscar smiled his little smile.

"Oscar should be driving one of those!" she said at another point.

"They'd never fit him in."

"Funny cars you could."

"You'd just need a bigger car," Doris said. "An Oscar-mobile."

Oscar put his hands before him, drove pop-eyed, then cross-eyed.

"That's it," Doris said. "Most of those cars appear to need a bit more weight on the back wheels anyway, don't they?"

Immediately several of them began to explain to her that this wasn't necessarily true.

"It's a tough sport," Oscar said. "You have to change gears without using the clutch, and the timing of it has to be really fine. Then the cars tend to sideslip, so one has to concentrate on steering and changing gears at the same time."

"Two things at once?" Doris said.

"Hey, drag racing is a very stripped-down sport. But that means they really get to concentrate on things. Purify them, so to speak."

Then what looked like freeway cars appeared, lurching and spitting their way to the starting line. These were funny cars, fiberglass shells over huge engines. When two of them took off Doris finally got a good feeling for how fast these machines were. The two little blue things zipped by, moving four times as fast as she had ever seen a freeway car move. "My!"

They loved her for that little exclamation.

When the races were over the spectators stood and mingled, and Oscar became the center of a group. Doris was introduced to more names than she could remember. There was a ringing in her ears. Oscar joined a long discussion of various cars' chances in the championships next month. Some of his friends kidded him about the Oscarmobile, and Doris spent some time with a pencil sketching the design on a scrap of paper: rail car with a ballooning egg-shape at the rear end, between two widely separated wheels.

"The three-balled Penismobile, you should call it."

"That was my plan."

"Oh, so you and Oscar know each other pretty good, eh?"

"Not that good!"

Laughter.

Ordinary clothes, "Americana" outfits, blue jeans and cowboy boots, automotive types in one-piece mechanics' jumpers . . . Oscar's recreations seemed to involve costuming pretty often, Doris thought. Masks of all kinds. In fact some of the spectators called him "Rhino," so perhaps his worlds overlapped a bit. Professional wrestling, drag car racing—yes, it made sense. Stupid anachronistic nostalgia sports, basically. Oscar's kind of thing! She had to laugh.

As they left the stadium and returned to their car they passed a group wearing black leather or intricately patched blue-jean vests, grease-blackened cowboy boots, and so on. The women wore chains. Doris watched the group approach the part of the parking lot filled with motorbikes. Many of the men were fatter than Oscar, and their long hair and beards fell in greasy strands. Their arms were marked with black tattoos, although she noticed that spilled beer seemed to have washed most of one armful of tattoos away.

The apparent leader of the group, a giant man with a long pony-tail, pulled back a standard motorbike and unlocked it from the metal stand. He sat on the bike, dwarfing it; he had to draw up his legs so that his knees stuck out to the sides. His girlfriend squeezed on behind him, and the little frame sank almost to the ground. The back tire was squashed flat. The leader nodded at his followers, shouted something, kicked his bike's motor to life. The two-cylinder ten-horsepower engine sputtered, caught like a sewing machine. The whole gang started their bikes up, *rn rn rnn,* then puttered out of the parking lot together, riding down Sand -Canyon Road at about five miles an hour.

"Who are they?" Doris asked.

"Hell's Angels."

"*The* Hell's Angels?"

"Yes," Oscar said, pursing his lips. "Current restrictions on motorcycle engine size have somewhat, uh . . ."

He snorted. Doris cracked up. Oscar tilted his head to the sky, laughed out loud. The two of them stood there and laughed themselves silly.

Tom and Nadezhda spent the days together, sometimes in El Modena talking to Tom's old friends in town. They went out to look at Susan Mayer's chicken ranch, and worked in the house's groves with Rafael and Andrea and Donna, and lunched at the city hall restaurant with Fran and Yoshi and Bob and a whole crew of people doing their week's work in the city offices. People seemed so pleased to see Tom, to talk with him. He understood that in isolating himself he had hurt their feelings, perhaps. Or damaged the fabric of the social world he had been part of, in the years before his withdrawal. Strange perception, to see yourself from the outside, as if you were just another person. The pleasure on Fran's face: "Oh, Tom, it's just so nice to be talking to you again!" Sounds of agreement from the others at that end of the table!

"And here I am trying to take him away," Nadezhda said.

Embarrassed, Tom told them about her proposal that he join her. But that was not the same thing as holing up in his cabin, apparently. They thought it was a wonderful idea. "You should do it, Tom!"

"Oh, I don't know."

One day he and Nadezhda cycled around Orange County together, using little mountain bikes with high handlebars and super-low gears to help them up the hills. Tom showed her the various haunts of his youth, now completely transformed, so that he spoke like an archeologist. They went down to Newport Harbor and looked around the ship. It really was a beautiful thing. Up close it seemed very large. It did not have exactly the classical shape of the old clipper ships, as its bow was broad, and the whole shape of the hull bulky, built for a large crew and maximum cargo space. But modern materials made it possible to carry a lot more sail, so that it had a clipper's speed. In many ways it looked very like paintings and photos of the sailing ships of the nineteenth century; then a gleam of titanium, or a computer console, or the airfoil shape of a spar, would transform the image, make it new and strange.

Again Nadezhda asked Tom to join them when they embarked, and he said "Show me more," looking and feeling dubious. "I'd be useless as a sailor," he said, looking up into the network of wire and xylon rigging.

"So am I, but that's not what we'd be here for. We'd be teachers." *Ganesh* was a campus of the University of Calcutta, offering degrees in marine biology, ecology, economics, and history. Most of the instructors were back in Calcutta, but there were several aboard in each discipline. Nadezhda was a Distinguished Guest Lecturer in the history department.

"I don't know if I'd want to teach," Tom said.

"Nonsense. You teach every day in El Modena."

"I don't know if I like that either."

She sighed. Tom looked down and massaged his neck, feeling

dizzy. The geriatric drugs had that effect sometimes, especially when over-used. He stared at the control board for the rigging. Power winches, automatic controls, computer to determine the most efficient settings. He nodded, listening to Nadezhda's explanations, imagining small figures spidering out a spar to take in a reef in high seas. Sailing.

"Our captain can consistently beat the computer for speed."

"At any given moment, or over the course of a voyage?"

"Both."

"Good to hear about people like that. There are too few left."

"Not at sea."

Biking through the Irvine Hills, past the university and inland. Sun hot on his back, a breath of the Santa Ana wind again. Tom listed the reasons he couldn't leave, Nadezhda rebutted them. Kevin could tend the bees. The fight for Rattlesnake Hill was a screen fight for him, it could be done from the ship. The feeling he should stay was a kind of fear. They pedaled into a traffic circle and Tom said "Be careful, these circles are dangerous, a guy was killed in this one last month."

Nadezhda ignored him. "I want to have you along with me on this voyage."

"Well, I'd love to have you stay here, too."

She grimaced, and he laughed at her.

At the inland edge of Irvine he stopped, leaned the bike against the curb. "One time my wife and I flew in to visit my parents, and the freeways were jammed, so my dad drove us home by back roads, which at that time meant right through this area. I think he meant it to be a scenic drive, or else he wanted to tell me something. Because it just so happened that at that time this area was the interface between city and country. It had been orange groves and

strawberry fields, broken up by eucalyptus windbreaks—now all
that was being torn out and replaced by the worst kind of cheap-
shot crackerjack condominiums. Everywhere we looked there were
giant projects being thrown up, bulldozers in the streets, earth-
movers, cranes, fields of raw dirt. Whole streets were closed down,
we kept having to make detours. I remember feeling sick. I knew
for certain that Orange County was doomed.''

He laughed.

She said, "I guess we never know anything for certain."

"No."

They biked on, between industrial parks filled with long buildings covered in glass tinted blue, copper, bronze, gold, green,
crystal. Topiary figures stood clustered on the grass around them.

"It looks like Disneyland," Nadezhda said.

He led her through residential neighborhoods where neat
houses were painted in pastels and earth tones. "Irvine's neighborhood associations make the rules for how the individual homes
look. To make it pretty. Like a museum exhibit or an architect's
model, or like Disneyland, yes."

"You don't like it."

"No. It's nostalgia, denial, pretentiousness, I'm not sure
which. Live in a bubble and pretend it's 1960!"

"I think you'd better board the *Ganesh* and get away from
these irritating things."

He growled.


Further north the sky was filled with kites and tethered hot air
balloons, straining seaward in the freshening Santa Ana wind.
"Here's the antidote," Tom said, cheering up. "El Toro is a
village of tree lovers. When the Santa Ana blows their kites fly
right over Irvine."

They pedaled into a grove of immense genetically engineered
sycamores. Tom stopped under one of these overarching trees and

stared up through branches at the catwalks and small wooden rooms perched among them. "Hey, Hyung! Are you home?"

For answer a basket elevator controlled by big black iron counterweights descended. They climbed in and were lifted sixty feet into the air, to a landing where Hyung Nguyen greeted them. Hyung was around Nadezhda's age, and it turned out that they had once met at a conference in Ho Chi Minh City, some thirty-five years before. "Small world," Tom said happily. "I swear it's getting so everyone's met everyone."

Hyung nodded. "They say you know everyone alive through a linkage of five people or less."

They sat in the open air on Hyung's terrace, swaying ever so slightly with the massive branch supporting them, drinking green tea and talking. Hyung was El Toro's mayor, and had been in-strumental in its city planning, and he loved to describe it: several thousand people, living in sycamores like squirrels and running a thriving gene tech complex. Nadezhda laughed to see it. "But it's Disneyland again, yes? The Swiss Family treehouse."

"Sure," Hyung said easily. "I grew up in Little Saigon, over in Garden Grove, and when we went to Disneyland it was the best day of the year for me. It really was the magic kingdom when I was a child. And the treehouse was always my favorite." He sang the simple accordion ditty that had been played over and over again in the park's concrete and plastic banyan tree, and Tom joined in. "I always wanted to hide one night when they closed the park, and spend the night in the treehouse."

"Me too!" Tom cried.

"And now I sleep in it every night. And all my neighbors too." Hyung grinned.

Nadezhda asked how it had come about, and Hyung explained the evolution: orange groves, Marine air base, government botan-ical research site, genetic engineering station—finally deeded over to El Toro, with part of the grove already in place. A group of people led by Hyung convinced the town to let them build in the trees, and this quickly became the town's mark. "The trees are our philosophy, our mode of being." Now there were imitations all over the country, even a worldwide association of tree towns.

"If you can do that here," Nadezhda said, "surely you can save one small hill in El Modena."

They explained the situation to Hyung, and he agreed: "Oh, hell yes, hell yes. It's not a matter of legal battles, it's simply a matter of winning the opinion of the town."

"I know," Tom said, "but there's the rub. Our mayor is proposing this thing, and he's popular. It might be he can get the majority in favor of it."

Hyung shrugged. "Then you're out of luck. But that's where the crux will lie. Not in the council or in the courts, but in the homes." He grinned. "Democracy is great when you're in the majority, eh?"

"But there are laws protecting the rights of the minority, there have to be. The minority, the land, animals—"

"Sure. But will they apply to an issue like this?"

Tom sucked air through his teeth, uncertain.

"You ought to start a big publicity campaign. Make the debate as public as possible, I think that always works best."

"Hmm."

Another grin. "Unless it backfires on you."

A phone rang and Hyung stepped down free-standing stairs to the window-filled room straddling the big branch below. Tom and Nadezhda looked around, feeling the breeze rock them. High above the ground, light scattering through green leaves, big trees filling the view in every direction, some in groves, others free-standing—wide open spaces for gardens and paths: a sensory delight. A childlike appeal, Nadezhda said. Surface ingenuity, structural clarity, intricate beauty.

"It's our genes," Tom replied. "For millions of years trees were our home, our refuge on savannahs filled with danger. So this love has been hardwired into our thinking by the growth of our brains themselves, it's in our deep structure and we can never lose it, never forget, no matter these eyeblinks in the city's grimy boxes. Maybe it's here we should move."

"Maybe."

Hyung hurried upstairs, looking worried. "Fire in the hills, Tom—east of here, moving fast. From the description it sounded near your place."

And in fact they could see white smoke, off over the hills, blown toward them in the Santa Ana wind.

Tom leaped to his feet. "We'd better go."

"I know. Here, take a car and come back for your bikes later. I called and they'll have one for you at the station." He punched a button on the elevator control panel, and great black weights swung into the sky.

A summer brushfire in the California foothills is a frightening sight. It is not just that all the hillside vegetation is tinder dry, but that so much of it is even more actively flammable than that, as the plants are filled with oils and resins to help enable them to survive the long dry seasons. When fire strikes, mesquite, manzanita, scrub oak, sage, and many other plants do not so much catch fire as explode. This is especially true when the wind is blowing; wind fans the flames with a rich dose of oxygen, and then throws the fire into new brush, which is often heated nearly to the point of combustion, and needs only a spark to burst violently into flame. In a strong wind it looks as if the hillsides have been drenched with gasoline.

Nadezhda and Tom rounded the last turn in the trail to Tom's place, following several people and a three-wheeled all-terrain vehicle piled with equipment. They caught sight of the fire. "Ach," Nadezhda said. The ravine-scored hillside east of Tom's cottage was black, and lightly smoking, and the irregular line that separated this new black from the ordinary olive gray hillside was an oily orange flickering, ranging from solid red to a transparent shimmering. White smoke poured up from this line of fire, obscuring the sun and filling the air downwind, filtering the light in an odd, ominous way. Occasionally fire leaped out of the burn line and jumped up the hill toward Tom's place, licks of flame rolling like tumbleweed, trees and shrubs going off suddenly, bang, bang, bang, like hundreds of individual cases of spontaneous combustion. It was loud, the noise an insistent, crackling roar.

Tom stood rigidly on the trail before Nadezhda, staring through the strange muted light, assessing the danger. "Damn," he said. Then: "The bees."

Hank ran by with some others. "Come on," he said, "can't fight a fire from a distance."

Kevin appeared shovel in hand, his face and arms streaked with black ash and brown dirt. "We got the beehives onto a cart and out of here. I don't know how many were smoked inside. Got the chickens out too. We've been watering your roof and they're cutting a break down this ridge, but I don't know if we're going to be able to save it or not, this wind is so fucked. You'd better get what you want out—" and he was off. Tom jogged up the trail to the cabin, and Nadezhda followed. The air was hot, thick with smoke and ash. It smelled of oils and burnt sage. Unburnt twigs and even branches blew by overhead. Just east of the cabin a big crowd of people worked with picks, shovels, axes, and wheelbarrows, widening an ancient overgrown firebreak. The cabin stood in a wide spot in this old break, and so theoretically it was well-placed, but the ridge was narrow, the terrain on both sides steep and rough, and Nadezhda saw immediately that the workers were having a hard time of it. A higher ridge immediately to the west offered a better chance, and in fact there were people up there too, and pick-up trucks.

Overhead a chopping sound blanketed the insistent whoosh and crackle of the fire, and four helicopters swept over the skyline onto them. Gabriela was shouting into a walkie-talkie, apparently directing the pilots. They clattered by in slow, low runs, dropping great trailing quantities of a white powder. One dropped water.

Billows of smoke coursed up and out, were shredded in the wind. The helicopters hovered, turned, made another run. They disappeared over the skyline and the roar of the fire filled their ears again. In the ravine below them the fire appeared subdued, but on their side of the ravine shrubs and trees were still exploding, whooshing torchlike into flame as if part of a magician's act, adding deep booms to the roar.

On the break line almost everyone Nadezhda had met in El Modena was hacking away at the brush, dragging it down the ridge to the west. Axe blades flashed in the eerie light, looking dangerous. Two women aimed hoses, but there was little water pressure, and they couldn't spray far. They cast white fans of water over everything within reach, firefighters, the new dirt of the break, the brush being pulled away. Down below the house Kevin was at work with a pick, hacking at the base of a sage bush with great chopping swings, working right next to Alfredo, who was doing the same; they fell into a rhythm as if they had been a team for years, and struck as if burying the picks in each other's hearts. The sage bush rolled away, they ran to another one and began again.

Nadezhda shook herself, followed Tom to the cabin. Ramona was inside with all the other Sanchezes, her arms filled with clothing. "Tom, hey, get what you want right now!" It was stifling, and out the kitchen window Nadezhda saw a burning ember float by. Solar panels beyond the emptied beehives were buckling and drooping.

"Forget the clothes!" Tom said, and then shouted: "Photo albums!" He ran into a small room beside the bedroom.

"Get out of there!" someone outside the house shouted, voice amplified. "Time's up!" The megaphone made it a voice out of a dream, metallic and slow. "Everyone get out of the house and off the break! NOW!"

They had to pull Tom from the house, and he was yelling at them. A huge airy rumble filled the air, punctuated by innumerable small explosions. The whole hillside between ravine and ridge was catching fire. Hills in the distance appeared to float and then drop, tumbling in the superheated air. People streamed down the fire-break they had just made, and those who had been in the house joined them. Tom stumbled along looking at the ground, a photo album clutched to his chest. Alfredo and Kevin argued over a map, Kevin stabbing at it with a bloody finger, "That's a real firebreak right up there," pointing to the west. "It's the only thing this side of Peter's Canyon that'll do! Let's get everyone there and widen it, clear the backside, get the choppers to drop in front. We should be able to make a stand!"

"Maybe," Alfredo said, and shrugged. "Okay, let's do it." He shouted instructions as they hurried down the trail, and Gabriela stopped to talk into her walkie-talkie. White smoke diffused through the air made it hard to breathe, and the light was dim, colors filtered and grayish.

At the gouged trail's first drop-off there was a crush of people. They looked back, saw Tom's cabin sitting among flames, looking untouched and impervious; but the solar panels beyond had melted like syrup, and were oozing dense black smoke. All the weeds in the yard were aflame, and the grandfather clocks burned like men at the stake. As they watched the shingles on one corner of the roof caught fire, all at once as if a magician had snapped his fingers. Poof! One whole wall gone up like newspaper in the fireplace. Nadezhda held Tom by the arm, but he shrugged her off, staring back at the sight, clutching the album still. His wrinkled face was smeared with ash, his eyes red-rimmed with the smoke, his fringe of hair flying wildly, singed to curls in one spot by a passing ember. His mouth was in a tight disdainful knot. "It's only things," he said to Nadezhda hoarsely, angrily. "Only things." But then they passed a small knot of smoked bees lying on the dirt, and he hissed, looking anguished.

He insisted on helping at the firebreak to the west, and Na-dezhda went along, packed into the back of a pick-up truck with a crowd of smoky, sweaty Modeños. She got the feeling they would have been joking and cursing with great vitality if it weren't for Tom among them. At the firebreak they leaped out and joined a big crowd already working there. This firebreak was on a long, level, broad ridge, and it had been recently cleared. They worked like madmen widening it, and all the while the line of rising smoke with the terrible orange base approached. The black behind the line seemed to extend all the way to the horizon, as if all the world had been burnt. Voices were cracked, hoarse, furious. Hills, ravines, canyons, all disappeared in the smoke. No colors but gray and brown and black left, except for that line of whitish orange.

Helicopters poured overhead in a regular parade, first civilian craft, then immense Marine and Coast Guard machines. When these arrived everyone cheered. Popping over the horizon like dragons out of a nightmare, fast as jets and only meters off the treetops, they bombed the fire relentlessly, great sheets of white powder trailing behind them. The powder must be heavy, Nadezhda thought at one point, not to be lofted like the ash and embers. She had a burn on her cheek, she didn't know where it had come from. She ran a wheelbarrow from workers to pick-up trucks, feeling a strange, stark happiness, pushing herself till she choked on the gritty air. Once she was drenched by the spray from a helicopter's water drop. Little bulldozers arrived, looking like Moscow snowplows. They widened the firebreak quickly, until it was an angry reddish strip nearly thirty meters wide, extending along the ridge for a few kilometers. It looked good, but with the wind gusting it was hard to tell if it would hold the fire or not. Everything depended on the wind. If it slacked they would be okay. If it grew stronger, Peter's Canyon was in trouble. If it stayed constant . . . they couldn't be sure. They could only work harder. An hour or two passed as they tore frantically at the vegetation, and watched the fire's inexorable final approach, and cheered or at least nodded in approval at every pass of the helicopters.

At one point Kevin stopped beside Nadezhda. "I think the

choppers might do it," he said. "You should get some gloves on."

Nadezhda looked down the line of the break. Gabriela was driving a dozer, shouting happily at a patch of mesquite she was demolishing. Ramona and Hank were hosing down the newly cleared section of firebreak, following a water truck. Alfredo was hacking away at a scrub oak with an axe. Stacey and Jody were running brush to a pick-up, as Nadezhda had been until just a moment before. Many others she had not met were among them performing similar tasks; there must have been a hundred people up there working at this break, maybe two. Several had been injured and were being tended at an ambulance truck. She walked over to look for Tom. "Is this your volunteer fire department?" she asked a medic there.

"Our what? Oh. Well, no. This is our town. Whoever heard about it, you know."

She nodded.

The firebreak held.


Hank walked up to Tom and held his arm. "House burns, save the nails."


Just before sunset Hank and Kevin joined Alice Abresh, head of El Modena's little volunteer fire department, and they drove one of the pick-up trucks back around Black Star Canyon Road, to search for the origins of the fire. In a wind like theirs such a search was relatively simple; find the burnt ground farthest east, and have a look around.

This point turned out to be near the top of a small knoll, in the broken canyony terrain east of Tom's place. From this hilltop scorched black trees extended in a fan shape to the west, off to the distant firebreak. They could see the whole extent of the burn. "Some plants actually need that fire as part of their cycle," Hank said.

"In the Sierra," Alice replied absently, looking around at the ground. She picked up some dirt, crumbled it between her fingers, smelled it. Put some in plastic bags. "Here they mostly just survive it. But they do that real well."

"Must be several hundred acres at least," Kevin said.

"You think so?"

"Smell this," Alice said to them. They smelled the clod of dirt. "This is right where the thing had to start, and it smells to me like kerosene."

They stared at each other.

"Maybe someone's campfire got away from them," Kevin said.

"Certainly a bad luck place for a fire as far as Tom's concerned," Hank said. "Right upwind of him."

Kevin shook his head. "I can't believe anyone would . . . do that."

"Probably not."

Alice shook her head. "Maybe it was an accident. We'll have to tell the cops about this, though."


That night Tom stayed at the house under Rattlesnake Hill, using a guest room just down from Nadezhda's. When they had seen that the second firebreak would hold, they had led him down to the house, but after a meal and a shower he had taken off again, and was gone all evening, no one knew where. People came by the house with food and clothes, but he wasn't there. The house residents thanked them.

Nadezhda glanced through the photo album he had saved. Many of the big pages were empty. Others had pictures of kids, Tom looking much younger, his wife. Not very many pictures had been left in the album.

Much later he returned, looking tired. He sat in a chair by the atrium pool. Nadezhda finished washing dishes and went out to sit by him.

The photo album was on the deck beside him. He gestured at it. "I took a lot out and tacked them to the walls, a long time ago. Never put them back in." He stared at it.

Nadezhda said, "I lost four shoeboxes of pictures once, I don't even know how or when. One time I went looking for them and they weren't there."

She got up and got a bottle of Scotch and two glasses from the kitchen. "Have a drink."

"Thanks, I will." He sighed. "What a day."

"It all happened so fast. I mean, this morning we were biking around and everything was normal."

"Yeah." He took a drink. "That's life."

They sat. He kicked the photo album. "Just things."

"Do you want to show them to me?"

"I guess so. You want to see them?"

"Yes."

He explained them to her one by one. The circumstances for most of them he remembered exactly. A few he was unsure about. "That's in the apartment, either in San Diego or Santa Cruz, they looked alike." A few times he stopped talking, just looked, then flipped the big pages over, the clear sheets that covered the photos flapping. Fairly quickly he was through to the last page, which was empty. He stared at it.

"Just things."

"Not exactly," Nadezhda said. "But close enough."

They clicked glasses, drank. Overhead stars came out. Somehow they still smelled of smoke. Slowly they finished the glasses, poured another round.

Tom roused himself. He drained his glass, looked over at her, smiled crookedly. "So when does this ship leave?"

It was strange, Kevin thought, that you could fight a fire, running around slashing brush with an axe until the air burned in your lungs like the fire itself, and yet never feel a thing. To not care, to watch your grandfather's house ignite, and note how much more smokily plastic burns than pine. . . .

Numb.

He spent a lot of time at work. Setting tile in Oscar's kitchen around the house computer terminal. Grout all over his hands. Getting into the detail work, the finishing, the touch-ups. You could lose yourself forever in that stuff, bearing down toward perfection far beyond what the eye would ever notice standing in the door. Or lost in the way it was all coming together. Oscar's house had been an ordinary tract house before, but now with the south rooms all made one, and clerestory windows installed at the top of their walls, they formed a long plant-filled light-charged chamber, against which the living rooms rested, behind walls that did not reach the ceiling. Thus the living rooms—kitchen, family room, reading room—were lit from behind with a warm green light, and had, Kevin thought, an appealing spaciousness. Some floors had been re-leveled, and the pool under the central skylight was surrounded by big ficus trees alternating with black water-filled pillars, giving the house a handsome central area, and the feeling Kevin always strove for, that one was somehow both out-doors and yet protected from the elements. He spent several hours walking through the house, doing touch-up, or sitting and trying to get a feel for how the rooms would look when finished and furnished. It was his usual habit near the end of a project, and comforting. Another job done, another space created and shaped. . . .

He never saw Ramona any more, except at their games. She always greeted him with a smile both bright and wan at once, a smile that told him nothing, except perhaps that she was worried about him. So he didn't look. He avoided warming up with her so they wouldn't get into another session of Bullet. Once they were in a four-way warm-up, and lobbed it to each other carefully. She didn't talk to him as she used to, she spoke in stilted sentences even when cheering him on from the bench. Deliberate, self-conscious, completely unlike her. Oh well.

His perfect hitting continued, like a curse he could never escape. Solid line drives these days, slashed and sprayed all over the field. He didn't care any more, that was the key. There's no pressure when you don't care.

Once he ran into her at Fran's bakery and she jumped as if frightened. God, he thought, spare me. To hell with her if she felt guilty about deserting him, and yet didn't act to change it.

If you don't act on it, it wasn't a true feeling. One of Hank's favorite sayings, the text for countless incoherent sermons. If the saying were true, and if Ramona was not acting, then . . . Oh well.

Work was the best thing. Get the breakfast room under the old carport as sunny and tree-filled as possible. Put the skylights in place, boxes into the roofing, bubbles of cloudgel onto the boxes, get the seal right, make it all so clean and perfect that someday when roofers came up here to repair something they'd see it and say, here was a carpenter. Wire in the homeostatic stuff, the nervous system of this rough beast. More kitchen tiles, a mosaic of sorts, the craft of the beautiful. Sawing wood, banging nails in the rhythm of six or seven hits, each a touch harder, the carpenter's unconscious percussion, the rhythm of his dreams, tap-tap-tap-tap-tap-TAP, tap-tap-tap-tap-tap-TAP. Rebuilding the northside roof and the porch extending out from it, in a flash he imagined falling off and his elbow hurt. Gabriela wore an elbow sleeve for tendonitis, carpenter's elbow, and she was the young one. They were all getting old. The master bedroom would be cool no matter what.

One day after work Hank pulled a six-pack from his bike box and plunked it down in front of Kevin, who was taking off his work boots. "Let's down this."

They had downed a couple of dumpies when Hank said, "So Ramona has gone back to Alfredo, they say."

"Yeah."

"Too bad."

Kevin nodded. Hank slurped sympathetically at the beer.

Kevin couldn't help declaring that Ramona was now living a lie, that she and Alfredo couldn't be happy together, not really.

"Maybe so." Hank squinted. "Hard to tell. You never really can tell from the outside, can you."

"Guess not." Kevin studied his dumpie, which was empty. They opened two more.

"But ain't none of it cut in stone," Hank said. "Maybe it won't last between them, and could be you might pick up where you left off, after they figure it out. Partly it depends on how you act now, you know? I mean if you're friends you don't go around trying to make her feel bad. She's just trying to do what's right for her after all."

"Urgh."

"I mean if it's what you want, then you're gonna hafta work for it."

"I don't want to play an act, Hank."

"It ain't an act. Just working at it. That's what we all gotta do. If you really want to get what you want. It's scary because you might not get it, you're hanging your ass out there, sure, and in a way it's easier not to try at all. Safer. But if you really want it . . ."

"If you don't act on it, it wasn't a true feeling," Kevin said heavily, mocking him.

"Exactly, man! That's just what I say."

"Uh huh." And thus Alfredo had gone down to San Diego.

"Hey man, life's toof. I don't know if you'd ever noticed. Not only that, but it goes on like that for years and years. I mean even if you're right about them, it still might be years before they figure it out."

"Jeez, man, cheer me up why doncha."

"I am!"

"God, Hank. Just don't try to bum me out someday, okay? I'm not sure I could handle it."

Years and years. Years and years and years and years. Of his one and only life. God.

"Endure," Hank would say, standing on the roof and tapping himself in the head with his hammer. "En-doourrr."

Pound nails, set tile, paint trim, scrape windows, lay carpet, program thermostating, dawn to dusk, dawn to dusk. Swim four thousand yards every evening, music in the headphones drowning thought.

He didn't know how much he depended on work to kill time until it came his turn to watch the neighborhood kids for the day. This was a chore that came up every month or so, depending on work schedules and the like. Watching all the adults leave as he made breakfast, herding all the tykes over to the McDows' house, starting up the improvised games that usually came to him so easily . . . it was too slow to believe. There were six kids today, all between three and six. Wild child. Too much time to think. Around ten he rounded them up and they made a game out of walking down the paths to Oscar's house. It was empty—with Kevin gone, the others were off to start a new project in Villa Park. So he got the kids to carry tiles from the stacks in the drive back to the hoist. Fine, that made a good game. So did scraping putty off windows in the greenhouses. And so on. Surprising how easily it could be made into a child's game. He snorted. "I do kindergarten work."

Onshore clouds massed against the hills, darkened, and it started to rain. Rain! First a sprinkle, then the real thing. The kids shrieked and ran around in a panic of glee. It took a lot of herding to get them back home; Kevin wished he had a sheepdog. By the time they got there everyone around was out getting the raincatchers set, big reversed umbrellas popping up over every rainbarrel and cistern and pool and pond and reservoir. Some were automatic but most had to be cinched out. "All sails spread!" the kids cried. "All sails spread!" They got in the way trying to turn the cranks, until Kevin got out a long wide strip of rainbow plastic and unrolled it along a stretch of grass bordering the path. The rain spotted it with a million drops, each a perfect half sphere; shrieking louder than ever the kids ran down the little rise between houses and jumped onto the plastic and slid across it, on backs, bellies, knees, feet, whatever. Adults joined in when the raincatchers were set, or went inside to break out some dumpies, singing "Water." The usual rain party. Water falling free from the sky, a miracle on this desert shore.

So Kevin kept an eye on his kids, and organized a sliding contest, and took off on a few slides himself, and got a malfunctioning raincatcher to work, and caught a dumpie from Hank as Hank pedaled past in a wing of white spray, throwing beer and ice cream like bombs; and he sang "Water" like a prayer that he never had to think about. And all of that without the slightest flicker of feeling. It was raining! and here he was going through the motions, sliding down the plastic strip in a great spray, frictionless as in a dream, heading towards an invisible home plate after a slide that would have had to begin well behind third base, he's . . . safe! and feeling nothing at all. He sat on the grass soaked, in the rain, hollow as a gourd.

But that night, after an aimless walk on the hill, he came home and found the message light blinking on the TV. He flipped it on and there was Jill's face. "Hey!"

He turned it on, sat before it. "—having trouble getting hold of me, but I've been in Atgaon and up to Darjeeling. Anyway, I just got into Dakka tonight, and I can't sleep." Strange mix of expressions, between laughing and crying. "I umped a game this afternoon back in Atgaon, I have to tell you about it." Flushed cheeks, small glass of amber liquid on the table beside her. She stood suddenly and began to pace. "They have this women's softball league I told you about, and their diamond is back of the clinic. It's a funny one, there are trees in left field, and right in the middle of right center field there's a bench, and spectators sit there during the games." Laughter, brother and sister together, a world and several hours apart. "The infield is kind of muddy most of the time, and they have a permanent home plate, but it's usually so muddy there that you have to set a regular base about four feet in front of the home plate, and play with that as home. And that's what we did today."

She took a sip from the glass, blinked rapidly. "It was a big game—the local team, sponsored by the Rajhasan Landless Co-op, was taking on a champion team from Saidpur, which is a big town. Landowners from Saidpur used to control all the local khas land, which is supposed to belong to the government. There's some resentment here still, so it's kind of a rivalry.

"The champions arrived, and they were big women, and they had uniforms. You know how unie teams always look like they really know how to play. I saw some of the local team looking at them and getting worried, and all in all it was a classic underdog-overdog situation.

"The locals were actually pretty good—they looked ragged, but they could play. And the unies could play too, they weren't just show. They had a big fat catcher who was what I would call neurotic, she would yell at the pitcher for anything. But even she could play ball.

"So they played the first few innings, and it was clear the unies had a lot of firepower. But the local team turned some great defensive plays. Their third baseman nabbed a couple of shots down the line, and she had a good arm, although she was so pumped up she kept almost throwing them away. But they got the outs. Their defense was keeping them in the game. They gave up a few runs, sure, but they got some, too—their center fielder came up with two women on base, and powdered a line drive that shot under the bench in right center, it scattered the spectators like a bomb!" She laughed. "Home run."

Another slug from the glass. "So that made it four to three in favor of the unies. A tight game, and it stayed that way right to the end. You know how it gets tense at the end of a close game. The crowd was going wild, and both teams were pumped up.

"So." She paused to take another sip. "Scotch," she said, shivering. "So it got to the bottom of the ninth, and the locals had their last chance. The first batter flew out, the second batter grounded out. And up to bat came that third baseman. Everyone was yelling at her, and I could see the whites of her eyes all the way around. But she stepped into the box and got set, and the pitcher threw a strike and that third baseman clobbered it! She hit a drive over the left fielder's head and out into the trees, it was *beautiful*. Everyone was screaming, and the third baseman rounded the bases as fast as she could, but the unies' left fielder ran around out there in the forest and located the ball faster than I would have thought possible, and threw between trees to the shortstop, who turned and fired a bullet over the catcher's head into the backstop, just as the third basemen crossed the plate!''

She stared into the screen, rolled her eyes. ''However! In her excitement, the third baseman had run across the *old* home plate, the permanent one! Everyone there saw it, and as she ran toward her teammates they all rushed out at her, waving their arms and screaming no, wrong base, go back, and the crowd was screaming too, and it was so loud that she couldn't hear what they were saying, I guess—she knew something was wrong, but she didn't know what. Saidpur's big boss catcher was running around the backstop chasing down the ball, and when the third baseman saw that she knew the play was still going, so she just *flew* through the air back toward the plate, and slid on her face *right back onto the old home plate again*. And that big old catcher snatched up the ball and fell right on her.''

Jill took a deep breath, had a drink of Scotch.

''So I called her out. I mean I had to, right? She never touched the home base we were playing with!

''So her whole team ran out and started yelling at me, and the crowd was yelling too, and I was pretty upset myself, but what could I do? All I could do was wander around shouting 'She's out! She didn't touch the God-damned home plate that we're playing with! Game's over! She's out! It's not my fault!' And they were all crying and screaming, and the poor coach was pleading with me, an old guy who used to live in Oakland who had taught them everything, 'It was a home run and you know it was a home run, ump, you saw it, those home plates are the same,' and so on and so forth, and all I could do was say nope, she's out, those are the rules, there's only one home base on the diamond and she didn't touch it, I'm sorry! We must have argued for twenty minutes, you can see I'm still hoarse. And all that time the unies were running around congratulating themselves as if they had really won the game, it was enough to make you sick. They really were sickening. But there was nothing I could do.

"Finally it was just me and the coach, standing out there near the pitcher's mound. I felt horrible, but what could I do? His team was sitting on the bench, crying. And that third baseman was long gone, she was nowhere to be seen. The coach shook his head and said that broke her heart. That broke her heart—"

And Kevin snapped off the TV and rushed out of the house into the night, shaking hard, crying and feeling stupid about it— but that drunken look of anguish on his sister's face! That third baseman! He was a third baseman too. That broke her heart. To step in the box under that kind of pressure, and make that kind of hit, something you could be proud of always, and then to have it change like that—Night, the rustle of eucalyptus leaves. When our accomplishments rebound on us, when the good and the bad are so tightly bound together—It wasn't fair, who could help but feel it? That broke her heart. That broke her heart.

And Kevin felt it.

# 9

*Night in the dormitory, in the heat and the dark. Sounds of breathing, hacking cough, nightmare whimpers, insomniac fear. Smell of sweat, faint reek, that they could do this to us. There's noise at the far end of the room, someone's got a fever. One of the signs. Bleeding gums, vomiting, high fever, lassitude, disorientation. All signs. Trying to be quiet. They're trying to talk him into calling the meds, going into the hospital. He doesn't want to go of course, who would? They don't come back. That there's a place makes people want to stay here. Smell of fear. He's really sick. They turn on the light in the bathroom to get a glow, and try to stay quiet and yet every man in the dorm is wide awake in his bed, listening. Meds are here. Kill all of them. Whispered conversation. Shifting him onto a stretcher, the sick man is crying, carried between beds and everyone is silent, no one knows what to say, then one shape rises up—"See you over there, Steve." Several people say this, and he's gone.*

He took off into the hills. Up the faint track switchbacking up Rattlesnake Hill. Late sun pierced breaking clouds, pencil shafts of light fanned down over the treetopped plain. The eucalyptus grove on the lower south knob of the hill looked like a bedraggled park, the trees well-spaced, the ground beneath clear, as if goats were pastured there. Nothing but packed wet dirt and eucalyptus leaves. There were chemicals in those leaves that killed plants.

Clever downunder trick. Stepping on soft green acorns and matted leaves. There are people like those trees, harmful to everything smaller around them, creating their own fine space. America. Alfredo. Tall, handsome, strong. But shallow roots. And fungicidal. Everything on this hill killed, so his space would be secure. So he would be a hundred. Where would he send his directable overhundred? Defense, no doubt. Create more business for his medtech. Business development, sure.

Everyone was a kind of tree. Ramona a cypress. Doris an orange tree, no a lemon tree. Old Tom a gnarled Sierra juniper, hanging on despite the dead branches. Oscar, one of the El Toro sycamores. Hank a manzanita, nature's bonzai, a primal part of the hills. Kevin? A scrub oak. Strong limbed, always shedding, looks like it's falling apart.

Up the wet root-rimmed trail to the real peak, feeling his quads. Onto the broad top. Sit for hours. Watch the sunset. Watch the dark seep out of the earth. Watch the dark leak into the sky.


Back down the hill, through the avocado trees. He was too restless to go inside the house. He got on his bike and started to ride. The cool air of the night, the foothill roads.

Thoughtlessly he coasted down into the roundabout where Foothill met Newport, circling into it to head up Newport to Crawford Canyon Road; and there was Alfredo, biking through in the other direction. Alfredo looked up, saw Kevin, looked down again. But as they zipped by each other Kevin caught a glimpse of the expression on his face, and it was a mix, so much in it, but the dominant emotion was—triumph. Triumph, pure and simple, suppressed and then he was past.

And at that moment Kevin hated Alfredo Blair more than he had hated anything in his life.

He was astounded at the virulence of the feeling, its power to dominate his thoughts. He rode and rode but he couldn't think of anything else. If only he and Alfredo could get into another

fight on the softball diamond, what he would *do* to him. It was
an incredible stimulant, hatred—a poisonous amphetamine, sending him into long wrenching fantasies of justice, retribution, revenge. Revenge! Fierce fights, both verbal and physical, all
complicated (even in fantasy) by Ramona's presence, which meant
that Kevin could never be the aggressor. Unless he were to catch
him out one night, alone—like tonight—crash bikes, leap on him,
strangle him, leave him dead—so much for his look of triumph!

Then again it wasn't hard to imagine scenarios where he was
defending himself, or Ramona, or the town, fighting to save them
all from Alfredo's malignant, arrogant drive to power. Punching
him in the face *hard*—the idea made him hunch over, in little
paroxysms of hatred. Oh to do it, to do it, to do it! It really was
astonishing.

At last, much later, he returned home. His legs were tired. He
walked through the garden to the house—

And there in the grove, movement. That shape! Instantly
Kevin thought of the patch of kerosene east of Tom's place—
arsonist, voyeur, intruder in the night (maybe Alfredo, there to
gloat, there to be killed)—"Hey!" he said sharply, and was off
running, jumping over the tomatoes and into the grove, movement
out there, black on black. Between the rows of misshapen avocado
trees, fallen avos like ancient grenades black on the tilled dirt,
movement, movement, nothing. A sound and he was off again,
trying to pant silently as he followed the weak clicks of dry avo
twigs breaking.

He turned and saw it again, fifteen trees down, dark shape,
still and large. A tiny sound, giggle-chuckle, and his anger shifted,
an electric quiver of fear ran up his spine; *what was it?* He ran
for it and it slipped left, downhill. He turned at the tree, looked
down an empty row.

No movement, no sound.

An empty still grove, black in the black. Kevin standing in it trembling, sweating, darting glances left and right.

One day he climbed the hill and there in the copse of trees were Tom and Nadezhda, sitting under the tallest sycamore.

They waved him over. "How's it going?" Tom said.

"Okay. And you?"

"Fine. Nadezhda's ship has gotten its cargo aboard, and they're under way soon. I think I'm going to go along."

"That's good, Tom." He smiled at them, feeling low. "I was hoping you'd do that."

"I'll just keep him one voyage," Nadezhda said.

Kevin waved a hand, sat before them.

They talked about the hill for a while. "You know I've been getting calls from my friends," Tom said. "About the information from Avending we sent them, and some other stuff. I think I know now why Alfredo has done all this."

"Really!" Kevin exclaimed. "And?"

"Well—it's a long story." Tom picked up a handful of leaves, began dropping them on the ground. "Heartech makes cardiac aids, right? Cardiac aids, artificial blood, all that kind of thing. Alfredo and Ed Macey started the company eight years ago, when they were finishing grad school at UCI. It was a way of marketing an improved heart valve they had invented. To start, they got a loan from the American Association for Medical Technology, which is one of the information associations that sprang up to fill the gap left in the thirties when the venture capital laws changed. In the years since, unfortunately, the AAMT has become the refuge for a lot of the greediest elements in American medicine. Bits of the old AMA, people from the profit hospitals, they all found their way into this AAMT, and started building their power base again." Tom laughed shortly. "There are people in this country, as soon as you set limits of any kind, their only goal in life becomes to break them. Being a hundred isn't enough—for a lot of them, the thrill is to have more power than they should. More than allowed! They love that.

"But Alfredo isn't like that, as far as I can judge. He wanted to build medical devices, that's all. You remember how he used to talk about it when they were beginning. And they got their start, fine. But like a lot of small companies beginning, it got rough. It wasn't clear at first that their valve was an improvement over the other models on the market, and they were struggling. It got to the point where it looked like they would go under—and that's where the AAMT stepped in again.

"They offered Alfredo and Ed another loan. This one would be illegal under the new laws, but they said they believed in Heartech's product, they wanted to help. The AAMT would start a black account for Heartech, and then they'd have a place ever afterward where they could go for help, deposit funds they didn't want to report—a whole program, a whole black bank. And Alfredo and Ed—they could have tried to find some other way out, I guess, but they didn't. They went for it."

Kevin whistled. "How did your friends find out about this?"

"First by looking into the AAMT's Hong Kong bank, which covers a lot of this action. And my friends have a mole in the AAMT who hears a lot, and from her the stories get to my friends.

"So." Tom spread his hands. "That was the start of it. Heartech got through its hard year, began to prosper. Some excellent evaluations of the new valve came in, and it became the standard for certain conditions, and then they expanded into other products. You know that part of the story. But all along, they were getting more deeply involved with the black side of the AAMT, using funds, and after they hit the size limits for a company of their kind, banking funds as well. They're iceberging, it's called. Most of their overprofit is going to taxes, but they're hiding a part of their operation in the AAMT in order to be able to do even more."

"But why?" Nadezhda asked. "Why do that?"

Tom shrugged. "It's the same impulse that got Alfredo started, if you ask me. He believes in this equipment, he knows it saves lives, he wants to do even more of it. Save more lives, make more money—the two are all mixed up in his business, and if you try to limit the latter in any way, it looks to him like you're limiting the former."

Kevin said, "But he could have started up an association of his own, and farmed some of the profit out to smaller companies, right? The procedures are there!"

"Yeah, yeah, he could have. But he didn't. They took the easy way, and the upshot of it is, they're in the AAMT's pocket."

"A Faustian bargain," Nadezhda observed.

"That's right." Tom picked up more leaves. "And he should have known better, he really should have. He must have felt desperate, back there that first time. Or else he's one of those smart people who is also fundamentally a little stupid. Or he's simply drawn to the power."

"But are you saying that the AAMT is responsible for this development idea?" Kevin asked.

Tom nodded. "They've been using the little companies they've got in their pocket as fronts, and funding developments like this all over the country. In one small town outside Albany, New York, they were getting resistance, and so they bought its whole city council—contributed illegally to the campaigns of several New Fed candidates for the council, and when they won, it was shoved right through. So they got that one built. They've done it all over the country. Once the developments are in place, the AAMT can use them. They've got a lot of control over them, and they can use them to build medical centers, or labs that generate profits that can be slipped into the AAMT and used to generate more, and so on. They no doubt would tell you they're doing it for the good of the nation's health care services. And maybe there's some truth to that, but there's a lot of raw power drive in it too.

Putting the complexes in prominent, attractive places—that's part
of it too, and that's mostly the drive for power, if you ask me.
Pretty places.''

"So was this one their idea?"

"That's what my friends have been told. In fact they were
told that Alfredo tried to resist it, at first."

"You're kidding!"

Tom shook his head. "Alfredo told them it was a bad idea,
and he didn't want Heartech involved. But he's in their pocket,
see? They've got the goods on him, they can twist him like a
dishrag.

"Still, he squirmed around trying to fight it. He said, listen,
the hill's protected, it's zoned open land, and besides the town
doesn't have any water to spare. Tell you what—I'll try the zoning
and water issues and see what happens. If they don't go, we can't
build anyway. Because he was pretty sure they wouldn't go. That's
why he started all this backwards, you see? And indeed the water
thing didn't go. But he's simply in no position to make a deal.
They've got him, and they said, Hey—propose it directly, and see
how that goes. And so that's what he's doing now."

"How did your friends find *that* out?" Kevin said, amazed.

"Their mole in AAMT has seen this one up close, apparently.
She knows for sure, I'm told."

"Well—" Confused, Kevin didn't know which of several
things on his mind he wanted to say. "Well, hey—then we've
got him, don't we. I mean, when this story gets out . . .''

Tom frowned. "It's a question of proving it. We'll need
something other than just the story, because the mole isn't coming
out for this particular case. So we'll need some kind of documentation to back the charge, or they'll deny it, and it'll look like a
smear campaign."

"Will there be any documentation?"

"Not much. They don't write these kinds of arrangements
down, they don't put them in computers. The black economy is a
verbal game, by and large. But my friends are looking—following

traces of the money, mostly. They seem confident they'll come up with something on the Hong Kong end of things. But they haven't yet."

The three of them sat for a while.

"Wow," Kevin said. "I just had no idea."

"Me neither."

Nadezhda said, "It makes sense, though. There wasn't much motive to go for this hill in particular."

"Oh, I don't know," Tom said. "I think maybe Alfredo likes the idea, now. Height equals power, after all, and he's fond enough of power. But it's true—now we've got more of the story, we can see he's . . . hoist on his own petard, to an extent."

"I had no idea."

"People's motives are mixed, Kevin."

"I guess." He sighed.

After a while he said, "In a way I wish you weren't leaving."

"I'm not going to stop working on it. Most of what I'm doing is by phone, and I'll keep doing that from the ship."

"Part of it's your presence," Kevin said.

Tom regarded him steadily. "If that's so, it's going to change. That part's up to you, now."

Kevin nodded.

"You'll do fine."

Kevin nodded again, feeling doubtful.


Time passed in silence.

Nadezhda asked him what was happening with Ramona.

Awkwardly, hesitantly, Kevin found himself telling the story. The whole story. The childhood stuff, the softball game, the ultraflight, the night in the hills, the birthday party, the following morning. The little that had happened since.

It felt good to tell it, in a way. Because it was *his story*, his and his alone, nobody else's. And in telling it he gained a sort of control over it, a control he had never had when it happened. That

was the value of telling one's story, a value exactly the reverse of
the value of the experience itself. What was valuable in the experience was that he had been out of control, living moment to
moment with no plan, at the mercy of other people. What was
valuable in the telling of the story was that he was in control,
shaping the experience, deciding what it meant, putting other people in their proper place. The two values were complementary,
they added up to something more than each alone could, something
that . . . completed things.

So he told them his story, and they listened.

When he was done he sat crouched on the balls of his feet,
feeling pensive.

Tom looked at him with his unblinking birdlike look. "Well,
it ain't the worst thing that could happen."

"I know." But this is bad enough for me! he thought.

He recalled Tom's long years of silence, his retreat to the
hills after Grandma died. Years and years. Sure, worse things
could happen. But at least Tom had had his great love, had gotten
to live it to its natural end, to live it out! Kevin's throat was tight.

"There is not much worse," Nadezhda said to Tom, rebuking
him. Then to Kevin: "Time will make a difference. When enough
time is passing—"

"I won't forget!" Kevin said.

"No. You never forget. But you change. You change even
if you try not to."

Tom laughed, tugged at the white hair over one ear. "It's
true. Time changes us in more ways than we can ever imagine.
What happens in time . . . you become somebody else, do you
understand?" His voice shook. "You don't forget, but how you
feel about what you remember . . . that changes."

He stood up suddenly, walked to Kevin and slapped him on
the shoulder. "But it could be worse! You could forget! And that
would be worse."

He stood by Kevin's side. Nadezhda sat on the ground beyond

them. For a long time the three of them rested there, silent, watching sunlight tumble down through clouds.

That night while they were making dinner Kevin said, "One thing that really bothers me is the way everyone in town seems to know about it. I hate people talking about me like that, about my private affairs."

"Hell, you can't ever escape that," Tom said. "People are talking about me and Nadezhda too, no doubt."

Donna and Cindy and Yoshi came into the kitchen. "The bad thing," Kevin said, "is that now when I fight Alfredo over the hill it looks like it's just because of Ramona."

"No it doesn't. Everyone knows you're against that development, and the Greens are too. This thing is only likely to get you sympathy votes. And you can use all the votes you can get."

As they ate Kevin brooded over Tom's departure. Mexico, Central America, across the Pacific to Manila, Hong Kong, Tokyo. Working the winds and currents as so many ships had before. Well, it sounded great. Good for Tom. But with Jill in Asia, his parents in space . . .

Hank would still be there. Gabby. The team. Yoshi, Cindy, Donna, the kids, the rest of the household. Doris would still be there. Doris.

Two days later Kevin was the only one who went down to Newport with Tom and Nadezhda to see them off. Everyone else was too busy, and said their good-byes that morning at the house, or over the phone. "Seem's like half the town is overseas," Jerry Geiger complained. "Don't stay away long."

They took a car to Balboa, and Kevin helped them get their baggage aboard. The ship seemed huge. Overhead the dense network of rigging looked like a cat's cradle in the sky. Gulls flashed across the sun in screeching clouds, mistaking them for a fishing trip. The pavilion behind the dock was crowded.

Eventually *Ganesh* was ready. Kevin hugged Nadezhda and Tom, and they said things, but in the confusion of shouts and horns he didn't really hear. Then he was on the dock with the other well-wishers, waving. Above him Tom and Nadezhda waved back. *Ganesh* swung away from the dock, then three topsails unfurled simultaneously, on the foremast, the second mast, and the miz-zenmast. Slowly, as if drifting, the ship moved downchannel.

Feeling dissatisfied with this departure, Kevin jogged down the peninsula to the harbor entrance. He walked over the boulders of the Wedge's jetty, looking back to see if the ship had appeared.

Then it was there, among the palms at the channel turn. The wind was from the north, so they could sail out on a single reach. With only the topsails set its movement was slow and majestic. Kevin had time to get to the end of the jetty and sit on the flat rocks. He couldn't help recalling the last time he had been out there, with Ramona, watching the ships race in. Don't think of it. Don't think.

The topsails were set nearly fore-and-aft, emphasizing the elegant transfer of force that propelled the ship across the wind. Always beautiful to see a square-rigged ship set so. People on both jetties stood watching it pass.

Then it was even with him, and Kevin could make out figures on the deck. Suddenly he spotted Tom and Nadezhda, standing by the bowsprit. He stood and cupped his hands around his mouth. "Tom! TOM!" He wasn't sure they would be able to hear him; the ocean's ground bass ate all other sound. But Nadezhda spotted him and pointed. All three of them waved.

*Ganesh* swung to the south, the yards shifting in time with the movement, so that the topsails were square to what was now a following wind. And then all the sails on the ship unfurled at once, mainsails, topgallants, skysails, moonsails, stunsails, royals, jibs. It was as if some strange creature had just spread immense wings. Immediately it leaped forward in the water, crashing across

the incoming swells and shooting broad fans of spray out to starboard. Kevin waved. The ship drew away from him and grew
smaller, the centerpoint of a wide V of startling white wake. Maybe
that was Tom and Nadezhda in the stern, waving. Maybe not. He
waved back until he couldn't see the figures any more.


Back in El Modena Kevin went to work campaigning against the
Rattlesnake Hill development, just as Tom had suggested. He and
Doris went down to the town's TV studio and made a spot to put
on the town affairs show, going over their arguments one by one.
They walked around an alternative model of the hill with the
development on it, one that showed the roads necessary, and had
the landscaping changed so the extent of the buildings was more
visible. Oscar directed the spot, and added points to their argument,
including a long section he had written himself on the water requirements of the new structure. Doris pointed at graphs of the
costs involved and the expected returns, the possible population
increase, the rise in the cost of housing in the town when people
poured in. "We set the town's general policy over a long period
of years, and it's been a consensus agreement about El Modena's
character, its basic nature. If we approved this construction all that
would change." Every graph made a different point, and Doris
walked from each to each, leading the watchers through to her
inescapable conclusion. Then Kevin showed videos he had made
on the hill, at dawn, in a rain shower, looking down at the plain
on the clear day, in the grove on the top, down among the sage
and cacti, with the lizards and ants. Bird song at dawn accompanied
these images, along with Kevin's laconic commentary, and an
occasional cut shot of South Coast Plaza or other malls, with their
crowds and concrete and the bright waxy greenery that looked
plastic whether it was real or not.

It was a good spot, and the response to it was positive. Alfredo
and Matt did a rebuttal show which concentrated on their economic
arguments, but still it seemed to Kevin that they had won the first

TV round, surely one of the crucial ones. Tom saw a tape on *Ganesh,* and in one of their frequent phone conversations nodded happily. "That will get you votes."

Then, at Tom's urging, Kevin went out door to door, stopping at all the big houses and talking to whoever was there for as long as their patience allowed. Four nights a week he made himself go out and do this, for two hours at a time. It was wearing work. When he got tired of it he thought of the hill at dawn, or of the expression on Alfredo's face that night on the bikes. Some people were friendly and expressed a lot of support for what he was doing; occasionally they even joined him for the rounds in their neighborhood. Then again other households couldn't be bothered. People told him right to his face that they thought he was being selfish, protecting his backyard while the town shares languished. Once someone accused him of going renegade against the Green party line. He denied it vehemently, but it left him thinking. Here was where the party organization could help—there should be lots of people out doing these visits, or making calls. He decided to go up and see Jean about it.

"Ah good," Jean said, looking up from the phone. "I'd been meaning to get you up here."

Kevin settled into the seat across from her.

She cut off the speaker on the phone: "Let me get back to you, Hyung, I've got someone here I need to talk to." She tapped the console and swung her chair around to face him.

"Listen, Kevin, I think it's time to slack off on this idea of Alfredo's. It's medical technology he wants to bring into town, not a weapons factory. It makes us look bad to oppose it."

"I don't care what it is," Kevin said, surprised. "The hill is wilderness and was slated to be made part of Saddleback Park, you know that."

"Right now it's zoned open space. Nothing ever happened with that park proposal."

"That's not my fault," Kevin said. "I wasn't on the council then."

"And I was, is that what you're saying?"

Kevin remained silent.

Jean swiveled in her chair, stood, walked to her window. "I think you should stop campaigning against this development, Kevin. You and Doris both."

"Why?" Kevin said, stunned.

"Because it's divisive. When you take an extreme position against a development like that, then it makes the whole Green party look like extremists, and we can't act on real issues."

"This is a real issue," he said sharply. She eyed him from the window. "I thought this was what the Green party was about—slowing growth, fighting for the land and for the way of life we've got here. It's the Green party that made this town the way it is!"

"Exactly." She looked out the window at the town. "But times are changing, Kevin, and having established the town's style, we have to see what we can do to maintain it. That means taking a central position in affairs—if we do that, all subsequent decisions will be made by us, see? You can't do that when you're at one extreme of community opinion."

"But this is exactly what we stand for!"

"I know that, Kevin. We still defend the land. But I think that land can be put to use, and it will actually be good for other land around the town."

She wouldn't say anything more. Finally Kevin left, frustrated to the point of fury.

"I just don't understand her!" he exclaimed when he described the meeting to Oscar. "What the hell does she mean, good for other land? She's just caving in!"

"No, she's not. I think she and Alfredo are working out a deal. I've been hearing rumors of it in the town offices. The work we've been doing has put pressure on Alfredo, and I think Jean feels it's a good time to get him to make concessions. The Greens lay off on Rattlesnake Hill, and in return Alfredo puts all the rest of the Green program through the council."

"You're kidding."

"No."

"Well why didn't she tell me that?"

"She probably figured you wouldn't go along with it."

"Well she's right, God damn it!"

He went back up to see Jean again. "What's this I hear about you making a deal with Alfredo?" he said angrily, the moment he walked into her office.

She stared at him coldly. "Sit down, Kevin. Calm down."

She went to the window again. She talked about the Greens' gradual loss of influence in the town. "Politics is the art of the possible," she said again at one point.

"The thing is"—finally getting to it—"we've taken a bunch of polls in town about this issue, and they show that if it comes to a town referendum, we're going to lose. Simple as that.

"Now that may change, but it's my judgment that it won't. Alfredo, though—he can't be as sure. It's a volatile situation."

And Alfredo knows things you don't, Kevin thought suddenly.

"So he's nervous, he's feeling vulnerable, and he's ready to deal. Right now. It's a matter of timing—we can get him to agree to do things now that he simply won't have to agree to later on. Now, this development could be good for the town, and it can be done in a way that won't harm the hill. At the same time, we can get Alfredo to agree to the back country plan and the big garden strip down by the freeway, and the road and path plan, and a population cap. He's willing to go along with all that. Do you see what I mean?"

Kevin stared at her. "I see that you're giving up," he said absently. His stomach was contracting to its little knot of wood again. Nothing but scattered images, phrases. He stood up, feeling detached. "We don't have to concede anything to him," he said. "We can fight every one of those issues on their own merits."

"I don't think so."

"I do!" Anger began to flood through him, gushing with every hard knock of his heart.

Jean gave him a cold stare. "Listen, Kevin, I head the party here, and I've talked with all the rest of the leadership—"

"I don't give a shit who you've talked to! I'm not giving Rattlesnake Hill away!"

"It's not giving it away," she snapped.

"I'm not trading it, either."

"You were elected to fill a Green slot, Kevin. You're a Green member of this council."

"Not any more I'm not."

He walked out.

He went to see Oscar and told him what had happened. Was it legal for him to quit the Greens while he was holding a Green slot on the council?

Oscar thought about it. "I think so. The thing is, while you're the Green on the council, your policy is the Green policy. See what I mean? You don't really have to quit the party. You can just say, this is what Green policy is. People may disagree, you may get in trouble with the party, and not get picked to run again. But there's no legal problem."

"Good. I'm not running for re-election anyway."

But after that, the nightly house-to-house campaigning got more difficult. A lot of people didn't want to talk to him. A lot of those who did wanted to argue with him. Many made it clear they thought he was waging a personal war with Alfredo, and implied that they knew why.

One night after a particularly tough walk around he came home and the downstairs was empty, and he went up to his room. Ramona was with Alfredo and Tom was on his ship and Jill was in Bangladesh and his parents were in space, and thinking about it he began to quiver, and then to tremble, and then to shake hard.

Tomas appeared in his doorway. "Home late, I see."

"Tomas! What are you doing?"

"I'm taking a break."

"You're *taking* a *break?*"

"Yeah, sure. Come on, everyone's got to take a break sometime."

"I wish I had this on videotape, Tomas, we could use it to pry you away from your screen more often."

"Well I'm busy, you know that. But I've been finding I get a twitch in the corner of my right eye when I look at the screen for too long. Anyway, let's go down to the kitchen and see if Donna and Cindy have left any beers in the fridge."

"Sure." So they went down to the kitchen and talked, about Yoshi and Bob, Rafael and Andrea, Sylvia and Sam. About themselves. At one point Kevin thought, I'm catching up on the life of the guy who lives in the room right next to mine. Still, he appreciated it.


Another time after an evening of campaign drudgery he went to the town hall restaurant to have dinner, thinking some chile rellenos and cervecas were just what he needed. Late summer sunset dappled the trees and walls of the courtyard, and it was quiet. The food was good.

He had finished, and Delia had cleared away his plate and was bringing him a last cerveca, when Alfredo walked out of the city chambers across the yard. He was at the wrought iron gate when he saw Kevin. Kevin dropped his gaze to the table, but still saw Alfredo hesitate, gate in hand—then turn and walk over to him. Kevin's heart pounded.

"Mind if I sit?"

"Uh," Kevin said, unsure. Alfredo looked uncertain as well,

and for an awkward moment they froze, both looking acutely uncomfortable. Finally Kevin jerked, shrugged, waved a hand, muttered, "Sure."

Alfredo pulled back one of the white plastic chairs and sat, looking relieved. Delia came out with Kevin's beer, and Alfredo ordered a margarita. Even in his distraction Kevin could see Delia struggling to keep surprise off her face. They really were the talk of the town.

When she was gone, Alfredo shifted onto the edge of his chair and put his elbows on the table. Staring down at his hands he said, "Listen, Kevin. I'm . . . real sorry about what's happened. With Ramona, you know." He swallowed. "The truth of the matter is . . ." He looked up to meet Kevin's gaze. "I love her."

"Well," Kevin said, looking away, intensely ill at ease. He heard himself say, "I believe it."

Alfredo sat back in his seat, looking relieved again. Delia brought his margarita and he drank half of it, looked down again. "I lost sight of it myself," he said in a low voice. "I'm sorry. I guess that's why all this happened, and, you know." He didn't seem to be able to finish the thought. "I'm sorry."

"There was more to it than that," Kevin said, and drank his beer. He didn't want to go any further into it. Talk about love between American men was a rare and uneasy event, even when they weren't talking about the same woman. As it was Kevin felt impelled to order a pitcher of margaritas, to cover the awkwardness.

"I know," Alfredo said, forging onward. "Believe me, I'm not trying to take anything away from you—from what happened, I mean. Ramona is really unhappy about what . . . well, about what us getting back together has meant for . . . you and her."

"Uhn," Kevin said, hating the babble the subject of love always seemed to generate.

"And I'm sorry too, I mean I never would've tried to do anything like what's happened. I was just . . ."

The margarita pitcher arrived, and they both set about busily filling and drinking the glasses, lapping up salt, their eyes not meeting.

"I was just a fool!" Alfredo said. "An arrogant stupid fool."

Again, as from a distance of several feet, Kevin heard himself say, "We all lose track of what's important sometimes." Thinking of Doris. "You do what you feel."

"I just wish it hadn't worked out this way."

Kevin shrugged. "It wasn't anyone's fault."

Had he said that? But it was as if he was taking something from Alfredo to say that, and he wanted to. He was by no means sure he believed any of the things he heard himself saying; yet out they came. He began to feel drunk.

Alfredo drank down his glass, refilled, drank more. "Hey, I'm sorry about that collision at third, too."

Kevin waved it away. "I was in the baseline."

"I shoulda slid, but I wasn't planning to when I came in, and I couldn't get down in time when I saw you were gonna stay there."

"That's softball."

They drank in silence.

"What—"

"I—"

They laughed awkwardly.

"What I was going to say," said Alfredo, "is that, okay, I'm sorry our personal lives have gotten tangled up, and for fucking up in that regard. And for the collision and all. But I still don't get it why you are so opposed to the idea of a really first-rate technical center on Rattlesnake Hill."

"I was gonna say the same thing in reverse," Kevin said. "Why you are so determined to build it up there on the hill?"

A long pause. Kevin regarded him curiously. Interesting to see Alfredo in this new light, knowing what he now knew about Heartech and the AAMT. "It doesn't make sense," he said, pressing harder. "If this center is all you say it is, then it could do well anywhere in town. But we only have one hill like that, still empty and left alone. It's a miracle it's still that way after all these years, and to take that away now! I just don't get it.''

Alfredo leaned forward, drew incomprehensible diagrams in the condensation and salt and spilled liquor on the table. "It's just a matter of trying for the best. I like to do that, that's the way I am. I mean sure, the better the center does the better it'll be for me. I'm not free of that kind of thinking, but I don't see why I should be, either. It's part of trying for the best you can.''

So interesting, to see him rationalize like that—to see the strain there, under the moustache, behind the eyes!

Kevin said, "Okay, I'd like to be a hundred myself, and I like to do good work too. But good work means doing it without wrecking the town you live in.''

"It wouldn't be wrecking it! To have a center that combined high tech labs and offices with restaurants, an open deck with a view, a small amphitheater for concerts and parties and just looking at the view—man, that's been the goal of city planners for years and years. More people would use the hill than ever do now.''

"More isn't better, that's the point. Orange County is perfect proof of that. After a certain point more is worse, and we passed that point long ago. It's gonna take years to scale things back down to where this basin is at the right population for people and the land. You take all the scaling back for granted, but you value the results of it too. Now you're getting complacent and saying it's okay for major growth to start again, but it isn't. That hill is open land, it's wilderness even if it's in our backyards. It's one of the few tiny patches of it left around here, and so it's worth much more as wilderness than it ever could be as any kind of business center.''

Kevin stopped to catch his breath. To see how Alfredo would rationalize it.

Alfredo was shaking his head. "We have the whole back country, from Peter's Canyon Reservoir to Black Star Canyon, with Irvine Park too. Meanwhile, that hill is on the town side of things, facing the plain. Putting the center up there would make it the premiere small center in southern California, and that would do the town a lot of good!''

Suddenly Kevin could hear the echo in the argument. Surely this was exactly what the AAMT representatives had said to Alfredo when they were putting the arm on him.

Fascinating. Kevin only had to shake his head, and Alfredo was pounding the table, trying to get his point through, raising his voice: ''It would, Kevin! It would put us on the map!''

''I don't care,'' Kevin said. ''I don't want to be on the map.''

''That's crazy!'' Alfredo cried. ''You don't care, exactly!''

''I don't care for your ideas,'' Kevin said. ''They sound to me like ideas out of a business magazine. Ideas from somewhere else.''

Alfredo blew out a breath. His eyebrows drew together, and he stared closely at Kevin. Kevin merely looked back.

''Well, hell,'' Alfredo said. ''That's where we differ. I want El Modena on the map. I want on the map myself. I want to do something like this.''

''I can see that.'' And behind the dispassion, the somehow scientific interest of watching Alfredo justify himself, Kevin felt a surge of strangely mixed emotion: hatred, disgust, a weird kind of sympathy, or pity. I want to do something like this. What did it take to say that?

''I just don't want to get personal about it,'' Alfredo said. He leaned forward, and his voice took on a touch of pleading: ''I've felt what it's like when we take this kind of disagreement personally, and I don't like it. I'd rather dispense with that, and just agree to disagree and get on with it, without any animosity. I . . . I don't like being angry at you, Kevin. And I don't like you being angry at me.''

Kevin stared at him. He took a deep breath, let it out. ''That may be part of the price you pay. I don't like your plan, and I don't like the way you're keeping at it despite arguments against it that seem obvious to me. So, we'll just have to see what happens. We have to do what we have to do, right?"

Taken aback, Alfredo didn't answer. So used to getting his way, Kevin thought. So used to having everybody like him.

Alfredo shrugged. "I guess so," he said morosely, and drained his glass.


Dear Claire:

. . . My living room is coming together, I have my armchair with its reading light, set next to the fireplace, with a bookstand set beside it, piled high with beautiful volumes of thought. Currently I have a stack of "California writers" there, as I struggle to understand this place I have moved to—to cut through the legends and stereotypes, and get to the locals' view of things. Mary Austin, Jack London, Frank Norris, John Muir, Robinson Jeffers, Kenneth Rexroth, Gary Snyder, Ursula Le Guin, Cecelia Holland, some others . . . taken together, they express a vision that I am coming to admire more and more. Muir's "athlete philosopher," his "university of the wilderness," these ideas infuse the whole tradition, and the result is a very vigorous, clear literature. The Greek ideal, yes, love of the land, healthy mind in healthy body—or, as Hank says, moderation in all things, including moderation of course! You can be sure I will remain moderate in my enthusiasm for the more physical aspects of this philosophy. . . .

. . . Yes, the political battle here is heating up; a brush fire in the canyons to the east of town burned several hundred acres, including one structure, the house of Tom Barnard. The fire was not natural—someone started it, accidentally or deliberately. Which? No one can say. But now Barnard is planning to sail off with my wonderful Nadezhda.

Then again, few are as Machiavellian as I. The police, for lack of other evidence, have declared it a fire started by accident

—with the file marked for the arson squad, in the event other questionable cases like this occur. In other words the Scottish verdict. It's the end of that, but I keep my suspicions.

Meanwhile the obvious parts of the battle continue apace. The mayor's party has started to do what is necessary to get a town referendum on the issue. If they get the referendum on the ballot (likely), and win it, then all our legal maneuvering will have been in vain.

I try to remain sanguine about it all. And I have assuaged my grief in the loss of Nadezhda by associating more with Fierce Doris. Yes, yes, just as you say, growing admiration and all that. She is still as hard as her bones, but she is sharp; and around here a little waspishness is not a bad thing. I have entertained her by taking her to see some of my more arcane pursuits, and behaving like a fool while engaged in them. Always my strong suit when it comes to pleasing people, as you know.

Doris responded in kind by taking me to see her new lab. Yes, this is the way her mind works. This was high entertainment. She has gotten a new position with a firm much like Avending, "but ahead in just the areas I'm most interested in." So, I said, her great sacrifice in quitting Avending was actually naked self-interest? Turned out that way, she said happily. Her new employer is a company called SSlabs, and they are developing an array of materials for room temperature superconducting and other remarkable uses, by making new alloys that are combinations of ceramics and metals—those metals known as the rare earths or lanthanides, I quote for your benefit as I know you will be interested. What do you call it when it is partly ceramic and partly metal? "Structured slurries"—and thus the company name. Exact elements and amounts in these slurries are, of course, closely guarded industrial secrets. Great portions of the lab were closed to me, and really all I got to see was Doris's office and a storage room, where she keeps rejected materials for use in her sculpting. Seeing the raw material of her art made me understand better what she had told me about allowing the shapes of the original objects to suggest the finished sculptures; the work is a kind of collaboration between her and the collective scientific/industrial enterprise of which she is a part. The artist in her stimulated by what the scientist in her reveals. Results are wonderful. I will enclose a photo of the piece she gave me, so you can see what I mean.

. . . Romance here has gone badly awry for my friend Kevin, alas; his beloved Ramona has returned to her ex the mayor, leaving Kevin disconsolate. I have seldom seen such unhappiness. To tell you the truth I didn't think he had it in him, and it was hard to watch—somewhat like watching a wounded dog that cannot comprehend its agony.

Because of my own experience with E in the last year in Chicago, I felt that I knew what he was going through, and although I am not good at this kind of thing, I determined to help cheer him up. Besides, if I didn't, it seemed uncertain that my house would ever become habitable. Work on it has slowed to a remarkable degree.

So I decided to take him to the theater. Catharsis, you know. Yes, I was wrong—there is theater in Orange County—I discovered it some weeks ago. A last survivor down in Costa Mesa, a tiny group working out of an old garage. It only holds fifty or sixty people, but they keep it filled.

Kevin had never seen a play performed—they just aren't interested here! But he had heard of it, and I explained more of the concept to him on our way there. I even got a car, so we could arrive in clothes unsoaked by sweat. He was impressed.

The little company was doing *Macbeth*, but only by doubling and even tripling the parts. Kevin had heard the name, but was unfamiliar with the story. He was also unfamiliar with the concept of doubling, so that in the first two acts he was considerably confused, and kept leaning over to ask me why the witch was now a soldier, etc. etc.

But the way he fell into it! Oh Claire, I wish you could have seen it. This is a society of talkers, and Kevin is one of them; he understood the talkiness of the Elizabethans perfectly, the verbal culture, the notion of the soliloquy, the rambling on —it was like listening to Hank or Gabriela, it was perfectly natural to him.

And yet he had no idea what might happen next! And the company—small in number, young, inexperienced, they nevertheless had that burning intensity you see in theater people—and the two principals, a bit older than the rest but not much, were really fine: Macbeth utterly sympathetic, his desire to be king somehow pure, idealistic—and Lady Macbeth just as ambitious, but harder, hard and hot. The two of them together, arguing over whether or not to murder Duncan—oh it crackled, there was a heat in their faces, in the room! You really could believe it was the first time they had ever made this decision.

And for Kevin it was. I glanced over at him from time to time, and I swear it was like looking at a dictionary of facial expressions. How many emotions can the human face reveal? It was a kind of test. Macbeth had taken us into his inner life, into his soul, and we were on his side (this achievement is necessary for the play to succeed, I believe) and Kevin was sitting there rooting for him, at least at first. But then to watch him, following his ambition down into brutality, madness, monstrosity—and always that same Macbeth, still there, suffering at the insane choices he was making, appalled at what he had become! Fear, triumph, laughter at the lewd porter, apprehension, wincing pain, disgust, pity, despair at the skyrocket futility of all ambition: you could read it all on Kevin's face, twisting about into Greek masks, into Rodin shapes—the play had caught him, he watched it *as if it were really happening*. And the little company, locked in, absorbed, vibrant, burning with it—I tell you, I myself began to see it new! Thick shells of experience, expectation, and habit cracked, and near the end, when Macbeth stood looking down at Birnam Wood, wife dead, tomorrow and tomorrow and tomorrow, I sat in my chair shuddering as much as Kevin. Then Macduff killed him, but who could cheer? That was us, in him.

When the "house lights" came on Kevin slumped in his seat

beside me, mouth open—pummeled, limp, drained. The two of us left the garage leaning against each other for support. People glanced at us curiously, half smiling.

On the drive home he said, My . . . Lord. Are there more like that?

None quite like that.

Thank God, he said.

But several of Shakespeare's plays are in the same class.

Are they all so *sad?*

The tragedies are very sad. The comedies are very funny. The problem plays are extremely problematic.

Whew, he said. I've never seen anything like that.

Ah, the power of theater. I blessed little South Coast Repertory in their little garage, and Kevin and I agreed we would go back again.

. . . I don't know whether to tell you about this or not. It was very odd. I don't know . . . how to think of it. The things that are happening to me!

One night I went out into the backyard, to pick some avocados. Suddenly I had an odd sensation, and as if compelled I looked back into the house. There under my lamps sat a couple, both reading newspapers, one on the couch, the other in my armchair. The woman had a Siamese cat in her lap.

I was startled—in fact, terrified. But then the man looked up, over his spectacles at the woman; and I felt a wave flow through me, a wave of something like calmness, or affection. It was so reassuring that all of a sudden I felt welcomed, somehow, and again as if impelled I went to the glass door to go inside, unafraid. But when I slid the door to the side, they were no longer visible.

I went in and felt the couch, and it was cold. But there was such a calmness in me! A kind of glow, an upwelling, as if I stood in an artesian well of kindness and love. I felt I was being welcomed to this house. . . .

Now I suppose I won't send this letter. You will think I am losing my mind. Certainly I have considered it. Too much sun out here, California weirdness, etc. etc. No doubt it is true. A lot of things seem to be changing in me. I who spent a night with geese and coyotes, I who saw crows burst out of a tree— But I didn't tell you about those things either. I'm not sure I could.

Still—and this is the important thing, yes?—I am happy. I am happy! You would know what an accomplishment that is. So if I have ghosts I welcome them, as they have welcomed me.

I suppose I can always cut this section and leave the rest.

# 10

For several nights running I barely slept, falling only into that shallow nap consciousness where part of the mind feels it is awake, while another part feels an hour passing between each thought. I would wake completely around three, feeling sick, unable to return even to the miserable half sleep. Toss and turn thinking, trying not to think, thinking.

At dawn I would get up and go to the canteen and drink coffee and try to write. All day I would sit there staring at the page, staring into the blank between my world and the world in my book. Until my hand would shake. Looking around me, looking at what my country was capable of when it was afraid. Seeing the headlines in the newspapers scattered around. Seeing my companions and the state they were in.

And one day I stood up with my notebooks and went outside, around the back of the canteen to the dumpsters. The book was in three thick spiral ring notebooks. I sat cross-legged on the concrete, and started ripping the pages away from the wire spiral, about ten at a time. I tore them up, first crossways, then lengthwise. When I had a little pile of paper I stood and threw the pieces into the dumpster. I did that until all the pages were gone. I tore the cardboard covers away from the spirals, and ripped them up too. The twisted wire spirals were the last things in.

No more utopia for me.

*After that I returned to the canteen and sat just like before,
feeling worse than ever. But there was no point in continuing,
really there wasn't. The time has passed when a utopia could do
anybody any good, even me. Especially me. The discrepancy between it and reality was too much.*

*So I sat there drinking coffee and staring out the window.
One of my dorm mates, he sleeps a couple beds down, came by
with his lunch. Hey Barnyard, he said, where's your book.*

*I threw it away.*

*Oh, no, he said, looking shocked. Hey, man. You can't do
that.*

*Yes I can.*

*Next day, same time, he came by with a ballpoint and a gray
lab notebook. Something from the hospital no doubt.*

*Here, man, you start writing again. Deadly serious look on
his face. You got to tell what happens here! If you don't tell it,
then who will? You got to, man. And he left the notebook and
walked away.*

*So. I will not write that book. But here, now, I make these
notes. To pass the time if nothing else. I observe: there is less
desperation here than one would think. There is a refusal of despair. There is a state beyond panic. There is a courage that should
shame the rest of us. There is a camp, an American internment
camp, where every day people are taken to the hospital, where
the others help them out, and carry on. There is a place where
people on the edge of death make jokes, they help each other, they
share what they have, they endure. In this hell they make their
own "utopia."*

Life at sea suited Tom. Nadezhda and he had a tiny cabin to bump
around in, a berth barely wide enough to fit the two of them. At
night the rhythmic pitch over the groundswell translated to the roll
and press of her body against him, so that she became an expression
of the sea, an embrace of wind and wave. He had forgotten the
simple pleasure of sharing a bed. At dawn, if she was still sleeping,

he rose and went on deck. The raw morning light. There he was, on the wide ocean's surface, where a few constants of light and color combined to create an infinity of blues. To sail on a blue salt world, ah, God, to think he had gone a lifetime without it, almost missed it! It made him laugh out loud.

At dawn he had the deck almost to himself. Those on watch were usually in the bridge, an enclosed glass-fronted compartment spanning the deck just before the mizzenmast. Once he came across a group that had stayed up all night, to see the green flash at sunrise.

The crew was about equally divided between men and women, and most of them were in their twenties. Their work, their play and their education all spilled into one another. Partying and romance kept them up late every night; they were the most high-spirited group of young people Tom had ever seen, and he could see why. Quite a life. The young women were especially rambunctious. That first rush into an independent life! All youth responds to it, but some are aware it wasn't always like this, that even their parents didn't have such opportunity. So these women cavorted like the dolphins that surfed in the bow wave during certain magic dusks and dawns, tall, dark, hair and eyebrows thick and intensely black. Tom watched them like Ingres in the baths, laughing at their sexiness. Perfect dark skin, rounded limbs, heavy breasts, wide hips, like women from the Kama Sutra who had stepped off the page and forgotten their purpose, become as free as dolphins.

Occasionally he went down to the ship's communications room and called home. He talked to Kevin and learned of the latest developments there, and gave advice when he was asked. He also called Nylphonia and his other friends from time to time, and conferred with them about the search through Heartech's records. There were tendrils of association between Heartech and the

AAMT, but they were tenuous. "We'd probably have to bust AAMT to get Heartech, and that won't be easy."

"I know. But try."


Thunderheads, slate below and blooming white above, showed how high the sky really was. A line of them lofted to the south like a stately row of galleons, and then the ship was underneath them. *Ganesh* rode waves like low hills, wind keening in the rigging. The sailors on watch wound the sails in on power reels, touching buttons on the bridge's huge control board. The masts' airfoil configurations shifted, metal parts squeaking together. Tom and Nadezhda sat in chairs behind and above the sailors, looking out the broad glass window. Their captain, Gurdial Behaguna, dropped by to look over the helmswoman's shoulder at the compass readout. He nodded at them, left. "He's pretty casual," Tom said.

Nadezhda laughed. "This is a small blow, Tom. You should see it in the North Pacific."

Tom watched spray explode away from the bow, then come whipping back on wind and crash to invisibility against their window. "That's the return route, right? So I suppose I will."

She smiled, reached for his hand.


Another day later Tom went aloft with the bosun, Sonam Singh, who had on a tool belt and was going to do some repairs on a tackle block at the starboard end of the main moonsail yard—that is to say, the sixth and highest sail up the mainmast, above the main course, the topsail, the topgallant, the royal, and the skysail. It was as high on the ship as you could get, some two hundred and forty feet above the deck; to Tom it felt like a million. He looked down at the little mouse-sized people scurrying around the model ship down there, and felt his hands clutch at the halyard. They were climbing the weather side, so that the wind would blow them into the halyards rather than away from them. The mast's movement was a slow figure eight, with a couple of quick catches in it. Glancing behind he saw the broad V of the wake, its edges a startling white against the sea's brilliant blue. Fractal arabesques swirled away from the ship's sleek sides. The horizon was a long way away; the patch of world he could see was as round as a plate, and blue everywhere.

"Clip yourself onto this line," Singh told him, pointing to a cable bolted at intervals to the underside of the slender moonsail yard. "Now put your feet on the footrope"—which looped three or four feet under the yard—"and follow me out. And if you would please grab these handles on top of the yard. One step at a time. Okay? Okay."

Tom was in a harness like a rock-climber's, which was clipped to the line under the yard. Even if his foot slipped and his arm gave away, he would still be there, hanging by his chest, swinging far above the deck, but it beat the alternative. "I can't believe sailors used to climb out here without these," he said, shuffling down the footrope.

"Oh, yes, they were a dangerous bunch of men," Singh said, looking back at him, "Are you okay? Are you sure you want to be doing this?"

"Yes."

"Very good. Yes, they would be standing on the footrope and giving their hands to the sails, reefing them or letting them out, tying frozen gasket knots, and sometimes in most wicked weather. They were quite the athletes, there is no doubt of that. Rounding Cape Horn east to west, that would be a trial for anyone."

"Some of them must have fallen."

"Yes, they lost men overboard, no doubt of that. Once a ship lost every man aloft when it gusted hard south of Cape Horn— five men in all. Here we are, at the end. Look at this block, the little runner inside it has pulled itself away from the side. A case of poor manufacturing, if you ask me. Now the line is stuck, and if you tried to reel it in it would snap the line or short the reel.

Here now, you can lean out in your harness if you are wanting, you don't have to hold on like that.''

"Oh." Tom let go and leaned back in his harness, felt the wind and groundswell swirl him about. Up here you could see the pattern the waves made on the sea's surface, long curving swells rippling the reflected sunlight. Blue everywhere. He watched the bosun repair the tackle block, asked him questions about it. "This line allows you to bring down this side of the sail. It is called bunting. Without it you can't use the sail at all.''

Singh concentrated on his screwdriver and the block, swaying about as he worked. He explained some of the network of lines matted below them. "They are beautiful patterns, aren't they? A very pretty technology indeed. Free locomotion for major freight hauling. Hard to believe it was ever abandoned.''

"Wasn't it dangerous? I mean, that last generation of sailing ships, the big ones with five and six masts, most of them came to grief, didn't they?''

"Yes, they did. The *Kopenhagen* and the *Karpfanger* disappeared from the face of the sea. But so did a lot of diesel-driven tubs. As for that particular generation of sailing ships, it was a matter of insufficient materials, and poor weather forecasts, and carrying too much aloft. And some design flaws. It was yet another case of false economies of scale—they built them too big. Bigger as better, pah! When you're burning fuel to transport fuel, then it might look true. Until the ship strikes a reef or catches fire. But if the fuel is the wind, if you're interested in full employment, in safety, in a larger definition of efficiency, then there is nothing like this beauty here. It is big but not too big. Actually it is as big as those old six-masters were, but the design and the materials are much improved. And with radio, and sonar to look at the bottom, and radar to look at the surface, and satellite photos to look at the sky, and the computer to be putting it all together. . . . Ah, it is a beauty, isn't it?''

* * *

They stopped in Corinto, Nicaragua, and had to wait a day to get to the docks, anchored in a long line of ships like theirs. Tom and Nadezhda joined a group going ashore, and they spent the day in the markets behind the docks, buying fruit, an old-fashioned sextant, and clothing light enough to wear in the tropics. Tom sat for an hour in the bird market, fascinated by the vibrant coloration of the tropical birds on sale. "Can they be real?" he said to Nadezhda.

"The parrots and the mynah birds and the quetzals are real. The New Guinea lories are real, though they aren't native to the area. The rest are not real, not in the way you mean. Haven't you ever seen gene-engineered hummingbirds?"

Flashes of saffron, violet, pink, silk blue, scarlet, tangerine. "No, I don't believe I have."

"You need to travel more." She laughed at the look on his face, kissed him, took his arm and pulled him along. "Come on, they make some fine bikes here, that's something you know about."

A day in a tropical market. Sharp smells of cinnamon and clove, the bleating of a pig, the clashing of amplified guitar riffs, the heat, dust, light, noise. Tom followed Nadezhda's lead, dazed.

In the end they spent all the money they had brought ashore. The ship unloaded some microchips, titanium, manganese and wine, and took on coffee, stereo speakers, clothing and gene-engineered seeds.

The following evening, the last before they embarked, they went back ashore and danced the night away, sweating in the warm tropical air. Very late that night they stood on the dance floor swaying slightly, arms around each other, foreheads pressed together, bodies all around them.

They set sail, headed west across the wide Pacific. Endless days in the blue of water and sky. Tom became a connoisseur of clouds. He took more of the geriatric drugs. He spent time in the foretop, he spotted whales and dreamed great dreams. They passed a coral atoll and he dreamed a whole life there, Polynesian sensuousness in the peace of the lagoon.

One balmy evening Nadezhda's class met on the foredeck, and Tom described his part in the struggle to make the international agreements curtailing corporations. "It was like trust busting in Teddy Roosevelt's time. In those days people agreed monopolies were bad because they were bad for business, basically—they cut at the possibility of free trade, of competition. But multinational corporations were a similar thing in a new format—they were big enough to make tacit agreements among themselves, and so it was a cartel world. Governments hated multinationals because they were out of government control. People hated them because they made everyone cogs in machines, making money for someone else you never saw. That was the combination needed to take them on. And even then we nearly lost."

"You talk like it was war," Pravi said scornfully. She was one of the sharpest of Nadezhda's students, well-read, quick-minded, skeptical of her teachers' memories and biases.

"It was war," Tom said, looking at her with interest. In the twilight the whites of her eyes looked phosphorescent, she seemed a dangerous young Hindu woman, a Kali. "They bought people, courts, newspapers—they killed people. And we really had to put the arm on the countries who decided that becoming a corporation haven would be a good source of revenue."

"Put the arm on them," Pravi said angrily. "You superpowers in your arrogance, ordering the world around again—what was it but another form of imperialism. Make the world do what you decide is right! A new kind of colonialism."

Tom shrugged, trying to see her better in the dusk. "People said that when the colonial powers lost sovereignty over their colonies, but kept the power by way of economic arrangements. That was called neo-colonialism, and I see the point of it. But look, the mechanisms of control and exploitation in the neo-colonialist set-up were precisely the corporations themselves. As home markets were saturated it became necessary to invest abroad to keep profits up, and so the underdeveloped world was sub-sumed.''

"Exactly.''

"All right, all right. But then to cut the corporations up, distribute their assets down through their systems to constituent businesses—this amounted to a massive downloading of capital, a redistribution of wealth. It was new, sure, but to call it neo-colonialism is just to confuse things. It was actually the dismantling of neo-colonialism.''

"By fiat! By the command of the superpowers, telling the rest of the world what to do, in imperial style! Putting the arm on them, as you put it!''

"Well look, we haven't always had the kind of international accords that now exist to take global action. The power of the United Nations is a fairly recent development in history. So some coercion by powerful countries working together was a political necessity. And at the time I'm speaking of capital was very mobile, it could move from country to country without restraint. If one country decided to become a haven, then the whole system would persist.''

"At that point third world countries would have been in power, and the superpowers would have become colonies. You couldn't have had that.''

"But the haven countries wouldn't have had the power. They might have skimmed away something in taxes, but in essence they would become functionaries of the corporations they hosted. That's how powerful corporate capitalism was. You just have no idea nowadays.''

"We only know that once again you decided our fate for us.''

"It took everyone to do it,'' Tom said. ''A consensus of world opinion, governments, the press. A revolution of all the people, using the power of government—laws, police, armies— against the very small executive class that owned and ran the multinationals.''

"What do you mean, a revolution?'' another student asked.

"We changed the law so much, you see. We cut the corporate world apart. The ones that resisted and skipped to haven countries had their assets seized, and distributed to local parts. We left loose networks of association, but the actual profits of any unit company were kept within it in a collective fashion, nothing sucked away.''

"A quiet revolution,'' Nadezhda said, trying to help out.

"Yes, certainly. All this took years, you understand. It was done in steps so that it didn't look so radical—it took two working generations. But it was radical, because now there's nothing but small businesses scattered everywhere. At least in the legal world. And that's a radical change.''

Accusing, triumphant, Pravi pointed a finger at him. "So the United States went socialist!''

"No, not exactly. All we did was set limits on the more extreme forms of greed.''

"By nationalizing energy, water and land! What is that but socialism?''

"Yeah, sure. I mean, you're right. But we used it as a way to give everyone the opportunity to get ahead! Basic resources were made common property, but in the service of a more long-distance self-interest—''

"Altruism for the sake of self-interest!'' Pravi said, disgusted. Her aggression, her hatred of America—it irritated Tom, made him sad. Enemies everywhere, still, after all these years, even among the young. What you sow you will reap, he thought. Unto the seventh generation.

"Sociobiologists say it's always that way,'' he said. "Some doubt the existence of altruism, except as a convoluted form of self-interest.''

"Imperialism makes one cynical about human nature,'' Pravi

said. "And you know as well as I that the human sciences are based on philosophical beliefs."

"No doubt." He shrugged. "What do you want me to say? The economic system was a pyramid, and money ran up to the top. We chopped the pyramid off and left only the constituent parts down at the base, and gave the functions that higher parts of the pyramid served over to government, without siphoning off money, except for public works. This was either altruism on the largest scale ever seen in modern times, or else very enlightened self-interest, in that with wealth redistributed in this way, the wars and catastrophes that would have destroyed the pyramid were averted. I suppose it is a statement of one's philosophy to say whether it was one or the other."

Pravi waved him away. "You saw the end coming and you ran. Like the British from India."

"You needn't be angry at us for saving you the necessity of violent revolution," Tom said, almost amused. "It might have been dramatic, but it wouldn't have been fun. I knew revolutionaries, and their lives were warped, they were driven people. It's not something to get romantic about."

Insulted, Pravi walked away, down the deck. The class muttered, and Nadezhda gave them a long list of reading assignments, then called it off for the night.

Later, standing up near the bowsprit, looking at stars reflected on the water, Tom sighed. The air was humid, the tropical night cloaked them like a blanket. "I wonder when we will lose the stigma," he said to Nadezhda softly.

"I don't know. We'll never see it."

"No." He shook his head, upset. "We did the best we could, didn't we?"

"Yes. When they shoulder the responsibility themselves, they'll understand."

"Maybe."

* * *

Another night he was called down to the communications room to receive a call from Nylphonia. She looked pleased, and said "I think you have Heartech and the AAMT in violation of Fazio-Matsui. Look here."

The AAMT had put Heartech's black account into a Hong Kong bank, but the funds were "washed but not dried," as Nylphonia put it. Still traceable. Some information had been stolen from the bank, and it corresponded perfectly with electronic money orders that had been recorded in passage through the phone system, going from Heartech to the AAMT. It would not be enough to convict them in court, but it would convince most people that the connection existed—that the accusation had not been concocted out of thin air. So it was sufficient for their purposes.

Tom nodded. "Good. Send a copy of this along to me, will you? And thanks, Nylphonia."

Well, he thought. Very interesting. Next time Kevin and Doris went into the council meeting, they could use this like a bomb. Make the accusation, present the evidence, show that the proposed development on Rattlesnake Hill had illegal funds behind it. End of that.

He thought of the little grove on the top of the hill, and grinned.


The next dawn he slipped out of their berth, dressed and went on deck. They were tacking close-hauled to a strong east wind, and rode over the swells at an angle, corkscrewing with the pitch and yaw. The bow was getting soaked with spray, so Tom went to the midships rail, on the windward side. He wrapped an arm through the bottom of the mainmast halyards to steady himself. The cables were vibrating. Time after time *Ganesh* ran down the back of one swell and thumped its port bow into the steep side of the next, and white spray flew up from the bow, then was caught by the wind and blown over the bowsprit in a big, glittering fan. The sky was a pale limpid blue, and the sun caught the fans of bow spray in such a way that for a second or two each of them was transformed into a broad, intense rainbow. Giddy slide down a swell, dark blue sea, the jolt as they ran into the next swell, blast of spray out, up, caught in the wind and dashed to droplets, and then a still moment, the ship led by a pouring arch of vibrant color, red orange yellow green blue purple.

Captain Bahaguna was on the other side of the deck, helping a couple of crew members secure metal boxes over the rigging reels. It was tricky crossing the deck in such a swell. "What's up, Captain?"

"Storm coming." He looked disgruntled. "I've been trying to get around to the north of it for two days now, but it's swerving like a drunk."

Tom toed the box. "We'll need these?"

"Never can tell. I do it if we have the time. Ever been in a big storm?"

"That one off Baja."

Bahanguna looked up at Tom, smiled.

Below decks Sonam Singh was showing a group of sailors how to secure bulkheads. "Tom, go check out the bridge, you're in the way." The young sailors laughed as they worked, excited. Immersion in the world's violence, Tom thought, the primal thrill of being out in the wind. In the tempest of the world's great spin through space.

In the comm room Pravi was studying a satellite photo of the mid-Pacific. Pressure isobars overlaid on it contoured the mishmash of cloud patterns, drew attention to a small classic whirlpool shape. "Is it a hurricane?" Tom asked.

"Only a tropical storm," Pravi said. "It might get upgraded, though."

"Where are we?"

She jabbed at the map. Not far away from the storm.

"And which direction is it moving?"

"Depends on when you ask. It's coming our way now."

"Uh oh."

She laughed. "I love these storms."

"How many have you seen?"

"Two so far. But it's going to be three in a couple of hours."

Another thrill seeker. Revolution of the elements.

Tom returned to the deck, holding on to every rail. Things had changed in his brief stay below; the sea was running larger, and the horizon seemed to have extended away, as if they were now on a larger planet. *Ganesh* seemed smaller. It sledded down the long backs of the swells like a toboggan, shouldering deep into the trough and then rising like a cork to crash through the crest and hang in space. Then a free fall, until the bow crashed down onto the water, and they began another exuberant run on the back of the next swell. Except for this moment of skating, it felt like the ship's whole motion was up and down.

The wind still drove spray to the side in fanned white torrents, but the rainbows were gone, the sun too high and obscured by a high white film, which dulled the color of the sea. Off to the south the horizon was a black bar.

A bit dizzy, and fearful of seasickness, Tom found he felt best when he was facing the wind, and looking at the horizon. Seeing was important. He went to the mizzenmast halyards, wrapped his arms around a thick cable, and watched the sea get torn to tatters.


The wind picked up. Spray struck his face like needle pricks. It was loud. The swells had crest-to-trough whitecaps, which hissed and roared. The wind keened in the rigging at a score of pitches, across several octaves, from the bass thrum of the mast stays to the screaming of the bunting. Behind these noises was a kind of background rumble, which seemed to be the sound of the storm itself, disconnected from any source in wind or water: a dull low roar, like an immense submarine locomotive. Perhaps it was the wind in his ears, but it sounded more like the entire atmosphere, trying to leave the vicinity all at once.

Nadezhda appeared at his side, holding an orange rain jacket. "Put this on. Aren't you going below?"

"It made me dizzy!" They were shouting.

"We had one of these on the way over from Tokyo," Nadezhda said, looking at the long hog-backed hills of water surging by. "Lasted three days! You'll have to get used to being below."

"Not yet." He pointed to the black line on the southern horizon. "I'll have to when that arrives."

Nadezhda nodded. "Big squall."

"Pravi said it was almost a hurricane."

"I believe it." She laughed, licked salt off her upper lip. Face flushed and wet, eyes bright and watering. Fingers digging into his upper arm. "So wild, the sea! The place we can never ever tame."

Above them narrow rectangles of sail got even narrower. Most of the ship's sails were furled, and the ones out were down to their last reef. Still the ship was pushing well onto its side. They hung from the halyards as the ship plunged up and down. "Can you imagine having to go aloft!" Tom cried.

"No."

The ship shuddered through a thick crest. White water coursed down the lee rail of the deck. "We'd better get below," Nadezhda said. And indeed Sonam Singh was in the hatchway gesturing fiercely at them. As the ship skated down a swell they dashed for the hatchway, were pulled roughly down it.

"Keep inside," Singh ordered. "Go to the bridge if you want to see, but stay out of the way."

Crew members rushed by, dripping wet and bright with exhilaration. "They're going on deck?" Tom asked.

"Setting the sea anchor," Singh replied, and followed them out.

The passageways seemed narrower. You had to use the wall for support, or be banged against it. Up broad steps to the bridge, which was split into two rooms, one above the other. The top room was the cockpit of action; Captain Bahaguna and the helmsman were standing before the window watching the ship and waves through crazy patterns of water dashed against the glass. The fourth mast stood before them like a white tree. The lee railing, to starboard, was running just above the water, and crests boiled right over it and coursed back to the stern. That gave Tom a shock—the ship, buoyant as it was, still shouldered through the water like a submarine coming to the surface. The sky was a very dark gray now, and the broken white sea glowed strangely under it.

The captain watched the control terminal. It had a red light blinking among the greens. "We'll probably lose that sail," Bahaguna said, then saw Tom. "That block is stuck again. Here, get into the room below and get strapped into a seat. The real squall is about to hit."

The horizon had disappeared, replaced by a gray wall. They got to the room below holding onto rails with both hands, sat in empty chairs and fastened the seat belts.

They were headed straight into the waves. The bowsprit spiked an onrushing white hill of boiling water, lifted up a big mess of it that rushed down the deck, sluicing off both sides, until a wave some four feet high smashed into their window and erased the view. The light had a greenish cast in these blinded intervals. The ship moved sluggishly under the weight. Then the wave fell to the sides, and they could see gray clouds flying by just over the mast. Irregular thickets of water flew by, rain or spray, it was impossible to tell.

"The sea anchor's out," Nadezhda said. "That's what got us head on."

Soon Sonam Singh and part of the sea anchor detail came

through, utterly drenched, moving as if in an acrobat's game. "We did it. Glad the storm lines are rigged on deck, I'll tell you."

So they were moving backwards in the storm, pulling a sea anchor. It was a tube of thick fabric, shaped like a wind sock, with its larger end connected to a cable that ran back to the ship's bow. As waves thrust the ship sternwards the sea anchor dragged before them, insuring that the bow faced into every wave, which was the only safe angle in seas like this. It was an ancient method, and still the most reliable.

The squall struck. The roar redoubled, the glass blurred completely. Nothing but patterns of gray on white. The sailors left the bridge like dancers on trampolines.

Bursts of wind stripped the water from the glass like a squeegee, and Tom saw a world transformed, no longer a place of air over water, atmosphere over ocean. Now the two were mixed in a bubbling white mass, and whole swells of foamy salt water were torn off the ocean surface and dashed through the air. The wind was trying to tear the surface of the ocean flat.

The bare masts themselves functioned as sails in a wind like this. All the rigging that extended forward was tauter than bowstrings, straight as theoretical lines of geometry; they gave off a thrumming that could be heard inside the bridge. On the other hand many of the lines supporting spars from the stern were slack, whipped back and forth so rapidly that they blurred in the middle. The masts and yards flexed in bows that were visible to the eye.

Another wave buried the window and it was back to the aquarium view, the murky green-black light.

Up and down the ship rode. They felt more than saw the bow shouldering through hills of water. The noise was unbelievable, like several jets taking off at once. Up and down, up and down, up and down. Tom got used to the motion, he was no longer dizzy, even in the weightless sweeps downward. Time passed. He fell into a bit of a trance, induced by the weird submarine light, interspersed with sudden glimpses of night-in-day chaos, seen with a strange clarity broken by lightning lines of water streaming over the glass. He was not getting used to the storm so much as being overwhelmed by it—making a psychic retreat from the infinity of watery assaults. The mind had to retreat from such mindless intensity.

A long time passed that way, with only occasional snatches of a view, always the same: flying mix of wind and water, under a black sky. Tom's hands and wrists were tired, weary from holding his chair arms. He needed to pee. Could he make it to the head?

Suddenly the noise dropped, the light grew. The motion of the ship eased, and when the window next cleared he saw white clouds scudding overhead. "The eye," Sonam Singh said, passing through on his way to the captain.

"I'm going to go to our berth and lie down," Nadezhda said. "I'm exhausted."

"Be careful getting there."

"I'll be wrapped to the rail."

"I'll come down later and see how you are."

"Fine." Off she went, balancing skillfully.

Up on the bridge they were discussing damage to the rigging. Tom stood carefully, staggered to the head. Peed with his shoulders banging wall to wall. The water in the bowl surged up and down. He felt battered, as if the little balancing mechanisms in his ears were still rattling about. Better to be seated, to have something to look at.

He got back to his seat and clipped in gratefully. Captain Bahaguna was giving rapid orders. "When it hits again it'll be from the southeast. We'll come about now.'' Crew members ran through. Pravi stopped to see how he was, said, ''Don't you think the water surface is higher, like we're on a kind of hill? A kind of big, low waterspout under the low pressure, don't you think?''

Tom saw nothing of the sort. Green swells covered with white foam, white clouds stuffed with green rain. Off to the south was a black island: ''Is that land!'' Tom cried, frightened.

''Other side of the storm,'' she said. ''We've got about twenty minutes.''

The captain shouted at Singh about the sail that wouldn't furl. ''It'll break the yard off and probably the pole too!''

''Nothing we can do about it, sir.''

Then the explosive roar of the wind hit again. The ship heeled far to starboard; Tom thought they were going to turn turtle. It seemed a bomb was going off continuously. The window cleared and he saw the waves grown huge again, iron flecked with ivory, tops torn off, but still thirty, forty, perhaps fifty feet tall! When they were in a trough the next crest dwarfed the ship, it struggled up the side of the wave like a toy boat. ''My God,'' Tom said, appalled. A wave engulfed them, and the glass showed only rushing darkness. The roar was muffled. They were underwater.

The ship shouldered up, broke to the surface and the howling wind.

Before them another wave as big as the one before, or bigger. Extending off to left and right as far as he could see. He was holding his breath, willing the ship to rise faster. The bowsprit seemed bent at a higher angle than before. The wave, a liquid hillside, a ridge collapsing on them, was dotted with a flurry of black dots.

''What are those!'' he shouted, but no one heard him. Then they were flying up like the bob on a fishing line yanked from the water, up the wave hillside to the avalanching crest, inundated as if the wave were a broken dam, and Tom felt it through the chair: *whump*.

* * *

The ship was struggling in a different way. Sluggishly. The bow
slewed off to port. Shouts came from above. Long minutes passed.
Sonam Singh staggered by on hands and knees. "We hit something!" he cried at Tom.

"I saw it!" Tom said. "Wreckage—lumber, maybe."

He couldn't tell if Singh had heard, he was shouting something
about the sea anchor.

Then the room rolled onto its side. Tom found himself hanging
by his seatbelt. Only his hipbones saved him from being cut in
half. Muffled roar, underwater again. In the gloom people shouted.
Singh was over on one wall. The ship shuddered violently, turned,
righted itself. Some noise and light returned. Tom glanced through
the window as he freed himself from the seat. Another white
mountain smoking toward them, in the mind-numbing howl. Mainmast and second mast were both bent, held in a tangle of alloy
and rope rigging. The deck around the foremast was twisted, perhaps buckled. The ship listed to port.

He got the seatbelt undone and hung from the chair back.
Time passed. People behind him were shouting, but he couldn't
turn his head to see. Then Sonam Singh grabbed him. Captain
Bahaguna was crawling down the ladder from the bridge, followed
by Pravi and the helmsman.

They had a shouted conference: "—lifeboats!" Singh said
into the captain's ear. Then mouth collided with ear, hard, and
they both cried out, held their heads.

"No lifeboat could survive in this!" Tom shouted loudly,
suddenly afraid.

Singh shook his head. "They're submarine, remember? We
go under. Then wait."

"The ship won't sink," Bahaguna said. He didn't like the
idea.

"No, but we don't know what compartments might flood.
The bows are breached, and the other masts might go. More dan-

gerous here than in the boats. While the launch bay is still clear perhaps we should be getting out. We can come back when the storm has passed.''

Inundated again. The ship listed far to port. Slowly water washed away from the glass. White foam, a moving hill of water. Under again. There were red lights all over the panel. The glass cleared and was instantly covered with water again.

A few more swells, sluggish response of the ship. Getting worse. A few more.

Finally the captain nodded, looking grim. ''Okay. Abandon ship.''

They all crawled to the passageway leading aft. Suddenly they were in the muffled dark again, crawling on the wall. Sonam Singh was cursing. ''Damned lumber ships, they lose their deck loads—'' He saw a group of tumbling bodies ahead, raised his voice to a bellow: ''Slow down up there! Slow down! Everyone to launch bays!'' But the bodies rushed on. The lifeboats were near the stern, Tom had remembered all about them. They would be fired out like ejection seats in an old jet fighter. He and Nadezhda had been given a tour—oh my God, he thought. Nadezhda!

Their cabin was just below and behind the second mast.

He turned down the steps to the tweendecks, ran forward on the meeting of wall and floor. He had been a sprinter most of his life, and now it all came back to him. A real scramble. He had done something to his left wrist, the hand wouldn't move well and the wrist hurt with a stabbing pain that went up his arm. He came to the passageway that led to their cabin. Several inches of water slopped over deck or wall, whichever was down. Thrown down, and on that hand again. He yanked open their door. The cabin was empty. Good. Water sloshed at knee height. The ship was permanently on its port side, but he needed to get starboard and aft, where the launch bays were. Storm muffled, ship underwater, he could hear his breath surging in and out of him in big gasps. Nadezhda must already be back there. This intersection of passageways didn't look familiar. Shit, he thought. Not a time to get lost! He held a railing, tried to recover his breath. Up steps, water sloshing, the compartment had been breached, or not sealed off from breached compartments further forward. Around a corner, down another passageway, up steps. Water followed him. Shocking to have water inside the ship. He cracked his forehead, a nice hard spot that, no harm done. Needed to get starboard, water at thigh level and his left hand didn't work. He was tired, arms and legs like blocks of wood, they didn't want to move. Okay, a long passageway fore and aft, hustle down it aft, almost there. Sonam Singh would be mad at him, but he had had to check.

The passageway turned and ended in a closed hatchway. Good enough, beyond that would be an unbreached compartment. But he had to get it open and get through. Warmish salt water foamed up around his waist as he worked the dogs of the hatch one-handed, left arm thrust under a railing to hold him. So many locks on these bulkhead doors! He was in danger of getting knocked over, drowned while inside the ship. Had to go under foam to get to the bottom dogs, and they were stiff as hell. Okay, last one. Flash of triumph as he put his weight on the handle and pushed out. The door was snatched from his good hand and the water behind him shoved him over the coping and right out the door—onto the open deck of the ship. Wrong hatch! He dug with his feet, trying to get a purchase and get back inside. Then water surged up around him and he was off and away, swept away helplessly. His leg hit something and he grasped for it. Caught it, had his grip torn away. Then he was tumbling underwater, thrashed in a soup as if body surfing. Instinctively he clawed upward, broke the surface with lungs bursting, took in a big gasp of air and foam, choked and was rolled under again.

Free of the ship, he thought. Probably so. Fear took all the air out of his lungs. Desperately he swam, up and up and up. He got to the surface and trod the boiling surface furiously. Yes, free of the ship. Couldn't see it anywhere. Overboard in a hurricane, "No!" he cried out, the word wrenched from him. Then under again and reeling, lungs burning as he held on. Drowned for sure, just a matter of time. He clawed madly to the surface, too frightened to let go. Another breath, another. He looked around for the ship, saw nothing. Too tired to move, and at the bottom of a trough with a wave forty feet high over his head. Hell.

Under again and somersaulting. Punched in the stomach. No way to tell up from down. This had happened to him body surfing as a kid, he had almost drowned three or four times. Swim to shore. He forced his eyes open. Green white black. He had to breathe, he couldn't breathe, he had to breathe and it was water he breathed; feeling it he choked in panic and thrashed upward and held his breath again, and then breathed in and out and in and out and in and out; and all of it water. Helpless to stop himself. He felt the water heavy inside him, lungs and stomach both, and marveled that he was still conscious, still thinking. You really do get a last moment, he thought. What do you know.

And indeed he felt an enormous liquid clarity growing in him, like a flash of something or other. It was quiet and blue black white, a riot of bubbles flying in every direction around him, glowing. Blue capture plate, white quarks. Done for. Relax. Concentrate. He cast his mind deliberately back to his wife, her face, his baby held easily in his hands, and then the images tumbled, a forested cliff over ocean, a window filled with blue sky and clouds, swirling like bubbles of nothing in the rich blue field of the life he had lived, every day of it his and Pamela's, and the crying out of his cells for oxygen felt like the pain of all that love given and lost, nothing of it saved, nothing but the implosion of drowning, the euphoria of release—and all the blue world and its blue beauty tumbled around him, flashed white and he snapped alert, wanting to speak, pregnant with a thought that would never be born.

# 11

*Out.*

*How I hugged that lawyer. He just looked tired. Lucky, he said. Procedural irregularity.*

*He drove me to a restaurant. Looking out the car window, stunned. Everything looked different. Fragile. Even America is fragile. I didn't know that before.*

*At the restaurant we drank coffee.*

*What will you do? the lawyer said.*

*I didn't have the faintest idea. I don't know, I said. Go to New York and meet my wife's ship when it comes in. Get cross country to my kid, find some kind of work. Survive.*

*There was a newspaper on the next table but I couldn't look at it. Crisis to crisis, we're too close to the edge, you can feel the slippage in the heat of the air.*

*And suddenly I was telling him about it, the heat, the barbed wire, the nights in the dorm, the presence of the hospital, the fear, the courage of all those inside. It's not fair, I said, my voice straining. They shouldn't be able to do that to them! I seized the newsaper, shook it. They shouldn't be able to do any of this!*

*I know, the lawyer said, sipping his coffee and looking at me. But people are afraid. They're afraid of what's happening, and they're afraid of the changes we would make to stop it from happening.*

*But we've got to change! I cried.*

*The lawyer nodded. Do you want to help?*

*What do you mean?*

*Do you want to help change things?*

*Of course I do! Of course, but how? I mean I tried, when I lived in California I tried as hard as I could. . . .*

*Look, Mr. Barnard, he said. Tom. It takes more than an individual effort. And more than the old institutions. We've started an organization here in Washington, DC, so far it's sort of a multi-issue lobbying group, but essentially we're trying to start a new political party, something like the Green parties in Europe.*

*He described what they were doing, what their program was. Change the law of the land, the economic laws, the environmental laws, the relationship between local and global, the laws of property.*

*Now there're laws forbidding that kind of change, I said. That's what they were trying to get me on.*

*We know. There are people afraid of us, you see. It's a sign we're succeeding. But there's a long way to go. It's going to be a battle. And we can use all the help we can get. We know what you were doing in California. You could help us. You shouldn't just go out there and survive, that would be a waste. You should stay here and help.*

*I stared at him.*

*Think about it, he said.*

*So I thought about it. And later I met with some of his colleagues, and talked about this new party, and met more people, and talked some more. And I saw that there is work here that I can do.*

*I'm going to stay. There's a job and I'll take it. Work for Pam, too. Talked to her on the ship-to-shore, and she sounded pleased. A job, after all, and her kind of work. My kind of work.*

*It didn't take all that much to convince me, really. Because I have to do something. Not just write a utopia, but fight for it in the real world—I have to, I'm compelled to, and talking with one of the people here late one night I suddenly understood why:*

*because I grew up in utopia, I did. California when I was a child was a child's paradise, I was healthy, well fed, well clothed, well housed, I went to school and there were libraries with all the world in them and after school I played in orange groves and in Little League and in the band and down at the beach and every day was an adventure, and when I came home my mother and father created a home as solid as rock, the world seemed solid! And it comes to this, do you understand me—I grew up in utopia.*

*But I didn't. Not really. Because while I was growing up in my sunny seaside home much of the world was in misery, hungry, sick, living in cardboard shacks, killed by soldiers or their own police. I had been on an island. In a pocket utopia. It was the childhood of someone born into the aristocracy, and understanding that I understood the memory of my childhood differently; but still I know what it was like, I lived it and I know! And everyone should get to know that, not in the particulars, of course, but in the general outline, in the blessing of a happy childhood, in the lifelong sense of security and health.*

*So I am going to work for that. And if—if! if someday the whole world reaches utopia, then that dream California will become a precursor, a sign of things to come, and my childhood is redeemed. I may never know which it will be, it might not be clear until after we're dead, but the future will judge us! They will look back and judge us, as aristocrats' refuge or emerging utopia, and I want utopia, I want that redemption and so I'm going to stay here and fight for it, because I was there and I lived it and I know. It was a perfect childhood.*

Kevin was working at Oscar's place when he heard the news. He was up on the roof finishing the seal and trim around the bedroom skylights, and Pedro, Ramona's father, came zooming up on his hill bike, skidding to a stop on the sidewalk. "Kevin?" he called.

"Yeah, Pedro! What's up?"

Serious look, hands on hips. "Get down here, I've got bad news."

Kevin hustled down the ladder, heart thumping, thinking something's happened to her, she's hurt and wants me there.

"It's Tom," Pedro said as he reached the ground. Kevin's heart leaped in a different direction. Just the look on Pedro's face told him. Deep furrow between his eyebrows. He grasped Kevin's upper arm. "Their ship was wrecked in a storm, and Tom—he was washed overboard."

"He what?"

It took some explaining, and Pedro didn't have all the particulars. Gradually it dawned on Kevin that they didn't matter. Killed by a storm. Lost at sea. Details didn't matter.

He sat on a workhorse. Oscar's front yard was cluttered with their stuff, dusty in the sun. He couldn't believe it.

"I thought ships didn't sink these days." Proud *Ganesh* flying away from Newport's jetties.

"It didn't really sink, but a lot of compartments flooded, and they judged it safer to get out into the lifeboats in case it did sink. It's still out there wrecked, dead in the water. I guess it was a typhoon, and they got hit by a load of lumber, tore the ship all up."

Pedro was holding his arm again. Looking up Kevin saw on his face the strain of telling him, the bunched jaw muscles. He looked as much like Ramona as a short gray-haired sixty-year-old man could, and suddenly a spasm of grief arrowed through Kevin's numbness. "Thanks for telling me." Pedro just shook his head. Kevin swallowed. From his Adam's apple down he was numb. He still had a putty knife in his hand. It was Pedro's kindness he felt most, it was that that would make him weep. He stared at the dirt, feeling the hand on his arm.

Pedro left.

He stood in Oscar's yard, looking around. Working alone this afternoon. Was that better or worse? He couldn't decide. He was a lot more solitary than he used to be. He climbed back onto the roof, returned to work on the trim around the skylights. Putty. He sat on the roof, stared at it. When he was a kid he and Tom had hiked in the hills together, sun just up and birds in the trees. Bushwhacking while Tom claimed to be on an animal trail. They'd get lost and Kevin would say, "Animal trail, right Grandpa?" Seven years old and Tom laughing like crazy. Once Kevin tripped and skinned both knees bad and he was about to scream when Tom grabbed him up and exclaimed like it was a great deed, an extraordinary opportunity, and pulled up his own pantlegs to reveal the scars on his knees, then had taken out his Swiss army knife and nicked a scar on each knee, touched their four wounds together and then actually sucked blood from Kevin's shins, which had shocked Kevin, and spit it in four directions rattling out the nonsense words of an ancient Indian blood oath, until Kevin was strutting around glowing with pride at his stinging knees, badge of the highest distinction, mark of manhood and oneness with the hills.


That evening and the next day, the whole unwanted raft of condolences. He preferred swimming alone. Laps at the pool, thousands of yards.

He made calls to Jill and his parents. Jill gone as usual. He left a message, feeling bad. He got his mother on screen: weird moment of power and helplessness combined as he gave her the news. Suddenly he appreciated what Pedro had done, to come over and tell him like that. A hard thing to do. The little face on the screen, so familiar—shocked by the news, twisted with grief. After an awkward brief conversation they promised each other they would talk again soon.

Later that day he watched Doris cook a dinner for the house, when it was his turn. "You know we don't have any way to find those friends of his," she said. "I hope they'll get in touch with us."

"Yeah."

She frowned.

*  *  *

He was angry at the crew of *Ganesh*, angry at Nadezhda. Then she reached him on the phone and he saw her, arm in a sling, grim, distracted. He recalled what Tom had told him of her life, a tough one it sounded. She told him what she knew of the wreck. Four other crew members missing, apparently they had been trapped in a forward compartment and had tried to make their way back over the deck. Tom had disappeared in the chaos of the foundering, no one sure what had happened to him. Disappeared. Everyone had thought he was in one of the other lifeboats. She went on until Kevin stopped her. He asked her to come back to El Modena, he wanted her to return, wanted to see her. She said that she would, but she looked tired, hurt, empty. When the call was over he couldn't be sure if she would come or not. And then he really believed in the disaster. Tom was dead.

They finished the work on Oscar's house a couple of weeks later, in the burning heat of late September. They walked around it in their work boots and their greased, creased, and sawdusted workshorts, brown as nuts, checking out every little point, the seal on the suntek and cloudgel, the paint, the computer (ask it odd questions it said "Sorry I fail the Turing test very quickly"), everything. Standing out in the middle of the street and looking at it, they shook Oscar's hand and laughed: it looked like a clear tent draped over one or two small dwellings, red and blue brick facades covered by new greenery. Oscar did a dance shuffle to the front door, singing "I'm the Sheik, of Ar—a—bee" in a horrible baritone. "And your love, belongs, to meee," pirouetting like the hippopotami in *Fantasia*, mugging Valentino-like swoops at Jody and Gabriela, who squeaked "Don't—stop—don't—stop" in unison, pushing him back and forth between them.

Inside they split up and wandered through the rooms, looking things over. Kevin came across Oscar and Hank standing together in the central atrium. Hank said, "These black pillars are neat.

They give it an Egyptian Roman wrapped in plastic look that I like.''

Oscar looked around dazed. "Egyptian Roman, wrapped in plastic,'' he murmured. "I always dreamed of it.''

Kevin went back out front to get a beer from his bike basket.

Ramona appeared down on Laurinda, pedaled up to him. He waved and put down the dumpie, feeling strange. They had talked briefly several days before, after the news about Tom came in. Condolences.

"Hi,'' she said, "How are you?''

"Fine. We're just having a little celebration here.''

"All done?''

"Yep.''

"Hopefully Oscar will have a housewarming?''

"I think so, yeah. This is just an informal thing, the inside's still a mess.''

She nodded. Pursed her lips. The furrow between her eyebrows appeared, reminding Kevin sharply of Pedro. "You okay?'' Ramona said.

"Oh yeah, yeah.''

"Can . . . can I have a talk with you?''

"Sure.''

"Now's not a bad time?''

"No, no. Here, let's walk up the street, if you want.''

She nodded gratefully, eyes to the ground. They walked up the bike path, her bike between them. She seemed nervous, awkward, uncomfortable—as she had been, in fact, ever since her birthday. It made Kevin weary. Looking at her, the long stride, the sun bouncing off glossy black hair, he felt an ache of desire for her *company*—just that, nothing more. That he would lose even her friendship. "Listen, Ramona, it's all right.''

She shook her head. "It's not all right.'' Voice muffled. "I hate what's happened, Kevin, I wish it never would have.''

"No!'' Kevin said, shocked. "Don't say that! It's like saying . . .''

He didn't know how to finish, but she nodded, still looking down. All in a rush she said, "I know, I'm glad too, but I didn't ever want to hurt you and if it means I did and we can't be friends anymore, then I can't help but wish it hadn't happened! I mean, I love you—I love our friendship I mean. I want us to be able to be friends!"

"It's okay, Ramona. We can be friends."

She shook her head, unsatisfied. Kevin rolled his eyes, for the sake of himself alone, for his own internal audience (when had it appeared?). Here he was listening to himself say things again, completely surprised by what he heard coming out of his own mouth.

"Even if—even if . . ." She stopped walking, looked at him straight. "Even if Alfredo and I get married?"

Oh.

So that was it.

Well, Kevin thought, go ahead and say something. Amaze yourself again.

"You're getting married?"

She nodded, looked down. "Yes. We want to. It's been our whole lives together, you know, and we want to . . . do it all. Be a family, and . . ."

Kevin waited, but she appeared to have finished. His turn. "Well," he said. He thought to himself, you make a hell of a crowbar. "That's quite a bit of news," he said. "I mean, congratulations."

"Oh, Kevin—"

"No, no," he said, reaching out toward her, hand stopping; he couldn't bring himself to touch her, not even on the forearm. "I mean it. I want you to be happy, and I know you two are . . . a couple. You know. And I want us to go on being friends. I mean I really do. That's been the worst part of this, almost, I mean you've been acting so un*com*fortable with me—"

"I have been! I've felt terrible!"

He took a deep breath. This was something he had needed to

hear, apparently; it lifted some weights in him. Just under the collarbones he felt lighter somehow. "I know, but . . ." He shrugged. Definitely lighter.

"I was afraid you would hate me!" she said, voice sharp with distress.

"No, no." He laughed, sort of: three quick exhalations. "I wouldn't ever do that."

"I know it's selfish of me, but I want to be your friend."

"Alfredo might not like it. He might be jealous."

"No. He knows what it means to me. Besides, he feels terrible himself. He feels like if he had been different before . . ."

"I know. I talked to him, a little."

She nodded. "So he'll understand. In fact I think he'll feel a lot better about it if we aren't . . . unfriendly."

"Yeah. Well . . ." It seemed he could make the two of them feel better than ever. Great. And himself?

Suddenly he realized that what they were saying now wouldn't really matter. That years would pass and they would drift apart, inevitably. No matter what they said. The futility of talk.

"You'll come to the wedding?"

He blinked. "You want me to?"

"Of course! I mean, if you want to."

He took a breath, let it out. A part of his mind under clamps sprang free and he wanted to say Don't, Ramona, please, what about me? Quick image of the long swing *no*. He couldn't afford to think of it. Find it, catch it, clamp it back down, lock it away. Didn't happen. Never. Never never never never never.

She was saying something he hadn't heard. His chest hurt, his diaphragm was tight. Suddenly he couldn't stand the pretense any more, he looked back down the street, said "Listen, Ramona, I think maybe I should get back. We can talk more later?"

She nodded quickly. Reached out for his forearm and stopped, just as he had with her. Perhaps they would never be able to touch again.

He was walking back down the street. He was standing in

front of Oscar's. Numbness. Ah, what a relief. No pleasure like the absence of pain.

Hank was around the side of the house, loading up his bike's trailer. "Hey, where'd you go?"

"Ramona came by. We were talking."

"Oh?"

"She and Alfredo are going to get married."

"Ah ha!" Hank regarded him with his ferocious squint. "Well. You're having quite a week, aren't you." Finally he reached into his trailer. "Here, bro, have another beer."

Alfredo and Matt's proposition got onto the monthly ballot, and one night it appeared on everyone's TV screens, a long and complex thing, all the plans laid out. People interested typed in their codes and voted. Just under six thousand of the town's ten cared enough to vote, and just over three thousand of them voted in favor of the proposition. Development as described to be built on Rattlesnake Hill.

"Okay," Alfredo said at the next council meeting, "let's get back to this matter of rezoning Rattlesnake Hill. Mary?"

Ingratiating as ever, Mary read out the planning commission's latest draft, fitted exactly to the proposition.

"Discussion?" Alfredo said when she was done.

Silence. Kevin stirred uncomfortably. Why was this falling to him? There were hundreds of people in town opposed to the plan, thousands. If only the indifferent ones had voted!

But Jean Aureliano was not opposed to the plan. Nor her party. So it was up to the people who really cared. The room was hot, people looked tired. Kevin opened his mouth to speak.

But it was Doris who spoke first, in her hardest voice. "This plan is a selfish one thrust on the community by people more interested in their own profit than in the welfare of the town."

"Are you talking about me?" Alfredo said.

"Of course I'm talking about you," Doris snapped. "Or did you think I had in mind the parties behind you putting up the capital? But they don't live here, and they don't care. It's only profits to them, more profits, more power. But the people who live here do care, or they should. That land has been kept free of construction through all the years of rampant development, to destroy it now would be disgusting. It would be a wanton act of destruction."

"I don't agree," Alfredo said, voice smooth. But he had been stung to speech, and his eyes glittered angrily. "And obviously the majority of the town's voters don't agree."

"We know that," Doris said, voice as sharp as a nail. "But what we have never heard yet from you is a coherent explanation of why this proposed center of yours should be located on the hill instead of somewhere else in the town, or in some other town entirely."

Alfredo went through his reasons again. The prestige, the esthetic attraction of it, the increased town shares. On each point Doris assailed him bitterly. "You can't make us into Irvine or Laguna, Alfredo, if you want that you should move there."

Alfredo defended himself irritably. The other council members pitched in with their opinions. Doris mentioned Tom, started to tell them what Tom had been working on when he died—dangerous territory, Kevin thought, since they had never heard from Tom's friends. And since much of the material had been taken from Avending by Doris herself. But Alfredo cut her off before she got to any of that. "It was a great loss to all of us when Tom died. You can't bring him into this in a partisan way, he was simply one of the town's most important citizens, and in a way he belonged to all of us. I think it very well might be appropriate to name any center built on Rattlesnake Hill after him."

Kevin laughed out loud.

Doris cut through it, almost shouting: "When Tom Barnard

died he was doing his damndest to stop this thing! To suggest naming the center after him when he opposed it is obscene!''

Alfredo said, "He never told me he opposed it."

"He never told you anything," Doris snarled.

Alfredo hit the tabletop, stung at last. "I'm tired of this. You're getting into the area of slander when you imply that there's illegal capital behind this venture—"

"Sue me!" Doris shouted. "You can't afford to sue me, because then your funding would be revealed for sure!" Kevin nudged her with his knee, but as far as he could tell she didn't even feel it. *"Go ahead and sue me!"*

Shocked silence. Clearly Alfredo was at a loss for words.

"Properly speaking," Jerry Geiger said mildly, "this is only a discussion of the zoning change."

"It's the zoning makes the rest of it possible!" Doris said. "If you want to go on record against the development, here's where you act."

Jerry shrugged. "I'm not sure that's true."

Matt Chung decided to follow that tack, and talked about how zoning gave them options. Alfredo and Doris hammered away at each other, both getting really angry. It went on for nearly an hour before Alfredo slammed his hand down and said imperiously, "We've been over this before, five or six times in fact. We have the testimony of the town, we know what people want! Time to vote!"

Doris nodded curtly. Showdown.

They voted by hand, one at a time. Doris and Kevin voted against the proposed zoning change. Alfredo and Matt voted for. Hiroko Washington voted against. Susan Mayer voted for. And Jerry voted for.

"Ah, Jerry," Kevin said under his breath. No rhyme nor reason, same as always. Might as well flip a coin.

So the zoning for Rattlesnake Hill was changed, from 5.4 (open space) to 3.2 (commercial).

* * *

Afterwards Kevin and Doris walked home. There it stood, a bubble of light in a dark orange grove, looking like a Chinese lantern. Behind and above it the dark bulk of the hill they had lost. They stopped and looked.

"Thanks for doing the talking tonight," Kevin said. "I really appreciate it."

"Damn it," Doris said. She turned into him, and he hugged her. He leaned his head down and put his face on the part of her straight black hair. Familiar fit, same as it ever was. "Damn it!" she said fiercely, voice muffled by his chest. "I'm sorry. I tried."

"I know. We all tried."

"It's not over yet. We can take it to the courts, or try to get the Nature Conservancy to help us."

"I know."

But they had lost a critical battle, Kevin thought. The critical battles. The *Flyer*'s polls showed solid support for Alfredo. People thought he was doing a good job, dynamic, forward-looking. They wanted the town shares higher. Things were changing, the pendulum swinging, the Greens' day had passed. To fight business in America . . . it was asking for trouble, always. Kick the world, break your foot.

They walked into the house, arms around each other.


Kevin couldn't sleep that night. Finally he got up, dressed, left the house. Climbed the trail up the side of Rattlesnake Hill, moving slowly in the dark. Rustle of small animals, the light of the stars. In the little grove on top he sat, arms wrapped around his knees, thinking.

For a while he dozed. Uneasily he dreamed: he was in bed down in the house when a noise outside roused him, and he got up, went down the hall to the balcony window at the north end of the horseshoe. He looked down into the avocado grove, and there by the light of the moon he saw it again—the shape. It stood upright, on two legs, big and black, a node of darkness. It looked up at him, their gazes met and the moonlight flashed in its eyes, vertical slits of green like a big cat's eyes. Through the window he could hear the thing's eerie chuckle-giggle, and the hair on the back of his neck rose, and suddenly he felt as if the world were a vast, dark, windy place, with danger suffusing every part of its texture, every leaf and stone.

He jerked out of it. Too uneasy to wake up fully, he dove back below again, into sleep. Uneasy sleep, more dreams. A crowd on the hill.

When finally he woke to full consciousness, he got up and walked around the hilltop. It was just before dawn.

He found he had a plan. Somewhere in the night . . . he shivered, frightened by what he didn't know. But he had a plan. He thought about it until sunrise, and then, stiff and cold, he walked back down to home and bed.

The next morning he went to talk to Hank about his plan. Hank thought it was a good idea, and so did Oscar. So they went to talk to Doris. She laughed out loud. "Give me a couple of days," she told them. "I can make it by then."

"I'll let people know what's happening," Hank said. "We'll do it Sunday."


So on Sunday morning they held a memorial service for Tom Barnard, up on Rattlesnake Hill. Doris had cast a small plate, ceramic overlaid on a bronzelike alloy, with the overlay making a bas-relief border, and in the corners, animal figures: turtle, coyote, horse, cat. In the middle, a brief message:

In Memoriam, Thomas William Barnard
Born, El Modena, California, March 22nd 1984
Lost At Sea In The Pacific, August 23rd 2065
There Will Never Come An End To the Good That He Has Done

Hank conducted a brief ceremony. He was dressed in his Unitarian minister's shirt, and at first he looked like he was in costume, his face still lined and brick-red with sun, his hair still a tangle. And when he spoke it was in the same Hank voice, nothing inflated or ministerial about it. But he was a minister, in the Unitarian Church (also in the Universal Life Church, and in the World Peace Church, and in the Ba'hais), and as he talked about Tom, and the crowd continued to collect on the crown of the hill—older people who had known Tom all their lives, younger people who had only heard of him or seen him in the canyonlands, members of Hank's congregation, friends, neighbors, passersby, until there were two or three hundred people up there—all of them listened to what Hank had to say. Because there was a conviction in Hank, an intensity of belief in the importance of what they were doing, that could not be denied. Watching him Kevin lost his sense of Hank as daily partner and friend, the rapid voice tumbling words one over the next picked Kevin up and carried him along with the rest of them, into a shared sense of values, into a community. How Hank could gather them, Kevin thought. Such a presence. People dropping by the work sites to ask Hank about this or that, and he laughing and offering his advice, based on some obscure text or his own thoughts, whatever, there was never any pretense to it; only belief. It was as if he were their real leader, somehow, and the town council nothing at all. How did he do it? A matter of faith. Hank was certain they were all of them spiritual beings, in a spiritual community. And as he acted on that belief, those who had anything to do with him became a part of it, helped make it so.

"People die, rivers go on. Mountains go on."

He talked about Tom, told some of Tom's life story, incidents he had observed himself, other people's stories, Tom's stories, all in a rapid patter, a rhythm of conviction, affection, pleasure. "See one thing he does, know the rest. Now some of you know it and some of you don't, but this hilltop was nothing but prickly pear and dirt till Tom came up here. All these trees we stand under were planted by Tom when he was a boy, to give this hilltop some shade, to make it a good place to come up and look around, take a look for the ocean or the mountains or just down into town. And he kept coming up here for the rest of his life. So it's fitting that we make this little grove his memorial. It was a place he liked, looking over a place he loved. We don't have his body to bury, but that's not the important part of him anyway. Doris has cast a plaque and I've cut a flat spot into this big sycamore here, and all of us who care to, can help nail it in. Take a light whack so everyone can get a shot at it, and try not to miss and hit Doris's handiwork. It looks like the ceramic might break off.''

"Are you kidding?" Doris said. "This is a new secret bonding, the ceramic and the metal interpenetrate each other.''

"Like us and Tom's spirit, then. Okay, swing away.''

And so they stood the plate against the largest sycamore in the grove, about head high, and passed out a few hammers from Hank's collection, and they swirled around the tree in a loose informal knot, chatting as they waited their turn to tap one of the four nails into the tree.

Wandering around greeting people Kevin saw Ramona, who gave him a big smile. He smiled back briefly, feeling serious, calm, content.

Ah. There down the slope a ways stood Alfredo, looking dark. Kevin felt a quick surge of bitter triumph. He decided that it wasn't a good time to talk to him. Best not to get into an argument at his grandfather's funeral.

But Alfredo brought the argument to him. Kevin was standing away from the crowd, watching it and enjoying the casual feel of it, the sense of neighborhood party. Tom would have liked that. Then Alfredo came up to him and said angrily, "I should think you'd be ashamed of using your grandfather's death like this.''

Kevin just looked at him.

"How do you think it would make Tom feel?''

Kevin considered. "He would love it."

"This doesn't change anything, you know. We can build around it."

Kevin shook his head, looking past Alfredo, up at the grove. "This changes everything. And you know it." All of the people there would now think of the hill as a shrine, inviolate, and as they all had friends and family down below . . . Little ghost of his hatred: "Don't fuck with this hill any more, Alfredo. There's no one will like you if you do."

Then he saw who was standing before the memorial tree, about to take a swing with a hammer. He pointed. Alfredo turned around just in time to see Ramona smack a nail, then pass the hammer along.

That would make the difference. Alfredo would never dare cross Ramona on an issue this charged, not given everything else that had happened, the way it had all tangled together.

"Build it somewhere else," Kevin said harshly. "Build it down in town, by Santiago Creek or somewhere else nice. Tell your partners you gave it a try up here, and it didn't work. Whatever. But leave this hill alone."

Alfredo turned and walked away.


Later Kevin went to the tree to put the final knocks on all four nails: one for Nadezhda, one for his parents, one for Jill, one for himself. He touched the broken bark of the tree. Warm in the sunlight. This living tree. He couldn't think of a better memorial.

After the ceremony, Hank's idea of a wake: a party in Irvine Park, lasting all that afternoon. A lot of beer and hamburgers and loud music, flying frisbees, ecstatic dogs, barbeque smoke, endless innings of sloppy softball, volleyball without lines or scoring.

In the long summer twilight people drifted away, coasting down Chapman, their bike lights like a string of fireflies flickering between the trees. Kevin biked home alone, feeling the cool sage air rush over him. A good life, he thought. The old man had a good life. We can't ask for anything more.


So it came about that one morning Kevin Claiborne woke, under an orange tree in his house. Big day today: Ramona and Alfredo were getting married in the morning, and in the afternoon they were having the reception down in the park, next to the softball diamonds. Half the town would be there.

A late October day, dawning clear and cool. Hot in the afternoon. The best time of the year.

Kevin went down to their street project to work by himself for a while, leveling the new dirt. Filling in holes, thinking about the day and the summer. Thought like a long fast guitar solo, spinning away inside him. It was hard to focus on anything for more than a second or two.

Back home he dressed for the wedding, putting on his best shirt and the only dressy slacks he owned. Admittedly still casual, but not bad looking. Colorful, anyway: light green button-down shirt of the young exec style, and gray slacks, with creases and everything. No one could say he had underdressed for Ramona's wedding. Hopefully he wasn't overdressed.

He had given the matter of a wedding gift some thought. It was tough, because he wanted it to be nice without in any way suggesting that he was trying to intrude on their daily life, to remind them of him. Kitchen implements were therefore out, as well as a lot of other things. Nothing for the bedroom, thanks. He considered giving them something perishable, but that didn't seem right either. Might look like a comment in its own way, and besides, he did kind of want them to have something around, something Ramona might see from time to time.

Ornamental, then. He decided on a flowerpot made from scraps of the oakwork in Oscar's study. Octagonal, a neat bit of woodwork, but rough in a way that suggested outdoors. A porch pot. Bit sticky with the last coat of varnish, and he needed to get a plant for it. But it would do.

He biked to Santiago Creek Park with a trailer to carry everything. Okay, he told himself. No moping. No skeleton at the feast, for God's sake. Just put a good face on it. Otherwise better to not go at all.

He did fine. He found himself numb, and was thankful for that. He sat with the Lobos and they joked about the possibilities of playing with a pregnant shortstop and so on, and he never felt a twinge. The Sanchezes swept in beaming and the Blairs too, and Ramona walked down the path to the sound of Jody's guitar, by the stream in a long white Mexican wedding dress looking just like herself, only now it was obvious how beautiful she was. Kevin merely breathed deeply, felt his strength. He was numb. He understood now how actors could take on a role, play a part, as in *Macbeth*. They did it by erasing themselves, which allowed them to become what they played. He was learning that ability, he could do it.

Hank stood in the gazebo by the stream, in his minister's shirt again. His voice lifted and again he took them away, just as always. Kevin recalled him dusty in the yard, saying, "Ain't nothing written in stone, bro." Now he led Ramona and Alfredo through their marriage vows, "for as long as you both shall live." It's not stone, Kevin thought, we write these things in something both more fragile and more durable. Hank made him see it. You could believe in both because both were true. These were vows, sure enough. But vows were only vows. Intentions—and no matter how serious, public, heartfelt, they were still only vows. Promises. The future still loomed before them, able to take them anywhere at all. That was their great and terrible freedom. The weird emptiness of the future! How we long to fill it in, now, in the present; and how completely we are denied.

The wedding partners exchanged rings. Hers went on easily, her fingers were so slim. Blank out, Kevin, blank out. You don't know anything about her fingers. His they had trouble with; finally Hank muttered, "Let it stay there above the knuckle, the beer's getting warm." They kissed. At Hank's instigation the crowd applauded loudly, cheered. Kevin clapped hard, teeth clamped together. Hit his hands against each other as hard as he could, sure.

Picnic party in the park. Kevin set about getting unobtrusively drunk. The Lobos had a game to play but he didn't care. Danger to his long-forgotten hitting streak! He only laughed and refilled a paper cup with champagne. It didn't matter, it meant nothing. The laws of chance had bent in his corner of the world, but soon enough they would snap back, and neither the bend nor the snap would be his doing. He didn't care. He drank down his glass, refilled. Around him people were chattering, they made a sound like the sea.

He saw the wedding couple in an informal reception line, laughing together shoulder to shoulder. Handsome couple, no doubt about it. Both perfect. Not like him. He was a partner for someone like, say, Doris. Sure. He felt a surge of affection for Doris, for her bitter fight against Alfredo in the council meeting, for her pleasure in the plan for Tom's memorial. They had almost become partners, she had wanted it. How had they ever drifted apart? It had been his fault. Stupid man. He had learned enough to understand what her love had meant, he thought. Learned enough to deserve it, a little. Stupid slow learner, he was! Still, if something as flawed as the wedding couple could be made right . . . He refilled, went looking for Doris.

He spotted her in a group of Lobos, and watched her: small, round, neat, the sharp intelligence in that big laugh, the sense of fun. Wild woman. Down to earth. Could talk about anything to her. He walked over, feeling warmth fill him. Give her a hug and she would hug back, she would know what it meant and why he needed it.

And sure enough she did.

Then she was talking with Oscar, they were laughing hard at something. Oscar hopped up and began doing a ballerina routine on a bench. He wavered, she took a chop at the back of his knee. "Hey there." He hopped down, staggered gracefully her way, she leaned into him and pretended to bite his chest. They were laughing hard.

Kevin looked into his cup, retreated back to the drinks table. He looked back at Doris and Oscar. Hey, he thought. When did that happen? All the desire he had ever felt for Doris in the years they had been friends surged into a single feeling. She's mine, he thought sharply. It's me she liked, for years and years. What did Oscar think he was doing? Doris loved him, he had felt it that night in Bishop, or after the council fight, almost as strong as ever. If he started over, asserted himself, told Doris he was ready now, just like Alfredo had told Ramona—

. . . Oh. Well, it was true. Situations repeat themselves endlessly; there aren't that many of them, and there are a lot of lovers in this world. Perhaps everyone has been at every point of the triangle, sure.

Kevin walked behind a tree. He couldn't see his friends, could only hear their two voices, ragging each other vigorously, to the delight of the teammates nearby. When had they gotten to be such friends? He hadn't noticed. Last he knew they were sniping for real, and Doris seemed serious in her dislike. And Oscar was so fat!

He felt bad at that. Oscar was a good friend, one of his best. Oscar was great. He learned things from Oscar, he laughed and he made Oscar laugh. There was no one like Oscar. And if something was starting between him and Doris—

Again the intense burning flush. Jealousy, possessiveness. "Hey," he said to the tree. Feeling betrayed. "God damn." How many people, how many things could go wrong? He had thought his cup full, there.

He shook himself like a dog just out of the surf. Remembered how he had felt about Alfredo. He laughed shortly at himself. Raised his cup to the couple behind the tree. Drained it. Went to get more, feeling virtuous and morose.


It was a relief when the game started. Make-up for a postponed game, it was supposed to count but no one cared. Kevin pounced on the grounders that came his way, threw people out with a fierce pleasure in the act, in the efficiency and power of it. Mongoose jumping on cobras. *Third baseman Kevin Claiborne.* The phrase, spoken in a game announcer's voice, had resounded in his mind millions of times when he was a kid. Maybe billions. Why the appeal of those words? What makes us become what we become? Third base like a mongoose, this announcer had always said. Third base like a razor's edge. And here he was doing it. That broke her heart.

They were playing Hank's team, the poor Tigers, who rose above their heads to give them a challenge. Ramona, looking much more like herself in her gym shorts and T-shirt, played a sparkling shortstop, so that between them it was a defensive show. "We've got this side shut down entirely," she told him after another hot play. Low scoring game.

He hit as always. Walk to the plate and turn off the brain. Easy today. Swing away. Line drive singles, no problem. Not a thought.

Bottom of the last inning they were down a run, confident of a come-from-behind victory. But suddenly they were down to their last out, the tying run on first. Ramona was up, and Kevin walked out to the on-deck circle swinging a bat, and out of the blue he thought, if Ramona gets out then the game is over, and I'll have batted a thousand for a whole season.

He took a step back, shocked at himself. Where had that come from? It was a bad thought. Bad luck and maybe worse. It wasn't like him, and that frightened him. What makes us. . . ?

Ramona hit a single. Everyone yelling. Two on, two out, one run down. Game on the line. If only that thought hadn't come into his head! He didn't mean it! It wasn't like him, he never thought like that. It wasn't his thought.

Into the batter's box, and the world slipped away. Make sure you touch the right home plate, he thought crazily. Tim, the Tigers' pitcher, nodded once at him, disdaining to walk the man who was batting a thousand. Kevin grinned, nodded back at him. Good for Tim, he thought—and that was his thinking, back in control. Good. Everything forgotten, the luck, the curse, the world. Tim's arm swung back and then under, releasing the ball. Up it lofted, into the blue sky, big and round, spinning slowly. All Kevin's faculties snapped together in that epiphany of the athlete, in the batter's pure moment of being, of grace. An eternal now later and the ball was dropping, he stepped forward with his lead foot, rocked over his hips, snapped his wrists hard. He barely felt the contact of bat and ball, right on the button and already it was shooting like a white missile over Damaso and out into right center. Clobbered it!

He ran toward first slowly, watching the ball. Hank, out in center field, had turned and was racing back; he put his head down and ran, thick short legs pumping like pistons. Forty-six years old and still running like that! And in his minister's shirt no less. He glanced over his shoulder, adjusted direction, ran an impossible notch faster, watched the ball all the way. It was over his head, falling fast to his backhand side—he sprinted harder yet, leaped up, snagged the ball at full extension, high in the air—fell, hit the ground and rolled. He stood up, glove high. And there in an ice-cream-cone bulge was the ball. Catch.

Kevin slowed down, approaching second. Confused. He had to laugh; he had forgotten how to leave the field after making an out. He stood there, feeling self-conscious. Game over, so there was no need to rush.

Hank had taken the ball from his glove. Now he was inspecting it with a curious pained expression on his face, as if he had, with a truly remarkable shot, killed a rabbit. After a while he jerked, shrugged, ran back in. He jogged up to Kevin and gave him the ball. "Sorry about that, Kev," he said rapidly, "but you know I figured you'd want me to give it a try."

"That was one hell of a try," Kevin said, and the crowd around them laughed.

"Well, what the hell—I guess batting nine-ninety-four for the year ain't such a bad average, anyhow."

Then everyone was cheering and clapping him on the shoulder. The Tigers mobbed Hank, and for a moment as they left the field Kevin was mobbed too, lifted up by the legs and carried on the shoulders of his teammates, so that he could look across at Hank, being carried the same way. Then he was back on the ground, in the dugout. Taking off his cleats.

Slowly the shoes slipped off.

Doris plopped beside him. "Don't feel bad, Kevin, it was a good hit. Hank made a super catch."

"It's not that," Kevin said, rubbing his forehead distractedly.

"Ah." She put an arm around his shoulder. "I understand."

She didn't, actually. But when people said that, it wasn't exactly what they meant. Kevin knew what she meant. He blew out a breath, feeling her arm over his back, and nodded at the dirty red concrete.


The reception rolled on through the afternoon, and the band set up and the dancing began. But after a few more drinks Kevin slipped away to his bike, uncoupled his trailer and rode off.

He was feeling low. Mostly because of Tom. He needed to talk to Tom, needed that grinning ancient face staring into his and telling him he was taking it all too seriously. Nine-ninety-four is actually *better* than a thousand, Tom would say. Could it really be true he would never talk to Tom Barnard again? The loss of that. Too much to imagine.

Biking down Redhill he gnawed at the thought, helpless before it. It was the worst of all the recent events, worst because it was irrevocable. Ain't nothing written in stone, bro—but death is written in stone, written in ceramic and bronze to outlive the generations of bodies, minds, spirits, souls—all gone, and gone for good. Lives like leaves. And he needed to talk to him, needed his advice and his jokes and his stories and his weirdness.

"Grandpa," he said, and shifted his hands down the handlebars to race position, and coasted for a second so he could yank up viciously on his toe clip straps, crushing his feet to the pedals. And he started to ride hard.

Wind blasted him, and the tops of his thighs groaned. They pulsed through the lactic build-up, a hot pain that slowly shifted to a fierce, machinelike pumping. His butt and the palms of his hands and the back of his neck bothered him as he settled through the other transient pains of hard biking. He breathed harder and harder, until his diaphragm and the muscles between his ribs were working almost as hard as his thighs, just to get the oxygen into him and the $CO_2$ out of him, faster and faster. Sweat dried on his forearms, leaving a whitish coating under the hairs. And all the while a black depression settled in his stomach, riding up and down rhythmically with every heave of his lungs, filling him from inside until he hurt, really hurt. Strange that emotion alone could make this kind of pain. That broke her heart. He was going to bike it out of him, the machine was nothing more than a rolling rack to expunge this pain, and the world that made it. He was south now, firing down Highway Five at full speed, dodging other traffic and taking the smooth curves of the downhill in tight, perfect lines. Toes pointed down to shift the calf muscles being used. Push down/pull up, push down/pull up, over and over and over and over and over, until the bike's frame squeaked under the stress. Fly south, flee that whole life, that whole world!

But in Dana Point he turned north, onto the Coast Highway. He wanted to ride within sight of the sea, and this was the best way. A moment of sharp mortal fear as he glanced down into the small boat harbor at Dana Point; something in the shape of it scared him. He fought it away, pushed harder up and down the roller coaster ride of the road, enjoying the pain. Eyes burning from sweat, thighs going wooden on him, his lungs heaved just as if he were sobbing, violently but rhythmically. Maybe this was the only way he could let himself sob so hard, and all without a tear, except those blown out by the harsh rush of salt wind scouring his face. Another moment of sharp fear as he passed the industrial complex at Muddy Canyon, like a vacuum in his heart, tugging everything inward. Harder, go harder, leave all that behind. Go harder, see what breaks first. Image of Ramona walking up the streamside path. That broke her heart.

On a whim he turned into Newport, onto Balboa Peninsula. It was a long sprint to the dead end at the Wedge, and he flew, final effort, killing himself on a bike. He came to the end of the road, slewed with braking, freed a cramping foot, put it down. The harbor channel, between its two stone jetties. Green scraps flying at the top of tall palm trees.

He freed the other foot, walked the bike to the concrete wall at the jetty's foot. His thighs felt ten feet around, he could barely walk. He was still gasping for air, and with the bike wind gone sweat poured out of him, ran down his burning face. All his muscles pulsed, bump bump bump with every hard knock of his heart. The whole world shifted and jumped with every heartbeat, bump bump bump, and things in the late afternoon sun had a luminous grainy quality, as if bursting with the internal pressure of their own colors. Ah yes: the end of a workout. Faint wash of nausea, fought, mastered, passed through, to something like sexual afterglow, only more total, more spread through the musculature—more in muscles than in nerves, some sort of beta-endorphin opiate high, the work-out high, best of them all. Sure, he felt pretty good for a man in the first great multiple grief of his life. Except he was cooking. The afternoon sea breeze helped, but not enough. He trod through the sand, every step sinking deep, calves almost cramping.

He stripped to his shorts, walked out into the ocean. Water perfect, just over seventy degrees and clear as glass. He dove in, delicious coolness all over him. He swam around dragging his legs, which pulsed furiously. Lolled back into the shallows and leaped off the bottom to ride the little tubes until they dumped him on the sand. Could even catch a miniature Wedge effect, side wave backwashing across the incoming ones for an extra push. He had done this as a child, with Tom, an old man even then, doing the same beside him. Old bald man yelling, "Outside! Outside!" Green flags ripping above the lifeguard stands, the big stones of the jetty. They had done a lot together, Tom and he. Coronado to Lassen, Yuma to Eureka, there was no escaping that.

Cooled off and tired, Kevin sat on the wet sand just above the reach of the white soup. The salt wind dried him and he could feel the rime of it on his skin and in his hair, warping lick into tangles of curl. Late afternoon sun glassed the water. Salty light in the salty wind. Sand.

He put on his shirt and left it unbuttoned, dropped his shoes by his bike and walked out the jetty, feeling each warm stone with his toes. They had walked out here many times, he used to scare Tom with his leaps. He tried one, hurt his arch. Only kids could do it. His moods rushed up and down on a wild tide of their own, hitting new ebb records, then curious floods of euphoria. How he had loved his grandpa, what friends they had been. It was only by feeling that love that he could do justice to what had happened since. So he had to feel this good, and this bad. He stepped over a big gap between stones, landed perfectly. It was coming back, the art of it. You had to dance over them, keep committing yourself to something more than a normal step. Like life: like *that,* and *that*, and *that*.

The sun was obscured by a cloud for a moment, then burst out again. Big clouds like tall ships coasted in, setting sail for the mountains and the desert beyond. The ocean was a deep, rich, blue blue, a blue in blue within blue inside of blue, the heart and soul and center of blue. Blinding chips of sunlight bounced on the swelltops. Liquid white light glazed the apricot cliff of Corona del Mar, the needles of its Torrey pines like sprays of dark green. Ironwood color of the sun-drenched cliff. Eye still jumping a bit here, oxygen starvation, then enrichment. What a glossy surface to the massive rocky substance of the world! These boulders under his feet were amazing pieces of work, so big and stony, like the broken marbles of giants.

He skipped from boulder to boulder, looking. From time to time his hands came together and swung the imaginary bat in its catlike involuntary swing.

He came to the end of the jetty, the shoulder-high lighthouse block. The wind rushed over him and the clouds sailed in, the waves made their myriad glugs and the sunlight packed everything, and he stood there balancing, feeling he had come to the right place, and was now wide awake, at the center of things. End of the world. Sun low on the water.

For a long time he stood there, turning round, staring at all of it, trying to take it all in. All the events of the summer filled him at once, flooding him from a deep well of physical sensation, spinning him in a slurry of joy and sorrow. There was a steel chisel someone had left behind. He kneeled, picked it up and banged it against the last granite rock of the jetty. The rock resisted, harder than he would have imagined. Stubborn stuff, this world. A chunk of rock about the size of two softballs was wedged between boulders, and he freed it for use as a hammer. Hammer and chisel, he could write something, leave his mark on the world. All of a sudden he wanted to cut something deep and permanent, something like I, Kevin Claiborne, was here in October of 2065 with oceans of clouds in the sky and in me, and I am bursting with them and everything has gone wrong! The granite being what it was, he contented himself with *KC*. He cut the figures as deep as he could.

When he was done he put down his tools. Behind him Orange County pulsed green and amber, jumping with his heart, glossy, intense, vibrant, awake, alive. His world and the wind pouring through it. His hands came together and made their half swing. If only Hank hadn't caught that last one. If only Ramona, if only Tom, if only the world, all in him all at once, with the sharp stab of our unavoidable grief; and it seemed to him then that he was without a doubt the unhappiest person in the whole world.

And at that thought (thinking about it) he began to laugh.